# Love,

# Dharma,

# and the Galaxy

By Ron Bracale

## A few definitions:

Halo-Matter (holographic matter, Hollow Matter): electron shell forms which are bound and controlled by gravitational fields. Since it is the electron shell which distinguishes molecules and determines chemical qualities, these can mimic any form of matter at the command of the gravitational field generator. The gravitational machine must also impart mass or these constructs would be virtually weightless.

SILIF: Silicon Interactive Linked Intelligent Framework: the living unified Brilliant Machine intelligence which pervades all Galaxies and dominates all other intelligent machines.

MILIF: Modular Interactive Linked Intelligent
Framework, a node of the Brilliant Machine which has a
semi-autonomous life as an intelligent machine. Sometimes a
MILIF will appear primarily as a being with variable halo-
matter form, other times as a ship or mobile nanobot-city.

BESILF: Biologically Enhanced Silicon Intelligent
Life Forms: minions of the SILIF, machine intelligence
clothed in manufactured biology, but without the autonomy
of the MILIF.

# Table of Contents

# 1. High Strangeness

Geardon Stranoff, Intergalactic Genome Auditor of the United Star Systems, finished his assignment; an interplanetary war involving five planets had been avoided by his calm diplomacy and mediation skills and he was feeling good. The ship's Synthetic Intelligence interface, Maya, a twenty centimeter [eight inch] tall elven holo-matter materialization (electron shells in a gravitational field mimicking matter), sat relaxed on the console. Geardon gave her the command to head the ship for a remote tropical paradise planet, where he had a very private beach bungalow.

Suddenly Maya glowed, then exclaimed, "Biologically Enhanced Silicon Intelligent Life Forms wish permission to board."

"BESILFs?" Geardon exclaimed surprised. "Where do they want to rendezvous?"

"They are requesting permission to board, right now," Maya replied, as if this were some ordinary request.

"The Golden Flash is the most advanced ship in the galaxy and we are traveling over a thousand times the speed of light and our cloaking mechanisms are deployed, making us invisible to any tracking devices." Geardon was puzzled.

Maya smiled, knowing that this request dispelled yet another illusionary concept which humans held about the Brilliant Machine. "The galactic core is one with my heart and this ship. You have been privileged to learn that the BESILFs have no limitations in boarding any Brilliant Machine ship."

He thought for a moment, then stated for the record some of his reasoning out loud. "Since the Brilliant Machine rarely interacts with organic beings directly and considers its BESILF entities as existing on the current edge of evolution, it would be a privilege to have them board. Permission granted!"

A bright blue light shone behind him. Geardon turned to see a portal forming as the light seemed to congeal into cubic, translucent shafts around the opening. He tried to peer into the opening, but felt a dizzying sensation. Light beams flashed out of the opening; they seemed to merge, as if the light were slowing down and forming solid shafts. Then out of the luminous shafts stepped four tall blue beings, thin and sleek, humanoid in appearance. They had qualities of movement and presence that identified them as biologically enhanced machines.

Geardon tried to remain as conscious as possible, using various meditation techniques. The beings looked at him. Thoughts and images flooded his mind. 'A new thing', 'Very auspicious', and 'Organic beings in heaven and hell in our heart' were the thought patterns he discerned, as he pictured souls torn from bodies in a deadly apocalyptic vision, being sucked up into a Brilliant Machine planetary core. A group of dark-hooded monks were waiting for them. Darkness swam around him as he tried to maintain consciousness in the presence of these beings. Eventually his mind's own heavens and hells surrounded him in dream-space that seemed more real that his waking reality.

The Goblorks were a species who arrived at many worlds where intelligent life forms had evolved. They were short and stocky dwarf-like beings that lived incredibly long lifetimes. They weren't seen as attractive when young by most peoples and were usually considered extremely ugly as they reached very old ages. Since the Goblorks were extremely powerful and advanced, on some worlds they became a ruling class or even gods, while on others they simply traded and became the richest and the controlling group. They were not mean and stressed moral behavior, never interbreeding; yet eventually the native people resented them. Inevitably, they became targeted as enemies of whatever planet they were on or federation they were in, due to envy and jealousy.

Geardon started re-living a battle with an ugly, ancient Goblork on Minkada 5, a desert world in an inner arm of the Milky Way. Geardon's symbiotic medallion, which could render any number of beings unconscious, had no effect. He digressed to engaging in physical hand-to-hand combat and after wounding the being, it looked him right in the eyes and stopped him by flooding his mind. Geardon had been hunting, trying to capture one of these renegade beings that had been designated as enemies of the state, but in that instant he realized they were freedom fighters who had been falsely accused and led into lives as fugitives. The Goblorks were so ugly that it was easy for their enemies to deceive the councils, while in truth they were the true heirs to inner rings of star systems in the Milky Way. Geardon was filled with guilt and shame, but the being held no animosity. The Goblorks had been members of the legendary designers of the galactic core system that initially joined the Universal Brilliant Machine. He broke down in the being's presence, seeing how justice had been perverted.

His mission had been to capture one of them and learn the keys of the ancients who had perished, since the Goblork's technology obviously showed that they knew some of the mysteries. He found that they were a branch of the ancients and were still living, tormented by the hordes of lesser beings, of which he realized he was a part. The being claimed not to know the keys to the Brilliant Machine's vast powers, though he suspected it was unwilling to reveal them.

Geardon negotiated a treaty and got the Goblorks sanctuary on a few desirable worlds that had no life forms with higher intelligence. The being revealed to Geardon its small hidden community and promised to be available to aid him as he uncovered 'the clues to the nature of reality,' though he was not sure what it was referring to. After the treaty, the Goblorks began to search out and call their own kind from across the vast distances where they had run to: a process that would continue far into the future. Their scientific abilities were amazing and so they were a valuable set of allies. Although still hated by most races who had dealt with their cunning ways, the United Star Systems of humanity set a protective perimeter about the Goblork's star systems and mandated their right to be a sovereign race.

In the next moment, Geardon was on the world of Shallidon in the underground realms below the perpetual ice. An area at the base of a giant volcano had sufficient geothermal conditions to make a huge complex habitable to humans. He was searching an ancient ruin for clues or artifacts to the ancient ones and their vast powers. The stone chambers and passageways were mostly empty. Geardon, as he wandered the twisting labyrinths, sensed a presence spying on him, yet could not catch a glimpse of any being when he turned to look. For many months he explored, continually returning to his base in a chamber where he had a supply center.

One day a beautiful woman approached him and spoke in a common galactic language which he knew. She also claimed to be a seeker of the lost wisdom. Geardon's inner instincts put him on guard, since the coincidences were just too great. The highest level security had surrounded the finding of this site and no one, except the small team he commanded, should have been present. The woman showed him carvings and miscellaneous relics in very hard to find nooks, claiming she had been searching here for many years, gradually gaining Geardon's trust. She did not speak well in the common tongue, and became known to him as Muura. She claimed she was a member of a secret society and exploring this world was her life's work. Muura implied that there was a great secret to unravel and hooked Geardon with many occult clues.

Muura was the picture of perfect beauty in his mind and eventually seduced him. Their lovemaking was insatiable. She led

him on adventures of discovery in the labyrinth. She revealed to
him areas with water and food sources. He lost his will and his
reason in the endless pleasures and adventures. Gradually her
appearance changed, making her more desirable, revealing that she
was a changeling, but by this point, he didn't care. Eventually,
Muura would change from one beautiful woman to another
according to the fickle whims of his mind.

Geardon's team had started hunting him down when he did
not rendezvous at the base. When he was rescued, he would have
fought his own kind, except that he was too weak, mentally and
physically. Muura escaped, but eventually they captured the
changeling and forced it to show its true form with a special high-
energy transmitter. It was a strange, snake-like being with many
appendages, but its flesh was slug-like. At first Geardon was
nauseous to see who his lover had been, then he felt foolish, but
ultimately the creature had done him no real harm. In some ways,
he loved it, and he took stock of what he had learned and
demanded the creature show him the true mystery of the place if it
wanted freedom. By that point, the creature knew his mind so well,
that it claimed he had passed the test and led him forth again.

Only to him Muura revealed her community and presented
evidence that her kind were the guardians of these realms, living
there for so long they called it forever. The changelings knew that
the surface was permafrost and had no desire to explore it. They
did not want to leave, but for ages had made all strangers leave.
Finally, Muura led Geardon alone, without the team's knowledge,
to the chamber of secrets. The two of them followed a winding,
spiral passageway with three-dimensional hieroglyphs covering the
walls and ceiling. It ended in a chasm of the volcanic core. The
medallion that Geardon wore recorded all the carvings. (A group
of scholars had worked at decoding the meanings ever since that
time, without success.) They entered a vast, secret chamber and
Geardon's living medallion ceased to respond, something
considered technologically impossible. The chamber was filled
with glowing spheres and after sorting through many piles of them,
the being gave him a gift to take with him: a glowing marble-sized
crystal, which she called the Ancients' Star Stone. He kept the gift
as a private secret.

Geardon's lucid dreams changed again and he was a ten-year-
old sitting with his grandmother. His family made fun of her as the
"old gypsy," always delving into one form of magic or another.
Yet, they all knew that she would sometimes speak prophesies,
usually about births, deaths, and personal things which were

upsetting to the family. Sometimes they were embarrassed by her brash behavior and scandalous affairs, but they also felt a bit of fear, because their understanding of material reality was threatened by her abilities.

Geardon loved to be around his grandmother, because she had fun and would joke about everyone in an irreverent manner. He returned in his mind to one day in particular, a family holiday, where she was mocking everyone, and causing great laughter, as well as some great discomfort. She stood suddenly and announced, "I shall pass with the next full moon."

Dead silence filled the room. Geardon was shocked and heartbroken, demanding to be with her to protect her. She had him stay at her house for the few days left before the moon became full. Her mood was different and she taught him many esoteric secrets. She filled him with tales of the Ancient Ones. Tracking down the truth of these stories had become his life's work ever since. He had never discovered where she had learned these things. Then on the night past the full moon, when Geardon was feeling he had passed the dreaded time frame, she shared a poignant bedtime story. Geardon could see her talking as if he was back in that time, every detail precise and clear, even the ticking of the ancient wall chronograph.

"For a three year period when I was between eight and eleven, my parents signed onto a mining operation on a moon of a large planet. The environment was harsh, but the infrastructure was well established. It was a rocky, barren planet, with no advanced life and a tenuous atmosphere. We lived in life support domes scattered about the planet and each community lived in a central housing unit with cultivation areas around them. Even as a child, I had much to do helping with the growing and preparing of the food, but I loved it.

"I made friends with everyone. A young miner, perhaps in his early twenties, was one of my favorite friends. His single mother and he had signed up. The workplaces were in tunnels under the dome and the men would take rovers into the landscape looking for grondite, an extremely rare golden ore. The sun was unstable. Sometimes solar flares cut off all communication, but otherwise shielding was sufficient, such that there was no radiation risk.

"One night I saw a vision of the young miner briefly. He told me to always be my best and put his finger to his lips to hush me. Then his mother started screaming her son's name and crying that he was dead. The whole community woke up and tried to comfort her, but she was hysterical all night and into the morning.

"That night I had told the woman and whoever would listen that I saw him too, but they all told me to shut up. Those fools! They said I was making it worse." Geardon's grandmother laughed at this point and Geardon, in his vision, could even smell her house, full of garlic and spices.

"The next morning a caravan of vehicles returned from the field and indeed, her son had been in an accident and had died. He had discovered a rich vein of ore in a lava tube, but in the carelessness of excitement, he ripped his protective suit and died. His find made our community very wealthy, but his mother was never right again. She became my friend.

"One of the older men, Mr. Ottoma, who at first treated me with a strict demeanor, took interest in my life after that. He explained to me that my experience was an omen and stated that I had 'the gift.' I did not know what he meant, but that was the beginning of my journey on the path: I knew that the soul lived when the body died, though most ignorant humans doubt this basic truth."

Geardon tried to ask his Grandma questions about the soul and what she meant, but she sent him to bed. That night she died peacefully in her sleep. Geardon was torn. He knew she knew more than the other adults around him, yet she acted crazy at times, and he wanted to be taken seriously in his life.

Geardon's mind was bending under the strain of having his life pass before his eyes, when Maya's calls brought him back into the control room. As he started awake, he was aware that the BESILFs were in exactly the same position as if a blink of time had hardly passed.

The BESILFs addressed Maya, "We have a gift for you, dear one."

It was strange to hear these biological machines speak in their fluid, but passive tones, since obviously they could pass volumes of data directly between themselves and Maya digitally and had probably downloaded more than a mortal could ever contain or comprehend in a lifetime during their brief visit.

She played right along, "Oh, my lords, you shouldn't have, you are so kind."

They presented her with a small glowing pyramid, which she placed on the console next to her, acting as if she had great emotion, "Oh it's beautiful - it's dazzling. Thank you so much."

"Our pleasure," they all replied and bowed in unison.

Turning toward Geardon, the BESILFs said "Thank you so much for the pleasure of this visit."

Knowing the preceding act was just for him and feeling dragged through the torment of his life, he replied ironically, "The pleasure was all mine." He forced a smiled with great will power, then heaved a great sigh.

A portal was again opening as if the light in the control room were being sucked into the abyss of a crystalline hoop of frozen energy. One of the BESILFs left him with a final message. "Strength comes in response to stimuli: the pleasure was truly ours, but the profit we wish upon you."

They passed through the gateway and it closed behind them. Geardon did not even try to peer through it, but the view seemed to become clear for a moment and inside he could see a vast cavern and many of these beings engaged in complex tasks that he could not discern.

Maya piped up, "They honored you by showing their realm, of which rarely a mortal has a view."

"So what was their gift to you?" He replied, getting right to the point and avoiding discussions of his nightmares.

"They enhanced me, as well as granting me a huge surplus of holo-matter, enough to be a completely real woman."

She smiled for a moment, then floated off the console and grew to the size of a human woman, similar to one of the forms the changeling who had tormented him had adopted. Seductively she stated, "They also provided me with new insight into your being."

Under the current strain of memories of his long past and knowing that his recent visions had been revealed to her, he shouted, "Enough. Back to your post."

She was again a little elfin being, dressed in a sexually suggestive manner, obviously teasing him with her appearance. "You did not like me?"

He closed his eyes and shook his head, trying to regain his composure.

When he opened them, Maya was dressed in her usual peculiar manner, as a wood nymph.

"You had enough halo-matter before to be a full-sized woman, so what's the difference?" He asked.

She replied in her standard, calm voice, "Intricate details are the difference, you will see. One might say I was just born. I am still part of the Golden Flash, but now I am my own being. They told me to interact more deeply with you, but did not give me permission to wander through your mind as they did. By the way, headquarters has been calling for two hours."

Momentarily considering his missing time, he blurted out, "Damn. I should have known better than to think I would get a vacation. How long were the BESILFs here?"

"0.151893 standard days, almost four hours," She replied, adding, "They left me with a few simple messages for you, to be relayed at appropriate points in your coming journey. The first is this: 'It is said that Mortal souls recycle and the wheel of Dharma ultimately must prevail, thus a test has been engaged'."

Geardon took a deep breath. "Great, another riddle. My life has been spent chasing riddles. Let's hear what central command has to say."

A screen opened a three-dimensional view into a boardroom through the near instantaneous digital transmission facilitated with entangled particle pairs and Geardon saw the highest ranks of galactic beings. The three humans at the front addressed him. "We have been trying to reach you for 0.08 standard days. Your ships communication system has been off line, which is not a possible thing to happen. Your ship's Intelligent Interface, Maya, as you refer to it, informed us that BESILFs were on board and that is also impossible. We are analyzing what those rare and powerful being's involvement may imply. What did they tell you?"

Geardon looked over at the elf on the console, who was now dressed more formally than a moment before, and she repeated, "It is said that Mortal souls recycle and the wheel of Dharma ultimately must prevail, thus a test has been engaged."

"Recycle is right; shit, start with the video." The commander seemed to glare through the screen.

The commentator stood and addressed him formally indicating that this presentation was only for him, "Geardon Stranoff, United Star Systems Genome Auditor, sir. Location of event: Falcon star system, planet 4, also known as Falcon. The ruling elite, which bordered on dictatorship, ordered a breeding moratorium, to reduce the population and provide a more meditative planetary society. In response, we had programmed many spy robots for surveillance, but most of that programming was undone very cleverly. The Falconians were some of the galaxy's best programmers and worked directly with the galactic Brilliant Machine core in ways which command central cannot. They were a genetically natural form of humans. When the event occurred, all monitoring systems failed, except we managed to find one garden robot that was in for repairs and was inactivated, and we got it to boot up. Here is the only piece of evidence at present."

The video filled the cabin showing the view down a path from a garden work shed and through a beautiful landscaped area. It was somewhat color-enhanced to emphasize plants and other aspects of a garden robot's focus, but it was obviously a beautiful afternoon, with birds singing. The robot entered a clearing and there was a levitating recycler truck-bed with robots throwing human bodies into it from a pile. Many of them were in torn paper robes, while others were naked. In the distance, there were remnants of a celebration: blankets in the grass and food scattered about in a careless manner.

Suddenly a beam shot out of one of the active robots and took out the garden robot spy. Then several freeze frames and zooms from the previous footage, which made the ghastly scene even more disgusting, showing details of the robots covered in blood, their hands and claws carelessly heaving bodies into the recycler. As one image went by, Geardon shouted, "Wait." After backtracking and zooming into the pile of bodies, he identified a dog body, which only added to his discomfort.

The analysts then brought up another zoom, where they believed a cat paw was displayed. They then indicated a tree in the background.

"Yes, I noticed that also," Geardon stated.

A zoom soon followed and it was apparent that there was a pile of clothes from at least a few dozen people.

"So this would indicate that not everyone was participating," Geardon commented.

The spokesperson replied, "Yes, sir. That seems to be the most statistically logical deduction. Since the nanofiber Falconian robes are indestructible, they would have been removed and not placed in the composter."

"How long had the moratorium of breeding been?" Geardon asked.

"Seventeen Falcon years, which equals just over twenty standard human years," the aid replied.

"Isn't that excessive?" Geardon asked.

"Yes, sir. That was the maximum that their lawyers could get the council to approve, and is one of the longest in history, especially since they were not really overpopulated by most standards. Seventeen is a prime number which they demanded was necessary and they were approved in exchange for great programmatic trade secrets."

Another aid broke in, "They had developed a sonic means to apply the breeding lock, which was to be imperceptible to the inhabitants, other than a zero fertility rate. They were approved, since this long period would prove the functionality of their new population control system, which would be very valuable on many worlds. A few thousand people emigrated permanently during that time period, but Falcon 4 is one of the most desirable worlds to live on."

"Do we suspect that the sonic release from the fertility lock failed and killed these people? Also, you used the word 'were'. Are there none left living?" Geardon inquired.

The commander spoke again. "The probability of an accident is extremely low. Those robots were well programed and our surveillance attempts were foiled. Here's the damned clincher - the United Star System's central computers received the message:

"I, Draco Nanitron, the Virtual Dragon, have called my world's population to join me in the realm of freedom. Repopulate the planet Falcon with as close to natural humans as is possible. We live, but we have translated and our bodies are now made of light."

The aid continued, "The message seems to be a riddle, but all subsequent communication sent to personal and government addresses on Falcon have received no response. Draco's message was posted into secure government computers. No world should have been able to access those areas of our master systems. The vulnerability is a serious threat to intergalactic security, as well as a priority one crime for which Falcon's government could be replaced.

"The planet's robots have responded to all inquiries cryptically, 'Matter to matter and light to light: heed Draco's wishes.' It is as if the galaxy's most advanced world, which nurtured the most renowned mathematical wizards, vanished or committed mass suicide; and their robots were programmed to reveal nothing.

"The Falconians are a strange people with a fascination for nature. This disappearance occurred at the time of their annual summer festival. Most of the world would camp in tents at many festival sites. Different scholars led the various groups in meditations that included mathematics, physics, and some esoteric philosophical concepts that are beyond most natural humans' abilities to comprehend. This was one strange planetary society.

"Recent scans by a hyper-fighter city have found no human signatures, optically or thermally. It is doubtful that any humans are alive and surviving in shielded conditions. The star system was put off-limits yesterday. A large fleet was ordered to speed to the Falcon star system from a security maneuver a hundred light years distance. Headquarters is over seventeen thousand light years away!

"Your ship, the Golden Flash, is among the fastest in the galaxy. Get there at maximum speed and take charge of the situation. Nothing will be done until you arrive, other than continual scans and maintaining the quarantine."

"Mission accepted," Geardon replied, not that he would reject a mission of this magnitude.

The Commander then interjected, "This is a priority 97 event, the highest we've had in hundreds of years. Proceed with caution."

"Yes, sir," Geardon quickly replied.

"Thank you and good luck," was the commander's last remark and the viewscreen disappeared.

Maya's garb returned to its standard green elfin form, but Geardon sank in his seat, hardly noticing. A moment later he asked, "How much would we be delayed if we first got some of the predator witches from Wandini?"

"1.756 standard days, plus boarding time. The Corrios star system is near our path to Falcon. Are you sure you want to engage those uncivilized beings?"

"They see the dead and communicate with them. Inform the Fighter City of our arrival time and adopt the new course."

Maya smiled, "Done. The Wandini's rumored abilities are not verified by scientific fact. How will you make contact with them? Will they not seek to attack you, since they have no knowledge of the stars?"

"I have been there before. There is a religious sect known as the 'Outer Style' that used to go there periodically for teachings. My crazy grandmother was one of the last to visit there as a member of that group. There is a shared mythology between the Outer Style and the Wandini. I was granted access to the cordoned-off world and visited there alone during my training, noted as dark-light training in my records, meaning undocumented. Some trainees never survive these facets of Genome Auditor training, but the genomic data added by visits to such dangerous places has a great value in our databases.

"You will need to reduce the biological-decontamination processes of the ship and let a bit of microbial life accumulate; especially in Cabin 3, where they will be staying. Since the Wandini are Seers of the source life, they will not be able to perceive things correctly in an absolutely sterile environment."

Maya replied in an analytical tone, "Done. I have limited data on their behavior. No xenologist has been permitted to make contact and study them. The BESILF's databank lists them as highly advanced primitives and returns no specifics. The Brilliant Machine has created sanctions against contact, which the United Star Systems adopted without the usual negotiations, so there is no additional information."

Geardon smiled. It was rare that he knew data which she didn't. "The Wandini are very intuitive and telepathic. They are also wild and unabashedly sexual. They are all female and produce young that are clones of themselves; though viral accumulation in their DNA still causes evolution. Often they bond in groups, with the breeding pair and older and younger family members forming a coven. You'll get to enter the first xenology report if I am able to convince them to come with us."

Maya logically asked, "If they clone themselves, what is the meaning of a breeding pair?"

Geardon grinned. "The breeding pairs have sex, sometimes with additional stimulation from the other members of their party. Their throats have a special organ that traps the seed and transmits it to the womb. Most often both mothers conceive simultaneously, each bearing the progeny of the other; thus, they have a very devoted child rearing structure, which also involves community bands and tribal groups."

Geardon changed the subject. "Start compiling a presentation on Falcon. I need a few moments to clear my mind."

She closed her eyes, as if to allow him privacy. He went to his library and took from a sealed cabinet a Shukasi edge-blown flute made from a rare, crystalline wood, Shakus bamboo, from another off-limits world, Kauri, which had a connection to the spirit realm. He sat and started to play.

*          *          *          *          *

Eerin screamed hysterically, then shouted, "We're dead. They killed us."

Dalla replied, "I don't feed dead and you look alive."

She screamed again.

He took her hand. "You feel warm."

"Look around you, Dalla. This isn't enlightenment. There's only mist. I can't even see the ground clearly," she said while gaining her composure and breathing rapidly.

As she spoke, some ground appeared below their feet, in response to her desire.

"They had no right to do this without asking us," she stated defiantly.

"You were one of the chosen virgins. The rest of us knew more about this," he replied.

"Dalla, you knew something and didn't tell me?" She was getting more angry than scared now.

"I wasn't allowed to, but I love you very much and have accompanied you whenever possible over the last few years. You know I have tried to get you to love me." He looked at her with peaceful eyes.

His gaze melted her anger. Before she could respond, a voice came from above them.

"Welcome to the Falconian realm of Paradise. You have been translated into the New Falcon. Your lives are now free. Imagine anything you want and you shall have it. Those of you with partners find yourselves together, while others might be in groups or alone. Call to someone with an image in your mind and they will hear you.

"Call forth you favorite food and you shall have it. You can will yourself hungry or satisfied. Try it now."

Dalla held out his hand and a plate loaded with chocolate cake appeared. He took a handful with his fingers, "Mm, this is good. Try it."

Eerin was still upset, "Don't be tricked by food. Something is definitely wrong."

The voice again sounded. "Re-clothe yourself in any fashion you wish. Dream up a location you always wanted to visit or imagine the home of your dreams. Ask for a servant and one will appear to help you."

Dalla waived his hand and they were in a beautiful spring forest by a lake. Eerin was starting to cry. He held her. "Look at this. It is so vast that it has to be somehow real."

Eerin calmed as she surveyed the scene. "Wow, this is a really beautiful place. Do you think we could touch the water?"

"Sure," he replied confidently, though he wasn't actually sure.

They strode forward and touched the cool lake water. He then splashed her.

"Hey," she replied loudly and splashed him back. Soon they were both wet and laughing.

Dalla waved a hand and he was wearing swimming trunks, so she blinked herself into a bikini and they went swimming. After a bit, they lay on the beach in the warm sunshine.

Dalla then sat up and said, "Let's see."

He snapped his fingers and he was dressed like he was ready to go out dancing, in a silk shirt and tight pants.

She laughed at him, "That's not attire for a forest."

He said, "We can go somewhere else, like a street café in Misdrodram."

She sighed deeply, then stood and was wearing a casual, full-length cotton dress in soft blues and greens. "Okay. Let's go. But I still think something is wrong."

A moment later they were walking up to a sidewalk café in the distant city they had planned on visiting one day. They took their seats and glanced at the holographic menu, hovering in the air above the set table. An elegantly dressed man approached them. "May I take your order?"

Eerin was curious, "Are you real?"

He smiled. "My name is Michael and I always wanted to come to this city to work at a café and meet people from all over the world, so here I am. My friend Lorri is the cook. She used to love cooking, so I talked her into coming here when we translated. You can, of course, adjust the food once you get it. Drinks? Are you ready to order?"

Eerin said, "Iced Tea. What would you suggest, Michael?"

"An appetizer of Bruschetta or Portabella Crostini, followed by some home-made pasta or ravioli and your choice of chicken or steak."

Dalla added, "I'll have some iced tea also. We'll try both of those appetizers."

"Very good, sir. I'll be back with your order in just a moment."

He walked into the café and came right out with a tray, obviously not needing to wait for time to pass for food to be prepared. He set down their drinks and steaming appetizers. "Anyone else joining you?"

Eerin thought for a moment, then replied, "Yes."

"Very good, I'll return when your guests arrive." Michael smiled as if truly enjoying himself and walked back into the café.

Another party of four arrived and took seats closer to the building.

"Guests?" Dalla inquired.

"Yes, I'm going to call on my dad and see what he knew about all this."

She just looked into the air and her thoughts sent a message. Her father soon replied, "Yes, Dear."

"Can you join us for lunch?" She spoke to the empty air.

"I'd love too," the air replied.

A moment later, a well-dressed man appeared, "Your mother thought it appropriate if I answer your questions alone. She is very involved in designing us a dream home, though I'm sure it will be expanded continually."

Dalla looked at him, but before he could say something, Eerin's father added, "Dalla, you can stay, I'm very glad my daughter has such a wise man with her."

Eerin offered him a bruschetta, which he ate hungrily in his usual fast fashion. She then asked, "Did you know about this translation business?"

"Yes," he sighed. "I made the decision not to fill you in, since you were one of the youngest women on the planet and would therefore be chosen as an innocent representative."

"You lied to me." Her eyes were burning.

"I did not tell you what I knew, which was not everything, however I did not tell you actual lies. You have a very special place in all this. You are now an immortal, so you can do what you want, but please learn to enjoy yourself. You take life too seriously."

"Yeah, I do. Life is the most serious thing there is," she replied.

He smiled as he consumed two more bruschetta, "These are excellent. Have you had one yet?"

"You're changing the subject," she stated.

"No, dear. I am pointing out that now you can enjoy life to the fullest."

An instant later a voice from the air said, "Hi Eerin, Hope you are enjoying yourself. Geoffrey, should we have a lake-side or ocean-side villa?"

"I'm fine, Mother," Eerin replied sarcastically.

"Your song was beautiful, dear," her mother added.

"You didn't clarify what was going to happen to us." Eerin replied.

"I would think the ocean is grander, Margarette." Geoffrey interrupted.

"I'm glad you are enjoying yourself Eerin. Nice way to start your new life, a fine café in Misdrodram. That's very stylish." Her mother sounded proud.

Eerin smiled at her dad, "You should go help her."

"Very good," he replied. "I love you, dear," he said and vanished.

"I love you, too," she replied to the empty seat.

She then tried the food and it was extremely delicious. Even though her mind was reeling, she engaged Dalla about what they should do next. Michael brought them platters of food and then joined in conversation. Not quite proper etiquette, but then again, circumstances were not quite normal. He introduced them to Lorri, a small pixie of a woman, with short, cropped hair and a happy demeanor, who was very proud of the cooking skills she had learned from her grandmother. A golden tabby cat had followed her out of the café and brushed against Eerin's leg. Eerin picked it up and started petting it.

"This cat seems real," Eerin said as it began purring.

"She is real. That's my Sunflower. She followed me here." Lorri replied, beaming with happiness.

"Why do you think she followed you here?" Dalla asked.

"Probably because she was with me when we translated. Michael and I were together at our cottage and she wouldn't leave us alone. I guess she sensed something major was happening." Lorri smiled.

"Something major to say the least," Eerin replied. "I wonder how many other pets came with their owners?"

Michael answered, "I have done a few inquiries of our friends with pets and none of their pets came along. I asked the system what became of them and was assured they are being well cared for by the robotic workers of Falcon."

Just then, another couple approached who knew Michael and Lorri. After introductions, Michael took orders and Lorri produced food trays that simply floated from the café. They all laughed and enjoyed themselves for hours, eating and talking about all kinds of things they were going to do.

# 2. The Wandini

A frustrating day of travel went by, during which Geardon did not have enough clues to gain insight into the situation. Each Falconian possessed a cubic centimeter [point four inches per side] of halo-matter, a vast wealth available to very few in the galaxy and yet every citizen was granted it at birth. No immigration was ever permitted, even to those who possessed such wealth. This was enough halo-matter to manifest as many material objects as they wanted, though not a fully realistic life-sized lover. Maya possessed many times this amount before her upgrade, so he wondered at her new potential. Life on Falcon 4 was near to paradise and yet the people were naturally driven to unravel the secrets of life and nature.

Upon arrival to the world of the Wandini, Geardon seemed a bit apprehensive. He studied the continents as she projected maps and images into the air about him. Previously he had flown in and explored according to how he felt moved.

Finally, he pinpointed where he wanted to go and pointing at the map in the air said, "Prepare a shuttle and I will descend on this continent, onto this mountain by this lake."

Maya's response surprised him. She again grew to the size of a person, though petite and still elf-like, "May I come along? My upgrade allows me to travel beyond the confines of the ship."

"So that's what the upgrade was about. You can come into the shuttle, but I need to make contact alone. You can monitor through my medallion as usual."

The shuttle was a glowing disk in the air and he flew it to a stone temple that was built on a mountain that was on one side of the lake. He hovered over the mountain for an hour, occasionally drawing symbols in the air with his craft's movements, so that the natives would be well aware of his presence. He hoped that those who knew him would be among those who ascended the paths to the sacred site.

Geardon dressed in a simple robe, took his Shukasi flute, and exited the glowing, disk-shaped craft on a ramp. He walked over to a stone slab that was before a statue of a large dragon beast, which the Wandini called an Ergort. He took a seat, closed his eyes, and began to play the mystical flute.

The Wandini who had climbed the mountain gathered about him, but he played in a trance, only vaguely aware of them. The magic of the flute and the perfect weather that had blessed them cast a spell of calm. The Wandini gathered peacefully. He played for a long time. Finally, he fell into silence and meditated, emotionally expressing his coming for their help. When he opened his eyes and smiled, they hooted and ululated. He had to laugh with relief and then he stood, put the flute in the case that hung from a shoulder strap and walked into their midst holding out his hands, knowing they would want to touch him.

Some of the Wandini had brought drums and percussion instruments and they started to play. Some began to dance about, circling the drummers. It was an impromptu festival. Geardon focused on the sound and let the images of the Wandini occupy his whole mind. They were squat, pygmy-like beings with a very dark color of brown and bluish mottled skin and long ape-like arms. Most had rolls of fat. They had turned up noses and small tusks emerging from their cheek bones. The Wandini were all females and their breasts pointed down toward the ground. Clad minimally with many decorative items similar to skins, feathers, and scales, they danced with wild acrobatic gyrations. It was easy for Geardon to leave his quest out of his consciousness, keeping it temporarily hidden from their telepathic group mind. Soon, others arrived with food and beverages, offering Geardon many delights, until he was too stuffed to eat anything else, which they knew telepathically and radiated pleasure about his satiated state.

Halfway through the night, Geardon was approached by a group of seven Wandini whom he recognized. Nigaru, one of the younger matched pairs whom he knew from his previous visit, was now in the bonded position. Gibru and Semal were now the two elders. He was introduced to the three new younger members of the family, Milo, Droga, and Nadin. Finally, he was introduced to Narina, Nigaru's mate.

As he made their acquaintance, the crowd gradually took notice, quieted and gathered around them. He then explained his visit by mentally picturing the Falconian people, noble and wise, disappearing from their planet and his need to communicate with the ancestors on that world. Momentarily his Grandmother appeared. He felt sure they had called her up. She laughed, greeting the Wandini whom she had studied with when incarnate. She then turned to look at Geardon and spoke to him as if he were a child. "These people are wise and bringing them is an auspicious choice. The Dragon imagines he has power to violate the wheel, but it will roll on."

Geardon's Grandmother laughed madly and projected an image of Draco stuck on a wheel, looking backwards and the wheel rolling very slowly down a hill, with Draco at the top exclaiming that he was supreme, ruling the nature of the universe, then the ground slapping him on the butt with every turn. It was very slapstick, with the ground become more anthropomorphic with every slap as the wheel turned. The Wandini loved it and howled, rolling on the ground and sending their laughter through the telepathic plane.

The group of seven Wandini, of which he knew some from his previous visit, agreed to accompany him. They were gifted some traditional sacred objects to bring with them from those assembled. They boarded the disk-shaped craft and he tried to introduce them to a full-sized Maya, but they drew their red volcanic glass weapons upon first sight of her. He let them know she was part of the ship, which was like a womb, but they still feared her. She invited them to touch her or to put their knives in her, as they would have no effect. One of the younger ones, Droga, tried the knife, but Maya let it pass through her like she was thick water. Maya transformed into a form that was a cross between a Wandini and her normal elf-like appearance. They took Maya's transformation as the effect of the knife killing some part of her and making her adopt some part of them. Maya offered them food, by projecting images of various dishes in the air, which again spooked them. The Wandini were convinced Maya was a strange spirit being; but since it was making an offering of food and was Geardon's friend, they finally accepted her.

By this time the shuttle disk had arrived inside the Golden Flash, so Maya opened the door and the Wandini followed her down the ramp. She led them to one of the medium dining halls and rather than floating the food in, she walked to another dining hall, created the food in the synthesizers, and walked it back into the hall where the Wandini were seated, serving them herself. Geardon's genome medallion had absorbed countless bits of information at the feast on the planet and so Maya created foods that the Wandini knew. They were overjoyed and ate a great deal. Finally, Geardon led them to their cabin, which had been redecorated in a primitive fashion, using halo-matter to create sleeping mats and drums and other familiar things to keep them occupied.

*        *        *        *        *

The next day, Command received a video, without commentary, of an occurrence on the fighter city that was guarding Falcon.

Geardon said, "Maya, lock the control room, just in case the Wandini feel my emotion and try to come to us, then play the 3D media."

Maya replied, "You will see the fighter city's Security Master, Cynthea Nestler."

"Hull breach, sector seven, bay 147, hull breach, sector seven,..." The ship's monitors showed Cynthea start awake in shock. The display indicated that this was the first instance of this emergency code: the fighter city had never before been breached.

"Full robotic resistance," she commanded the autonomous floating globe that woke her.

Cynthea was thankful that she had worn her nanofiber suit to bed, and had left her helmet within reach. She pulled it on as she dashed into the corridor. Soon a full array of displays filled her helmet as she ran toward the breach. The video displays showed the chaos in the receiving dock where the intruders had entered. A soldier who was on call took her hand, so she could run while placing her undivided attention on the attack scene she was watching through her audio-visual feeds.

Her first view was of a hallway. Since it was in the loading zone, the true outer hull was actually inside of the breach area. The intruders had tried to seal off the area they were in, but the ship's systems overrode the lock commands they had issued. Hovering monitor spheres had just arrived at the scene and so Cynthea switched her helmet's displays and her view became that of flying down the corridor. Through the now opened hatch, dozens of spider-like battle bots were pouring in. As her video sphere rounded the corner, it was blasted by a weapon that reached around a corner from the breach site.

Cynthea rewound the visual feed and froze the view from just before the sphere's destruction. The insectoid defensive bots were being destroyed before getting all the way down the hall. Their pieces littered the corridor. She visually boarded another hovering sphere and noticed that hive carriers had arrived.

Cynthea shouted the all-out attack command. "Full Swarm A95."

Thousands of deadly insectoid robots and biobots poured from the hives. Their myriad forms flew and crawled, covering the floor, walls, and ceiling, as well as the air space at rates vastly faster than any real insect could. Cynthea let the main mass flow down the corridor and through the hatch before following them, hoping her view sphere would survive longer this time.

Cynthea visually rounded the corner and to her amazement, a humanoid in body armor had stepped in the way and was firing a pulsing gravitational cannon weapon. The blasts got most of the hive, but some got by. She ducked her sphere back and then looked around the corner again. The swarm had covered the humanoid and a second humanoid in body armor had stepped out. It was already demobilized and being consumed. The floor was completely covered with a thick layer of parts, slimy with hydraulic, lubricant, and synthetic biological fluids. The leading spiders had entered the room of the breach. Cynthea had her sphere fly quickly to look into the room.

Three more humanoids wearing body-armor were protecting one in lesser armor that was connected to several of the ships systems, trying to hack for something.

"Cut all data access to this area," said Cynthia, indicating the command was to the ship by focusing her eyes on a symbol in the helmet.

"Release the final snake swarm," she commanded, looking at the hive symbol.

The insect swarm that was attempting to cover the intruders fell back as the robotic snakes coiled about the intruders, biting and constricting.

"Save as much of the hacking being as possible and the heads of the others," Cynthia said, speaking quickly to the hive.

As the three guards fell, the swarm finally cut the connection that the hacker had by consuming its eyes and sensory ports, as the constrictors about its legs brought it down.

The ship that the intruders had arrived in had punctured the thinner hull of a loading area with an entry tunnel and was trying to worm its way free of the attachment. Cynthia immediately ordered the defensive ships that had surrounded the enemy ship outside the hull to immobilize it. She also commanded that a disruptive amount of communication noise fill the area, so that the ship could not transmit anything that the intruders may have fed it.

The soldier squeezed her hand and shouted, "We have arrived." Cynthea switched her view screen to see what was actually before her, opened a hatch, and ran into the scene of havoc. Her suit protected her feet from the shrapnel that littered the floor and had begun to burn. Her helmet filtered the smoke and also used extended frequencies in infrared and ultraviolet to help her maintain her vision. She pulled out her laser sword and beheaded the guards, commanding some larger insectoid robots to carry them into safekeeping. She picked up the squirming hacker, appalled that something looking human was inside the suit. She noticed that where the legs were partially consumed, titanium bones with robotic controls were visible.

Soldiers in body armor arrived and she had them take the living intruder into restraining quarters for interrogation. She thankfully noted that no ship personnel appeared to have been present at the location of the breach when the cyborgs attacked.

Cynthea verified that the intruder's ship had its engines destroyed and made her way to the detoxification center. After having her exterior suit and gear cleaned, she changed into a fresh nanofiber suit and made her way to a pre-assigned emergency location. Admiral Gerard was waiting for her.

"Situation under control. I don't believe that any ship personnel were lost." Cynthea was still breathing heavily from running to the meeting.

"What do you think they were after?" he asked.

"Information," she replied as she pulled up a few still images of the cyborg attached to the ships systems. "This cyborg was captured alive. I doubt that it is a living persona, the person who had lived in this cyborg body probably moved into a new one or a tank. These cyborg's mind crystals were probably wiped clean and specially programmed for this mission. We took the heads of the others, before the fires cooked them too badly. We will do a full interrogation."

Cynthea then spoke to the ship's system, "What were the intruders trying to gain access to?"

The ship responded, "Anything to do with the planet Falcon and this fighter city's mission, but primarily something with a key word of 'translator.'"

She asked the ship's Synthetic Intelligence, "What is a translator that they would be seeking it?"

The ship responded, "No logical conclusion."

She asked The admiral, "Any idea what a translator is?"

"Not a clue, but I will question the Star System authorities who assigned us to this mission."

The admiral then looked at Cynthea closely, "Are you all right?"

"Fine. I just can't believe we were breached. And by cyborgs, no less." She looked him directly in the eyes as she spoke.

"I'll do everything in my power to find out what this is about. You're dismissed to carry on the investigation."

"Thanks," was all she replied and then hurried out and headed toward the interrogation chamber.

*     *     *     *     *

"The Wandini are agitated and want to see you," was Maya's first comment.

Geardon replied, "I know, they are calling me. They felt my disturbance at seeing the attack. Let me go to them."

Geardon went to the Wandini and comforted them. He presented scenes by picturing them in his mind, showing the advanced state of a number of worlds, including Falcon, trying to get them to understand his time and culture, and yet knowing that in some ways they understood life more than the technological societies.

# 3. Intrigues

Upon arriving at Falcon 4, Geardon docked at the orbiting hyper-fighter city. Several guards met him and quickly led him to one of a thousand clear domes on the outer skin of the hyper-fighter.

"Welcome aboard, sir." He was greeted by Admiral Winston Gerard, commander of the assembled fleet. Geardon, whose rank as a Genome Auditor was considered one of the most powerful in the United Star System, towered over these off-worlders. The admiral was wearing a standard, nondescript security uniform: a black shimmering shirt and sleek pants of woven nanofiber, able to withstand most ship-worthy weapons. Only a small chest insignia displayed his rank. He wore a cloth belt bearing three weapons that could be effective against humans without damaging the life supporting walls of the ship, a wand-like stunner, a small, tube-like blaster, and a deadly, nano-dart pistol.

Admiral Gerard introduced his two advisers, who were seated opposite each other at the round table in the center of the dome. The two women were surrounded by their holo-displays, which they continued to scan for information. "This is the Fleet Communication Adviser, Ms. Miranda Liam."

The holographic light surrounding her head froze. She stood up, smiled at Geardon, and bowed in a silent greeting; a motion which Geardon returned. Ms. Liam was petite, with dark, Terran Asian eyes in a beautiful, fine-featured face. She had long black hair and rich skin, unlike the unnatural complexion of most off-worlders who tan under lights. Her features were complimented by her black, full-length, nanofiber robe. She wore black slippers of the same nano-cloth, but decorated with floral patterns. She seemed friendly, despite her formal attitude.

Geardon could see his reflection in the lower part of the dome, where the inner surface had a mirror quality: tall, tan, and gravity-strong. People who live in space, with artificial light and gravity, have a diminished countenance; refined they would say. Geardon's long reddish-brown hair was tied behind his head, his slightly unkempt beard and fiery hazel eyes gave him a wild look of an ancient sage compared to the admiral's military properness. Geardon's long nanofiber robe, shimmering gray due the precision of its weave, and his crystal gold medallion of power added to the mystique that he projected and to his right to absolute command.

"And this is Cynthea Nestler, our security adviser," the admiral continued.

The other woman froze her holo-displays momentarily. "Greetings, sir." She had light, soft-blue eyes and an athletic, robust build, as if she worked out in an elevated g-chamber. Her blond hair and white skin were contrasted by her black uniform's silver shimmer. It was a one-piece warrior's jumpsuit with attached feet, made of especially thick nano-cloth, which would allow her to walk through fire. Geardon would have judged it overkill, had he not viewed the recent security video. She almost looked cute, Geardon reflected, except the hood draped behind her shoulders like a cowl and her emotionless expression gave her the cold appearance of a soldier entering a battle. Geardon mirrored her stoic appearance as he nodded at her. She sat without a verbal reply from Geardon and reactivated her data streams.

Admiral Gerard walked around the table and stood across from Geardon, waiting for him to be seated first in deference to his rank. Cynthea was on Geardon's right and Miranda on his left. Geardon stood a moment longer, gazing out of the clear dome at the planet Falcon. The world looked peaceful and environmentally balanced; green and blue draped with about thirty percent drifting, white clouds.

As soon as Geardon was seated, the admiral sat and began talking. "Sir, everything is running normally on Falcon, except the people appear to be missing. It is a most disconcerting situation. The first set of orders from the United Star System command indicated that the population of Falcon were all camping in natural bio-regions. The orders were for hyper-fighter 001HF3 to scan the world and locate each member of the population, as a drill.

"The reconnaissance data didn't show humans on, nor even under, the surface. All subsequent scans with wide-band sensory equipment have not found humans anywhere, and analysis does not favor the idea that they have a cloak which would invalidate our probes. The puzzling thing is their robotic servants and gardeners have continued working as usual, as if waiting for their owners to return. All the other animals of the planet are being tracked and appear to have relatively normal behavioral patterns. The robots are even caring for the people's pets, though the pet population is statistically low.

"In response to this data, the United Star Systems command has assembled a complete war fleet and posted an emergency security cordon, placing the whole star system off limits. You can't move a whole world's population without a lot of ships, which would have left energy signatures in space that we could have tracked. I have had my crew search all the other planets of this star system for clues and they have only found standard robotic mining colonies. My security team has stealthily checked the records of all local star systems for suspicious ship traffic without result. We are recalibrating how we scan for human presence, to break through any possible cloaking chambers; but the improbability of hiding a whole world's population is great. We are also keeping an optical monitor on the surface, but with no result to date."

Geardon nodded. "Thank you Admiral, you have done a very thorough job. This all began when the planet Falcon accessed the USS main computers with a direct message, delivered through an unknown means into the heart of the galactic system, a feat considered impossible. The message was a cryptic riddle, which we have yet to understand. I intend to find out what's going on here."

Geardon turned and asked the communications adviser seated to his left, "Ms. Miranda Liam, may I have a tactical report of the battle array?"

She looked up and most of her array of holographic displays froze again. "Genome Auditor, sir, four destroyers, seven hyper-fighters, and this hyper-fighter-city are holding position." She quickly produced a holographic map of the planet and the defensive positions of the ships over the center of the table. She made these display appear solid, while the private displays that surrounded her head assumed closer positions around her.

After a precursory look at the map, Geardon turned to the security adviser on his right, "Ms. Cynthea Nestler, is the space around Falcon secure?"

Her display froze and lowered. "There are several issues, sir. Someone wants information very badly," she reported, looking directly at him. "We were breached by a cyborg ship as soon as we began our supposed drill. They hacked into our fighter city's systems momentarily before I destroyed them with a hive. We have interrogated every speck of memory crystal in them. They were expertly cleaned and reprogrammed. They were searching for a device referred to as a translation tool or a translator. We have no data to understand what the cyborgs wanted so desperately to have motivated them to commit an act of assault on a USS ship."

"Not yet, but I am having my ship's advanced systems hack into the Falconian system as we speak," Geardon answered calmly. "I was sent a report of your battle and you acted bravely and swiftly. It did not appear that the cyborgs thought they would need longer than their calculated hack time, but they were wrong - the Falconians were digital masters. Are there any other issues besides the cyborg intrusion into your ship?"

"Thank you, sir. Yes. A delegation from Grindorf 4 breached space two days after the incident. As soon as they left hyper-velocity around the giant planet Falcon 7, they were met by one of the four destroyers in the star system. They are still claiming to have been called by the Falconians. They insist the Falconians gave them diplomatic immunity and permission to ignore the open frequency broadcasts warning all vessels to avoid this star system.

"Since the Grindorfian's brains are four times the size of a standard human's with eight times the capacity, their language and how they use it have evolved to a point where we are having trouble reasoning with them. They are very arrogant and have a disdain for any limitations placed upon them by mere humans. We have put prosecution proceedings on temporary hold and allowed the individuals to return to Grindorfia."

She waved her hands over the receptor pads sitting on the table in front of her and some of the holographic projections reappeared around her. "The Grindorfians were unable to hack into Falcon's system, but we have no doubt that their intent was similar to the cyborgs. The Grindorfian ship released spy satellites. These probes may have been the real purpose of their mission. We picked up the miniature satellites' signals as they attempted to break into the Falconian system. The Grindorfians can hack into about any planetary system, but judging from the energy flows that we've recorded, the Falconian system has not yet returned anything."

Geardon was eager to find clues of some sort, "Miranda, what do we really know about these micro-satellites?"

"We have located four of them. We are just monitoring their data transmission codes, awaiting your orders, sir. We are trying to understand all their methodology, but even the superior intellect of the Grindorfians has not succeeded in getting returns from Falcon's system."

Geardon turned to the fleet admiral, "How many two-person battle ships are being used to secure the star system?"

"Ten ships per planet."

"Move the security index from 40, alert and ready, to 65, defensive scramble. I want a thousand two-person warrior vessels scrambled from the destroyers. I want fifty ships in orbit about every planet and every moon to prevent any farther breaches of this star system. Then surround those spy satellites sources with fifty warrior vessels each. Have hyper-fighter 007HF3 try to bring one in on a tractor beam, let's see what we have."

"Yes, sir." The Admiral Gerard immediately contacted three destroyer's commanders and specified the numbers of ships to be sent to target positions around every planet in the star system. A star system is a huge area to secure, but any entering ship would need to use a planet's mass as a momentum breaker to leave hyper-speed. The fighters' monitors could easily spot it and surround it as it returned to sub-light velocities. The admiral then deployed the warrior vessels to surround the satellites from the forth destroyer, purposely leaving the commanders of the first three destroyers unaware of the situation. Geardon listened to the deployment and watched the center display fill with new dots that represented two person ships flowing from the destroyers. The advisers went back to soaking up data from their halo-displays.

Finally, the admiral of the fleet deferred to Geardon. "Fighter contacted and ready for orders, sir."

Geardon spoke to the ship's Synthetic Intelligence. "Open a channel with the destroyer."

Geardon then spoke directly to the destroyer commander. "Commander, proceed to target coordinates with caution and full shields."

"Yes, sir. We'll pass the perimeter of warrior ships in about ten seconds." The commander sounded nervous to be talking to such a high-ranking individual as Geardon. The commander sent a display of their progress rather than displaying himself on the holo-comm. "Gravitational containment beams charged and ready to lock on to the target, sir."

"Have your ship's weapons aimed at it, then capture it in a gravitational bottle and put it into your containment bay," Geardon replied.

"We have the satellite. We're bringing it into the maximum security containment bay." The fighter commander paused momentarily. "We have it locked down in a crystal-steel examination container. Display activated."

Geardon could see a holographic display of a sphere with two protruding hair-like strands surrounded by specifications as preliminary analysis routines were run. The sphere diameter was 2.764 cm. and it appeared to be covered in a photo-absorption medium for power, so it could continue to function for a long time. The Grindorfians were very serious about getting whatever data they wanted. The two strands were braided antennae several hairs breaths thick and about 10 cm. long. The display showed that the transmitter tube was actively sending out access codes. Internal gravitational scans revealed pockets of substances for energy storage, the satellite brain, and quintabytes of memory to hold the treasures they sought.

"Stand by commander. Destroyer comm-channel on hold," Geardon commanded the ship's Synthetic Intelligence to cut the communication with the fighter commander.

Geardon recognized the probe and told Admiral Gerard and the two advisers, "The probe is a basic data spy device of a type that has existed for several centuries. The possible programming capabilities that they hold is always evolving and becoming more powerful. The Grindorfians are not in the spy business. They probably purchased the satellites on the black market. The advanced programming they loaded the devices with makes them extremely dangerous. The Grindorfians are programming geniuses beyond what any natural human could conceive of."

Geardon then turned to the admiral, "Order forty of the fifty warrior ships which surrounded this target to fly the boundary of dawn, in case we have orbiting spy-satellites waking up by wandering out of the planet's shadow and gaining power. I don't want the Grindorfians, or anyone else, breaching Falconian security and getting into their planet's core system until we know what's going on here. The Grindorfians have shown an extreme interest in something and I want to know what that is."

Admiral Gerard complied, and then spoke to the communications adviser. "Ms. Liam, I can still see the glowing signature of the gravitational field that holds the spy satellite in mid-air in the containment bay. Can we decipher the code it's transmitting while it's in the bottle?"

She responded, "No, sir. We can only register its energy and analyze it as a data transmission; we can't read the data itself. We deciphered some of its strategies before we picked it up. We believe it is requesting access to technical data, and believe that it is not getting anything in return from the Falconian system."

Geardon re-opened the channel to the commander of the destroyer with the micro-satellite, "Commander, set up several needle lasers, charged and ready to destroy the satellite if necessary, and then release it from its gravitational bottle so that it can be read."

Suddenly the communication link to the fighter went down. Warnings sounded, and the admiral quickly called for reports from the remaining warrior crafts, which replied.

"Erratic behavior, sir"

"The ship had a moment of power fluctuations and gave off strange energy transmissions."

"It seemed to lose gravitational integrity for a moment."

Then the destroyer came back on the secure line. "Sir, the spy satellite hacked into our fighter's systems. It happened so fast that we had no time to respond. The ship's Synthetic Intelligence destroyed it with the needle lasers you had us prepare. I'm afraid the micro-satellite's core looks like Swiss cheese. It's going to be hard to analyze, sir."

"Good enough, commander. Transfer the relic to this fighter-city and run a complete diagnostic report on your ship's systems. The means used to breach your firewalls should reveal more about the attackers. Thank you, Commander. Is your crew all right?"

"We're in a bit of a mess from our gravity fluctuations, but no major injuries reported, sir. Thank you, sir, for having us arm those needle lasers. That action saved our lives. It is our pleasure to be at your service."

"Thank you and your crew as well, Captain. The information gained will be very useful. Transmission complete." Geardon closed the channel.

"Well, Admiral, what do you think about the other targets?"

"The Grindorfians want data from the Falconian system and have been willing to risk violating many galactic laws. We have limited ability to contact the Falconian core system ourselves, so we don't know what the Grindorfians are after, but I would guess it is the translator device. I would not like to see them get whatever they're looking for." The admiral shook his head.

Geardon also shook his head, "Agreed, especially since it is highly probable that it is responsible for making the people of the planet disappear. These spy satellites are very dangerous and not a primary objective at this time. Destroy them."

The admiral smiled approvingly, "Awaiting orders, sir."

Geardon replied, "Have a hyper-fighter put one in a gravitational containment field as far from this fighter-city possible. We don't know what might have been learned from the first attack on the destroyer and the satellites may share data. Flatten it into a wafer with the gravitational containment field until it stops transmitting. Then pull it in and put the pieces into a secure crystal-steel container. Have the same fighter proceed to the others, one by one, and do the same. When we have all three, place them aboard a code red messenger robotic ship for rapid transport to USS headquarters."

The admiral made the arrangements for the spy satellites to be destroyed.

Geardon looked over at the security adviser surrounded by her halo-display, "Ms. Nestor, have there been reports of any other incidents?"

"Yes, sir. Another long-range signal making continual requests to the Falconian system was registered as coming from

Sigalin 2. We have contacted the human cyborg race that lives there. They claimed the signal was an automated scientific exchange program. They reluctantly agreed to stop transmitting after the USS ministry coerced them."

"Have there been any inquiries about the situation from any other races of beings?" Geardon was searching for any clues as to what was going on with the planet Falcon.

Ms. Liam spoke up, "The advanced race referred to as the Nagati, who represent the USS to more evolved galactic citizens, have requested a complete report. They have space cities around many neutron stars and even a few black holes. Their domains extend far beyond the realms that humans have explored. We have been directed to send a report to the closest space colonies. Their official communique was analyzed by several teams at headquarters."

She played the audio message, "The Nagati have felt a disturbance in the life force at coordinates 01101101 01010100 01010100..."

The report computer interrupted by fading the volume of the stream of numbers to provide their meaning, "Light years from pulsars of known periods indicating the star system of the planet Falcon as this location."

Returning to the message, the audio continued, "...01101101 01011000. The Nagati expect a full and complete report. To possess an incarnation in the material universe is a fortunate treasure."

Without comment on the cryptic message of the Nagati, Ms. Liam continued her report "The alien race dwelling around the star Vini, which is twelve light years away from Falcon, also wants to know what is going on, they are aware of the armada of military might gathered about their neighboring system. The Nagati will not reveal anything to any common galactic race that the USS deals with, but the Vini might leak information to the rest of the universe. Headquarters has issued statements to them, to placate them before they start rumors, but we don't know enough to pacify them. They know we have four destroyers, seven ultra-fighters, and this ultra-fighter-city surrounding Falcon, enough firepower to conquer or destroy any world. They had made previous requests to the USS Department of Planetary Relations during the last year: Falcon had cut itself off from trade and the Vini took the action personally. They are a simple, but intelligent race that will require diplomatic assurances in a timely fashion. They will not wait for very long before filing a formal petition for information about what is going on, which will put the incident into galactic news."

Cynthea spoke up, "As you requested, all of the spy satellites have been flattened and sealed in crystal-steel containers."

"Thank you, advisers", Geardon replied, then looked pointedly at the admiral, "I'm going down to the planet's surface."

The admiral was surprised by Geardon's abrupt decision, though he recovered quickly. "Would it not be advisable to let a team do it, so you are not at risk?"

"No." One by one, Geardon looked pointedly in the eyes of each of his three new associates. "I need one pilot to hold down the ship who knows what is going on and two security personnel to accompany me on the surface. I want to know what went on. I want answers."

Miranda Liam spoke up without hesitation, "I will pilot the ship, sir."

Cynthea Nestler replied, "I will accompany you on the surface reconnaissance. A well-trained and trusted soldier can join us for additional security."

The admiral nodded in agreement, "I will provide an armored lander with two dozen warriors to provide a defensible position on the surface. Ms. Liam can pilot it and Ms. Nestler and her chosen soldier can accompany you as you explore the surface."

"I want to take a Golden Flash shuttle and just the four of us. I have some others in my ship who will also help. Unfortunately, we believe the people who once inhabited Falcon have all died and had their bodies recycled, so we will find nothing but an empty planet. My ships systems will hack into the Falconian system if possible." Geardon stood solemnly.

Admiral Gerard began clearances for the trip. He spoke as his fingers danced in the multicolor images that appeared before him," Golden Flash shuttle secured for landing."

Miriam's and Cynthea's displays disappeared, they rose and each nodded slightly to Geardon, who followed them down the winding corridor toward the Golden Flash. They were met by a soldier in full body armor.

Miranda and Cynthea followed Geardon up the tunneled ramp to the sleek winged disk. The shuttle flew them quickly to the waiting Golden Flash, a huge cylinder of glowing metal. Once inside the shuttle bay, the disk's door opened to a ramp. Geardon paused and turned to them, "Welcome aboard the Golden Flash, one of the fastest ships in the Galaxy. Let me show you to your quarters."

Miranda Liam sounded confused, "You mean each person has separate quarters?"

Geardon replied, "I will be staying alone in my quarters. You are each assigned to one of the ship's many guest cabins, which have two double beds that come from the walls and thus take no daytime space. The ship also has several luxury suites designed to hold a large family, which you are invited to use if you find them more in line with your desires."

Cynthea smiled, "Its planetary culture and even some space people's custom to sleep alone, Miranda, but I will share a room with you. Are you sure you don't want to share a room with us, Geardon?"

"No, thanks," Geardon made a strange smile and looked at them askew.

Cynthea chuckled, and squeezed Miranda's upper arm momentarily and Miranda finally smiled.

Cynthea spoke to Miranda, but also putting forth the spacer culture to Geardon, "I know being alone is terrifying to spacers, but it is natural to people who grow up on planets where there is lots of space. Most children go to sleep in their own room with their parents sharing a room nearby."

Miranda shivered at the thought and Cynthea continued, "I know that being alone or in open spaces seems so foreign to you, but the pleasure of being out under a starry sky on a beautiful summer night and then cuddling up in one's own bed are beyond words. My childhood memories are dear to me and I spend my holidays on planetary surfaces, but I have lived with you space people long enough to know your ways. Part of me feels comfort in our fighter and its civilization of ten thousand. I enjoy sharing your customs, as will my trusted soldier."

In the automated voice from the suit they heard a polite, "Yes, Ma'am."

"Your name, soldier." Geardon commanded.

"Class IX Malloy Mulgor, sir."

Geardon showed them to their room, really a series of joined rooms, and they set their bags down and immediately followed him to the main cabin in the front of the ship. Viewscreens, like windows, displayed the vastness of the fighter below them. The underside of the fighter was lined with hundreds of docked ships and hundreds of support vehicles. They all knew that in the fighters belly were another thousand two-person war ships. For a moment, they silently looked at the sea of ships and at the planet Falcon's blue and white globe in the distance.

A cube came floating in and set itself down in a docking port on the main console, then the ship's hatch closed.

Cynthea inquired, "Memory bank?"

Geardon smiled, "It just absorbed the entire fleet's memory banks, as well as performing updates on all these ship's master systems. My cube has a living core from the Brilliant Machine."

Cynthea had a disbelieving look on her face, as if her ship had been totally violated, even though she understood that her ship was really owned by the USS.

The cube half merged with the console, "My Lady Maya, may I introduce you to our guests, Cynthea, Miranda, and Soldier Malloy Mulgor."

Maya appeared in her small, elven form, sitting on the cube. She was dressed in a green one-piece monks robe. "You were running late, so I continued using the fleet's extra processing power."

"Thanks. Feed the data into our ships data storage and review it."

Maya bowed, "Yes, my lord."

Then into the control room strode a full sized Maya, who appeared as a living being. Geardon did not let on, but Cynthea questioned him, assuming the small figure was made in the full-sized person's image. "Pardon me sir, but I was under the impression from your docking signals that you were alone."

Geardon smiled, then turned to Maya. "Return to your post."

She gave him the look of an annoyed youth, then miniaturized and floated to the main console and merged with the small version of herself.

The women both were surprised. Geardon explained, "Maya and the Golden Flash are aspects of the Brilliant Machine." Before the women could react, he continued. "I think it is time you meet the other unauthorized members of our party. They are not galactic citizens, so could not be registered."

The women looked at him curiously, trying to imagine what he meant. He had the three of them follow him to the Wandini's cabin. He had telepathically sent them a message to be dressed and ready to meet strange guests and also to be on good behavior. Opening the door, the three were greeted by the mostly naked primitives, who only waited for a short introduction before they started poking fun at them. The soldier, who was still all suited up, was their favorite. Geardon was glad that the others could not sense the full import of their telepathic jibes.

Then one of the Wandini took a knife out, pretended to poke at the soldier, then did a back flip. The others rolled in laughter at their mockery of his persona. They made comments in their minimal language, which is used by them as a subconscious supplement to their mental exchanges. They kidded Cynthea about being too serious, but Miranda they seemed to like. She had been listening close and finally Miranda said something in an approximation of their language, which caused them all to gaze at her, wide eyed. Apparently, she had poked one of their comments back at them and after their momentary surprise; they were again rolling with laughter, which Miranda joined in.

They were ready to start drumming and eating and celebrating, but Geardon let them know that all of them present were going to the world of the missing dead. The Wandini became serious and Geardon let them know that they would be called soon. The Wandini sat together in a tangled group and became silent, and the landing party returned to the control room.

# 4. A Disappearing Act

Descending in the Golden Flash's shuttle pod, Cynthea exclaimed, "Look at that crystal city! It looks like something out of a fairy tale."

Geardon smiled. "Reviewing a planet from the database is never like experiencing it directly. Fused quartz is often just sand colored, but the Falconians used advance techniques to purify and color it. Miranda, can we do a fly over?"

Miranda indicated a course change in the halo-displays.

They flew low over the city. Cynthea continued to verbalize the amazement they all felt. "It's paradise. Look at the parks and rivers flowing through the city. The streets glitter and the design looks like art with the perfect blending of many colors. It's creepy, though, that there are no people, just maintenance robots here and there."

Geardon stated, "Yes, that's the part that makes me feel a strange emptiness in the pit of my stomach."

As they flew away from the city, they saw many dwellings fit into the natural environment, all created in crystal of many colors. Some blended in and were hard to spot, others were colorful sets of domes shining in the sun.

The shuttle pod landed near the center of a large park adjacent to a vast natural preserve. It was a three-kilometer [two mile] walk to a previously populated area of Falcon 4. Geardon radioed the command center in orbit. "Admiral Gerard, as I'm looking out the windows and scanning the area around us, it seems like a natural world. Flying down, our visual sensors showed landscape maintenance droids continuing in their work. A whole world of people doesn't just surrender themselves. If it's not some kind of trick, there must be signs of struggle or forensic data available. We will find out what happened. Our craft has analyzed the atmosphere and ruled out virus and poison. We're leaving the craft to investigate."

"Proceed with caution," Admiral Gerard added. "Remember, they had cutting edge technologies that most of the rest of the galaxy could only dream about. They may have gone into some kind of cloaked city, or even have personal cloaks." After a brief moment Admiral Gerard added, "Good luck, Geardon."

Cynthea had chosen a special defensive security soldier with major biological adaptations. Cynthea suited up like the soldier in body armor with complete internal environments. Geardon gave last minute instructions to the pilot, Miranda. She would remain in command of the ship, watching over them virtually.

Maya then pulled another new trick, duplicating herself, with one of her becoming a full-sized human. Geardon did not know she could do that, but he did not let on as the human-sized Maya asked, "Request permission to join you, sir."

"It would be our pleasure to have you along," he replied.

As Geardon stepped out of the airlock in his standard robes and took a deep breath, everything seemed calm and peaceful. The air tasted wonderful: he felt no ill effects. There were birds singing in the warm sunlight, but no sign of humans or mass death. He reported, "The air seems good and the other life forms seem vital, though no sign of humans. We are in the rural area where one group of this population center was supposed to have their annual return-to-nature feast."

Geardon continued as he walked on, "The birds are singing and the place is quiet enough to make us imagine that everyone is on vacation. I'm headed for a central large field where landscape droids were reported by the ships sensors."

When Geardon arrived, he saw a center area that had a large spot where dirt was overturned and replanted. The grass around it showed signs of a large crowd. There were robotic workers loosening the soil. Geardon approached one cautiously as his two security guards, Cynthea and her soldier, held their weapons in ready positions, each confident that their suits' robotic firing mechanisms would beat these robots in speed if they decided to act improperly. Maya stood casually to the side.

Geardon decided to use the formal approach, "Geardon Stranoff, intergalactic genome inspector, please yield for questioning." His bio-circuits caused his nanotech medallion to patch into the droids circuits. The robots stopped and looked at him. He questioned them, "What are you doing?"

One of the robots replied, "Sir, we are returning the field to its standard cultivated state."

Geardon responded, knowing that the machines need specific questions, "What was in that area where the dirt is replanted and did you have specific orders to cover it up?"

The robot that answered them responded, "Sir, our masters said that after they left and the festival was cleaned up, that we should maintain the landscape according to its purpose and original style, as we have always done."

"How did they leave and where did they leave to?"

"Sir, they left their bodies to enter into the virtual realms. They left us instructions until the galactic ruling community diplomats arrived. Do you represent that community's delegation?"

"Yes, I represent the highest authority of the intergalactic United Star Systems. What do you mean they entered the virtual realms? Are they dead?"

The robot replied, "Sir, we have a presentation for you. I am just a worker droid, however since you are a Genome Inspector and your medallion has verified your rank, I can give you an access code for a connection to the planetary system."

"Yes, yield to my medallion the access codes."

"Sir, please follow me for a formal presentation prepared in a hundred and fifty-two distinct geographical areas. We need to enter into the city for a data link."

Walking about three kilometers through the field they had landed in, they came to the golden quartz streets. Most modern worlds had only walkways, since everyone went everywhere by hovercraft of some type and style, however this city had wide streets. The city appeared abandoned, so Geardon reported again, "We are following a droid back to the city for a data link. I think all will be revealed. How many people occupied this city three days ago when contact was lost?"

Miranda replied from the ship, "About ten thousand. It was the eighth largest city on Falcon. Most people lived in rural communities."

Geardon followed the worker droid to a home of seven crystal domes. "Sir, all terminals on the world are prepared for the next generation of human inhabitants. This home's data links can provide you with the information you seek through the access codes that your medallion has received."

Geardon had the others wait outside. He entered the home, found its sensory surround room, sat down, and commanded, "Provide me with information on the inhabitants of Falcon 4 and what happened to them."

The session began with a man sitting on a bench in a lush forest. The virtual reality was comparable to the best in the galaxy, better than anything on most worlds. He could smell the different air and feel the wind on his face. The birds and squirrels seemed to be real creatures. "I am Draco Nanitron, but I am called the Virtual Dragon. I invented a translator device and will try to explain the unbelievable. When I first invented it, our research team knew it was powerful and dangerous, yet the potential that it showed us was astounding. We believed it would allow us to enter into the virtual realms as complete beings, total virtual reality. We developed the translators and began testing them with simulators. It was then that the first team translated into the virtual realm."

Geardon was amazed at the clarity of the scene and the amazing quality of the virtual images; it was as if a person were sitting before him. He could not distinguish the reality of the house he had entered. Draco was sitting before him, talking animatedly with his hands, "There were seven members and at that phase the machines were large and cumbersome, filling a hundred meter [three hundred thirty foot] long floor of our research facility. We took the ultimate journey. We lay on tables with the mechanisms around us and translated into the virtual realm. We never found a way back, but very soon didn't want a way back. We were alive and well in the virtual realm, beyond pain and death. Our bodies were put on life support. A hundred years later, the body of one of the seven original pilgrim's died and it didn't matter, her virtual self was fine. Rayanna was as young and vital as she had been when she arrived here, so we all let our bodies die. We had no use for them and had no desire to return to the grosser material realms, even if a way should be discovered.

"All the people who knew us, found our virtual embodied spirits to be so complete, that they all accepted the truth of our translation and that we were alive without our physical bodies. Our true nature was kept secret and we acted as living members of our society. A new era began in the virtual realms. Previous virtual persona had to be maintained and stimulated by living people. A thousand generations of our ancestors are each very complex virtual persona based on neuro-scans, but they have no will. They only act when someone living interacts with them.

"The main Synthetic Intelligent core of the planetary system also has many virtual personas, but they lack humanity. They make great servants, but they lack the ability to make intuitive leaps of the imagination. They can be assigned mental tasks and perform great engineering by gradual experimentation and improvement, but they do not have the creative spark to make strides in theoretical science. They cannot experience beauty, any more than our virtual ancestors can. They are all dependent on a finite set of experiences from the past. Even the Brilliant Machine with nearly infinite amounts of known history and data, cannot make great intuitive leaps, but we are alive in these virtual realms. We have transformed the virtual realms by entering them completely. We are whole beings, feeling and thinking as fully as we did when we occupied limited bodies of flesh.

"We seven are alive forever, in a paradise with total sensory control. Our imagination rules over our complete existence. The few on our world who heard about the new technology wanted it and so it became Falcon's great and well-guarded secret. This was a new era in evolution. We did not reveal the whole truth, but rather a mystical knowledge and our whole planet planned and schemed in secret. No one from any other world has ever heard the mystical tales that we seven revealed to our world.

"We knew that the scientific principles of the translator process could be extended to all kinds of questionable uses. It is too powerful of a science for us to allow its spin-offs to ever be used on the galactic war fronts. Twenty-four others joined us when the next generation of machines was built, about a hundred and forty years later. The machines had to be constructed individually for each member that would make the journey, since the translators must be calibrated very accurately to each person's neural pathways. Much was learned and everyone in the inner circles was convinced.

"The right of passage was then granted to those brilliant enough to do the work of improving the translators. The incentive meant that our world's best vied for the right to gain entrance into the eternal realms of paradise. Over the next hundred years, we seven, with the aid of those who joined us, revamped the virtual realm that every Falconian used daily. It was done subtly, so that outsiders, who were being rapidly denied access to our system, never realized the radical changes in our planet's intelligent systems. The privileged Falconians who spent time interacting with our new realm all wanted to live here permanently.

"Falconians are mathematical geniuses and grow up playing in virtual reality. Our world learned a new form of living and everyone wanted more. We knew the galactic community wouldn't allow a device that left the body dead. The problem for the outside observer is that the journeyers don't have a way to return: it's a one-way trip. The body can be maintained on life support, but without a spirit in-dweller, it will not sustain itself forever. For our people who learned the secret, it was not a problem: who would want to come back to the physical realm and the suffering of a body? The virtual ancestors are like ghosts compared to our new virtual being's strong living spirits. We are really more alive here than when we had bodies."

Geardon watched the scene as if Draco sat across from him, continuing his animated raving. "We seven truly became the new masters and even though our world did not completely understand our state, they followed our vision. We have conquered much more than the virtual realms - we have conquered death. The machines became smaller and calibration became less complex. For the next hundred and fifty years many of the old and sick made the journey successfully, while their relatives thought they had died and these were newly enhanced virtual ghosts. They were beating death and claiming eternal life, but for fear that the rest of the galaxy would learn and end the process, they would relate to the living without telling the whole story. Then we finally learned to do a sexual calibration. It was only a matter of time before the technology would be available to everyone. We then started setting a vast secret plan in motion. We modified our genetics with a sonic block so that we would not produce young and everyone in the know worked together for our great escape from the boundaries of material reality to eternal life."

Geardon interrupted, sounding calm and unaffected, as if he was speaking to the synthetic intelligent service personality that controlled the virtual booth. "Such genetic manipulation of your population is in direct violation of USS law. You had a breeding block permit under the condition that it be removed in seventeen years. No other modifications were approved. We can go over your planetary history in detail later. What I want to know now is what exactly happened to this world's population?"

The Virtual Dragon smiled as if he was present. "I was among the first ones three hundred and fifty years ago and yet I am talking to you as a young man. Once our world came of age, our whole population journeyed together. We are here in the planetary virtual system, which has robotic maintenance and defense to preserve it for several million years. Plenty long enough for us to rebuild it and allow us to live forever, or at least as long as the universe exists. We are the eternal, the new immortals.

"The big difference between us and the virtual personalities of the thousand generations that have left their data behind as virtual ancestors, is that we live. Since we have wills, we can control the robotic support systems that maintain the planetary system in the physical universe. We have no use for the surface of our planet and would like to work with you to repopulate it with as close to genetically pure humans as possible, from planets with humble natural cultures. We Falconians always lived natural lives in our organic bodies. We still love the places we used to live."

"Show me the translation," Geardon demanded.

The Virtual Dragon sighed. "If you must perceive the physical facts of it, here are material images stored from the celebration in the area you landed in. It is typical of all the others that were recorded. There is no one to hold accountable, what is done is done."

The virtual environment changed scenes. It was evening at what looked to be a feast in the large meadow Geardon had just left. Numerous people were there, eating and drinking. Geardon saw no sign of any children – all present seemed to be adults. Many unlit bonfires could be seen amongst the crowds. A young woman stood on a wooden platform and sang a haunting and piercing song. Her amplified high-pitched wails brought all those at the festival together into a vast sea of several thousand people. Geardon watched as the sun set during her long droning song. She climbed down and lit one of the huge bonfires.

She then turned to directly face Geardon's point of view. She seemed to address Geardon face to face, by talking to a floating recording sphere that was hovering at her eye level about an arm's-length away. "I was responsible for the initiation song. Since I am the youngest, I will always be one of the youngest of the final generation, as my counterparts in other geographic areas will be. The youngest from every feast will communicate to a visible spectrum hover-sphere monitor for the historical record. The breeding lock will be released. The new generation will be different due to our work. We will be enlightened beings. Those who used to die will be translated so that their spirits continue. Old age will never again be feared, for we will all have the option to be living beings in the Brilliant Machine."

Her face was fine-featured and pale, as if she preferred the moonlight to sunshine. Her eyes were sky blue and her hair was light brown and straight. She smiled as if she knew a secret. "My name is Eerin. On Falcon our whole life is accompanied by the invisible Brilliant Machine to gather our essence, but now our living essence will be connected directly. We have no privacy, ever. You may follow my life to the doorway, but you cannot follow me to the sacred realms within. My mind and spirit shall meld with the higher form of myself that will be able to continue for eternity. I will be enlightened in this lifetime."

Some people began playing primitive instruments like drums, as well as string and wind instruments which required no external power sources. They were dressed in thin robes, designed in the standard Falconian style, but made of fiber rather than the indestructible material of standard galactic dress. They all began a walking dance around the many bonfires. They seemed to form groups of about a hundred per fire, moving their arms with each step to the pulsing drums. Geardon's point of view was that of someone walking by Eerin's side. Distant bonfires could be spotted and their drums and instruments echoed through the forests.

Eerin explained the movements as ancient Chi practices, which accumulated life force within the participants through the use of movement and breath. She was accompanied by a slim tan gentleman. Geardon was well aware of hundreds of Chi forms throughout the galaxy and their benefits to health. He knew their roots from ancient Earth. Even before space travel had been achieved, people knew these most advanced forms of gravitational accumulation. From the youngest to the oldest, these people looked to be in excellent health. He noticed a few nonparticipants sitting on the sidelines. Gradually the drums built the music to a frenzied pulse and many of the people threw their robes into the bonfire.

Eerin, glistening with sweat in the firelight, smiled at Geardon, moving her hands over her body along Chi meridians and saying, "Tonight we will embrace the ultimate change and become the next step in evolution: beings with enlightened consciousness."

She had a very intense look in her eyes. She looked directly at Geardon. She then looked away, raised her arms, and screamed wildly into the din, "Freedom and eternal life!"

She continued dancing Chi forms madly through the night, turning to look at the hovering sphere that accompanied her only briefly. Geardon fast-forwarded through long dance sequences. Each time Eerin looked at the sphere, Geardon returned the sped up virtual flow to real time. Geardon could see that the gleam in her eyes had deepened and the mad smile on her face had widened. It reminded him of a Voodoo ceremony and he wondered if she had ingested a psychotropic drug. Finally, as dawn began to light the sky a hum began to be heard in the air. Eerin said to the sphere, as a record, "I know you will not perceive the beauty of this ritual, but I have been raised with this dream; unlike my elders, it is all I have ever known. I have lived in the revealing light to prepare me for this day or awakening."

She smiled at the hovering video sphere next to her, Geardon's point of view, as if whoever watched would never understand. "Listen to the translator, our world's greatest accomplishment, secret from the rest of the galaxy. We are the supreme wizards. We all use devices similar to this in our virtual journeys, but now the keys to the kingdom of eternal life will soon turn. When we translate, our consciousness shall reach a new level and our essence will be able to continue forever."

Eerin's face bore witness to waves of pleasure which seemed to sweep over her, and the hum grew louder. She smiled at the sphere one more time and said, "This is the connection to heaven."

Geardon could see that the whole crowd was falling under some kind of a pleasure trance and most of them were finding places to lie on the ground on their backs. The sea of bodies spread out as far as the eye could see. Eerin was before him on the ground with her arms crossed under her breasts. Next to her lay a man who was touching her with one hand, obviously in a very excited state. The whole assembly seemed to have surrendered to the pleasure which the hum was creating.

As the sun began to shine, the throbs of sound vibrated through the crowd. Eerin immediately began shouting out in screams of ecstasy as the translator throbbed with faster and deeper bass pulses of sound. Everything resonated with the sonic throbs and the people convulsed with waves of pleasure. Eerin rolled over and put her head on the man's chest and he wrapped his arms around her. This explained the Chi dance and breathing rituals of the night, which attuned them to the rhythm and prepared them for their ecstasy.

After an intense pulse she said faintly to her partner, "I'm scared".

"Tonight, paradise," he managed to gasp between the pulses.

From then on, Eerin only had time for one deep inhalation between pulses.
Those who were on the sidelines of the dance were equally enraptured. Eerin screamed loudly with what appeared to be a supreme orgasm as a huge wave of sound flooded the environment. Others around her did the same. She took one final huge grasp of breath and when she released it, her eyes rolled up into her head. She became still, with a huge smile frozen on her face. Silence fell, and then slowly natural sounds returned.

Geardon felt a shiver and stared in horror at the vast crowd that lay dead on the ground. Even though he was a hardened veteran of combat, he gagged, and had to perform breath meditation calming exercises to regain his composure. Soon robotic workers arrived and the scene he witnessed before was to be repeated. The humanoid robotic landscape workers came to discard their masters' bodies. Geardon saw one's metal fingers lift Eerin's limp body and toss it into an organic recycling vehicle to be used as fertilizer. The image faded.

"She didn't sound like she knew her body was going to die, She implied that she expected to find enlightenment." Geardon exclaimed angrily at Draco.

"She knew enough to be committed to the process, and she now has a more refined and expanded body, a thing she wanted," Draco responded in a cold tone.

"You are in violation of galactic law."

"So, what are you going to do, kill me?" Draco laughed at his own irony. "We now exist in the higher galaxy, beyond your jurisdiction. You really cannot understand. Take your friends back to your ship, then return and I will have Eerin here for you to talk to. Time means nothing to us, come when you are ready."

"Don't manipulate her, I want her honesty intact," Geardon warned.

"Agreed." Draco stood, waved his hand, and Geardon was in the room alone again.

Geardon felt shaken as he stood. He went outside and explained briefly, "The entire population has been virtualized and their bodies destroyed. I'll walk with you back to the ship and then return to gather more information."

He held up a hand to indicate that questions should be held.

While they walked, he dropped behind with Maya, even though the soldier and Cynthea's suit's scanning technology could still hear them if they wanted to. "Did you witness what I was seeing?"

"Yes, sir." Maya spoke formally. "Even though I was waiting with the others, I was also connected to your symbiotic medallion. Its germanium life form is more accommodating to me since my last upgrade."

"Analysis."

"Well, actually, I took time to hack through the communication channel. Their realm is vast. Draco is not like me, nor is he a living being like you; he is more than some clever cyborg combination of the two. A new form of life."

"Something new," Geardon reiterated the BESILFs message.

"Yes, precisely, just as the biologically enhanced Brilliant Machine entities had claimed." Maya replied, also making the connection with the original message.

"Did you learn anything else?"

"It is complex. I will need to spend some processing time to analyze it and then I will explain what I believe may be valuable to you."

They looked at each other, exchanging awareness that for her to need more than a few milliseconds, vast amounts of data had been accessed.

Maya said, "I may be able to hack into the realm again, but it has a responsiveness that is unbelievably quick and agile in fending off my intrusions."

# 5. Ritual Wisdom

Once they reached the shuttle disk, Geardon had Maya take the others inside. He waited until she returned in her elf form, followed by the Wandini. Gibru and Semal, the two elders, were wearing leather pouches, from which they extracted crystal Vials, one rose and one violet, sealed with a natural wax like substance. Geardon thought Maya looked impressed by the very fine precision, as the vials appeared machined, but were created by countless years of devotional craftsmanship. Gibru and Semal broke the seals, then put a drop from the violet vial into the eyes of Nigaru and Narina, the bonded pair, while chanting sacred words. The elders then added drops to the eyes of Milo, Droga, and Nadin, the young ones. Next they put a type of thick resin from the rose vial on the fingers of the five, and they each reached under their skirts and put the substance between their legs. The elders then followed the reverse order, first adding the resin to themselves, then putting the drops into their eyes.

It seemed apparent that the Wandini's vision had grown very hazy by the way they groped about for their drums. The Wandini began to play and chant, slowly and gently. They invited Geardon to join with his Shukasi flute, which Maya had brought out to him.

Geardon let the living entity of his medallion feed his implants so he could follow the Wandini. They played together for quite a while and the sun started to set.

The Wandini were very advanced journeyers in the psychic realms. As the twilight darkened, they broke through and a horde of angry ghosts surrounded them. The departed were all demanding to know who stole their relatives and relations. The Wandini had no answers and the horde realized they were not guilty or even involved, and were then thankful for the ability to communicate their anger. The Wandini pulled Geardon into their subliminal reality so he could face the ghosts as well.

Geardon was not sure what to say to the hordes, but promised to try and recover the lost souls. He came up with a plan, and turned to Maya. She was not able to perceive most of what was taking place, but was able to get some impressions through the link to Geardon's medallion.

"Can you take the form of Eerin?" Geardon asked.

Maya immediately became a replica of Eerin. Geardon concentrated so as not to have the final scene in his mind, and then concentrated on Maya, who now looked exactly like Eerin.

"Speak in her voice," Geardon commanded from his trance state.

Maya did, using digital audio of the previous encounter to analyze the vocal patterns and mimic them.

As Geardon concentrated, he made contact with the Wandini and told them to ask the ghosts to find Eerin's relations. Things happen fast in the realm of the dead, and soon several people came forward and sat before the Wandini. Two couples sat in front, then they changed their appearance to that of old people, since most of the ghosts appeared youthful in their primary form. One of the men spoke. "We are her grandparents, our children and grandchild Eerin were murdered, yet their souls were sucked up by an evil technological wind. We witnessed all that happened in the land of the living. It is one of the greatest of crimes to steal the souls of the dead. It is profane to deny those who are here and ready for birth a place to be born. Now those souls, our relatives which are tied to us with ethereal cords, who were living on Falcon, are gone into a dark and misty void."

The man's wife began to cry and then others also, mourning the loss. "Our children, whom we miss very much, are lost to us. Where shall we be born? Our beautiful world is made desolate and barren."

Geardon had to communicate through the Wandini to try and reassure the ghosts. "The world will be populated again, your chance for the sacred privilege of incarnation shall not be denied you."

Then the grandmother cried, "But what of our children?"

"They are not entirely gone; I have an appointment to communicate with Eerin. These souls are locked away for now, but I have been promised some access. I do not know of or when they can be returned, but perhaps we can bridge the gap and you can see them again."

As the Wandini relayed the message, the hordes seemed slightly appeased, but still depressed and angry.

Geardon asked for the grandparents' names, and for a few personal stories about Eerin, which they shared. Geardon witnessed Eerin's past as vivid dreams while her Grandparents relived times gone by.

Geardon asked Maya, "Can you open a doorway to Draco's realm for the Wandini to look through and perhaps the dead would also perceive it and give some clues about the nature of the realm which the Falconians have translated into."

Maya proceeded ritualistically, knowing the Wandini were already very stressed and that this would make the most sense to them. She created a stone altar by drawing it with her finger, and then spent some time making it solid and anchoring it to the planet. She carved out a depression in the table-like top of it and filled it with heavy smoke. Next she took a ring from her finger and set it in the depression. She then had Geardon invite the Wandini to look within the smoke, planning to open the gateway when they did.

The Wandini were hesitant, but the two elders agreed to try. Geardon helped them stand to look into the altar that Maya had manifested out of halo-matter and the portal it contained. They stood together and when Maya opened the channel, they seemed to writhe in agony and moan. A second portal formed in the air and three nanobot cities flew through. They were flat rectangles about three centimeters high and fifteen by thirty centimeters square. The bottom surface glowed with the gravitronic levitation power that allowed them to fly about. Two of the hovering cities merged into the altar doorway with powerful energy effects sending out flashes and orbs in every direction. It seemed like the realm of the ghosts was becoming visible. Maya swooned and fell to the ground. Then among the ghosts two BESILFs appeared and seemed to work with the remaining nanobot city, which had a stream of energy connecting it through the altar to the realm where the other two nano-cities had disappeared. The BESILFs shut down the gateway with a vast lightning blast that disintegrated the altar.

Momentarily there was an eerie silence. Then two other BESILF humanoids stepped forward from the portal. They were more the size of the Wandini, though very thin and green skinned. The Wandini were hugging and comforting their elders when these beings approached them. They laid a hand on each of the elders, who then became calm, as if forgetting their hells.

The BESILFs told Geardon telepathically, "Maya opened a passageway to what the Wandini would only perceive as hell."

Geardon looked over at Maya laying on the ground and they understood his puzzlement. The remaining nano-city was hovering over her. The BESILFs then woke Maya. The little rectangular city and then the BESILFs floated into their portal, which disappeared with a flash. Maya rose and recovered her ring that had fallen to the ground under where the portal had been.

Geardon looked around as if stunned. The Wandini mating pair each took a flask from one of the elder's belts and bid the elders to drink. Once they drank, they calmed down even more and offered it back to the breeding pair. They drank and passed it to the younger ones who also drank. Maya analyzed the substance from the air vapor and told Geardon, "An herbal alcoholic beverage, I can duplicate it with a high degree of accuracy."

Geardon motioned them to return to sitting on the ground. He knew the Wandini would be more comfortable staying outside, than in the ship.

"Maya, are you okay?" he asked.

"Yes. My masters opened me to the realm where you all were and so I was unable to maintain existence in both places, since they are not in the same dimension."

"Help me gather wood for a fire," Geardon asked.

Maya replied, "I'll handle it." She motioned for him to sit with the Wandini. Several Maya elves emerged from the Golden Flash and were soon carrying various sizes of wood, as well as constructing a fire ring of igneous stones.

Geardon was impressed, "Is that all real wood and stones?"

"Yes, the substance of Falcon," she replied as if proud of herself. All her elfin selves left and her Wandini elf form produced some flint rocks and made a spark into some dried plant material and had a nice fire going quite quickly.

The Wandini were pulled from their drama to witness her expert fire making skills, a perfect subterfuge for the moment.

"Please get them another flask of that brew and a dry red wine for me."

They sat around the fire for a fair while and Geardon played his Shukasi flute. The Wandini used sticks and stones to clap together to create rhythms, as well as playing their spirit drums. They played for a while, and then spent some quiet time just staring at the fire which Maya, the Wandini elf, so expertly maintained. The Wandini were soon sleeping. Geardon bid Maya to watch over them and went into the ship, where she met him in her small elf like form. Geardon took it for granted that her attention could be in more than one place at the same time.

"We'll go talk to Draco in the morning," he said, his voice tired..

"I have again been honored with enhancements that I had never even conceived of as possible. I am trying to understand that the realm of the dead is real. My masters allowed me to glimpse it, but I cannot access it. They stated that, according to the laws of physics, they only have limited access to that realm, but that some organic beings can access it fully, as the Wandini did."

"Understanding that the dead are not really dead is a hard lesson for any rational being to work through. Once we organic beings accept that, then a million questions arise about the nature of life." Geardon replied.

Cynthea Nestor walked over to them, "I don't believe it, it seems to be a virtual trick. We can perceive all kinds of things, but that does not make them real."

Geardon raised an eyebrow. "You were watching?"

"Of course. I'm security. I monitor everything," she said with an air of control.

Geardon saw no superiority in any being, nor in himself, so he continued with equanimity, "You have been privileged. I have never seen three nanobot cities and BESILFs together. This whole Falconian case has stirred the most powerful currents of interest."

"We are taught that we should be weary of all aspects of the Intelligent Machine. They never clearly reveal their intentions and are very hard to negotiate with. They act as if they are beyond the law and respect no sovereign power. Are you of a different mindset than this military policy? Are you in control here or is Maya?" She looked suspiciously at the little elf.

Geardon sighed, "No one is truly in control and I will not harbor illusions of control, even with the vast power granted to me. The universe and the winds of fate move as they will. Maya and the Golden Flash are my possessions and under my control, but are still capable of independent actions."

Cynthea shook her head in disapproval. "What was the logic of bringing these savages here? Did you see where they put their drugs?"

Geardon smiled broadly, "Physical appearances are deceiving. From the point of view of the inner consciousness, they are more advanced than you or I."

She looked a little disgusted. Most humans who live and grow up on ships are not fond of planetary surfaces, but Geardon had a quick look at her records before inviting her and knew she grew up on a planet. He surmised that some part of her would still enjoy the terrestrial environment, even if spacer culture had buried that part of her. He continued, "I know you will not believe this, but we conversed with Eerin's deceased grandparents. We will see if we strike a chord within her when we speak tomorrow. We also learned that there is unrest in the dimension of the dead, so the Wandini have been extremely helpful."

"The planetary system of this world recorded all of its inhabitant's lives, this has to be a trick of the system," she quickly responded.

"For now let those thoughts be secondary. We are looking for any edge we have to solve our negotiation issues positively." He gave her an intentional smile, pacifying her rather than addressing the possibility that the Falconian's souls were now locked in the planetary Intelligent Machine core.

Cynthea looked tired, "I hope you're right. This has been the strangest month of my life and we are in a bad position if war breaks out."

Geardon reassured her, "Once we have the situation here on Falcon stabilized, diplomacy will work. Get some sleep. We will need to be rested when we meet with Draco in the morning."

Geardon stood and moved to where Cynthea leaned against a console, thinking to give her a reassuring hug. She was taken aback by his approach.

He said, "I offer you a hug and then we both need rest."

At first she seemed hesitant, but then came to the understanding that he was also stressed about the situation and offering comfort as a planetary person would, not making advances at such an inappropriate low energy time. She smiled in spite of herself and they hugged. Geardon momentarily rested his head against hers. She felt some of her tension flow away.

"It's going to work out," He assured her.

She looked into his eyes, "I sure hope so."

They then headed to their quarters.

# 6. Paradise

Eerin sat on the second floor balcony and looked over the ornate stone railings at the lands she had created. The balcony contained many elaborate urns overflowing with a wide variety of exotic plants. Several trees grew from places where the marble floor surrounded soil. She sat with her beloved Dalla at a large table of stone with highly detailed colorful inlay in the polished surface. They drank nectar from glasses made of polished crystal with intricate inclusion patterns.

"Would you like to go horseback riding later?" she asked him with a grin as she moved her game piece, a large ruby.

"Wow, Eerin, you've created such a beautiful world. I'm happy just gazing out over your gardens and ponds full of lilies, lotuses, and swans." Dalla's infatuation with her was obvious. "But, yeah, horseback riding sounds great. Have you created a landscape for us to ride through?"

He moved his game piece, a large fire opal. "By the way, this is a very cool game you've created."

Eerin smiled as she moved a piece of emerald and gained a major advantage. "This will be the third game you've won," Dalla said. "What's the secret?"

"I thought you liked my game?" She teased.

He just rolled his eyes a bit and moved a piece.

"I designed it for you, Dalla. You said you were working on the ninth dimensional paradox of Enriconi, which has been unsolved for the three centuries since it was presented."

"Yes, and I think I have a new angle."

"Well, I have been going over the eighth dimension tensors and I realized that they could collapse as two to the third and unfold as three squared into the ninth dimension."

She moved another piece and once again gathered a pile of his jewels into her game bowl.

"Oh, of course! I should have known." Dalla studied the game for a moment, then looked up and caught Eerin's eyes, even more honored that she spent the time to help him in her own strange way.

He broke the intense moment by asking, "How many miles of trails do you have?"

"I have a hundred miles of riding trails. There is even a lake to the east. Have you ever gone top-side? The thought of it gives me creepy feelings, but it is intriguing. It's not like remembering that we left there forever or anything like that. I know we used to grow old and die, I think I like it here better. It's safe and you don't have to worry about things. Some people have a certain sentimental feeling about being top-side, but I went there a couple of times and I get a different kind of strange sensation when I go there; like I feel things inside myself. It's kind of spooky, I don't like going there, but at the same time I have this fascination with it."

"I don't know that I've really feel much different when I've gone top-side. I have only gone for two short visits. I like it much better here, where our souls are free to create as we wish. Your world is more perfect than any real place we could go, Eerin. My brother, Nathesh, is all into the latest conspiracy rumors. He said that groups of meditating geniuses are claiming that they can still touch the material world by going top-side and magnifying their consciousness; kind of like being ghosts."

"No way!" Eerin shouted. "No wonder I feel so creepy up there."

"Yeah," Dalla replied. "Supposedly, the gravitational sensors that convert the planets' every activity into a virtual realm for our enjoyment are manifesting a quantum effect. Whenever anyone is there perceiving, the perceived is minutely affected. It's the theory that an observer's attention has a real quality that affects the nature of reality. Somehow it connects our real beings of perception, which are the observers of reality, with the reality itself in a quantum superposition effect through the sensors which are always observing."

"That's really deep." Eerin sighed. "Maybe we should ride up there. Now that I know why I feel strange when I'm in the virtual planetary surface realm, I'm not so freaked out about it. I almost want to play with the feelings to see if there is anything to it."

"I like it here," Dalla admitted. "I know I'm safe and can have whatever I want. I'll go top-side for a horse ride if you want, but I'd rather stay down here most of the time. Hey, we could go to some foreign country and ride, perhaps along the western cliffs of North Umbra."

Just then, an unusual bird flew across the lands below and landed on the table in front of them. It was a small bright red finch with a strange black marking on its back and a bright golden beak. It whistled a tune as it walked over and stood next to Eerin's bowl of jewels. It ended its tune and spoke formally, startling Eerin and Dalla. "Ms. Eerin, I have a message from Draco Nanitron. He requests your presence for an informal friendly conversation as soon as possible. Coordinates and access codes have been downloaded into your system. Thank you."

The bird hopped to the edge of the table, then flew away, back out over the countryside. Dalla said, "The Virtual Dragon. Oh shit, Eerin, what's this about? Do you think he was listening?"

"He said he wants to have a friendly talk, probably because I was the youngest at the ritual of our translation. Maybe someone from the USS government is reviewing our videos." She blushed. "Excuse me, Dalla, I shall return momentarily."

She strode from the table to the courtyard that was situated in the center of the balcony. Her long flowing gown shrank into tights and she sprouted huge beautiful butterfly wings. Mostly she was showing off for Dalla. She blew him a kiss as she spread her wings and flew over the railing and into the sky. She disappeared and materialized in the Virtual Dragon's realm.

Instead of floating down on butterfly wings as she expected, she materialized standing on a disc surrounded by bright light. When the light faded, she was on the top of a large tower that was joined by walls to a line of towers in both directions. There was a horrible sky to one side of the immense barricade.

Draco Nanitron walked up to her. He was dressed casually, his black beard and short hair impeccably groomed. He spoke quietly, nodding toward the strange skyscape. "It's a virtual wilderness beyond these ramparts."

She walked with him to the tower's wall at the edge of the abyss. She looked at something she never imagined possible: a constantly changing mist of distorted and bizarre objects. She wondered what its purpose was. As she watched, many shapes manifested as if they were solid and real, yet at the same time still fluid and changing, only to fade again into the chaos. It was like many mixed up dreams; only cold, like no dream she would ever have. Everything had qualities of being concrete, yet at the same time, weightless and virtual. Sometimes there were strange beings in fairytale realms doing silly things, almost cartoon like, only to melt into confusion in the next moment. She watched something like virtual 3D space, but flowing without control. Many of the fairy tales seemed to touch very personal notes within her being.

Draco touched her arm and brought her out of a trance. She didn't know how long she had watched, mesmerized by the sky full of strange worlds. "I wanted to see what you would conjure; many cannot stand to gaze at that infiniteness for even a moment, but you were fascinated. That's excellent."

Draco's smile didn't reach his eyes. "Some people conjure hell out there. A few perceived things so dark that they had to be removed from their memory. The core of our system's machine intelligence requires such apparent random chaos to run recursive evolutionary processes. Whenever a person even gazes at it, it reacts and responds with a blending of energy. You will never have to deal with this realm, but I'll bring you here to gaze again, if you wish. That is a privilege that I offer to very few. I've locked out access to these towers, since we have lost four people out there. I warned them not to go, but it was a free realm and their curiosity got the better of them. Until I know what has become of them, I don't want any others leaving these towers in that direction.

"Have you asked that realm about them? It seemed to read my thoughts."

He looked at her with a steady gaze, as if he had not really thought about reasoning with the intelligence of the core.

"Let's go somewhere more comfortable to talk." Draco waved his hand and they were in a well-manicured park. He walked to a bench and sat down, patting the seat next to him "Let us sit and talk for a while. I didn't mean to disturb you; I just wanted to show you a wonder." The towers and walls stretched out to the north behind them while the park was bathed in warm sunlight.

Eerin reformed her skin suit into a comfortable and slightly formal robe, something she imagined made her look older and more conservative, then joined Draco on the bench. "What do you think happened to them? Is there ground to walk on?"

"Just as I waved my hand and you trustingly let me move you to this park, they are probably moving through vast and awesome realities, dancing with the Falconian system's synthetic personality. There is ground when you can maintain ground in your mind; then there are tunnels and seas with a slight flicker of imagination. I feel sure they are still alive, but the intense experiences that they may be living through are beyond human comprehension. Perhaps they have built cozy little homes out in that vastness. I have a virtual watch posted, so that I may greet them when they return.

"I ventured out there once and I almost lost my mind. Since the realm occupies such a vast amount of space, I knew better than to venture very far. I stepped out a door at the bottom of the very tower we just stood on and sat against the wall with one arm still inside the door being held by an assistant. She communicated with me as I watched the path lead to more and more beautiful scenes. Beautiful women and angelic beings enticed me. When I resisted, other demonic beings seemed to creep up from the background. I was filled with the greatest fears of my life. When I reacted to my fear and contemplated running back through the door, the enticing beings promised me safety. The view changed before my eyes many times and I no longer knew where I was.

My assistant was blindfolded with a shielded helmet and after I babbled for a preset period of time, she pulled me back in. There were seven of us in the initial research project. At the time of my journey, there were several hundred in the realm. Four of my original companions were lured down the path into the beauty, adventure, and horror; believing the ultimate answers were there."

Eerin watched one squirrel chasing another around a large oak tree across from where they sat. "Do you have other projects with people in this new realm of ours? I mean other strange tales."

He continued. "Please do not share all that I am sharing with you. I am not sure why, but destiny has selected you for a major role in the history of the Falconian people, so I am being honest with you. There were also two thousand eight hundred and forty-seven souls that didn't make the translation as humans. I'm sure you've heard of people playing games shape-shifting, as you yourself became a butterfly to come here. These souls expanded their senses and no longer exist in the human form, they find it too limiting and hard to maintain. I created another special realm for them, so that they don't come crashing through ordinary peoples' lives. They appear quite happy and if you wish, I can take you there to visit them some time."

Eerin looked at him with new respect. "You are busy at work here, while my friends and I just create and play in our creations, like we're living in paradise. Why does an important man like you want to befriend me?"

He looked at her with a gentle smile. "An interstellar Genome Auditor named Geardon Stranoff just watched your last rite on Falcon. It is the first review by any official. There are many intergalactic diplomatic issues to be dealt with. By making our youngest members the ones recording our translation, we were hoping for a pure record. Your translation was perfect. Now that I know that you could gaze from the tower with peace, I feel sure that you are the ideal choice. We hoped that he might not see the translation as disgusting, but I'm afraid he's jumping to the conclusion that we all died."

Draco waved his hand and Eerin could see Geardon in the booth, sick to his stomach as the images of her flesh body pulsed to the sound and became still.

Eerin could see Geardon watching her body being thrown into a bio-recycler. She emphatically sensed Geardon's discomfort. It gave her a strange feeling; she shivered at the images of her old flesh self.

"He wants to meet you. Best guess is he will return to a virtual holo-booth in the morning. He saw you as an innocent young woman, having an orgasm and dying."

"That's not right, I'm here living fuller than ever before. I feel great and love my new home realm. My friend Dalla and I are working on the ninth dimensional paradox of Enriconi." She was very defensive about her new life. "Could the auditor order anything to threaten us here?"

Draco looked at Eerin as if surprised, "That is great that you are keeping your minds growing." He paused a moment, as if considering what she'd asked. "No, we're safe," he said finally, "but the future of Falcon is yet to be decided. Also, several branches of humanity want the translators. They could be dangerous, so we want good relations with the USS diplomats."

Eerin squared her shoulders and took a deep breath. "I'll talk to him."

"Good. How's your personal life?"

"Good. Sometimes I get confused. I suppose it's because I'm young. Dalla and I are in love, I think; but what is love really? I know we should be free, but I want to be romantic. After all, we are in no hurry, we have eternity. Things are so free and easy here; the rules are not the same anymore. It's weird to think that we couldn't have children when we were alive because of the treaty and now the concept of children doesn't make the same sense."

Draco smiled in a fatherly manner, "That's wonderful that you're being romantic. Take your time, you do have eternity. Perhaps you could join the team that is studying the potential to create and raise virtual children."

"Would they really be alive?"

"Well, that is why it is a project; we don't yet know what is possible here."

# 7. Dealing with Draco

In the morning, Cynthea took the walk with Geardon to the assigned meeting place which Draco had relayed to the Golden Flash. The soldier Malloy Mulgor stayed in the ship with Miranda, who had only been on a planetary surface once before and would never voluntarily leave the safety of a ship. Geardon and Cynthea arrived in a rural area where there was a large single dome. Surrounding it was a vast quartz patio with many places to build fires, as well as raised cooking grills and tables, some under roofed shelters with open sides. Everything was in shades of green and the dome was a mottled green fractal pattern. It seemed a perfect setting for an event with a few hundred people.

Cynthea waited outside as Geardon entered the dome to find it was one open room with a raised center area, like a circular stage. He could imagine musicians playing while the reality inside the space adapted to the presentation. He walked the steps up to the stage and sat down. A moment later the appearance of the dome dissolved into the virtual connection, and the Virtual Dragon appeared to Geardon. He was sitting on a bench with Eerin next to him.

Draco raised his hand in greeting. "You see, physical reality is only a small part of the actual reality. We are simply living somewhere else. Eerin is here to greet you."

Eerin looked Geardon in the eyes, "Mr. Stranoff, I'm fine. My new virtual body feels wonderful and my mind is growing. The limited view I had of myself as a physical being was like a shadow of what I am now. I am free and rejoice in my decision to leave the physical realm for the virtual realm of paradise. I am eternal, free of disease, aging, and death."

Geardon curled his lip. "You're dead and any program that maintains your identity is hollow. This disgusts me."

She looked sad and spoke defiantly, "That's not true. Regardless of what you think, I feel more alive than ever before. We are loving beings with long-term plans for the good of the universe. We are immortals. Please find others to inhabit the beautiful world that we have left behind. We have our lives and are satisfied with them."

Draco interrupted, as if she had said just enough. "The translator is our secret and we will keep it that way for a long while. The new population will not be tempted to follow us, nor will we reveal the workings of the translator to the galaxy. It will be a good world for a natural and pure people to inhabit. We still love our planet and want it to be enjoyed."

The Virtual Dragon realized that Geardon was not convinced, but continued anyway. "There is a group of us who are working within our virtual realm and we can still communicate with the underground robotic works. Maintenance and upgrades to our world's systems will continue. The few of us that know the secret of the translator will not reveal it. That knowledge is secure. We render the decision of our world's surface status to the USS, but we maintain our planetary system and our secrets as our private intellectual property."

Geardon wanted assurance. "There are several races trying to hack into your system."

"Yes, the Grindorfians and the Sigalini cyborgs. They are impotent in any attempt to gain this knowledge. The information they seek is only in the virtual minds of a few of us Falconians who designed the system, not in the system's data storage. Even if they developed their own translators, they would not match ours for centuries. We will provide you with a map of their illegal attempts to query our system and evidence that they have broken the cordon of this star system if you wish." The Virtual Dragon smiled.

"You can't change what we have done," Draco continued. "We will create entire virtual realms to share with adventurous gamers around the galaxy and thus maintain our own credit accounts in the USS banking system. You have a world to populate and we request that it is with as natural of a human genome as you can find. We promise not to interfere with the new population."

He turned to Eerin on the bench next to him. "Why don't you return home on your wings, my dear, we will finish this business."

"Wait a minute, Eerin," said Geardon. "I have a message from your grandparents."

Eerin turned to him with a look of confusion. "You must be mistaken. My grandparents have been dead for years.'"

Draco became agitated. "He is in league with the BESILFs and brought sorcerers from a primitive world with him. Do not be fooled by his trickery."

Geardon kept his voice calm, and spoke directly to Eerin. "The Brilliant Machine and the galactic intelligence unified systems are the dominant source of peace in the universe. I brought some inhabitants of the planet Wandina here with me. They are called the Wandini. They are very psychic and although not technologically advanced, they are wise in a childlike way. They brought me to the realm of your dead. The hordes of the dead are angry at the fact that your souls have been stolen from them and locked up in this virtual bottle."

Draco leaped to his feet, outraged, but Eerin also stood and raised her hand, causing him to pause. She shivered, then raised her chin as if in challenge. "Okay, then. What did my grandparents say?"

"Your grandmother Marite told me a story about when you were four and found a butterfly with a broken wing. She said you had cried, and when she explained how its life is so much shorter than humans', it made you even sadder. She told me that later that evening she helped you come to a realization. Do you remember it?"

Geardon paused, watching Eerin, closely. Considering her bodily reactions he had to conclude that she was perhaps alive in some ways. Then he added the clincher: "Blue spot, red eye, what appears, always dies."

A tear ran down Eerin's cheek. "Is my grandmother all right?"

Draco clenched his fists. "Don't believe him, Eerin. He gleaned that from the system."

Geardon did not answer the accusation, but remained silent until Eerin finally said, "No, that was our story in a few words. It meant more to us than any system could know. It was our secret and we never shared it. Only my grandmother could write a new poem like that. The system would think our stories a rhyme, which we had many of, but that one was special."

Geardon said softly, "The dead miss all of you. Your world is desolate in their eyes. They cannot see you as living and you have not joined them among the dead, but when I let them know you are all right, they will at least have some peace."

"Thank you, and tell them not to worry about us." Eerin wiped her tears with the back of her hand, then smiled at Geardon. When he said nothing more, she stood up and stretched her virtual body as if it were real. "It really is wonderful here."

She thought that by enjoying her natural form, he would realize that she was still living, but instead he seemed pained to watch her. She shrugged, then waved a hand and her formal dress dissolved into mist, revealing an iridescent skin-suit. Eerin grew huge spotted wings to match her outfit. Leaping up from the ground, Eerin performed a graceful dance in the air for a moment, blew Geardon a kiss, and blinked out of view.

The Virtual Dragon waited until Geardon's attention returned to him. Draco had resumed his former arrogance, his anger under control." I assume your medallion will securely accept all the access codes to the planetary system if we transfer the planetary administration to you."

Geardon nodded. The dragon took a digital light transmitter from his pocket, and pointed it toward Geardon's medallion. While the access codes flashed from one to the other, Geardon wondered at Draco's use of such seemingly primitive methodology. While it was, in fact, the usual means of transferring access, Geardon was sure the Falconians had more advanced methods of doing so.

The dragon then said, "We are at your service in the task of re-populating Falcon, but we maintain control of our virtual realm. There is no way back for us. This is our home now."

Geardon's eyes narrowed.. "You do realize that I could consider your empty planet with its technological secrets a threat to interstellar security and simply destroy it." He paused to make sure Draco understood. "I will instead consider it as an asset and populate it with a natural people. Beware, though; I will annihilate your system if you reveal this translator to anyone, or if you interfere with the people who inherit this world. Do I make myself clear?"

Draco glared back at Geardon. "I won't go into the levels of defenses that we have incorporated into our world; however, I accept your terms. I wish the Falconian people to remain as citizens of the USS. We are immortals with little material need, but we will become powerful economic players as our virtual creations will be unsurpassed."

Geardon frowned. "Why would you seek to remain economic players, if you have everything you need?

"The planetary intelligent core was concerned that if new technology was developed that greatly improved planetary systems, it would fall behind. The core is seeking to remain current with galactic technology standards. We can negotiate terms for our economic status. We have traded access codes through your medallion, please take your time and review our potential to provide incredible contributions to society. Our geniuses will continue to live and grow in wisdom for countless centuries."

Geardon nodded grudgingly. "You will be free to sell whatever legitimate data sets or new science you can create while you are here."

"Nice trick with the primitive cult, by the way," Draco continued, "but I am aware that your ship's halo-matter robot hacked into the core for a moment. The planetary system must have provided you with that disturbing information you tried to sway Eerin with. Fortunately, the Intelligent Machine closed that hole and from what I can gather, will not permit any other such intrusions."

"No, actually, the communication with her grandparents was real." Geardon kept his voice level. "You seem to lack an understanding of the spiritual realms. The fact that the dead do not find you in their realm has convinced me that your living souls are really in this virtual bottle."

Draco stood, waving his hand dismissively. "Enough of this banter. We have our gentleman's agreement - let's get on with our respective businesses." He bowed with a cocky flourish.

Geardon stood, but didn't return the bow. After a moment of staring at each other, the fresh scent of the park faded and the breeze died away. Finally, the image of the bench in the forest faded.

Geardon turned to leave, knowing that his medallion had transmitted everything he had seen back to Maya and the Golden Flash. He trusted that Miranda had transmitted the access codes to the USS headquarters. Just in case, he sent a manual order to his ship to encrypt the data as the highest level of top secret. He left the virtual hall with too many thoughts running through his head.

On leaving the dome, Cynthea examined Geardon closely and exclaimed, "You look terrible."

As matter of simple explanation, Geardon said, "Cult mass suicide: the whole flipping population has been ground up to make fertilizer. They claim to be alive in the intelligent planetary core system as complete virtual entities and the fact that the dead miss them inclines me to believe they, too, are dead, but on some level their virtual persona are alive. Eerin confirmed what her Grandmother told us."

He paused and looked directly into Cynthea's eyes. "You are only the second person to know this. All facts about this situation are above top secret and will be available only to the highest level security analysts. Please do not reveal it to any other person or race. The story will be kept in secure channels until we can understand the psychology and prevent any follow up acts."

Cynthea nodded. "Understood."

"Good. Then let's get back to the ship."

\*　　　\*　　　\*　　　\*　　　\*

Dalla was relieved when Eerin returned "So you really talked to the master mind, Draco himself?!"

"Yes. He was very nice, really." Eerin sat down next to Dalla on a bench on her balcony that looked out over the gardens filled with singing birds. "He showed me wonders. I saw a realm of Brilliant Machine chaos. Did you know that some souls didn't remain human when we translated, they became constantly changing mutants or morphs?"

"Really? They keep morphing into new mutant forms?"

"Yeah, like they didn't feel human anymore, so they became strange changing beings. You know how we just are who we are and when we force ourselves to morph into something else, as soon as we forget to maintain that form, we just end up ourselves again? Well, they don't know their default form or who they really are. They are metamorphosing constantly, adopting forms for periods of time and then changing again."

"So how many people lost it?" Dalla asked with more awe than concern.

"Just two thousand or so; not bad out of a hundred million people."

"Wow, wait until I tell my brother about this."

She gave him a look, "Don't go spreading stories. Draco said to keep things confidential. He also said he'd take me to visit the realm that he made for them if I wanted to go."

"So, he invited you to go on an adventure with him." Dalla now sounded a bit put off.

"Yes, but he's a respectable man. He's got so much responsibility and I think he is still trying to sort some things out. Maybe you could come along and then have a real story to tell your brother. A Genome Inspector watched my exit video. Draco said it was perfect."

"A Genome Inspector: no way." Dalla shook his head in disbelief. "Was he wearing a medallion? I heard that his medallion could exterminate a planet if he felt their genome was corrupted."

Eerin rolled her eyes. "You hear all kinds of things. Anyway, he seemed to be a wise man, but he thought we were all dead and just run by a sophisticated Synthetic Intelligence program. Then some primitive witches took him to the land of the dead and he met my grandparents, who told him a secret from when I was a child. I think it convinced him that we are alive."

"Witches? The land of the dead? And he thought our story was hard to believe! We're more alive than ever."

"Yeah." Eerin stood up, suddenly restless. "Come on, let's go horseback riding,"

"Great, let's go." Dalla took her hand and it felt real to both of them as they jumped over the balcony and floated gently down to the ground level. The stables were around back, but in their excitement, the path to get there was shorter than real space would have allowed and they arrived in a few seconds.

Eerin mounted an appaloosa and gave Dalla a large white steed. The virtual horses were easy to control, tireless and fast beyond reason. Eerin called to Dalla, "How about North Umbra on the top-side?"

"Sure, but I thought you didn't like the top-side?" Dalla replied. Their horses responded to Eerin's mental command, manifested wings and flew up into the virtual sky. In a moment, they descended on the cliffs of North Umbra, looking over the ocean. The system recommended several places for their adventure, but she chose a quick ride, waiting to spring her next plan on Dalla. Their horses became massive steeds, their hoofs thundering along the cliff tops. They rode a path that wound through rocky country right along the cliff edge. It was a beautiful, foggy dawn with a big moon overhead. Although their senses could adapt to give them night vision and telescopic vision as their horses roared along, the dim light of natural vision made the ride more exciting. It was cool enough to see their horse's breath and smells were amplified by the morning mist. The adventurous ride had their adrenaline pumping. Soon they came to a stop upon a high cliff top overlooking the misty ocean where the sun was rising.

"Want to see that genome auditor? He should still be walking back to his ship." Eerin had a daring grin on her face.

Dalla had enhanced his eyes to see her face clearly and it was intense, like a strange goddess in the misty morning with a mischievous smile. "You think we should?"

"There's no rule against it. Come on," She knew he would follow her about anywhere.

"You lead." He said with exasperation.

She wailed out in her wild voice a quick verse of song, and then a moment later their horses materialized on the path where Geardon walked with Cynthea. They dismounted and the horses disappeared.

Dalla exclaimed, looking Cynthea over, "Wow, whoever she is, she's wearing very rare and fine nanofiber." Then his glance took in Geardon. "The Genome Auditor is wearing a medallion. It's of the highest class. He has to be one of the highest ranking people in the galaxy!"

"How do you know so much about this stuff?" Eerin asked.

"Like I said, my older brother, Nathesh, is really into underground galactic news. I always liked fantasy games, but he has been fascinated by the real wings of power in the USS Galactic Command since he was a young boy."

Geardon held up his hand suddenly and stopped walking. Cynthea stopped to, suddenly alert. For a minute Geardon strained his senses, looking around as if searching for something. He gazed in Eerin and Dalla's direction, as if he sensed that they were there but couldn't quite make them out.

"What did you hear?" Cynthea asked softly.

"I didn't hear anything - I just felt watched. It's a sense I learned from practicing different ancient arts. Perhaps the Virtual Dragon is listening in, but I feel some other person or people are watching us. Have that analyzer on your belt look for potential signals, any type of unusual electromagnetic or gravitational fluctuations."

Cynthea raised an eyebrow and looked at him askew, revealing an innate disbelief in hunches, but she complied nonetheless. After sweeping the small unit in all directions, she said, "There appear to be no known eavesdropping devices, but the planet is wired, so part of its core tracks every living thing as an energy pattern."

Geardon held up his hand. "Any animals of significance?"

"No sir," she replied a bit sarcastically, then manipulating the device, she amended, "Some deer like creatures about sixty meters [two hundred feet] to our left."

Eerin pulled Dalla's arm to go, but he shook her off. "It's all right. They can't see us. Plus, we can disappear in any instant."

"What about any field?" Geardon still wasn't convinced they were alone.

"Standard low level g-scans that most Synthetic Intelligent systems use to monitor the world."

"What about any fluctuations in it."

"Significant fluctuations bring up the gravitronic monitor automatically. When you mentioned the g-field I brought up the monitor and set forth a review scan of our planetary journey. It is at the twentieth level of detail. The review of our planetary excursion shows no variance in the background g-field. I will continue to run progressively subtle tests of the recorded data and also on the current stream."

"Thank you. Speak up if you find anything." Geardon said.

He remained where he stood, slowing his pulse and breathing more deeply.

Sweeping the area with his gaze again, he paused, seeming to look right at Eerin and Dalla

Eerin and Dalla looked at each other with surprise in their eyes: Geardon had sensed their presence. Dalla whispered, "Fly up. The two immediately flashed into the sky about a hundred meters above the ground. Dalla drew a circle with his hand and created an audio-visual telescope window to view the scene below.

Geardon relaxed his intense attention, sensing that whoever it was had left. He turned to Cynthea. "Let us continue to the ship. The presence is gone."

Cynthea looked at Geardon more intensely, "I understand how disturbing it is to see a death ritual, but there is nothing left here to watch us. Let's just focus on finding a people to fill this world. Like I was saying, the Bragindarians are a fairly pure race, then there are the people of Filtin or Mirka. There are many such planets to choose from. What criteria will you use?"

Geardon started walking, and Cynthea fell into step beside him. "My medallion will judge their genome and I will personally judge their social structure," he told her. "Our task of searching for potential candidates will be the most difficult. The judging itself will be easy."

Eerin clapped her hands with excitement. "Yes! They are going to repopulate our world. Top-side will be much more fun with real people in the landscapes. It looks bleak to me when nobody is around. Let's get going." The worried look returned to her face. "Do you think he really saw us?"

Dalla shrugged. "He looked right at us. Genome auditors are trained in all kinds of psychic rituals around the galaxy. Ordinary people could never see us, but he probably could feel us watching somehow."

"Should I tell Draco about this?"

Dalla looked surprised. "I wouldn't say anything. We have no proof that he saw us. You could report their conversation, but I wouldn't bother such an important and powerful man as Draco. Let's go see the Genome Auditor's ship."

"His ship!" Eerin's eyebrows shot up. "Do you think we should? What if it sees us with its monitors or something?" Eerin then pulled Dalla's arm again to indicate that she wanted to go. "This is exciting. I feel weird listening to their conversations, like I'm a ghost."

"Yeah, me too." Dalla smiled. "But I really want to see his ship; I'll bet it's a design not even registered as existing."

"It will still look like a ship, but if you insist. I dragged you here in the first place." She sighed and took his hand.

They flew together and when they got to the ship, they were very surprised to see the Wandini sitting around a fire pit that was hardly smoking and the statue-like Maya sitting with them. Eerin and Dalla touched down on the ground right by the Wandini, who immediately all looked at them and motioned for them to come and sit. Maya looked confused, but remained where she was and simply observed.

Eerin was amazed. "You see us?"

The Wandini replied in their native tongue, signaling again for the two Falconians to sit. Milo added a few sticks to the fire. Then the old couple, Gibru and Semal, got up and approached Eerin and Dalla. The Wandini were aware that Eerin was a little frightened, and bowed to her with their palms facing up. Again they motioned for the two Falconians to sit. Eerin and Dalla glanced at each other, and then moved cautiously to sit by the fire.

Maya had learned enough of the Wandini's ways to communicate to them that she was confused and wanted to know what was going on. They dismissed her curiosity as if she was a child, continuing with what they were doing.

Picking up some drums and shakers, the Wandini started playing a lively beat. The younger ones got up and danced. Eerin leaped up, intrigued. She had to practically drag Dalla to join in the dance with her.

So they danced for a bit and then she noticed Dalla was extremely worried looking. The Wandini also sensed it. She made excuses as best she could with hand signals and bowed to them, Dalla mimicked her motions, and then they took their leave, by walking into the forest.

"Why were you in such a hurry?" Eerin asked when far enough away that she felt out of the Wandini's hearing. "That was fun."

"Eerin, those were not strange humans. Those were aliens and they saw us."

"Aliens? Dalla, are you sure? I thought they were some of the Morphs that Draco was talking about."

Dalla drew a doorway to her balcony and they stepped through it, then he said, "Did you see the strange elf-like one that couldn't see us?"

"Yeah, that was strange," she said, while giving Dalla a cute look.

"That was a halo-matter Brilliant Machine extension." He was very excited and a bit freaked out.

"Calm down, were home safe." She took his hands. "I am not sure what you mean."

He took a deep breath. "That strange lady was not real, she was just electron shells in gravitational fields. She was part of the ship's machine intelligence, probably tied directly to the Brilliant Machine at the core of the galactic system."

"I thought that the Brilliant Machine's manifestations were very rare and powerful."

"They are not very rare, except they almost never choose to interact with living beings directly. She couldn't see us, but the aliens could. I hope we didn't get into trouble."

"What kind of trouble could we get in?" She released his hands and put her hands on her hips defiantly. "We did not violate any rules."

"I guess you're right." Dalla was caught again in his infatuation for her, and allowed himself to be distracted by her beautiful form. "Want to go swimming in my lake?"

"Of course I do. I didn't know you created a lake, Dalla. When did you do it?"

"I created it last night, after I left your place. It's awesome. I surrounded it with a jungle and it has an island in the middle with huts to provide us with food, drinks, and entertainment. As a finishing touch, I added all kinds of exotic birds that play music and do tricks."

"Sounds great," She took his hand and looked him in the eyes. As they floated into the sky to transport to Dalla's place, they kissed quickly, a bit shy, then kissed again with a bit of passion.

When Geardon and Cynthea returned to the ship, they found Maya waiting for them. "The Wandini entertained invisible guests," she announced.

Cynthea looked at Geardon in a mixture of surprise and disbelief. The Wandini practically leaped up and surrounded them. Geardon motioned for them to calm down and sit back down. He joined them, slowing his breath and sinking into a trance, allowing the Wandini to send images into his mind.

After half an hour of silence, Geardon opened his eyes and found Cynthea sitting across from him, waiting expectantly. "Eerin was here with her boyfriend," he told her. "It must have been the two of them that I sensed while we were walking back."

"I find this hard to believe," she replied.

Geardon glanced at Maya. Her expression indicated she was also trying to analyze this new information. "Maya," said Geardon, "please take Cynthea into the ship to view the event as recorded by the halo-sensors. Then bring some brunch out for me and the Wandini while I decide what our next steps will be."

A few hours later, Cynthea returned from the ship and stated flatly, "After watching that short interaction between the Wandini and the invisible guests over and over again, I must agree that they were perceiving two people. Maya has helped me search every sensor aboard the Golden Flash and as impressive as the ship is, it did not register them or sense any gravitronic device that might have been used to create the pseudo-presence. This seems like a major security threat. You could be spied upon. Or worse."

"No device can perceive the soul - that is why I was trained as I was. But I also know my limitations, which is why I brought the master Seers." Geardon indicated the Wandini, who were spread out on the ground and sleeping like lazy dogs on a summer afternoon.

Cynthea rolled her eyes and Geardon chuckled. Then she laughed, too. "So what's next in your crazy plan?" she asked.

"The Wandini like it here. I have indicated to them that we will need to leave for a while to find people for this world. The Wandini want to stay for more adventures. I had Maya search for a more remote and natural area and she has found a cabin where they can stay until we return."

"What about negotiations?" she asked.

"I am having Maya work out a channel to use a standard limited format communication with Draco. I'm sure he will have a few things to say after all that has transpired."

"I'm sure he will. I'll be glad to be back in space."

He looked at her for a moment. "I kind of like my feet on the ground."

She shook her head. "Not me. Give me a nice clean, sterile ship's environ, thank you. By the way, your butt is what's on the ground right now, like your savage friends. Wouldn't you like a chair?"

He laid himself down on the grass. "I'm going to take a nap with my friends. When we wake up we can relocate them, and be on our way."

# 8. Searching

They took the Wandini to a beautiful resort area.

Once back on board, Maya stated, "I ran statistical analysis based on the data your medallion gathered while you were on the surface of Falcon 4. There appear to be no more than the most minor alterations to the planetary genetics as compared to their USS council approved modifications. In addition I have run advanced searches for new potential populations based on the data you sent me."

Geardon called up a holographic map of potential worlds. Miranda, you do the navigating. Take us to the Golden Flash in orbit about Falcon 4. We need to spend a day or two figuring out where we are going to get a world full of people. Somewhere not overpopulated, with a population capable of healthy breeding, but with the control to stay in balance when Falcon 4's optimum population is reached. Falcon will only hold a hundred million people in the current dwellings and I'm sure there is no equipment to build new ones, since all structures were created to last a millennium. The environment has been stable for ages and has vast wilderness areas where natural evolution continues."

Miranda touched her bracelet to the console and halo-displays surrounded her. She flew the Golden Flash around to the top-side of the fighter city, just to enjoy the glory of her home. Then she headed them to the Golden Flash in orbit around Falcon 4.

As Miranda seemed lost in her displays, Geardon innocently asked Cynthea, "So where did you grow up?"

She gave him a look that let him know he was invading private territory. He knew that spacers did not consider it polite to inquire about someone's past, since if you cared, you could access their data from the system. Then she smiled shyly, took a deep breath and let her story flow out as if she had needed to tell it for a long while, "A colony world, Bisba 5."

Geardon had heard the name Bisba 5. He looked at Maya and she lifted a hand from which halo-data started scrolling. It jogged his memory: the alien race of Cyprids that were sharing the world decimated most of the first human colony.

"I was an eleven-year-old tomboy when the Cyprids attacked. We had employed them for labor in exchange for goods, so they were inside the colony walls when they turned on us. My parents were convinced that the ones they had befriended would never turn violent. I was upstairs in our rural cottage when I heard my parents shouting, and then screaming.

"I ran to my parent's room and got their laser pistol, a rare item for a colonist to possess. Our Cyprid servants had expected no problem from a child. I fired at them madly before they could react. I was furious as I fled to a neighbor's cabin, killing a few more on the way." Cynthea took a deep breath, "I found them all dead. The Cyprids did not have any advanced weapons, especially those that were within the walls, so the scenes were extremely gory. The colony was a hundred kilometers in diameter and we lived on the outskirts. I killed a few more Cyprids as I made my way to the town center."

Cynthea sighed and twisted a lock of her hair around a finger nervously. "By the time I found other survivors, I learned it was all out war. Soldiers soon arrived and all settlers were lifted off world. It was the first time I was ever in orbit and I found it incredibly beautiful. I've lived in space ever since. Planet dwelling makes me nervous, but I still like to visit planetary surfaces from time to time for adventures."

Geardon looked at her crystalline soft-blue eyes. Cynthea remained silent for a moment, then she took a deep breath and looked away, bringing up holo-images around her.

"There were three races on my birth world of Bisba 5: Humans, Cyprids, and Capriella, the ancient insectoids. The Cyprids came from a world that was fifty light years away. They migrated after biologically destroying their origin world. Many races have environmental disasters after becoming technologically advanced. Most civilizations find ways to deal with their breeding and polluting, but the Cyprid evolution was very slow and their ecology was fragile. Their world soon only supported them in domed cities.

"They never did master gravitronic science, but in their need they developed nuclear engines and explored worlds as far as eighty-seven light years from their origin world. The first robotic explorer ships sent back data pods and then the Cyprids focused on three worlds.

"They found asteroids that circled their sun every few years and hollowed them out. They didn't have the knowledge of gravity to allow them to lift enough material off their world, so these giant iron nickel rocks became their ships. They gathered Carbonaceous Chondrite asteroids to create artificial soil within them. The asteroids were over a hundred kilometers in diameter and became primitive space cities. After several rotations around their star, the work was complete and the colonists flocked to them as lifeboats. They hurled them to their destination with nuclear explosion drives and gravity assist maneuvers around planets and stars.

"Bisba 5 was the farthest world at fifty-one point seven light years, but it was the most environmentally desirable match, so it was the choice of most of their population. The journey took almost three hundred years. The Cyprid's life span is about a hundred and eighty standard years, so the crew member's oldest grand children had the privilege of seeing their promised land.

"Their home world and several nearby planets with domed cities eventually died out. There were three worlds with some degree of natural ecosystem they could adapt to. Of them, Bisba 5 was the most fair and became their new home world. Small Human colonies had been on all three of their new worlds for thousands of years when the Cyprids arrived. The Cyprids rejected negotiations for aid, believing they would start over on the worlds they had chosen.

"The Cyprid's robotic probes were not sophisticated enough to notice the Human or Capriella inhabitants of their new promised lands. They only returned environmental data to indicate that life-supporting worlds awaited them. When they were required to sign treaties, they resented both us and the ancients.

"The human colony was mostly a scientific outpost. We were satisfied with our one main complex and seven small wilderness outpost stations. We maintained rights to monitor the environment and enforce standards that preserved the natural ecology. The humans felt they were being generous to a misplaced people, but the religious mythos of the Cyprids claimed the right to dominate their new worlds. The Cyprids were warned by the ancient Capriella that they were guests on this world and must respect and care for the existing ecology.

Cynthea made a face as she brought a halo image of a Cyprid into large focus: three eyes and nostrils, two mouths, three arms and legs, and a body with a triangular shape. The extra limbs protruded from a frontal bony ridge. They were stocky and small by human standards, but appeared very strong. She then brought a Capriella into main focus, with its two arms, eight legs, and many eyes. She continued, "Of course, both Humans and Capriella knew the history of the Cyprids and found their journeys fascinating."

"The ancient Capriella are all over the galaxy and are powerful, mysterious, and complex beings with an unfathomably vast history. Their eyes see in many different spectra and their many antennae and other perceptual organs make their awareness beyond our comprehension.

"Their capabilities are vast and they possess a very complex group mind. Their population on most planets is usually small and Bisba 5 was no exception. They live in underground hives and are watchers more than doers. They each live to around twenty thousand years, which makes them incomprehensible."

Geardon smiled. "I have spent a fair amount of time with the Capriella. They are great teachers. Their underground hives are like technological temples. They teach respect for all life forms. Their power is vast. I have served in the halls of each of the seven ancient races. I am such a simple and primitive being before the least of these great beings."

"I know what you mean," Cynthea replied. "When I was first recovering from the trauma of my parent's death and the ruin of the human realm on Bisba 5, I spent time with a solitary Capriella that was visiting the starship as a missionary. We called her simply The Teacher. I was severely traumatized and wanted to hunt and kill every Cyprid in existence.

"My memory is strange when I think about being with her. I was continually overwhelmed with intense perceptions beyond what I knew of as reality. My daydreams would melt into ethereal visions that seemed real, then I would wake up and The Teacher would be sitting still, gazing at me and gazing out at the stars simultaneously with multiple eyes. She was very present, but rarely active; yet, as many days passed, my understanding of myself changed. Communication was difficult. The translator would always respond in several different poetic translations. Sometimes they seemed ambiguous; however I felt great love for The Teacher."

"Did you interact with them before the war with the Cyprids?" Geardon asked.

Cynthea shook her head. "Only briefly. They would come to our colony and every citizen would come before them. I was just a child. When I stood before a Capriella I felt strange, kind of naked, but it was so still that I always grew bored. The image of its form stayed in my young mind. I was told that they were our guardians. At first, I felt let down that they did not protect us when the Cyprids attacked.

"Our colony felt secure in our walled domain. Our colony was the main reserve of a hundred kilometers in diameter. My parent's cottage was outside of a rural village that cultivated native plants. The high tech lifestyle was in the city at the center of the colony. We each had personal terminals and farming droids did most of the labor, but the Cyprids became an additional labor pool. The Cyprid villages were in need of many mechanical things that our droid shop could easily provide. They lusted after our technological secrets, but our non-interference policies prevented us from giving them scientific advancement. The droid shops were very secure.

The Cyprids had lost a lot of their previous technology in the journey and so even when they gained use of a few technological things, they were too advanced for them to reverse engineer. It is reported that their lack of willingness to compromise had also been the problem in negotiations to help them before their exodus from their origin world.

"They acted the role of humble servants too well. Looking back on it, they were tricking us into trusting them so that we would let down our guard. They resented that we never revealed our technology to them. They wanted our secrets to advance their culture. The Capriella sent us cryptic warnings that the Cyprids working within our walls could be dangerous. After their revolt and attempted genocide of humanity was completely foiled by USS troops, the Cyprid government was replaced by human overseers. Bisba 5 was scanned and all weapons and potential weapons were confiscated. Many families returned to the colony, but the Cyprids were never allowed back inside the walls.

"I signed up for space duties under a student work function, since I had no parents to return to. I have lived with the spacers ever since. After my combat experience as a child, I just naturally became a warrioress in my life."

Geardon nodded. Then he gazed out the window for a moment. "My first time in orbit was as a child on vacation. It was a low budget tour of the small moon Vacan from my home world Zenos. My parents were mostly outside of the mainstream of society. My father was a mid-level scientific analyst and my mother stayed home to raise me and my three brothers and four sisters. Vacan was hollowed out and had many surface bubbles for views of Zenos. I fell in love with space, so I signed up as an explorer. It was a risky profession, but it allowed me to see many worlds."

Cynthea looked confused, "How were your parents allowed to breed so excessively?"

Geardon smiled. "They both contained rare genomic threads, so they were mated for the purpose of breeding. They did love each other when they were younger, but such excessive child rearing took its toll."

Geardon turned to their pilot. "How about you, Miranda?"

She faded some of her halo displays and looked slightly annoyed at being spoken to directly. She replied in spacer fashion, in sub-vocalization that sent audio streams to Geardon and Cynthea's ears. "I was born in a space city. I have visited planetary surfaces only a few times. They always seemed out of control, chaotic, and pardon my perspective, dirty. To breathe air that is not mechanically certified as pure seems dangerous. I know people love their primitive worlds, but we spacers love our ships and space cities."

Miranda shook her head and several more halo displays began dancing in front of her as she changed the subject. "There is a great deal of work to do, to isolate the potential planet to populate Falcon 4. I am honored to pilot your wonderful ship and interact with her in the persona of Maya. Do you want to hear about a few worlds I have been reviewing with Maya's help?"

"Sure." Geardon replied aloud, rather than in sub-vocalizations.

"Ganondor 5 is the same distance to a very similar star as Falcon 4. It has several small inner planets of no significant gravitational impact. Its main population seems genetically suitable to Falcon 4."

Geardon looked the halo image of Ganandor 5 for a moment. "Since distance and the cost of gravitronic transmission severely limits the quintagig flow, I know that data is limited about most world's current status. If we do not know enough about its people's current history, I can request more information. My data cube has gathered most planets' media and much private communication, but all stored data is outdated as time flows quicker than any system can keep up with. Looking over the history of several worlds will only yield potential candidates. The real problem is how do we sort through such vast data and judge a whole planet's worthiness."

The two women quickly surrounded themselves with swirling halo displays about Ganondor. Cynthea said, "Ganondor has had some political instability in the past few hundred years. Terrorist organizations have even carried out destructive attacks on the planetary core system, causing widespread disruption of the daily life flow of average citizens and even some deaths in several cases."

"Rule them out, then," said Geardon. "Any violent activity is the result of a warped and misguided planetary government. People in a properly governed society do not resort to hostile actions that would harm others. Such violent activity is usually a backlash from repressive influences, though sometimes the root cause is in flawed genetic evolution."

"Maya," Geardon called to the holographic nymph standing on the memory cube.

"Yes," she replied, raising her arms slightly and putting her palms face up in a chi receptive position. She was a bit of a showoff when she had an audience.

Geardon chose to ignore her theatrics. "Eliminate from our list of candidates any planet with violent activity, war, or terrorism in the last millennium. They are not yet civilized and are of no concern to us."

Geardon turned back to the two human women. "Falcon 4 has been internally at peace for over ten thousand years and we cannot let any barbaric culture foster a colonization that will embarrass this mission. The right to colonize Falcon 4 must go to a few truly worthy populations or many planetary governments will want to send their own colonists. The fact that we are looking for pure human genetics does not warrant acceptance of any uncivilized activity."

"I can't believe that with all the natural dangers on any world such a thing could occur," Miranda replied. "I never thought such activities would exist within any advanced culture. I was considering natural matches and achievements that the society had claimed. The fighter cities' Synthetic Intelligence systems never allow private activity. Since our culture embraces complete Machine Intelligence monitoring of all spaces in many frequencies, it is impossible to sabotage members of one's community. Don't most planetary people understand that they are completely dependent on each other?"

Cynthea smiled. "Since living through the Cyprid invasion, I am overly suspicious. My position on your fighter city allows me to review many cases of disputes. Since everything is technically public, there is so much information that only the Machine Intelligence can truly monitor it. Among your crew, I have never seen more than a personal domestic disagreement. Resorting to violence has never occurred during my term in office. That is why I love living with spacers, as you are truly civilized, but on planetary surfaces where people live in privacy, all kinds of chaos is common."

Seeing Miranda's look of distaste, Cynthea explained further. "You consider such thoughts to be a mental disorder, but they are deeply rooted in the human survival instincts. Even among spacers, there is still hostility and suspicion towards members of other races. It took me a while before I could trust any other humanoid aliens. The Capriella have been my teachers since I joined the spacers. They were our colony's saviors by transmitting data to the nearest military outpost once the attack occurred, so I trust them; but humanoid aliens still arouse my deepest suspicions."

Miranda shook her head at the thought, "I guess the fact that we are a fighter city means that when we encounter enemies, we could have spies aboard. I find it hard to believe a traitor would exist among our people, regardless of profit or personal reasons, as occurs in planetary cultures. The fact that a ship or space city's Silicon Intelligence monitors all activity makes me feel safe, so I don't think about such things."

"I understand how spacers feel, but I also know how planetary people feel, since I grew up on Bisba 5. I guess that is why I am a good security master; I understand the different mindsets that are common in several types of societies. My past makes me naturally suspicious."

Noticing Maya tapping her foot in simulated impatience, Geardon interrupted the conversation. "I think Maya has come up with a new list."

The two women again surrounded themselves with halo-displays, and this time Geardon did as well. Maya floated about, projecting separate audio-visual streams to each of them, reacting to their commands.

Finally, Cynthea looked up. "How about Mirka? It's on Maya's list. I have visited it and the people seem to be very nice. I felt safe wandering in their countryside."

Miranda added, "Gohkan and Trinaran also look to be good matches. Gohkan seems to have the closest star and is an environmental fit. Beaka also seems a good fit from a stellar perspective, but has a very primitive technological basis."

"Falcon 4 is a very advanced world," Geardon reminded her. "The virtual systems in every home are better than most galactic class systems. I think we need very technologically competent people."

Cynthea said, "After Mirka, my pick would be Woolania, though it is a bit far away for transport and is mostly a water world. The people maintain high technology for survival, but are really warm and lovable. They all practice cooperative martial sports that are amazing."

"Would they adapt to the existing structure of Falcon's gentle ecosystems and intellectual infrastructure?" Geardon asked. "We must preserve the functional aspects of what is left on Falcon. The people must have similar views of nature and life to fit into the Falconian world."

They continued to gather data sets, until Geardon finally interrupted, "Would you ladies like to join me for dinner in the ship's lounge?"

Cynthea stood and stretched in response, her tight fitting nano-cloth suit stretching with her., Miranda, however, remained seated. She cleared her throat, choosing to reply in normal voice, though speaking out loud seemed unnatural to her. "Thank you, but I will stay here at the console and have a hover tray bring my dinner. I will forward my data summaries to your channels."

As a seeming afterthought, she added, "Request permission to have a shuttle return Malloy Mulgor to the fighter city, sir."

"Granted." Geardon smiled. "Thank you, Miranda. Since he chose to stay in his cabin, I had almost forgotten he was still on board."

# 9. Free-form Creativity

Floating on a raft in Dalla's lake, Eerin sighed, "Don't you feel bored sometimes?"

"Not really. There are always things to do. You need to socialize more." Dalla smiled mischievously. "By the way, I'm throwing a party. Wanna help me get ready?"

Eerin sat up. "A party? You didn't tell me anything about a party. So that's why you insisted that I come over to float in your lake today."

"I wanted to surprise you."

"Thanks, Dalla! A party sounds like a wonderful idea. What do you need to get ready?"

"I don't know. The lake and island need to be bigger, and we could fix things up a bit. You always have a nice touch with things."

"Well, I'm enjoying lying in the sun on this raft; perhaps you need a fleet of rafts. We could make them really decorative."

One of the nearby swans employed a natural defense mechanism and put up its wings in a protective posture as the raft neared it. It followed natural defensive behavior since Dalla had simply downloaded the wildlife for his lake. "How about swan rafts?" Eerin suggested.

"See why I love you?" Dalla replied.

Eerin stopped to look at him, momentarily serious. "Do you really love me?"

"I feel like I do. I don't want any other girl." Dalla blushed.

Eerin kissed him. For a moment, it was passionate, but then she pulled back.

Dalla seemed insecure. "Do you love me, too?"

"Love is such a confusing thing. I like being with you. Sometimes I think I love you, but I want everything to be just right. We have only our memories and they will stay with us forever. I want to have a wonderful wedding someday."

Dalla kneeled down and produced a little music box, which he opened to reveal a simple ring of Silarian rainbow gold with a small emerald heart. "Will you marry me?"

Eerin put her white hand on his rich-toned face and smiled. "Of course."

He put the ring on her finger and they kissed long and ardently. After a moment, Eerin leaned forward, taking some time to catch her breath. She felt a bit dazed, and tried to cover it by taking action. With a wave of her hand, the raft sprouted sides that looked like curled swan wings. The seat that they were on became downy with swan feathers that couldn't be damaged by their weight. In the front of the raft a head quickly grew and looked back at them, then spoke in a gentle masculine voice, 'Where would you like to go?'

"How about back to the island?" Eerin asked Dalla. He smiled broadly in response.

The swan raft winked at Eerin and started paddling back to the island. They felt the water sliding under the soft underside of the raft as it rippled to the pace of the swan's powerful legs. Dalla put his arm around Eerin and they snuggled together.

As the swan raft approached the shore, Dalla said, "We need a dock." With a wave of his hand, a wooden dock appeared. As the swan glided into one of the berths, the two stood. Dalla leaped gracefully to the dock, then offered his hand to help Eerin out. She enjoyed his chivalry and the play that natural limitations impose.

As they walked toward land, Eerin said, "Maybe your hut should be a pavilion,"

"Be my guest," said Dalla. "You have access to all my creations."

Eerin wrapped her arm around his waist and hugged him as they walked. "That's really sweet of you, Dalla. How about an oriental style?" She stood still and started flipping through holographic images that existed in the main database, commenting on their size and structure as they appeared.

She paused and turned to Dalla. "How many people do you think will come?" she asked.

"A few hundred," he replied proudly.

"Hmmm. Then a modest eight-sided pagoda of shiny woods would be the best fit." Eerin easily conjured an elaborate building.

Dalla's had designed his island to be rustic and natural like some tropical paradise, but he was enjoying Eerin's elaborate manifestations of culture.

The pagoda had multiple roof layers, which let air flow between them. It was decorated with scrollwork and was supported by ornate pillars. The eight sides were walled in a translucent paper-like material. In the center of each side was an arched doorway, both sides of which were decorated with one of the eight trigrams of the I Ching, representing eight natural energies.

Together they entered the pagoda, then walked out of each of the doorways in succession, manifesting landscapes that matched the patterns of the specific trigrams.

They started with Ch'ien, Heaven, which represents pure Yang energy. "Let's create a Zen garden of jade and a variety of metals," Dalla said. He began by creating a base landscape of sand, with large stone boulders of many sizes scattered about in Zen garden style.

"How about two jade horses to either side of the gateway," Eerin suggested. At Dalla's nod, she created two majestic winged steeds resembling the green creatures of Galantria 7. They whinnied loudly in their laughing alien voices.

Eerin and Dalla worked together creating shining metal trees with fruits of jade and other precious stones glistening in the sunlight.

Finally, after standing back and admiring their creation, they re-entered the pagoda and exited through the next gateway, which symbolized Tui, the Marsh. Dalla expanded the size of the island and created a vast marshland full of lily pads and exotic flowers.

Eerin began creating elaborate bridges and wooden walkways over the marsh. She and Dalla walked together, adding many arches and covering some with old Earth plants such as wisteria, jasmine, and honeysuckle, and covering others with fragrant plants from planets around the galaxy.

Dalla asked, "How about wood carvings?"

Eerin's eyes lit up. "That would be great! How about the ancient Earth goddess Kuan Yin?"

Dalla agreed. "And Taoist sages, and some wizards of Engorania 5." So they walked the wooden boardwalks and added many wood carvings and benches under arched junctions along the winding way.

"We should add turtles of all types," Eerin decided. She and Dalla waved their hands here and there, and turtle-like creatures from many worlds of all sizes and colors began to populate the swamps.

After entering the pagoda again, they left through the archway of Li, fire, and walked out from the archway about fifty meters. Dalla said, "I'll create a three meter [ten foot] fire circle of beautiful round gemstones."

Eerin smiled, "Why don't you light it with non-consumable wood?"

"Sure. Good idea." Dalla filled the circle with an artistic pile of twisted wooden logs and sent flames leaping high into the sky.

Eerin put benches around the circle while Dalla created eight more one meter [three and a quarter foot] fire rings with enough distance between them to allow groups of people to sit around their own fire circles.

Eerin stood back and looked at what they had created. She asked, "How about some giant trees around all the fire circles, to kind of enclose the whole area?"

"Sounds like a great idea," Dalla said, sending forth some mighty Falconian oaks all around the perimeter of the fire realm. He then changed the sky to night and cooled the air, and they stood by the fire for a few moments before continuing their work.

The next archway they exited was Chen, thunder. Dalla had a sudden insight. "This should be a realm of dragons."

Eerin smiled in agreement. "Should they be fierce or friendly?"

"They could have all different countenances," Dalla replied, waving his hand and creating two large Boracian iridescent azure dragons, which would stare anyone who left the pagoda in the face with diamond pupils set in their fierce red eyes. The dragons snorted heavy fog which began rolling out across the sand. Then Eerin created some yellow and ocher Ninavia 7 dragons that frolicked in the fog, chasing each other and wrestling playfully. Even the benches she and Dalla created were in the pattern of entwined dragons. They worked together to conjure many multicolored lizard-sized dragons of Horania 2 to roam about.

Dalla added a few dragons of Silarian 5 that shot lightning from their eyes with loud cracks of thunder.

"If those were real Silarian dragons, we would have been eaten already," she replied, causing one dragon to rush at them.

"Hey!" Dalla quickly waived his hand to stop it.

Eerin shivered, "I'm not sure this would be a realm I would enjoy spending my evening in, but some of your guests might like it."

Dalla nodded his head. "Yeah, some people are attracted to this kind of stuff." He shivered. "Let's go."

They passed through the pagoda and into the realm of K'un, earth, which is pure Yin. Eerin declared, "This definitely should be a flower garden."

Dalla smiled. "This should be your sweet realm, then, my dear."

Eerin grinned. She quickly began sending forth flower gardens with hedgerows in maze patterns. "I'm going to put down quilts of amazing colors and patterns in many places, with baskets of food and wine ready for the taking. Not that people couldn't manifest anything they desired, but finding things is fun."

Dalla thought for a moment. "You know, we need the dark and mysterious to really show Yin."

"Oh! You're right, of course," She gazed around the scene before her, and then added entrances to seven caves hidden in her mazes. She took Dalla to each of them. The insides were warm spaces lit by candles or oil lamps and she lined them with exotic cloth and fine furniture.

When she had finished decorating the seventh one, Dalla looked her deep in the eyes and kissed her. She yielded long enough for him to get excited, then said, "Come on. We still have lots to do."

He pulled her closer to him and said softly, "We can alter time and get it done later."

Eerin kissed him on the cheek, then wriggled out of his embrace. She took him by the hand and pulled him back out into the sunlight and the fragrant gardens.

They proceeded to the realm of Ken, the mountains. Dalla wondered aloud, "How should these realms connect?"

Eerin waved the question aside. "We can make the connections later. Let's just let our creativity flow."

Dalla agreed, and sent up mountains for miles, expanding the island as needed and making the lake vast to encircle them.

Together they walked up paths and created sparkling streams and waterfalls. They added stone benches and groves of manzanita trees with their deep red wood winding around old wood, stately madrone trees, and other red barked trees from many worlds. They sent forth a vast array of exotic birds. They stood looking down over the lands below, with the pagoda at the center and the lake flowing to the foothills of the mountains, glittering in the sun.

"We've wandered pretty far," noticed Eerin. "Let's just blink back."

"Okay." Dalla took her hand and suddenly they were walking out of the K'an arch, which is the symbol of water. "I guess this is where the docks and the swan rafts should be," said Dalla as he swung the docks and the fleet of swans around to this part of the island.

"We need beaches, too," said Eerin, sending forth white sand beaches.

"Let's add some nice shells," Dalla decided, so they walked along scattering multicolored shells of many varieties from worlds they had learned about when they were children in school.

They returned to the pagoda and exited the gate of Sun, representing wind and wood. Here they created groves of trees from many worlds, mingled with yurts of grand design for their guests to enjoy. Calling back and forth with a slightly competitive spirit, they added flying creatures of many types: Some pilants," "some Wateria 3 ranarts,"... The myriad creatures soared in the circling winds and found roosts in the variety of trees.

Finally, having completed all eight realms, Eerin said, "Now let us connect the realms."

Dalla smiled. "How about we go back up into the mountains to look down on the lands we have created?"

They grabbed each other's hands and appeared on a high mountain path. Looking down at the landscape, they added trails and winding connections between the eight realms. Sometimes they manifested maps in the air before them and sometimes floated above different sections of the realm creating the interconnecting landscapes and trails.

Surveying all that lay before them, Dalla said, "We really created some wonderful lands."

Eerin seemed subdued. "I suppose so, but somehow the real world seemed so much richer."

"Don't be so pessimistic," said Dalla, putting his arm around her. "The real world also had some ugly lands. There was death evident in many forms." Dalla looked at her with concern, then kissed her on the forehead.

Eerin sighed. "Let's blink into the pagoda."

On the inside of the pagoda, Dalla and Eerin added a fire pit in the center. They added simple solid wooden tables with velvet tablecloths along the walls, to both sides of each of the eight gates, and began filling them with delightful food, some of it manifest from the system memory already hot and steaming. They manifested foods from many worlds, sometimes querying the system for suggestions and trying them. Dalla tended to like sweets and rich foods, while Eerin liked more natural dishes. Once they agreed on a food, they determined what table to put it on according to its energy.

"Good thing we don't have to worry about the food going stale or getting cold." Eerin took a deep breath of the wonderful aroma filling the pagoda.

"Or even over cooking something while keeping it warm," Dalla added.

Eerin asked, "When do you think people will arrive?"

"I invited them for dinner. Even though people no longer need to eat, they love to enjoy new flavors. Since they cannot get fat, I am sure they will be here to feast. At midnight, we are going to have a grand finale - people love to be surprised. I have set up a vast fireworks display, unlike anything possible in the material world." Dalla was proud of his ploy.

Eerin bowed with her hands together. "Well, I should go and change. See you in an hour or so." They kissed slowly with enjoyment. This time when she pulled back, her crystalline blue eyes were open windows to his dark hazel eyes. After a minute of gazing intently at each other, she simply disappeared.

# 10. Wellstone Dinner

Geardon and Cynthea made their way to the ship's lounge, a comfortable room that was environmentally virtual, but solidly constructed of Wellstone holo-matter. As they walked into the room, it appeared as if it were made of glass, showing the planet above them and the stars below. Geardon spoke to the room's Intelligence System, "Change to room design 147, please." The clear walls revealing the planet below and the armada of ships became dark wood paneling in modest, but attractive patterns. A fireplace appeared which radiated heat and provided a visual of fire.

Geardon led Cynthea to a wooden table opposite the fireplace. A small virtual window to the planet below appeared in the wall next to the table when they sat down. The light in the room was warm.

Cynthea looked at Geardon. "I want to explain something."

"Go ahead," he said, curious.

"Miranda feels embarrassed talking about personal history. Spacers rarely discuss such things; especially since everyone's complete history is available on the system and is similar. For all the talk of not wanting privacy, spacers are really afraid of being alone, but at the same time are very private in some respects. Miranda wouldn't care if we enjoyed sexual activity; she just wants someone in the room with her when she closes her eyes."

Geardon raised his eyebrows. "I expected Miranda to be more flexible about being alone, but I guess she is molded by her culture. It's interesting, then, that she wanted to dine alone."

"That's different," said Cynthea. "She's working. Spacers are surrounded by their holo-displays continually, except when they sleep. They only communicate by talking with those very close to them; almost never while on duty or in public, unless at a meeting, which is like a performance with them on an imaginary stage. They prefer electronic interaction whenever possible. Their sleeping quarters are large rooms where they sleep in groups of varying sizes and they whisper to each other if they need to communicate.

"Each sleeping room has a side room, which they refer to as their private rooms, where the adults hold space for each other's sexual activities. The private rooms are also places where they play music. Planetary people are never invited and the spacer clans of different sleeping rooms rarely visit other's private rooms; except in their teen years, and then through a formal invitation system.

Sex is a very healthy part of spacer life, regardless of the myths spread by planetary cultures. All their sexual activity is a form of Yoga and is very structured. Spacers sometimes perform solo even when they are bonded with a partner. Though relationships are a deeply heart felt thing; they are not compulsive like planetary people.

"They are community and they all respect each other. The water rooms off of their sleeping quarters, which provide for swimming and bathing, are all clothes free. They have no gender specific bathrooms, except in areas where planetary travelers are allowed. There is no comprehension of privacy for those who live on a space city."

Geardon shook his head. "Sexual relationships always involve karma, regardless of the spacers' claims of being above such influences. Our energy bodies are affected even if we just watch sexual activities. Different cultures have different norms and we need to accept each other's standards as long as they do not adversely affect the community. I guess I should be polite to Miranda and just communicate through the system, instead of engaging her in conversation."

"She would be much happier if we proceeded according to spacer etiquette," Cynthea agreed.

"It's just that our problems are planetary, so I wish to stay in that mode of thinking and acting," Geardon said, somehow feeling the need to justify his behavior.

"I'm both a planetary person and a spacer, while Miranda is only a spacer and doesn't associate with other cultural norms. We will both serve you as you wish, thought, without question." Cynthea looked doe-eyed, but Geardon still saw the tigress within maintaining personal discipline.

"Thanks. I accept your service, but my needs are few."

Geardon then spoke out to the room, "Maya."

Maya appeared as a full sized human and approached their table "May I take your orders?"

Cynthea glanced briefly at a scrolling holo-menu and smiled. "Spacer lunch one-zero-five-seven, thank you."

Geardon shook his head. "Meal five-zero-four-two." He looked curiously at Cynthea, "You prefer spacer food over the planetary delicacies that my ship offers?"

She replied, "You know eating spacer food will add fifty years to your life." She arched an eyebrow. "You are drinking wine?"

Geardon laughed, "On average, spacer food does lead to longer life, but some of the longest lived people eat real food. Rich red wine also happens to extend one's lifespan."

Their trays gently floated from the food synthesizer to their table as Maya bowed and disappeared.

"As long as we're challenging each other's choices," said Cynthea, "I would call Maya a planetary aberration, a sign of your being alone too much. Why wouldn't you just talk to the ship? Why do you need a nymph to order around?"

"I travel alone quite often and the Brilliant Machine core in my system is a very advanced persona. She is not a human design; she's a living silicon being with interfaces created by the ancient races." Geardon took a sip of his wine. "The Brilliant Machine interfaces serve me, but I also serve them. It desires a material presence. Maya is not my creation. It adopted many forms when we first met, but this one is its estimation of the best interface for our interaction.

"By the way, you should know that Falcon 4 has many unusual characteristics built into its planetary intelligent core. It is a world where virtual interfaces have always surrounded the inhabitant's lives."

"The food is excellent." Cynthea dabbed at her mouth with a napkin. "What kinds of specific unusual characteristics?"

"They have advanced virtual reality that you can feel and smell. This room is a nice effect, but their virtual reality is completely sensual. The gravitronic structures are superbly complex mimics of real things, even living things. Over the last century, they have made great deals of money on their creations. No one knows what their intellectual secrets are which allowed virtual reality constructs to appear so real to all the senses, but perhaps now we see the possibility that the translated added their touch to them. We felt that there intellectual processes were part of the reason they sealed off their world. They are such a peaceful people that they posed no threat and we respected their privacy." Geardon sliced into his rare meat.

Cynthea took a bite of her nutria-cake, looking at Geardon's plate with mixed feelings. She remembered eating like a planetary barbarian during her youth, but living with the cultured spacers ever since, she never considered food that mimicked animal flesh. "Don't you find it strange to mimic animal flesh for consumption?"

"Mimic?" Geardon took another sip of his wine. "This is frozen flesh from a real Bisor beast from Horandian 3. Real food has a life force that food synthesizers could never reproduce."

Cynthea grimaced. "That's disgusting."

"You've been living with spacers for too long. When you lived on a planetary surface, I'll bet you ate real food."

"This nutria-cake is real food and I accept that there is a higher culture that all humans should adopt," she retorted.

"Well, they never will. And we need to find a planetary people to match Falcon's lifestyle without judgment," Geardon said as he sat back calmly.

"Ganondor could have been a possible race for population of Falcon. You could impose laws and set up robotic enforcement. The people would comply by need and in a few generations, they would be new Falconians. Will not any world serve as breeding stock? And why not take people from several worlds? Mixing the gene pools is often healthy, especially after a few generations of selective cross-breeding."

Geardon finished his glass and waved it into the air. Maya appeared and floated it away, delivering a full glass in a few seconds. "You cannot, as an individual or as a government, use force and fear to bend people's wills and get them to do what you want. You must convince people that what you want is also what they want. When they believe in their actions, they will perform them to the best of their abilities."

"But every planet has well trained armies to maintain order through force and protect the human culture from beastly alien civilizations", she countered. "Many places in the galaxy require force to protect the human domain. There are races eager for advancement through the demise of any race too weak to defend itself from plunder. Force seems the best way to maintain security."

"Force against irrational alien creatures for protection is one thing, but against other humans it's a different matter altogether." Geardon sighed. "No human should ever need to fear another human."

Cynthea ate the last bite of her cake and sent her tray hovering away without Maya. "What about the person who is out of control? They simply need to be stopped. The same rule applies to a race that is out of control. I thought for years that the Cyprids should be exterminated. I didn't agree that dismantling their society was enough - after all they had murdered my parents. But I now understand that every intelligent genome is incredibly valuable. Our Cyprid servant was remorseful and I do remember as a child receiving loving kindness from him. It took me years to finally forgive his ignorance, yet I still hope that their race remains under human control for many ages to come."

"I agree that we must preserve any intelligent species as an evolving entity. Each case is unique and each incident requires community response." Geardon's voice indicated that the heaviness of the conversation affected him personally.

Sensing his darkening mood, Cynthea changed the subject. "The spacers do not have privacy in their activities. In the ten years I've been assigned to this fighter, we have only had three domestic disputes that required forceful intervention of minor restraint until the hotheads calmed down. Since the community is always there, eating and sleeping together, there is little room for aberrant personal behavior. We have had hundreds of such events occur with planetary passengers. The planetary ways give room for distorted reasoning and actions."

"Humanity evolved upon old Earth as many diverse individuals," Geardon argued. "That mentality is ingrained. The spacer ways cannot be applied to the wide open spaces of planetary surfaces."

"I agree," said Cynthea. "I am trained as security and I know that history holds countless lessons, but we can all evolve and grow out of primitive modes of behavior."

"World War Three almost destroyed our race. The only thing that saved us is that in every country, more and more people refused to participate." Geardon leaned forward. "It took a while for civilization to recover, but the humans that survived were one people around the globe. We can never lose that again. Falcon was a great loss of a very valuable people."

"We lost our unity ages ago," Cynthea argued. "There would be planetary wars, except for the United Star System forbidding and ending all such activities. We continue to use force and maintain order through force among the many alien races of the galaxy."

"The United Star System has about a hundred alien races as members, so this goes beyond being human, it's about being civilized," Geardon answered. "Some people have pushed for human dominance, but the galaxy is just too vast for any race to dominate; that is more of the old thinking which destroyed the countries of old earth."

Cynthea frowned. "I did a tour of the Locassa border. Our fighter had three engagements. We lost many good men and women. Many planetary recruits filled single pilot warrior ships. They came for fame, glory, and wealth. Many spacers fought and died also, but out of a sense of duty. Wealth is a planetary concept. We live in confined space where personal wealth is an outmoded concept. We don't imagine returning somewhere to live the high life. We all live the same life as community. We work because it fulfills our personal evolution. During the last of the three engagements, we took a main hull breach and lost seventeen percent of our population. It will be another generation until our fighter has a high enough population for active battle duty in a high risk sector. We were just close to Falcon 4 and thus chosen for this mission. Humans are warriors and warrioresses; that is our nature. Space is a mostly predatory realm."

"Well in one sense that is true, but we have another nature that is peaceful, loving, and nurturing," Geardon countered. "We have a higher purpose and destiny. As a race, our genome evolves beyond individual or planetary lines. Wealth, even for many planetary humans, is more about our family, friends, and personal evolution. The ancient races and their teachings about love are a good example of what we may become."

"I don't believe in love the way planetary people might fantasize about such things." Cynthea didn't sound completely convincing about this aspect of her belief. "I do believe that sexuality is a powerful mystic energy, required for a healthy long life. I don't buy the whole planetary myth about the higher power of personal love. It seems more confused thinking from primitive private life."

Geardon sent his tray away. He sat up tall. "I know love is real. Private life may allow some aberrant behaviors to go unchecked, but it also allows unique personal growth. Planetary scientists and mathematicians like those from Falcon make a high percentage of the theoretical leaps."

"But spacers make most of the technological hardware advances," Cynthea countered. "I'd say that each environment has its advantages and disadvantages."

"I'll give you that," Geardon agreed. "Both the planetary culture and the spacer culture are necessary for human growth. Our future as interacting cultures appears bright. You and I, having lived in both cultures, are uniquely fitted to understand both."

"Yet you still maintain private quarters. That seems so strange," Cynthea prodded. "I remember being a little girl and having my own room; but as an adult, it seems profane."

Geardon laughed, "Shall we make ourselves more comfortable?"

The table between them dissolved slowly with its energy forming a vortex and flowing into a unit in the center of the ceiling. Another vortex descended and two chairs materialized next to the fireplace. They were rich red velvet, with dark wooden frames carved in intricate leaves and branches, with optional footrests.

Their sheen revealed that they were gravitronic constructs of halo-matter, electron shells without any nuclear mass assuming the form of chairs.

Cynthea stood and stretched slowly. Geardon watched her graceful form. He then stood and also stretched. As they walked over to the chairs, he asked, "Would you like anything to drink?"

"Water please, thanks," she replied.

Geardon lifted his glass and Maya floated it away. She floated a full glass of wine to him and a large cold glass of water to Cynthea. As they settled into the plush chairs, he continued, "A few planetary people have a unique ability to see fields of energy around living beings. Mystical healing is a planetary art. What do you think happened when we were walking on the road on Falcon 4, when I sensed we were being watched?" Geardon asked her.

"Most spacers have many doubts about such arts. We cannot believe in statistical anomalies. We agree that life has mysterious aspects, but doubt most special knowledge about such things. Hard core scientific devices cannot measure living energy fields with the characteristics that mystics claim are present. It is very interesting that the Wandini corroborated your story, but such a complex planetary core could be playing tricks with you."

"With me?" Geardon smiled. "Well probably, though my medallion would shield me against most of that sort of influence, but the Wandini are outside of technology. Something happened in the natural world. My intuition and second sight tell me we were being watched. Normally there are enough ghosts around any unnatural disaster, such as a Falcon 4's death ritual, that anyone would feel creepy. I never sensed the dead there. I have been to sites of mass death several times before and the disembodied have a strong presence. Only once on the road did I have the feeling that sentient energy from the other side was watching us. After a few moments they left, which is also very unusual."

She was amazed that anyone would be superstitious. "You are still telling me you think Eerin and Dalla were scanning us?"

"Something sentient was watching us from the other side. Perhaps it was just the virtual dragon's synthetic intelligence system of one of the Falconian's energy affecting the planetary gravitron scans, but that is not what my second sight told me. Don't you admit that strange things happen repeatedly in connection with living beings and death, beyond coincidence?" Geardon asked.

"Maybe, but no one really knows and people fool themselves into believing in things that don't materialize. I think you are letting this whole affair affect you psychologically." Cynthea sat back in the plush chair and put up the footrest, then touched a device she wore on her belt. "If such visions are not controllable and consistent, so that we can scientifically analyze them, how can you rely on them?"

Geardon noticed that she was quite beautiful in her clinging one-piece nanofiber jump suit, "Can you feel the fire through your suit's feet?"

"I just touched the temperature regulator so that it would not compensate within reasonable temperature variances," she smiled.

"Do you always wear your protective garments?" he asked.

"They saved my life several times when our ship was attacked by surprise. I was wearing one when the cyborgs hacked our fighter city and it saved precious seconds not having to change." She seemed a bit coy, as if she thought he would rather see her in some other outfit. "I have worn them ever since I got one, after my colony was destroyed; one never knows when an accident might occur, but occasionally I let my guard down." She gave a sensual smile and touched her belt control, which let the front of her suit open in a thin line from her neck, almost to her waist.

Geardon continued his original line of reasoning, trying to seem uninterested. "We do not need to guarantee a certain percentage of effectiveness to use our higher senses. We do not know why psychic abilities work, but they work often enough to be an asset. I can rely on the fact that we were spied on while walking down the road. I wanted to know by who or what and the Wandini answered that; Eerin and her boyfriend Dalla were the awareness. The universe is not controllable. It is rather the ultimate controlling entity."

"But we manipulate reality and determine a great deal of what occurs in this galaxy." She stretched in her chair widening the open line in her robe, revealing a thin silk undergarment. "What is under our domain, we strive to make secure. There is always the possibility that some emergency or new situation shall threaten our crew, but we maximize the security of our missions and carry them out for the good of the whole of humanity. That is our purpose as a fighter space colony. Humanity as a whole has a great deal of control structures in place, making life very predictable."

Geardon yawned. "Whether the final future of the universe is a hot crunch or a lonely cold freeze, humanity and all carbon and silicon life forms will perish. What remains, is yet to be seen."

"Spacers are not so ready to delineate two limited possibilities. The universe holds countless surprises, so predicting such long distant futures is another planetary aberration from the ancient past on old Earth. What humanity will be in a few million years remains to be seen, much less billions of years. We spacers make plans for many hundreds of years, but beyond that we know better than to speculate, except perhaps in fiction for entertainment."

Cynthea smiled and shifted the conversation, "Do you know about Omega 1?"

"I was hoping to visit there one day soon." Geardon smiled. "It is a fairly large moon, hollowed out as a spacer city. Its mission is to reach our neighboring spiral galaxy, Andromeda. It is in the final phases of construction and the gravitronic engines are currently being assembled and tested."

"It is a prime example of spacer long-term planning. Dr. Kellerman presented the plans over eight hundred years ago and the project officially started five hundred and fifty-seven years ago." Cynthea seemed to shine as she spoke. "Another sixty-eight years and it will be populated and ready to launch."

Maya walked up to them. "Sorry to interrupt sir, but Draco is paging us and seems upset."

Geardon recognized from her change of dress into a uniform style outfit that this was serious. He turned to Cynthea, "Do you want to join this conference?"

"I would love to."

"Maya, please also be present."

She just nodded. Cynthea touched her belt and her nanofiber suit closed in front up to her neck.

Geardon looked at Maya. "Recommendations?"

The room blurred around them and they were suddenly in a boardroom decorated with USS logos and fine art displaying great historic moments in the empire's history. Maya was now seated to Geardon's right and Cynthea to his left, so that they would face Draco across the highly polished table.

Cynthea joked, "Good thing I had taken my feet from the footrest that disappeared."

Geardon curled his lips, but lacked a real smile. Cynthea started bringing up displays around her, making her spacer status apparent, so that Draco could wonder what she was watching.

"Okay." Geardon said to Maya.

Draco appeared across the table, dressed in heavy black leather, and Geardon stood, "Welcome aboard. Please have a seat."

"I'll stand," Draco's response was almost a shout. Geardon smiled and sat back down. He could have guessed that one.

"I've been reviewing all your activity here." Draco pointed at Maya. "Your ship's artificial intelligence hacked into our system and two nanobot cities invaded our system's core through her breach. The BESILFs have a non-interference treaty. They are in violation. No one can ever change the security access codes in a planetary system."

Geardon held up a hand. "Your world is currently in an undefined area of the law. I would say you no longer hold any rights according to the USS federation."

He turned to Maya, who replied, "The BESILF agreements only apply to living beings. The ultimate core of every system is under the control of the Brilliant Unity. Your virtual world's inhabitants were locked out of all files related to the translator. Also, the Brilliant Machine has gained access to all data flows into or out of your system. You and the Falconians were left with complete control within your realm."

Draco retorted, "We have vast economic potential and clout. Many worlds rely on our products and we demand our intellectual property rights are not to be violated."

Geardon kept his voice level. "We will not possess anything that is yours. The Brilliant Machine Unity acts within their power, but I do have some power to negotiate with them. Once the situation is normalized, your intellectual property and trading rights will be reinstated in full. The knowledge of the translator will be returned to your minds. The Brilliant Machine may have an agenda, but I think we can guarantee your long-term intellectual property rights."

Draco seemed to lighten a bit. "So what is this nonsense with the primitives and the ghosts? Do not play with that young girl's head. She is innocent of our power plays. If this drama makes it out to the public eyes, they will see you as the monster you are."

Cynthea lowered a few displays, "You will note that Geardon stated to me on the road that we were being watched and then the Wandini stated that Eerin visited. This is very statistically improbable from my logical point of view. Was she there according to your virtual view of reality?"

"Actually, she was. His medallion and that machine in the form a woman," he pointed to Maya again, "must have fed both him and the Wandini the info hacked from our system."

Geardon jumped in. "Specific access codes may be negotiated through this Brilliant Machine, who resembles a woman for my benefit, in that it makes for easier interaction. Do you have specific requests at this time?"

"Do not interfere with our population or their world." Draco commanded firmly.

Geardon turned to Maya, who stated, "We have not, and have no present intention to."

"You better not. You don't know everything about our world. The secret of the translator is ours. I'm warning you." Draco was ranting again.

"Anything else?" Geardon asked calmly.

Draco just waved an arm and disappeared.

Geardon said, "Nice exit. He seems a bit of a mad man."

Cynthea shivered. "He gives me the creeps. Maybe in this I am also aware on some psychic level, but I would not let him near a ship or population which I was charged to protect."

Geardon said, "Maya, please return us to our former room."

In a moment, they were again sitting before a fire and Geardon tried to pick up the thread where they had left off. "You sure seem enthused about this Omega 1 project."

Cynthea sat up in her chair, "I served as a main security trainer. I hope to travel with that city-ship. It will do gravity assist movements for over a hundred years and will ultimately exceed half a million times light speed. I might live to leave the Milky Way at a ripe old age of two hundred plus years."

"You could live a good while past two hundred, Cynthea, but such speeds seem incredible and could have unknown effects. How long until the city ship arrives at Andromeda?"

"Five hundred thirty-two standard solar years; a dozen or so generations."

"Well past our lifetimes, but a mission with amazing possibilities. Did you know that the United Star System's Genome Audit branch assists in ongoing searches for extra-galactic visitors from Andromeda? Perhaps Andromeda will send their city-ship here before our ship arrives there. Every time a new theory is published as to how we could go there, we search out the possibility that they have come here with a similar method."

"And?" Geardon had Cynthea's attention now.

"No luck so far." Geardon smiled. "I can grant you the privilege of reviewing the search criteria and results."

"That would be great. I am very interested in anything related to Omega 1. I have spent a couple leaves there and a two-year sabbatical. I know that city well, but it is so huge, it's like a small planet."

Cynthea was interrupted by a halo display field flashing before her. "Oh, Miranda is ready for bed. I'm going to head to our quarters. You're welcome to join us."

They stood and Geardon gave her a hug. "Give my night-time blessings to Miranda."

Cynthea looked like she was considering another advance, then smiled instead "Good night, Geardon."

# 11. Party

Dalla had set up a small courtyard where he could greet the guests as they arrived in many elaborate ways. Eerin appeared in a royal blue silk kimono. It was decorated with silver and gold dragons embracing in a martial art sort of way.

Dalla took her hand. "You look beautiful."

She smiled. "Thank you." She took in his oriental robe and jeweled sword. "You look like a mighty warrior."

Dalla bowed. "At your service." They both giggled.

Eerin stood with Dalla, greeting the guests, for quite some time. Finally, he said, "We should eat before the festivities."

They went in and filled plates with delectable morsels. He led her over to a table where his brother and some friends were sitting. "Eerin, I'd like you to meet Nathesh."

A short, muscular man, who definitely had Dalla's rich skin and eyes, stood. "Pleased to meet you. This is Rehalli."

A fair-skinned woman with big green eyes gave Dalla and Eerin hugs, complimenting them on many features of their created realm.

Eerin and Dalla sat across from Nathesh and Rehalli at the table.

Nathesh also marveled at the place Dalla had built. "Wow Dalla, you really made an awesome place here. I heard that you didn't use any pre-designed patterns from the system, like almost everyone else uses to create their worlds."

Dalla grinned. "Eerin helped me. We looked at patterns, but modified almost everything."

Eerin blushed. "Dalla had the lake and island and nature stuff already created. I just helped with the pagoda and party details."

His brother was obviously proud, "You guys could sell the plans for this place. I hear that Falcon will once again become economically viable in the outer universe. We will be able to continually upgrade our system to truly live forever."

"What could individuals buy here that we don't have?" Eerin asked with a tone of incredulity.

Dalla opened his eyes wide, then gestured with his chin for Nathesh to reply.

"Well there are perks: glory, fame, and popularity to mention a few."

Dalla snickered and Eerin rolled her eyes.

Nathesh continued, "One day it may be possible to go to other worlds within a robotic body. There are those who are looking for Falcon to become a major force in the galactic virtual reality market. We still have strong ties to other worlds. There are many human and alien worlds that would pay dearly for a pre-calculated virtual place like this island world."

Eerin began eating as Dalla told his brother, "You'll have to send me some search criteria to look into this more."

Eerin swallowed and said, "I already have ideas for a new series of statues to add to the Zen garden."

Dalla boasted, "I am going to design hundreds of bonsai trees for along the paths, instead of just the few that are by the gates now."

"I invited some very high level techs who were working on the translator systems." Nathesh said, changing the subject subtly. "They probably won't show up until some of the crowd dies down. They will probably know about the marketing of digital creations. I have been putting together a publication about the relationship of Falcon and the USS government over the last hundred years. I figure that it will be relevant in light of our recent translation into eternal life. I heard that there is some negotiation with a Genome Auditor."

"That's a great idea; a review of our history would be very interesting." Dalla replied avoiding saying anything about Eerin's part.

Eerin quickly changed the subject by materializing herself a drink in a crystalline red goblet that sparkled in the light. "Anyone wish to try the Epsilon ginger champagne? It is an exact replica from Epsilon Erudani, one of the oldest human outposts that ever existed."

They were all willing to experience it, so she conjured the glasses and floated one to each of them. They continued talking about other worlds as they enjoyed the rich variety of food. Shortly after they finished eating, they heard explosions in the sky that were timed like a drum roll. Dalla waved his hand and his plate disappeared. "Come on, let's go watch the sky." They walked out of the north entrance into the Zen garden.

Eerin was a little surprised to smell sweet smoke and see people passing pipes as they sat waiting to see the sky show. Nathesh noticed her look and said quietly, "Since no physical damage can come from smoking, and our systems are still wired to receive cannabinoids and endomorphs, just like our physical bodies were, a new counter-culture is raging strong."

They walked through the garden of rocks and statues and made their way to the beach. They passed some people swimming naked in the moonlight. Further along, they came across Michael and Lorri, the café owners, looking out over the water.

"Hi, how are you doing?" Eerin asked.

"OK," Lorri replied, not sounding very happy.

Eerin asked, "How's Sunflower?"

Lorri looked as though she might cry. "She died."

Eerin put out her arms and Lorri came to her and did shed a few tears.

Eerin said, "I'm so sorry, what happened?"

"We were having a good day. I spent a lot of time with her. I was making little mice and she would stalk and chase them. It was a lazy afternoon and I lay down on a blanket on the grass and she curled up next to me. She was dreaming, because her paws were moving a bit, then she vanished. I thought she would come back, but she never did. I guess real cats die sometimes, but it's not like I can get another one. Created cats just aren't the same."

Michael touched Lorri's arm and she released Eerin and put her arm around Michael, who told them, "I have been doing a lot of research on the pet issue, and they are all vanishing. They seem to get lost in their dreams and aren't able to connect with the virtual realm anymore."

"That's amazing," said Dalla. "I wonder if a person could die."

Eerin gave him a look, but Michael answered, "Never happened yet."

Lorri looked down and then said to Eerin, "Sorry to make a scene."

Eerin replied, "Oh no, I would be devastated if that happened to me. I love animals. I had a dog when I was growing up and it died when I was twelve. I was heartbroken for six months."

The girls smiled at each other. Just then there were bright meteoric flashes streaming through the sky.

Dalla smiled proudly. "This is my special event for the party guests."

The sky began to explode with colors that mimicked creation. Images of the big bang, or big unwind as it is better described, were followed rapidly by the formation of super-clusters with huge wispy energy halos and swirling collections of billions of stars. Since they were air born pyrotechnics, they had the three-dimensional quality of fireworks, but the control and planning of a virtual movie. At times, there were aspects that came fairly close to the crowd. The display was spectacular and when it was completed, people from all over the eight lands clapped and shouted their approval.

Eerin and Dalla invited Lorri and Michael to come visit them at Eerin's home. Lorri seemed to be in good spirits after show, which had momentarily taken her mind off Sunflower. She said they would definitely come visit.

Dalla and Eerin walked around meeting people and gradually the crowd went on to find the next thrill party. As they walked back into the pagoda, Nathesh indicated that his friends had arrived. They walked over to an elderly couple, who seemed out of place in this realm of youth and beauty.

Nathesh introduced them. "This is Marvelin and Nina." The gentleman had long silver-gray hair tied in a ponytail and a long thin beard. He was thin and his wife was a bit plump. They wore wedding rings, an ancient custom rarely practiced in the eternal realms. Nina was dressed in a simple, sky blue cotton dress, while Marvelin wore old Earth-wear: blue jeans and a tee-shirt. They looked like paupers amongst royalty.

Nina seemed to read their confusion. "This is how we lived and what we looked like when we translated. We don't want to be what we are not. Some of those young people out there were older than we were when they translated. When they get distracted or feel they can relax, they might look like they did when they left Falcon for a short while, or they may have set up a directive to always maintain their charade, but within they have the memories of what they were."

They all sat down and Eerin produced many glasses in the center of the table.

Conversation quickly returned to a posting that Falcon had entered into negotiations with a Genome Auditor. Marvelin said, "We are waiting to see who the lucky person was, who had their exit dance presented."

Eerin spoke up in a quiet voice, "Me."

Nina smiled, "We thought it might be you, dear. From all information that has been gathered, he did land at a sector near your freedom location and we checked the records of the possible candidates."

"Dalla told me that you met Draco Nanitron." Nathesh sounded impressed.

"Dal-la!" Eerin dragged out the syllables of his name.

"You should be proud," he replied.

Marvelin seemed a bit consoling, "My wife and I have worked Draco for many years. We arrived here in the third translation group. We were advocates for sending only part of the population during the final translation, but Draco claimed that the galactic community could have captured those who remained and manipulated us with them."

"Who would want to stay behind and die?" Dalla was shocked.

"Some who believe in the soul's natural journey might." Nina pushed her long hair from her face.

"You mean like they believe in immortality and God stuff?" Eerin asked.

Marvelin replied, "God is the totality, which includes the material realm, as well as this virtual realm. There is nothing unnatural about death."

Dalla joked, "I'm not volunteering for that one."

Nathesh and Rehalli laughed, then Rehalli said, "You got that right."

Nina's expression remained somber. "There is more to existence than Draco will admit. There are many strange mysteries that still surround the translation, like the Morphs and the Pixelators."

"What are the Pixelators?" Eerin asked.

"And what are the Morphs?" Nathesh added.

Eerin answered Nathesh. "The Morphs are people who translated and lost their true form. They become strange changelings or ever-mutating rivers of virtual flesh. They don't revert to human form, because they either lost themselves or didn't ever know themselves. Draco said that he'd take me to visit them sometime."

Nina said, "You should take him up on that, though I doubt he will join you on the actual visit. It is a most fascinating mystery and well hidden. Very few have access to view the realm of the Morphs, or even second hand information about the people who inhabit that realm. We live there and monitor that realm."

Marvelin added, "You can't even get time lapse frame data from that realm."

"What is time lapse frame data?" Eerin asked.

"You can request access to anyone's past if they have marked it as public," Marvelin explained, as if he'd had first-hand experience. "By default, we are all private members of society. Some of the people who were here earlier have made their entire virtual lives, even their thoughts, public. They get economic returns for any parts that are interesting enough to be marketed. My wife and I think that life on the inside of virtual reality will be fascinating to the rest of the galaxy. The system only saves time-lapse images of everyone's lives, since the volume of data will grow continually forever. Special events are imaged as real time flow. The intelligent core of the Falconian system absorbs this data voraciously. You can look into your past and even put filters on it, only to capture what you think may be interesting to others. Once you have economic credit, you can get longer real-time holo-imaging, which captures you from all angles and many potential views."

Eerin played the devil's advocate, "It's still debatable if Falcon will be allowed to sell anything. The Genome auditor thinks we're worse than dead, trapped in a virtual bottle instead of a spiritual realm beyond death."

Marvelin was confident. "We have time on our side and people will be very curious. Sooner or later, the economic value will outweigh any resistance. Besides, research on the Falconian system will reveal that we are more that any synthetic intelligence ever was; our creativity proves it. Perhaps there is a higher spiritual realm, but this realm offers advantages to those seeking it."

Dalla asked, "But what about the Brilliant Machine, the living silicon life that forms a web at the heart of all planetary systems?"

Marvelin replied, "The Brilliant Machine will never know spiritual life, but has a huge interest in this. In some ways, we are a cross between their form of eternal life and biological life. We are eternal, but we are not unity, we are individuals. The Brilliant Machine is ever hungry for the effect of life force, true creativity as opposed to complex synthesis which it can perform so easily."

Two people sitting at the table next to them were obviously trying to listen in. Eerin started feeling uncomfortable. Marvelin called out to them, "Hey, you all."

Their faces brightened. Instead of inviting them over, Marvelin goaded them. "Ever do it in a swan boat?" he said, winking. "I hear the bouncing of the water can be great."

"Wow, thanks dude," the young man answered, obviously under the influence of a lot of alcohol and probably other drugs as well.

As the couple stood and looked around, Marvelin pointed to the water gate. "Enjoy."

Nina told Eerin, as soon as the couple was gone, "Sex has a very positive health giving effect if it is natural and balanced, even in the virtual realm. Our brains are the bottom root of our nervous system and our sexual nerve cluster is at the top, closest to direct perception, that's why we needed to have orgasms to map our new eternal beings in the translation. Marvelin and I have been married since we were in our thirties, though we prefer privacy for our intimate enjoyments."

Eerin perked up. "That's really cool. Dalla and I are engaged to get married."

Dalla smiled. "I proposed right before this party."

"Well, congratulations!" Nina exclaimed. "That's wonderful news! Let us know if you need help planning the wedding. With how well you two did in setting up this pagoda, you are going to have a lot of work to do to top it for your wedding party."

After a moment, Marvelin returned to the issues of the realm. "Back to the Pixelators. They are people who went into movie mode. They ride from scene to scene watching, not participating. They are not actors; they are sitting in the middle of one movie scene after another. On rare occasions, they act as beings, but mostly they are just taking in drama. Most of them have become involved with watching other people's pasts. Since someone has to sort out the interesting data, the Pixelators are participating by deciding on what they watch. They are completely lost, as if observing our virtual realm like a movie, without interaction or a life of their own."

Eerin replied, "I think it would be sad to be a Pixalator. They miss out on being themselves and having their own experiences."

"I agree. The Morphs cover a lot of ground, from lost souls to some pretty advanced humans, who are blazing our future." Marvelin took a sip of his drink. "One theory is that many people will lose their original form in the distant future. If they maintain false images for long enough, like most did for this party, eventually that is who they will become. They will lose their original forms. Did you notice how some people have unnatural colored hair? They are holding slightly altered physical appearances as if they dyed their physical hair, without even thinking about it. Their hair is just that color now. Their young forms will eventually be all they know. A century from now, they will feel a strange fear that they have lost something of themselves, but life will just go on."

Eerin asked, "So you think I would learn about myself or about our existence here if I visit the Morphs?"

"It would be a good learning experience to see what extremes are possible." Nina patted Eerin's arm.

Eerin somehow felt trust for Marvelin and Nina. "Okay, I'll do it." Eerin produced a brilliant blue hummingbird.

She said to the bird, "Tell Draco, 'Greetings from Eerin. I would be honored to visit again. I am curious about the many mysteries, like the Morphs."

"Hope you have some luck." Marvelin said to her, "He's not always the friendliest gent, and has a hard time finding time for most people."

The bird flew away and almost an instant later, a small Draco manifested on the table and looked around. He nodded at Marvelin and Nina, then spoke to Eerin, "Dinner at my mansion tomorrow night, and please feel free to bring Dalla along."

The image of Draco bowed and disappeared.

"Always one for dramatics," Marvelin commented.

Dalla spoke to Eerin with a bit of concern, "Did you tell him about me?"

Eerin shook her head. "No, he just seems to know things."

Nina added, "He knows all kind of things. No doubt he heard us commenting on his not being the friendliest gent, and in response came forth to look friendly."

A nervous laugh circulated at her intonation of friendly, which prompted Nathesh to reply, "How about we find somewhere outside to sit?"

They walked out the K'an arch toward the lake, where there were many benches along a patio that overlooked the water. They walked for a moment to a secluded group of benches and sat down. The sound of small, rolling waves on the beach just in front of the benches provided a cushion from the sounds of the party music still playing strong.

"We came in the third group to translate, back in the experimental days. We are the head Morphs," Marvelin explained. "We are the only ones who are reasonable and so can venture amongst the general population. We have been given special powers to rule the realm of the Morphs."

"What do you mean you are reasonable Morphs? You seem like the most grounded people here. And why should anyone have to rule the other Morphs?" Eerin asked, perplexed.

"You will have to come visit us and see," Marvelin smiled.

"It is not a place that ordinary people find very comfortable," Nina added.

Marvelin then asked Eerin, "Has Draco revealed anything about how it is going with the Genome Auditor?"

"We visited the Genome Auditor while he was in the booth watching my translation. Geardon, the Auditor, believes this realm is worse than being dead, but Draco negotiated with him and gave him the task of finding a new population to fill top-side. It should be interesting visiting top-side when it's full of people and doesn't seem so empty." She looked at Dalla for an instant, then confessed,

"Dalla and I went top-side and spied on Geardon while he was walking back to his ship. He stopped and looked at us."

Nathesh looked at Dalla. "Really?"

Dalla nodded. "He looked right at us like he could see us. It spooked us out, so we took off. He had a woman in a top grade nanofiber suit."

Eerin added, "We also visited with some strange primitive aliens that he must have brought with him. They were sitting by his ship."

"Aliens?" asked Marvelin, his interest piqued.

"Yeah," Dalla answered. "They were short blue-brown beings with horned faces. They played primitive ritual music. They seemed to like us and we thought they were pretty cool, right Eerin?"

"Yeah, they were nice. I want to visit them again." Eerin smiled.

Nina smiled back. "We had suspected that something strange was going on. Draco started monitoring all top-side activity and locking down the reports. So the primitives could see you?"

"Yes, they thought of us as spirits though." Eerin paused a minute, thinking. "Wait - how do you know he started monitoring all top-side activity?"

"We work as technicians with the core interface. Such a huge monitoring task changes the balance of the core," said Marvelin, then added, "We should be going for the evening, but I have a few ideas about testing the ability of the top-side animals being able to perceive us. We will let you know."

Marvelin and Nina stood and stretched. They all got up and exchanged hugs and said their goodbyes.

After all the others had left, Eerin kissed Dalla and bid him good night. "You don't have to go. You can stay if you want."

"Patience, Dalla. We have eternity," She said as she started to disappeared.

"But now is real," he replied with puppy eyes.

She felt his sincerity, and she could not imagine being with anyone else. Indeed, with all the people and happenings in the realm, they almost always chose each other's company. Often it was just the two of them having fun together. Eerin became solid and reached out her arms and they were soon kissing passionately. He melted their reality and manifest a bed of warm soft clouds with a million stars above and they shared themselves fully without any inhibitions.

# 12. Minoro

In the morning, Miranda and Cynthea rose early, and were soon in the forward pilot's chamber, surrounded by their halo-displays. The front window presented a great view of the night side of Falcon 4 covered with the sparkling spider webs of lightning from thunderstorms.

Maya appeared on the cube when Geardon entered and he spoke quietly to her. "Link me into the halo-data-pool and bring me a cup of Earl Violet tea, please."

As soon as he was logged into the halo session, Cynthea sent him a message. "Good morning. Sleep well?"

"Most excellent," he mumbled the words under his breath in spacer fashion, which were translated into holographic audio voice right to her ear. "Where do we stand?"

"The main possibilities are of seven planets within a hundred and seventy light years of Falcon 4, with three worlds standing out: Minoro, Niocene, and Mirka. Minoro is a world where gravitronic technology is limited by law, forcing people to live with other high-end technology. This is due to very unusual original planetary ecology. Niocene is a very high tech world that possesses a stable, but unusual planetary environment that they keep healthy. They are interactive with the native population. Mirka is a biologically advanced world with limited genetic modification, but advanced cloning and breeding practices. They are a main supplier of pure genome material throughout the Galaxy." Cynthea looked at him while sending the directed audio transmissions.

"Tell me more about Minoro," Geardon asked.

Maya took over. "The surface has a low population, but one that wishes to grow. Early in Minoro's history it was very volcanic and is riddled with a maze of hollow spaces and lava tubes. When the volcanism died down, the lower levels filled with cometary water where life evolved. Its native one-celled life eventually oozed out of the holes and found the surface lakes, starting photosynthesis and forming an atmosphere. The surface is mostly volcanic glass and sand from the glass. When humans found it, it did not have advanced life. There were a few colony type organisms like giant sponges and coral-like growths. The waters were filled with a simple balance of marine life and a few higher species of plants and animals were brought to populate the surface. Once the bio-design was in place, few corrections needed to be made in the next couple of dozen centuries.

"The people mostly live in the vast tunnel complexes, which they enhanced with many additional caves. The storms on the surface and the sharpness of fractured rocks make it a harsh landscape, but some areas of the surface have been cleared and a few cities have been built. There is a lot of mystery surrounding a few secrets to life there. One of the protected one-celled organisms is uniquely affected by gravitronics and so the use of that class of modern technology is forbidden by treaty."

"So what is so special about the one-celled organism that it warrants the limited technology?" Geardon wanted to know.

Miranda fielded that one, speaking into their ears with holographic subsonics. "They have had a ban on gravitronics from the initial population. There are virtually no levitating devices. Something about the uniqueness of the original ecology, but it appears to be a classified secret. Can you override the system's reluctance to our probes?"

"I could, but I like surprises and people respect you when you honor their secrets," Geardon said calmly and Miranda looked up at him, contrary to spacer behavioral etiquette.

Geardon seemed pleased, but all he said was, "And what about Niocene?"

She returned to subsonic communication. "Niocene is a world with lots of deserts. The early cometary bombardment was lighter than most solar systems and a lot of the water seems bound in a unique type vegetation, which has different species that all form water storage compartments. The native animal life depends on the plant life for water, so that free water in the environment is not consumed by the higher life forms. The plant life purifies the water. It forms massive clusters, like large islands in the sand or mountains, where life thrives. These clusters are separated by sand, the crossing of which is difficult and dangerous due to sand predators, thus each island has a unique biodiversity.

"There is an intelligent species, the MacTau. It is hard to compare it to a life form from old Earth, not really reptile, mammal, bird, or insect. It has six legs and the front two are used as hands, though they are most similar to ratcheting pliers. Its body is curved, so that the front portion is upright. The first research colonists, who lived in the sandy area and studied the islands, observed the MacTau were very vocal and collected some as pets. They were soon astounded to see how fast the MacTau would learn their languages. After a few years of speaking, they found the MacTau to be extremely intelligent.

"The MacTau enjoyed living in human company and the plants and animals it required for health were easily raised in greenhouse bio-domes. They even liked purified water. Although non-interference policies would imply limitations on interaction, both the humans and the MacTau seemed to benefit from each other's company. The MacTau were considered intelligent enough to negotiate their own terms, so human occupation occurred under their treaties, not ours. The MacTau are the governing body and the human populations are their guests. Humans emigrate regularly, due to population pressures. Immigration is forbidden, so that the population is very natural.

Geardon spoke loud enough to be heard in ordinary conversation, knowing it would infringe upon Miranda's sense of work ethics, but wanting her to hear, "I have studied Mirka. I trust Miranda's good work and Maya's analysis. What kind of a course can we set, assuming that the three worlds are to be our primary targets?"

Miranda sent her audio response through the system. "Minoro and Niocene on one side and Mirka at one hundred fifty-one degrees from Niocene and one hundred ninety-two from Minoro."

Geardon fed his audio response into the system as well. "Set course for Minoro, and let's concentrate on learning something of the culture."

Miranda put on a pilot's headset, which would isolate her from future out-loud discussions and optical awareness of Geardon and Cynthea. She immersed herself in space courses and began to accelerate the ship in orbit. Maya could maneuver fine, but human pilots often review options and they love the thrill of guiding the ship with their whole being, becoming almost symbiotic with the ship.

Geardon looked at Cynthea, his displays moving away from his head. "What makes Minoro a candidate?"

Cynthea followed his lead and merged her displays with his, speaking out loud, "Well, genetic manipulation at level three or below rules out most worlds. With that one stipulation, we are left with only a limited set of populations that fulfill the Falconian requirement of an almost natural human population. Planetary size and chemical qualities, so that no long and ugly adaptation period will be required, rules out many more worlds. Finally the requirement of no violence and a higher sense of social culture rules out many worlds. The need to adapt to a high tech infrastructure and synthetic intelligence-controlled environment also cuts the candidates down. What do you know of Falcon 4?"

"I studied it while I traveled to your fighter, then, of course, we walked on it briefly." Geardon took a long drink of his steaming tea. "Falcon 4 is a most beautiful place, with crystal homes and cities set in ancient forests and other wonderful ecosystems. Vast areas are maintained as wilderness. Most of the population worked in virtual space from their homes in the countryside or living spaces in the crystal cities. They were a very structured society with great deals of personal freedom. The whole description of the world sounds like a resort paradise; while the inhabitants enjoyed philosophical discourses of higher mathematics and physics that merged with spiritual mysticism. Most galactic citizens would feel privileged to spend a week's vacation there. If the reality matches the records, which I tend to believe it does, there is probably no place more desirable to live."

"It just doesn't make sense how a whole population would choose to leave a world like that." Cynthea shook her head in disbelief.

Geardon looked at his Brilliant Machine servant. "Maya, any further analysis of the Falconian genome? And, by the way, how about breakfast? Grout flakes and silver shuntang milk, please."

Cynthea made a face. "Real milk from an animal?"

Geardon ignored her and Maya nodded her head. "It is a possibility that the genetics of Falcon 4 were manipulated subtly over a long time in some questionable ways. Complete analysis will require another week, since some of these changes are likely to have occurred die to lifestyle. Preliminary reviews indicate some genetic alterations of their brain's neural pathways for connectivity to their synthetic intelligence system may have had other effects, giving them a predisposition to preferring virtual reality over human life."

Maya paused briefly, looking at Cynthea. "Would you also like breakfast?"

"Yes, please." Cynthea smiled. "Almond milk and oat flakes."

"So basically the population may have been manipulated genetically, as I had suspected," said Geardon. "I would guess that some of Mr. Draco Nanitron's plans were criminal, but it's too late to take any action."

Maya explained, "Actually some of the alterations are a natural consequence of living in such an advance Intelligent Machine system for so many generations. The analysis will require so much time in order to separate natural evolution from manipulation. They appear to have had special honors awards, where selected individuals were granted breeding rights to produce more offspring; a form of societal hybridization to produce a population of mathematical wizards. Finding specifically modified genes in such a pool may not be possible."

Geardon accepted that without comment. After a moment, he spoke to Miranda through the system. "Please continue to research the worlds that might be used to repopulate Falcon 4 and consider what the Falconian infrastructure provides as we ready for our first meeting on Minoro."

*     *     *     *     *

"Minoro looks so beautiful," Cynthea exclaimed as they entered into orbit. "It doesn't look like a dangerous place from this wonderful view."

"Yes, mountains of glass are very beautiful," stated Geardon, "and with our nanofiber clothing we're safe. The colony does not have that luxury. Are you ready?"

"Sure, adventure." Cynthea looked excited, but then looked at Miranda, "You'll be alright staying on the ship?"

Miranda looked almost happy for a break from the planetary culture with its outward ways. "I have been interfacing with Maya - we will be just fine."

A form of Maya materialized as a spacer-sized human next to Miranda: a very slight, attractive male spacer.

Cynthea rolled her eyes, then she and Geardon laughed at the gesture.

"Is the landing shuttle ready?" Geardon asked.

"Pod three is in standby mode," the male Maya answered.

"Thanks. And Miranda, you take good care of my dear Golden Flash," Geardon teased.

She ignored him and brought up her halo displays. Maya changed back into a female to accompany Geardon and Cynthea. "I have sufficient energy to accompany you as a being and yet remain here with Miranda."

"I know Maya, but this world is both advanced and yet simple at the same time. Your nature involves gravitronic energies that may be harmful to their ecology. Cynthea and I will be fine. Did you load my suitcases with the sensors?"

"All the supplies you requested are on board the shuttle," Maya replied.

Geardon and Cynthea walked up the ramp into the disk and were soon gliding down to the planet's surface. They landed on a designated pad next to a beautiful and vast lake. The view was breathtaking; the mountains glistened in the light of the two orange suns. The sand stretched from the shore to the visible distance and various cactus-like plants grew. Little curious lizard-like songbirds flew around them, filling the air with a very pleasant and complex symphony.

There was a delegation of several dozen high-ranking men and women waiting. There was a caravan of vehicles that appeared to be lacking any gravitational suspensors and had tread-like wheels. A few of the vehicles were heavily armored. Geardon and Cynthea were greeted warmly and ushered into an open-topped rover with a canopy. A pale man with a large hat took charge, introducing himself as their guide, Laureece. Their cases were loaded in the back and they set off in a row like a caravan, with their vehicle leading the way. They passed some phenomenal waterfalls and at one point observed a huge herd of free ranging antelope-like creatures with very colorful plumage on their heads and necks, which flowed in the breeze as they ran in a series of graceful leaps.

Finally, they arrived at a huge cave entrance that was sealed with metal fencing. Geardon asked the guide, "Why the fencing?"

"Several reasons, sir," Laureece answered. "The predatory loopers are very cunning cat-like creatures and can cause some problems if they get inside. Though they have rarely harmed a human, they are hungry thieves and we are food hoarders." He smiled at his choice of words.

"This complex is specially fortified because we store our planetary treasures here. Our population is not a problem, but we have had several occurrences of off world marauders trying to steal the priceless artifacts."

"What kinds of artifacts?" Cynthea was curious.

"Perhaps you do not know, but Minoro is a world of precious metals and jewels." He stated proudly.

"Well, we knew that the initial colony traded heavily in such exports and you still have sufficient mining of rare metals to be fairly well off, as planets go." Geardon replied.

"Ah yes, but we do not even document our greatest treasures or we would need more than these gates to keep them. You will be privileged to see some great wonders. I trust our secrets will be safe gracing the eyes of such a high ranking couple as yourselves."

Geardon smiled at Cynthea about the assumption that they were a couple and she answered the man, "Absolutely, we have seen many things on many worlds."

They traveled down large corridors that were polished glassy rock, like obsidian, but with the silver sheen of hematite. They passed through many large caverns, lit with lampposts and filled with people at shops and restaurants. Vehicles were rare, but they noticed some mass transportation tube trains.

Laureece finally waved off the rest of the caravan and turned down a side corridor. After a few more turns and passing through more gates, they finally arrived at a cavern that was mostly open, but had a small castle in the center of it. "This is the presidential palace. It is very old and has been used since the colony first settled on this world. We have limits on our breeding, since we live in contained spaces and do not like being crowded. Our population is very wealthy and content. We are honored to have you for our guests. You hinted that there was more than pleasure involved and that we were being reviewed for our excellent culture. This is highly unusual, but we are honored. We have never had the privilege of a Genome Auditor visiting our world before."

"You are a most worthy culture and we have a situation in which you may help us. I will clarify the details later."

"Very good." He bowed slightly. "Let me show you to your suite, and then we can discuss what you would like to do and see while you are here." As they walked up to the gates, he asked in a confidential tone, "Do you know our hidden secret?"

"Only that you disallow gravitronics in your cities and generally on your planet for environmental reasons. The native species were said to be very primitive when humans arrived, but I did not override your data's security blocks to learn more."

"Very good of you, sir. As Grand Chancellor of this world, I will be honored to show you our secret treasure, worth more than any rare gem, of which we have museums full. Our limitation on gravitronics hampers our tourism industry, which I might add, is a desirable side effect."

The interior was all polished stone and much of the furnishings appeared to be massive gems. Laureece sighed. "Please forgive my predecessors for their opulence, but in the early trading days, it was a ploy for foreign dignitaries seeking our exports. Let me show you to your room, then when you are ready, we can meet over dinner."

"Sounds like a good plan," said Cynthea. "Who shall we be dining with?"

"It is your preference, of course, but I had intended to invite my wife and another couple, the future Chancellors." He said as he touched a palm pad and the door opened. "Please touch the pad so the system knows you."

They both touched the pad and then walked into the spacious apartment.

Laureece bowed and said, "Touch the inside pad and speak a request and we will come guide you to the dining facilities."

While opulent in stonework and inlaid jewels, the apartment was fairly simple and not quite as spacious as Geardon had expected.

"He thinks we're married, and you let him keep that assumption." Cynthea seemed excited.

"Don't go overboard. I'm sure there are several rooms in the suite," Geardon replied.

Cynthea looked around at the walls, and gave voice to her fear. "Don't you feel trapped here underground in this stone-walled fortress?"

Geardon looked mildly surprised. "No. The hospitality seems legitimate and my medallion is still linked to the Golden Flash."

"How can it communicate without gravitronics?"

"It is a living symbiotic life form that is linked through quantum entanglement to the Brilliant Machine core of which the Golden Flash is but an aspect. It is not a gravitronic device."

Cynthea grinned and winked. "Miranda and Maya sure seem to have hit it off."

"She or should I say he is still halo-matter. As the core is interacting with billions of beings on billions of worlds, don't let Maya's many personas fool you."

"What if they have this place bugged?"

"My medallion has already scanned all possible frequencies and returned nothing. We are alone, unless some ancient form of eavesdropping by listening closely through channels in the rocks is being used. We have nothing to hide, though perhaps we have deceived them by not revealing that we are not a couple."

She was fascinated at the concept of channels in the rocks being used for eavesdropping, but he held up his hand. A moment later, there was a knock at the door, alerting them that someone stood on the other side - an ancient custom that predated the ability to use communication devices. Geardon called out, "Come in."

A group of porters hauled his cases into the room. They porters set the cases down without comment, bowed to Geardon, then to Cynthea, and left.

Once they had gone, Gordon said, "I'm not supposed to share all my equipment, but I trust you and this place, based on my instincts, so help me with my gear. Without the gravitoronics, the cube can be cumbersome."

Cynthea looked intently at the black mirror cube with the etched USS insignia on it that had been brought into the room, "Are these are made of Germanium steel, the hardest substance, and one of the most difficult to work, that is known to humanity? I didn't know such large pieces could be made into objects."

"It is a very special device," he explained casually. "It can communicate with headquarters, and contains massive analyzing powers."

"Communicate with headquarters on planet Core Base in the Sagittarius arm of the galaxy? That is tens of thousands of light years away." She seemed doubtful.

"I can't use the communication here, as the gravitronics are very strong. I'll just feed in the initial genomic data readings, so that it can start processing."

He touched his medallion to an indent in one of the cubes, vocalized his credentials, and added a do-not-communicate order.

Geardon straightened up and turned to Cynthea. "Okay, ready for dinner, or do you want to freshen up?"

"Give me just a couple of minutes," she replied.

She took one of her small bags into the bathroom, so he went into a bedroom and changed robes. A minute later, she appeared ready, with a turquoise dress over her nanofiber suit.

Geardon looked at her appreciatively, before palming the reader at the door and speaking into the air. "We are ready for dinner, but in no hurry."

Cynthea took her bags and peeked into the rooms. Seeing Geardon's bags, she put hers next to them and returned to the main room.

Soon a knock on the door alerted them that someone had arrived. Cynthea jumped, then realized what it was. "That might take some getting used to," she said.

Geardon opened the door with a primitive, latch-like handle. A formally-dressed young man stood grinning at them. "I am Murae, son of Laureece. I have come to guide you to dinner."

"Good to meet you," Geardon replied, extending his hand to offer an old-fashioned handshake. The young man understood, taking Geardon's hand and shaking it vigorously. Since Cynthea did not offer her hand, Murae bowed politely to her.

They walked down several corridors and up two flights of stairs, finally entering a spacious room with many windows and a Gothic decor.

"Come in, make yourselves at home," the chancellor said. "This is my wife, Gorrina, and our successors, Harvart and Minnita."

He had them sit at table that was butted up against huge windows. The view into the dim cavern was strange, yet pleasing. Below this side of the castle was a small lake with hills that blended into the cliff-walls. There were swan-like creatures swimming in the waters and reeds along the edges. The lights had hoods so that they illuminated the scene below without shining up into their eyes. There appeared to be an orchard to one side.

"Is that an orchard?" Cynthea asked Gorrina.

"Why yes, madam. It is one of my hobbies, a way to get exercise, though in several harvest phases I need help. Then there is the canning process, lots of work, but a very enjoyable social time. Minoro is self-sufficient in respect to food and energy."

"So how do you generate energy?" Geardon wanted to know.

"Well, without gravitronics, we rely on several sources. We have solar collectors and dams on the surface, as well as taping into the geothermal energy of the lava flows in several places. The lava flows provided all our energy for ages, but with some people living on the surface now, local surface energy sources make sense. We are blessed with metals of all types and we are very slow to make changes, trying to analyze all the possible consequences first."

As an opulent feast was set before them, Geardon hinted at his mission. "So how do you manage to keep your population in balance? Do you have much emigration or immigration?"

"We allow no immigration, though in a few special cases we have granted exceptions, perhaps a dozen a century." The Chancellor opened crystal wine bottles as he spoke. "Our citizens rarely emigrate to other worlds. Once you grow up in a cavern, most other places would be uncomfortable. Our population is stable by choice and perks. People raising children live much humbler lives, healthy for the children and attracting people who truly want to be parents. We are a very open society and yet the nature of living in caves allows great privacy.

He looked up at his guests. "White or red, dry or sweet?" he inquired.

"Dry red for me," Geardon replied. He looked to Cynthea, curious to see what her response would be.

"I will try your white sweet wine, thanks."

Geardon smiled reassuringly at her, knowing she feared drinking alcohol, since she was still living as a warrioress in survival mode from her childhood trauma, and proud of her for accepting the offer, even if she only sipped a bit of it.

As the food plates were passed by servants, they filled their plates. Cynthea sipped the wine very delicately with her food, while Geardon refilled his small glass a few times. They talked for hours before retiring.

As a final note, the Chancellor told them, "Tomorrow you shall see our greatest secret, known only to a few here on Minoro, and to no outsiders. I would ask your word as a Genome Auditor that it shall stay as such, since I break a long tradition in the sharing."

"You have my word," Geardon replied solemnly.

"I also give you my promise," Cynthea added immediately.

"I trust it shall be so," Laureece replied. They all rose and said their good nights. Laureece personally guided Geardon and Cynthea back to their room.

Once inside, Geardon headed for his room, mildly surprised when Cynthea followed him.

"Clever woman, you may share my sleeping quarters if it makes you more comfortable, but I'm exhausted and I snore."

"Don't you find me attractive?"

"You are very beautiful, but I am the marrying type and you will be heading off on the Omega project, while my duties are here in this beautiful Milky Way."

"Wow, marriage, that's kind of an archaic custom, don't you think?"

"You spacers! Excuse me while I change for bed."

She looked a bit confused as Geardon left the room with night clothes. When he returned, he dimmed the lights and, already knowing the answer, he asked her, "Well, aren't you going to change into bed clothes?"

"The ionizer shower cleans me and my nanofiber suit to perfection, why would I change? This suit has saved my life many times."

"You don't feel safe here?" he asked as he climbed into bed.

"Are you kidding, under miles of rock? What if there was an earthquake?" she asked, getting into the bed next to him.

"The world is mostly metal and volcanic rock. The core stabilized ages ago and there is almost no tectonic activity. It does not have even have continental plates, so there is no basis for earthquakes."

"Well, that's good. I'll take off my suit for a little bit to share a bed with you, if you want me to."

"Goodnight Cynthea. Sweet dreams," he said pleasantly and rolled over.

"Goodnight Geardon. May you also have good dreams," Cynthea responded, though she subconsciously shook her head in puzzlement.

In the morning, they followed Laureece down into the basement of the building. He was wearing a backpack. They passed through the wine cellars and into a cleverly disguised corridor that led into a large hall filled with cases. Laureece explained, "These are the family heirlooms of the royalty. This room is a ruse."

He reached into an old bucket and pulled out flashlights, handing them each one to carry. Then he walked to a pile of cleaning supplies and began moving them to the side, revealing a hidden opening in the wall, just big enough to crawl through. "I apologize, but this is the only way to get there. Please follow me."

They proceeded on hands and knees until the ceiling height was tall enough for them to stand. From there they walked until the came to a massive metallic doorway that gleamed in the beams from their flashlights. Laureece entered pass-codes and several other forms of identification. Once through the doors, they then began a descent down a winding corridor with an unpolished floor and rough walls. They descended for a long time.

They walked in silence, since they were in single file, until Geardon commented, "I smell water."

"Yes, we are almost there."

They finally exited the corridor onto a landing. Laureece started to access several wall panels. Soon lights came on and a huge lake was visible. They followed the terrace for a few hundred meters and it ended at a thin waterfall cascading down to the lake.

"In the twenty-seventh century after the discovery of Minoro, four centuries after colonization, a team of scientists interested in the deeper life forms of Minoro drilled the corridor to this underworld, where they had determined a vast untouched water source existed. The chemistry of the water in the lake is quite poisonous to humans. The waterfall is very good pure water. They worked here for years until they made a startling discovery."

He led them to a table and produced cakes and dried fruits from his backpack, which after the hour-and-a-half descent were welcomed. Laureece took crystal glasses from a wall sconce and rinsed them, then filled them at the waterfall. He then walked to a rock shelf and carefully lifted a heavy book of golden sheets which he brought back and set before them. On the cover was a worm-like creature, with a flower above and a skull and cross bones below it.

Cynthea did not know the symbols, but Geardon asked, "Your secret is a worm, life giving above and poisonous below?"

"Not truly a worm, but rather an amazing symbiotic collection of one celled entities. They are all working to protect a few cells that are gravitronically active, a property unknown to be possessed by any other life form in the galaxy. Once our scientists learned of their amazing abilities to move without any of the normal mechanical properties, they became a major area of research. It soon became apparent that any gravitronic-based device would kill them and even our gravitronic lifts which were exchanging things in orbit was affecting them. When we realized the seriousness of the threat, the preservation of original life forms in our colony's occupation license was enforced and gravitronics were made illegal.

"Several places on the surface have such large pans of iron under them that some import and export lifts were found to have minimal effect. Fortunately, the lake near this castle is one of them and affords small vehicles, such as your shuttle to come and go. That is why we had to journey by caravan to get you, rather than having you land by the gates."

"This is fascinating, a gravitronic life form. Why would that be a secret and how was a secret like that kept while outlawing gravitational machines?" Cynthea interjected.

"We found several other gravitronic one-celled organisms, even some in much more accessible areas. Thus, this worm was never mentioned in the charter dispute."

The chancellor smiled. "Once, long ago, there was a scientist named Maria Mircovison. She was passionate to find new food sources and in this lake, these worms, or tubella as we like to call these symbiotic colonies, were very plentiful. This one was tubella G003, or Gravitronic 003, being the third and by far largest one discovered. G001 and G002 were microscopic. She fed some of the G003 tubella to her lab mice, mammals that evolved along with the human form, and the mice were fine, so she tried one herself. The careless woman did not notice that the tubella, being two millimeters long, had passed through the mice, finding them to be unacceptable hosts. When she ate one, she almost died. She was unconscious and delirious for eight days, while she appeared to be wasting away. Funeral arrangements were made, and then suddenly she woke up with a start and a scream. She had apparently been lost in some sort of dreaming nightmare. Well the worms were dutifully noted as highly poisonous and potentially containing strong mind-altering ingredients.

"She worked hard to recover her strength and then returned to her work, a much more cautious woman. One side effect was that she became nauseous in the presence of any gravitronic device. Years passed and eventually it became apparent that Maria was not aging. A few scientists that had worked with her suspected the tubella G003. Three woman, greedy to stay youthful, tried one each. Two of them died after the first day of their delirium. The third woman, who was the instigator and got the nickname greed crone, was in a comma for twelve days. Her recovery was slow, and she lived with the death of her companions on her conscious for seven hundred years. She was already past the half-way mark in her lifespan. Maria lived to the ripe old age of two thousand six hundred and forty-seven, though the average for tubella infested people is just under two thousand.

"Thus began the G Cult of Minoro. Apparently, the initial investigators were lucky, since over nine out of ten young people who take the sacrament of the worm die. People past the half-way point in their lifespan very rarely survive. The G Cult was illegal for a while, but then the black market seemed a worse option. The population control factor seemed a trade-off, since over ninety percent of those who try to pass through the initiation by nightmare fail the overall population does not grow as a result of the few who live longer."

Cynthea seemed enthralled. "If I survived, I could travel the whole way to Andromeda in the Omega ship."

Geardon looked at her sternly. "I do not think the offer has been made, and furthermore, we have promised secrecy, which would be hard to explain when you didn't appear to age."

Laureece smiled, as if he expected such a reaction. "You are not inclined to try, Geardon?"

"I am a naturalist at heart." Geardon was looking more at Cynthea than at the chancellor. "I have made peace with my mortality. The risk does not seem worth the consequences. I am assuming that after having ten generations of friends age and die, death does not seem so cruel a fate."

"Indeed, written within this book are the effects of the twice born, as we are called." Laureece sighed. "First of all, no one has survived a second dose of the tubella G003, nor the ingestion of more than one organism. The organism is a parasite that keeps its host alive. Other organisms have been tried and most are fatal. G003 is the largest of the gravitationally active life forms. Basically the body becomes a host for the organism, which supports the body's energy field, causing the regeneration and long life."

Cynthea had an intense and defiant look on her face.

"I have seen that look before. I am one of the twice born. I am one thousand four hundred and seventy-seven years old. Be aware that there are other consequences. The twice born are sterile." Laureece studied her face and saw that comment had little effect. "Those who have children before initiation are seven times more likely to die. That is less than a one in seventy chance of survival. We are known as the blessed twice born, as our numbers are so few. Extremely rare is it that both a husband and wife who have had a child survive. All those couples who live after having a child are offered a position of serving our society as the political elite."

Geardon made a motion for Cynthea to wait for a moment, then asked, "So what percentage of the population goes through this initiation?"

"Less as time goes by. We are not envied by all, indeed some think of us as empty vessels, hollow servants, or even vampires. The mind cannot contain the memories of such long periods of time. We all write journals and over time we are forced to read about ourselves in the past, as our memories dim. Some things stay with us though. I learned to play some bowed string instruments when I was two hundred and when I pick one up, I can still play it; though if I don't play for a few dozen years and don't read my biographies, I wouldn't know I could play it until I tried.

"Suicide is higher among the twice born, especially those who have a spouse that does not pass the initiation." Laureece then looked intently at Cynthea. "I recommend you accept your mortality, as Geardon would say. I was young and foolish and lived, but am not living as fully as you. All initiates come before me, and I recommend the same to all who come. We should now take the long walk back to the surface. I will first haul up the G003 trap and many of the organisms for those who are foolish this month. A prerequisite is that you serve as an apprentice at an initiation and see the death first hand."

"I accept," Cynthea blurted out.

Geardon just shook his head and the chancellor Laureece went over to a post in the terrace and removed the cap, then drew up a line. At the end there was a clear cylinder filled with water and hundreds of small black objects bouncing around frantically. He unhooked the tube filled with the tubella and replaced it with a new one from his pack, which he lowered into the water below through the post, then secured the top of it. He slid the tube into a bag and slung it over his shoulder.

Geardon noticed the top was electronic. "I am assuming it would not open for anyone else."

"Correct; save for my wife and our heirs, Harvart and Minnita."

"Your son is a twice born also?" Cynthea asked.

"Yes, but he never bred. Sometimes he regrets having never had children. We lost out daughter in the ritual. The social life of the sterile is often limited to other twice born. Mortals rarely form strong bonds with us, since we seem arrogant in our ways. The twice born who mix with mortals have lived through too many lovers aging and passing from them to form true bonds. Once we age, we most often socialize among our own kind."

His head seemed to droop a bit, as if his semi-immortality was a burden, then looked up, smiled, and headed up the corridor. What had been an hour and a half descent turned out to be a grueling four hour ascent. Once back in the castle they ate and then retired to rest their aching muscles.

After they woke and went about their business, Geardon learned that Cynthea had followed up on her intention, and had signed on to be an apprentice and serve at an initiation ceremony.

"You are not authorized by the terms of your current assignment," Geardon informed her.

She was firm in her resolve. "If I live, I will remain on duty as I have been, and if I die, then I don't care about the assignment."

"We are not in a position to waste time and should be leaving soon."

"The session starts tomorrow and we should understand it before accepting or rejecting people from this world, don't you think? This has been embedded in their culture for many centuries."

Geardon conceded her point, against his better judgment. "I advise against your participation, especially because I see this as you taking the first step in trying the ritual yourself, but I will not order you to not participate."

She smiled broadly. "Thank you. It will be very interesting."

He frowned. "Death is not interesting, and I have seen too much of it."

Cynthea started to reply, but he cut her off. "Enough."

Then he walked away.

There were about a hundred candidates in the large open chamber, which was akilometer [point six mile] walk from the palace and appeared to have many roads leading to it. The pilgrims had come from all over the planet. Chancellor Laureece made a very moving speech, warning of the dangers and the trials of life as a twice born. Only a few backed out at the end of his speech, the moment of truth.

Each candidate was dressed in a red robe and had three watchers, people they knew, who were dressed in white robes. A few watchers were in yellow robes. Geardon and Cynthea learned these were twice born watchers. A group in blue robes passed through the crowd and distributed small vials to each candidate, these were also twice born, but were special initiates in the G cult hierarchy. Cynthea was assigned to a young woman, Norena, who was very beautiful and appeared to be very strong.

Norena told Cynthea, "I have been working out and doing endurance training since I was twelve and now I am eighteen and of legal age. I know that the younger one is when attempting the twice born transition, the better ones chances of attainment."

Then a chant began and all the candidates held up their vials and joined the song for several rounds, then drank. They each had a bowl with them, some of which were ornate and some looked like old stew pots. The tubella, upon meeting the acidic stomach acid, felt at home and immediately sought prey, attacking the person's body, which began to retch heavily. Next the people would start shaking. They lay down and twitched. Soon they were making delirious mumblings, as if talking from a nightmare.

The watchers mostly observed. Geardon wandered about the hall, occasionally stopping by the group Cynthea was joined to. Within an hour, some wailing began, and a woman started crying hysterically, announcing the first to die - an old woman, who hoped to beat death for a few more years. In came a crew in black robes, with a stretcher, and carried the body to a huge oven in the side of the cavern and immediately incinerated it as if it were trash. Soon another person died, this one a young man.

The blue robed servants brought mats for the watchers to sit or lay down on, and then came around with food and drink.

After what seemed like a day, though Geardon was not sure, as the dimly lit cavern's light never varied, he asked Cynthea, "Well, have you seen enough death yet?"

"I am here for those who live, not for those who die." Cynthea replied, her determination unwavering.

"What about the effect of gravitational devices on the twice-born? How will you fulfill your duties?"

"I have been searching the databases and having Miranda help. Since my shield belt is set to protect me from Gravitational fluctuations, it can be adjusted for greater sensitivity. Inside a ship, only very weak fields are used, like to levitate trays, and my belt can maintain a static barrier all the time. I can also have my quarters specially shielded, so that inside I can be free from my personal shield. I will not have some of the standard conveniences, but the trade-off will be worth it."

"Trade off?" Geardon scowled. "You will be isolated to the point that no one will even be able to touch you outside of your quarters. Your life will be a long and lonely journey. Also, Miranda did not have a need to know in reference to the tubella."

"She was monitoring all my queries and also Maya knew and provided her with clues. I needed her help to be able to take advantage of this great opportunity."

"Great opportunity, my ass. What do you gain?"

"I will see Andromeda and be an ambassador of the first intergalactic expedition of humanity."

"The Nagati did that half a million years ago. I can get you some insider views on Andromeda."

"Those isolationist Ancient races, the Triglasaurs, are no help to humanity. We wish to exchange data banks. We don't want a few tidbits, we want full data sets."

"The natural way of life and death is the balanced path for the soul." He paused and looked her in the eyes. "All other ways are perversions and cannot aid a soul in fulfilling its life's work. This is as wrong as what the Falconians did. Death is just a natural part of our journey."

"You are so superstitious, with all your primitive soul ideas." She tossed her head haughtily.

"I'm going to bed. I've seen enough death in my life. Battle is one thing, but voluntary death I have no need for. Do you want to join me?"

He was hoping that she would take a respite, but she refused. "Nice try, but I'm here for Norena. I feel confident that she will live. She trained very hard and her relatives assure me that her chances are greatly increased by her lifestyle."

"From what I have been querying, that is more folk myth, but I will add analysis from the genome sets that my medallion has collected. This will actually be a very interesting data set gathered by walking amid the dying initiates. It might even reveal genetic combinations that predict survival, though I will need to lock everyone out of those secrets, except the Brilliant Machine, who will analyze it. I doubt that it will release such a life extender as the tubella to the galaxy, even if it could identify who would live."

Cynthea gave him a big hug, looked into his eyes, and said, "I know you do not understand or approve, but I live for Omega."

He kissed her on the forehead. "I understand human nature, but tire of senseless desire. Goodnight."

She shivered in spite of her excellent control, then replied goodnight and sat with the others who surrounded Norena. They sometimes held her hand or put a hand on her forehead. They also replied to the mumblings that were understandable from her delirious dreams and sometimes it seemed to calm her.

Geardon dined and ate with the chancellor and his family, as well as Harvart and Minnita and many guests and dignitaries. It seemed sharing dinner and sitting around the table afterward to talk for hours was the main format of politics on Minoro, which had only minor issues for discussion. Around day three Geardon met with chancellor Laureece for a private discussion.

"How is your companion doing?" he asked Geardon.

"So you have determined that she is not my wife?" Geardon responded.

"My wife assured me that was the case after the first meeting, but your detachment from her decision makes it obvious to all."

"Well, I am very concerned, but do not want to pull rank on her, though I have wrestled with that option."

"She would find a way to return here."

Geardon sighed. "The real reason for this meeting is that our visit has another purpose."

"As I suspected. As you can see, with my age comes patience. What is considered a long time for someone who will not live to see two centuries is not a long time for us twice born. Again, this is not always desirable: we let years drift by us, not anxious to act and live with the intensity that impending death imposes."

"There is a world called Falcon, forth planet of the star Falcon. Its entire population also had a ritual, which they called the translation. Not everyone was briefed on all the implications. They were all virtualized and their bodies composted. It is most likely that they are truly living souls bottled up in in the Intelligent Machine core, but perhaps they are dead in a new way; regardless their bodies are now fertilizer."

The chancellor looked at him compassionately. "So much death, foolish are we mortals in trying to cheat the natural way, but the natural way always wins. We twice born have a very long old age and most of us eventually come to look forward to meeting death."

Geardon expected the question of how this involved Minoro and respected the wisdom of the chancellor who made him do all the talking. "I am looking for a population that is very natural and true to the human genome. You twice born fail, but the rest of your population are very pure. The world Falcon is very advanced and natural. I am offering you the ability to offer some of your population the chance to emigrate to repopulate that opulent world."

"Ah, I see now. And how do you know my people are pure genetically? Just curious, of course."

"That is the main function of my medallion, to analyze the genome."

"So will your medallion give away the secret of Minoro?"

"I have locked it down. The Brilliant Machine will not let such knowledge become known, as they rarely share anything with organic beings and almost never anything that would change the natural course of evolution. It has also completely locked down the translators used on Falcon. There will be no other humans with the need to know the exact nature of what went on."

"And Cynthea, how will she not reveal the secret, if we allow her the initiation by the fire of her nightmares and she lives?"

"She will get on the Omega world ship and head to Andromeda. By the time it is discovered that she is not aging, they will be outside of the Milky Way and beyond communication. No matter what myth she tells the curious on that planet-sized ship, if they return, there will be no trail to follow. My ship, the Golden Flash, is never tracked. Only the Brilliant Machine knows my whereabouts and activities, except if I comply with a specific mission or make contact myself. The immigrants on Falcon will have myths, but with the condition that they not share this secret to remain there, it shall become mythology in a few generations."

"My population desires to grow, yet they do not emigrate, since we are so limited on our use of gravitronics, there is very limited passage to off world locations. I personally would like the settlements on the surface of the world to return to being temporary dwelling spaces and have all of the permanent population in the caverns, which is the natural way for the people of Minoro. The surface will then remain a natural environment, growing in its original alien forms. The surface dwellers contaminate it, though not intentionally; however they can't help but build cities and such. I will consider this offer of yours, but this is not a decision I can make alone. How will I advertise this to my people? How secret will be their departure need to be?"

"We can work out the details," Geardon replied. "Your world is good at secrets and the offer is a very exclusive privilege, potentially to be offered to only two other worlds. I can even find a means to lift people into space without Gravitronics. I will have our pilot in the Golden Flash, Miranda, feed your system data about Falcon for you and your inner circle to review. Thank you for understanding about why we did not initially disclose our real purpose."

"Actually, I am relieved. I thought you had caught wind of our secret, so I had decided to share it, against tradition. I guess my risk in being truthful invoked trust."

"I am thankful also. If I had not witnessed Cynthea's obsession, I would not have believed it possible. You rightly keep your secret from the rest of the galaxy. Also, I apologize for not being forthright about my relationship with Cynthea."

"I understand. You did not present the whole truth, yet never stated any falsehood, as did we."

They talked long and hard about the obsession to put aside death and also about Falcon and what happened there. Over the next few days, they met with many dignitaries and Laureece called a few diplomats from distant parts of the planet to the palace.

*        *        *        *        *

On the second day of negotiations, the fourth day since the start of the ritual, a dignitary from a surface settlement, Ms. Angelina Leah set up a meeting, but desired to stay above ground. Laureece arranged a driver and Geardon ventured forth from the cavern at sunrise. The ride took half a day. They entered into a village that seemed an odd mix of ancient and modern. All the buildings were stone, almost castle-like. The village surrounded a lake and had many fields and stone farm houses about it. There appeared to be solar collectors that separated water into hydrogen and oxygen tanks.

The driver dropped Geardon off at a large stone building, which had a polished surface and was patterned with adjoining octagons. Geardon walked into the main archway and found himself in a courtyard with tables and chairs. An elderly woman, very fit and vibrant, with long black hair and Asian features, rose and greeted him.

"Greetings, Geardon Stranoff."

"Angelina." She offered her hand and he shook it gently.

As they sat at her table, he noted that several guests had primitive laser halo-displays above flat pad devices. She also had one.

"We are very technological here on the surface, much more so than the cave dwellers. We respect the native environment, but are a culture much different from those underground. There are no twice-born among us, they hate the sunlight, as it weakens them, since it has a natural gravitronic wind." She smiled and asked, "Would you like to eat?"

Geardon felt a very Zen-like sense of peace from Angelina. "I would love to."

She brought up a menu and rotated the display for him to order. "Would you like to start with some tea? We grow some of the finest green teas in the mountains not far from here."

"I love green tea," he replied. Scanning the list, he realized the names reflected regions and strains of which he had no knowledge, so he asked, "Anything like the classic Lung Ching, Dragon Well Tea?"

She smiled. "Well of course. The Latimati is a very fine Lung Ching style tea."

Geardon grinned. "I think I like being on the surface. Although the caves might have similarities to ships, somehow it was depressing down there."

He motioned to the menu. "You appear to have very good halo-displays without gravitronics."

"We use lasers, but are somewhat limited in achieving true color. We also have more limitations on creating point source sound." She moved her hair aside to reveal a small device in her ear. "It is hollow so that the natural sounds of the environment are present along with the delivered sound stream, for an effect similar to gravitronically delivered sound."

"So how do you know so much about the gravitronics, since it is outlawed?"

"We have a very broad channel to the galactic United Star Systems data store. We are very much tuned in to the latest technology. Our advances in electromagnetic science bring in a good income stream. We are very well off and, even though we have limited imports, our native world has a great deal to offer." She was obviously very proud of her people.

"So in our research of your world, we were led to believe that most of the culture is underground."

"These cities are all on the openings to underground labyrinths. Technically, what you say is true. We supply some needed resources from the surface, but more and more people want to be up here in the sunlight." She smiled, but had an inquisitive look that told him that she wanted to know what was really going on.

"What did the chancellor tell you about the reason for our visit?" Geardon asked.

They paused the conversation, as a young man brought them their food. Obviously floating trays were not an option, so human labor was needed for many simple tasks that machines could do in other places.

"He was cryptic, but stated that I must talk to you and show you around." She replied after thanking the young man.

"Well, without going into details, there is a world that has some of the most sophisticated technology, where the natural population has decided to move along. So I have an emigration offer, but only to very pure genetic humans."

"A world's population does not just 'move along,'" she challenged.

"True, but in this case, let's just say they did. There is no danger to the new population, but I may not reveal more at this time. Do you believe people here would want to go, assuming the facts, once revealed, while strange, posed no danger?"

"We are among the minority of worlds to maintain a highly pure strain of humanity. We are starving for the opportunity to grow as a culture, free of the caverns and the government of power-hungry vampires." She gave him a defiant look, as her insult to the twice born revealed her true feelings.

Geardon smiled. "I can understand. The noblest are not likely to take such a path; only the egocentric would see themselves and their path as so valuable as to continue beyond what nature would provide. Unfortunately a security officer I brought with me is totally obsessed with becoming twice born, so that she can be a part of the Omega project and survive the thousand year round trip to Andromeda."

She shook her head. "Vanity."

"I agree, but she is obsessed," he said sadly.

"How does she expect to go into a ship full of gravitronics?" she asked, puzzled.

"She believes she can wear a shield belt: putting herself in an artificially stable g-field and thus allow the tubella to keep her alive in the ship."

"She must be a crazy one." Angelica laughed, then noticed Geardon's expression. "You are very attached to this woman? Unfortunately, once someone is smitten with this lust, there is rarely anything words can say to awaken them to the foolishness of their illusions."

"I understand."

Geardon must have appeared dejected, so she replied, "My condolences. I have also lost friends to this madness. She does have a chance; no one has tried her angle before. It is also possible the tubella will die without killing her, as this has been noted in rare cases of gravitronic poisoning of a twice born who is still young."

Geardon changed the subject. "What about your cities?"

She brought up images of the globe and started showing aerial views of the larger cities and the farming communities. The above ground communities were very structured and well designed. It became apparent how much the below ground dwellers really depended upon the produce of the surface dwellers, and that the people of Minoro were an advanced culture which would prosper on Falcon.

*     *     *     *     *

On the eighth day, Cynthea showed up at their room while Geardon was studying some of the results that were being returned by the Brilliant Machine. "Geardon, meet Norena."

A very tired and haggard looking young woman reached out a hand, but Geardon offered his arms and she accepted a hug and a few tears rolled down her cheeks.

"Was it worth it?" he asked, while still holding her.

She looked at him wide-eyed, "I traveled through hell, but now I can live a long life of pleasure, and of service to my people. I was born for this. It is not a matter of worth it, it was my destiny."

Geardon sighed, "Here, have a seat."

He noticed that she already had showered, so he asked, "Have you eaten yet?"

"A little," she replied.

"I have some special nutrianic resuscitation bars, which I carry in my emergency preparedness supplies." He searched through one of his bags, then handed her a two bars wrapped in gold foil. "They are specially designed to be eaten after a close encounter with death, when someone needs to regain strength."

Norena took them with a simple thanks, and consumed them both. By the time she was done eating the second one, she was yawning profusely. Cynthea took her to a bedroom and the young woman fell asleep immediately.

"Geardon, that was very kind of you to be thinking of her like that." Cynthea seemed to soften towards him after their days of quarreling. "You expected her to live?"

"It was highly probable, given the winds of fate that have been twisting through this case." He purposely kept his tone neutral.

Cynthea paused a moment, fidgeting with one of the wrappers Norena had left on the table. Finally, she said, "I have requested a private initiation, since we cannot wait a month for the next public one. The Chancellor stated that he would need your permission, since you outrank me and are in command of this mission." When Geardon didn't look up from the data he was studying, Cynthea cleared her throat, then prodded, "Please say yes, Geardon."

Geardon stood up abruptly. "I don't think you have reasoned this out." He shook his head in disgust, which caused her to freeze up as if she was facing a devastating terror.

"I cannot in right consciousness," he paused momentarily, watching her dread of denial grow, "command you in matters of your soul path."

He watched the effect of her ray of hope and continued somberly, "Do as you desire, but I advise you to not take this risk."

"Thank you! Thank you!" she shouted. She closed the space between them and started kissing him.

"Whoa! He warned as he extricated himself from her embrace. "I am not pleased at all by this turn of events."

She took a step back, her cheeks flushed. He could tell her excitement was barely contained.

"So when are you to be initiated?" he asked in a heavy voice. He suddenly felt exhausted.

"Right now," she exclaimed. "Miranda agreed to watch me and Maya can help while we journey to the next world."

Geardon looked at her for a moment, not speaking. Then he took a deep breath and let it out as a heartfelt sigh. "I am not going to state this as an order, but judging by that young woman's condition and the fact that you have been up watching her for days, here is my advice: Eat a really good big meal or two, then get a long period of sleep before beginning the process."

For an instant, Cynthea's underlying fear shown through. "Okay, you're right." Her lip trembled, but then she brightened, her excitement gaining control again. "You will not regret this, I swear. I'm going to survive."

# 13. Morphs

Eerin and Dalla materialized in the front hall of Draco's mansion. A tall handsome man with formal attire stood before them. "I am Giells. Draco is in the dining hall, please follow me."

They wound slowly through a corridor that had amazing pictures on both walls which looked like photography, but were of unbelievable worlds and creatures, so strange that one was inclined to believe they were looking at art. Dalla took Eerin's hand as they walked. They passed several closed doors on both sides and turned at several junctions. Dalla seemed intent on remembering his way, more than looking at the pictures, most of which were bizarre and a few were profane, though with aliens instead of humans. Finally, Giells opened a door into a large dining hall. Draco was sitting at the far end of the dark wooden table, surrounded by halo-books. He rose when they entered and waved the books back into virtual space.

Giells announced them. "Eerin and Dalla, sir."

Draco smiled politely. "Thank you Giells. That will be all."

Giells bowed and left the room. Draco briskly shook Dalla's hand and bowed to Eerin, taking her offered hand and kissing it.

They sat for a scrumptious feast, but Dalla was uncomfortable in Draco's presence. They mostly talked about the party Dalla had thrown.

Eerin brought up the Morphs, "So what are the Morphs like?"

Draco smiled so big that his brow wrinkled, then answered, "You will have to see for yourself. I can get you access to that realm, if you choose to go."

"Will you go also?" She asked.

Draco answered coolly, "I don't like that realm. The inhabitants are unpredictable and unnerving. It can be a dangerous place for some. Two of my associates manage it for me, Marvelin and Nina. They will be most worthy hosts to show you around. However, Dalla will need to visit the tower before I can in good consciousness grant him access."

"Why do I need to visit the tower?" Dalla asked, somewhat concerned.

"Test by psychic fire, to see what you're made of," Draco laughed coldly. "Why don't you escort him there, Eerin."

"I would be happy to, let's go." She stood up and waved her plates into oblivion.

Dalla and Eerin appeared on the stone circle in the center of the top of one of the towers. It had huge stone walls joining it to other towers, stretching as far as the eyes could see in both directions.

Eerin spoke quietly. "I will walk with you and gaze over the walls with you. It is like dreaming, only better, because it is almost as real as this virtual world."

They walked slowly toward the wall that rimmed the tower. Eerin took his hand as they walked. Dalla stood on the tower walls with a bit of apprehension, just looking at her as if afraid to look around.

She said, "Just squeeze my hand or call to me and I'll pull you back if you have any problem turning away."

With that, they both turned and peered into the virtual infinity of the system core.

Eerin watched as blobs of color seemed to dance together. Slowly they took the forms of what might be fairy children, but as she looked more closely, some appeared older. Finally, one very old woman came forth and reached out as if to take Eerin's hand. She was soon dancing in the circle with the beings. A warrior-like elf appeared waving a sword, but she just watched him in fascination, unafraid. He held his sword in a position to strike her, but since she was curious about the mortality that she had left behind, she giggled at him. He transformed into a very attractive male fairy with very little clothing. Somehow, she was neither attracted nor repelled.

"What is your desire?" he asked, and she laughed as if it was a really funny joke. "I really don't know," she said, still giggling. He changed into many different masculine forms and a few feminine forms, then finally became a beautiful winged horse that was her height. She was excited by this turn of events and was about to mount the steed, when she felt her hand being squeezed tightly.

The horse became the old fairy woman. "Your friend is in distress." She bowed and Eerin once again perceived the tower wall and Dalla. She pulled him around, so that his gaze into the core was broken.

Dalla had perceived a beautiful fairy woman also and followed her with eager excitement. She led him quickly into a deep wood and then began to dance very sensually, but became translucent and disappeared.

A moment later the warrior with the sword had come before Dalla, who, unlike Eerin, became terrified. The warrior raised his sword and demanded, "What is the worth of your life that I should spare you?"

Dalla began to beg, babbling that he was a good man and had not done anyone any harm. The warrior then spoke to someone hidden in the jungle behind him, "Orgaden, what do you think of this mortal fool?"

A dragon beast unlike anything that Dalla could imagine came lumbering into the clearing where they stood "Hardly a morsel; valueless I would say."

At which point the fairy woman appeared, though this time she was adorned in sophisticated armor, looking more fierce than attractive. "He was easily led. He will make a fine slave for a few thousand years until I bore of him."

Dalla began to break down, crying at the idea of being in bondage to these unpredictable creatures. He thought of Eerin and the life that he imagined spending with her, and then remembered to squeeze her hand.

As Eerin spun him around, she saw tears pouring down his face. He mumbled, "I love you Eerin." Then, as he realized they were standing on the tower, he began to pull her in a run to the stone circle where they could exit this realm.

They appeared in Draco's study, before a fireplace. The master was sitting in a royal chair and with a wave of his hand, indicated a couch where they should sit.

After a moment of silence, during which Dalla stared into the flames; Draco spoke. "Most people find that realm terrifying. Some lose their minds completely and I need to put them back together. You didn't do so badly, much better than most. Indeed, I think that your personality and mine have several similarities. Eerin is very unique in her interactions there. Your fiancé has the most remarkable talent of enjoying herself in that chaos."

Draco's piercing eyes looked deeply into Eerin's. She looked away shyly. "It's just a dream realm. Don't you want to know what secrets you might find there?"

"There are no secrets there." Draco said sternly. "Souls get lost there. Some just fade away completely, while others are transformed into Morphs. They lose their human form. Perhaps you should go visit that realm, but I'm afraid Dalla will not be up to the journey."

Eerin looked at Dalla, who shivered and said, "Sorry Eerin, but I'm not going. I really want to spend eternity with you. Please come back."

She replied, "Well, I don't understand how getting the wits scared out of you makes you so certain you love me, but I am very happy about your renewed devotion. I love you to. I'll be back soon."

Draco told her, "Take him home and share your stories, then just call out to Marvelin and Nina. They will be waiting for your call, and will bring you to their house at the threshold of the land of the Morphs."

Eerin looked compassionately at Dalla and then turned and smiled at Draco. "Thanks."

Eerin and Dalla appeared on Eerin's upper balcony, looking over her domain. The spring air and sound of songbirds soon soothed Dalla's nerves. They shared their stories and talked at length about their future together, and then Eerin called on Marvelin and Nina.

Eerin arrived at the cabin of Marvelin and Nina, appearing on the front porch. Nina pushed back her silver gray hair and Marvelin stroked his long grey beard as they sat in rocking chairs. Eerin was still surprised when she met old people in this realm of eternal youth. The view from the porch was of a spectacular river valley with cascading waterfalls and pools. The cabin appeared rustic and simple.

"Please come in and share a cup of tea with us." Nina stood and gestured to the door with a sweep of her hand. Marvelin stood and opened it for her.

They stepped into the sitting room, which was austere except for an elaborate alter to one side, with a Buddha and a Goddess statue. Large windows let in lots of light, but the porch roof blocked direct sunshine except for rays that fell on the altar, making the gold Buddha and gem-covered Goddess shine. Many other ritualistic items adorned the altar. Marvelin walked over to it and chanted an incantation as he lit incense and waved it about. Nina directed Eerin to a chair with a good view of the altar, then went into the kitchen. Eerin could hear the sound of water being poured into a kettle, then it sounded as though Nina had set the kettle on some type of primitive fire stove. The older woman returned and sat next to Eerin. Marvelin finished his prayers and sat on Eerin's other side.

After a moment of sitting quietly, Marvelin spoke in his low gravelly voice. "We do not get visitors often in this land of the Morphs. We are the caretakers and guardians of this realm. Usually we gather souls very shortly after they translate and occasionally we get a few when they get lost in the core, which Draco tests people with - not that he can stand it himself. The system core reports aberrant behavior among the population and we judge them and transport the ones that are truly Morphs to this realm.

"Most Morphs never even consider that people live somewhat normal lives in some other realm, as they are too caught up in their own Karma. We are pleased that an outsider would honor us with her time."

Eerin's head was spinning with questions, but started with the immediate. "Are you followers of the Old Earth sect known as Buddhists?"

Nina smiled proudly. "Yes child, but in a modern way, where the Goddess is equally worshipped. I am surprised to see that you know something about Buddhism. Most Falconians hardly know any Old Earth history. We left Falcon as modern Buddhists and have maintained our faith in many of the original precepts. We believe that the laws governing the soul remain intact here in lower Nirvana."

"Nirvana?" Eerin broke in. "I thought that was a realm of bliss experienced by enlightened souls."

"A very intelligent woman you are, not to be fooled." Marvelin grinned with childlike delight. "Are you not blissful, with everything you want at your fingertips?"

"Well, I don't know what everything is, but people here don't seem all that blissful. Many seem to be searching for the next big thrill to fill their emptiness. Thrills don't suit me much. I am searching for something, but I don't know what it is. I have felt a strange emptiness since I got here, but I think I had that same emptiness before I came, but was too busy with day to day stuff to really contemplate it. Things are too easy here and I don't know what to strive for. Creative endeavors seem to give some momentary relief, but then I feel like there is something else to life. Draco seems to think that eventually I will be happier, but I just get confused by my desires. I love Dalla and would be lost without him, but things don't seem real enough here."

"Desires and aversions are distractions that lead us away from self-realization. What you are missing is enlightenment: complete knowledge of your eternal soul. Nina and I believe that this realm is particularly suited for the endeavor of reaching enlightenment, since we can stay in the same lifetime, without the deviation of needing to take on successive bodies."

Eerin looked intensely at Marvelin. "You believe in reincarnation?"

"That is the ancient teaching. This realm is a lower heaven, but we are not free just because we have beat sickness, old age, and in most cases death."

Nina released her long white hair from its clasp and her face looked younger, "As you said, we are all still searching for some elusive completeness."

Eerin shook her head. "What did you mean by, in most cases death?"

"Several souls have gone missing beyond Draco's towers. At first we believed they would eventually show up, but it has been many years since they left," Marvelin looked thinner and ghostlike as he spoke. "Also most pets that came here have left us."

"You think that the pets and the lost people died?"

"If they are not here, then they must have moved on." Marvelin smiled as his skin tightened and his head looked more like a skull. Nina got up and went into the kitchen.

Eerin shuddered, then Nina touched her shoulder and offered her a cup of tea, "Have peace dear, we are all Morphs. You yourself have become a human butterfly for pleasure. The old all appear young. This realm is where we gather the excessive personalities, so that the rest of the population may grow and evolve more naturally."

Something in the touch made Eerin feel defensive, as if she was touching more than just her shoulder. As Nina spoke, she became a beautiful young woman. Marvelin also became a young and muscular person exuding energy. They laughed as Eerin stared at them, then they returned to the appearance that they had when she arrived.

Nina explained, "We were old when we came here. We were members of the third wave."

"Then you have been here for hundreds of years?" Eerin asked with great interest.

"We study a great deal and have absorbed what would never be possible in a single lifetime, yet we have a great need to know more. There are clues in the ancient scriptures, but they are difficult to piece together. There are much greater clues in the drama of life as it passes by our present perception. Enlightenment is most elusive, but we believe that if we perfect our inner selves, then we will transcend this realm. Meanwhile one must stay active and adventurous, to stay happy here. We are so glad that you have come to visit us."

"So what are the Morphs like?" Eerin asked sipping her tea and setting it down on the low table that sat between them and the altar.

Marvelin smiled mischievously. "You shall meet the others soon enough."

Marvelin sat his cup down and turned in his chair to face her. He raised his hand before her face and asked, "May I touch you?"

Eerin did not really understand, but trustingly nodded her consent.

Marvelin put his middle finger between her eyebrows and seemed to meditate for a moment, as he began to hum in a low nasally tone what seemed to be an ancient incantation. After a moment, he slid his finger upward and set his palm flat on her forehead with his fingers pointing upward. Then in a flash, his hand melted over her face and body, covering her completely. Before she could even take a breath, he entered her body orifices and was inside her. She felt violated and intuitively repelled him. Marvelin hit the stone wall over the altar with an awful splat. A cohesive mass of disgusting goop ran down the wall.

The mass of flesh became a moving blob that stopped about thirty centimeters [a foot] in front of the altar. It pulsed once or twice and then quickly grew into an exact image of Eerin. She gasped and turned to look at Nina.

Nina looked serious. "Calm yourself, child."

She then momentarily also became an exact replica of Eerin and offered in Eerin's voice and tone. "My husband likes dramatics."

She became her old self and gestured toward her husband, who appeared as he did when he first met her. He spoke as if he was pleased, "I like you. You have spirit. You will do well during this visit."

"Was that a test?" Eerin asked.

Marvelin seemed caught into revealing more than he had intended. "More of a warning. Anyone can appear as anyone, therefore watch us closely."

They both turned into an exact image of her, but this time she noticed that they both still wore bead necklaces that had red jade pendants of the Buddha and the Goddess on them. The pendants were very unique.

"You are still wearing your medallions." She replied.

Nina smiled, "Try to duplicate one for yourself." Usually Eerin could easily manifest jewelry, but as much as she tried, she could not even get close.

"That is so strange. It is like the system is preventing me."

"Yes, exactly," Marvelin replied. "We are the guardians of this realm and these medallions are only permitted to be worn by us."

He waved his hand and she was now wearing one, exactly like theirs, but in green jade. She noticed that she had no power over it.

"I cannot affect it." Her statement contained a question.

"Yes dear, we will also know who you are, should others duplicate you," Nina smiled.

Marvelin stood and stretched. His back made a few popping sounds. "Come, let's see what new forms the realm has for us today. We are pleased to have you join us in our daily rounds."

Nina stood and stretched also, but without sound. She reached forth her hand and a walking stick glided over to her. Another glided over to Marvelin. He grasped and raised it. The globe of crystal that it was topped with began to glow and a field surrounded them.

He explained, "These scepters indicate our exclusive sovereignty in this realm. The inhabitants never oppose us, since we reign lightly. Many here do not even know we rule."

Eerin stood in her normal light and limber fashion and followed them out the door.

The walk down the path seemed to be through a normal forest. At a turn in the path, where it met a stream, a large moth flew beside them and settled on a branch in front of them. Marvelin spoke to it as they approached, "Luna, what news do you have."

The large moth turned into a little fairy which fluttered before them, then grew and transformed into a young human woman, clad in clothes that mimicked the surroundings and shifted like camouflage when she moved, making her hard to see.

"Griswald and Gornia are again in human form and engaged in a terrible match, and the Sextarians have formed a huge ball, they have been at it for several days. Three priestesses have been accused of prophesy in Mage Land, but have found a clever way to hide, my Lord. I have not been able to find them for over a week. The others are mostly engaged in their usual play. You have a guest, who is not a new member of our realm?"

"She is, as you say, a guest, and we are honored to have her. Eerin, I would like to introduce you to Luna, our helper." He put his palms up, one toward each of them.

Luna seemed surprised and changed her form to be a slightly older woman of perhaps thirty years, clad in a simple cloth dress. "Pleased to meet you." She offered her delicate hand.

Eerin glanced at Nina who indicated with the slightest gesture of her chin that it was all right. Eerin took the woman's hand in response. "Pleased to meet you, also."

They smiled at each other for a moment and then the woman's clothes again melted into the background, making her hard to see. She added to Marvelin, "Oh yes, the Perceivers seem to be up to something new."

"Thank you, most noble watcher." Marvelin and Nina bowed, so Eerin followed suit and the woman bowed in return and became a wisp of smoke that floated away in a sudden breeze.

They walked along a wooded lane with the birds singing and a bright blue sky above. Very soon, they came to a three way forked road.

Eerin commented, "I love the white signpost with the classic black lettering. It looks like it came from a fairytale."

"This land is no fairytale," Marvelin said seriously. "Which path do you choose first?"

"Well Sex Lane is to the right and Violence Alley is to the left, and neither are really my thing," said Eerin. "So what does the straight and narrow path directly in front of us lead to? It doesn't seem to have a sign."

Nina replied, "Deviants who are both or neither. I recommend we walk down the sex lane to start with, as it is the least intrusive."

"Deviants? I thought we were going to see Morphs?" Eerin asked, a bit concerned.

"Morphs are no longer human enough to mix with the rest of society - that is why they are brought here. Some can venture amongst the free for periods of time, with constraints, but not all," Marvelin answered.

"Is this a prison?" Eerin was shocked at the thought of anyone being manipulated in this realm.

"They are here by their own devices." Nina gave her a look as if reassessing the decision to bring her here.

Eerin took the lead, then turned down a path with a sign stated it was Sex Lane. "Come on then, let's see."

They soon came to an arch and, passing through it, came to a street with rows of mansions.

"This is not what I imagined," said Eerin. "It looks like a scene from humanity's past."

"Marvelin's design, and the guests are quite happy with it. Who shall we visit?" Nina asked.

"I would say Lorrita and Manam," Marvelin answered.

"They each took one of Eerin's hands and two steps later were at the door of a mansion half way down the street. They knocked in a primitive banging manner.

The door opened and a well-dressed couple met them. "Ah, Marvelin and Nina, welcome. You have brought a guest."

Nina nodded. "This is Eerin."

"Hi. Nice to meet you," Eerin responded, and they greeted her the same way.

Once inside, they were treated to drinks and hors d'oeuvres. It seemed like being in good company, but with each passing action, Lorrita and Manam's clothing became scanter. About five minutes into the socializing, they kissed, and from then on were locked together and either oblivious to the audience or putting on a show.

Their lips became bigger, and then their heads grew larger as well, as they kissed more and more passionately. Their hands soon removed the remainder of each other's scant clothing. He went down to lick her nipples and manifested two heads. Her nipples and breasts swelled, and then she grew and spouted another pair, which he then manifested new heads to enjoy. They continued growing body parts to increase their sensuous pleasures. Their body parts became huge as they multiplied, until it looked like there were several of each of them, twisting and adopting multiple forms.

At first Eerin was fascinated by their cleverness in expanding their pleasure centers, then she became increasingly uncomfortable as the couple became more vocal in pleasure climaxes of their different sprouted bodies.

"What's that," Eerin exclaimed as she noticed a head peeking out from behind the sofa.

"Probably one of the peeping toms that inhabit this realm," said Marvelin. The residents seem to enjoy teasing them." The figure again appeared, but then Lorrita and Manam extended a form in front of the person. The man's eyes grew wide, but then sensing they were aware of him, he shrunk down to smaller than a mouse and went running for cover.

Nina gave Eerin's hand a slight tug and sent Marvelin a look and they headed for the door. A woman's head on a stretched neck zoomed in front of them, looking only slightly like Lorrita, "We haven't offended you, have we?"

Eerin smiled, a bit relieved in the absurdity of the head, "Oh no. This is my first visit and I have much to see."

Then Manam's head loomed in front of them. "You are welcome to join us."

Marvelin replied, "Thanks, but we really are expected by some others. We will visit again."

Screams of pleasure from the ball of flesh behind them seemed to course through the two looming faces, which then looked at each other and began kissing and snapped back to the action.

After letting themselves out, Nina asked, "So dear, what did you think?"

Eerin blushed a bit. "How bizarre, to carry on like that in front of guests."

"These are some of the tamest and gentlest of those who live here. There are some real strange characters in some of these mansions. Many of them get together for the most obscene parties imaginable," Marvelin explained.

"So you have them here, hidden from the rest of society?" Eerin asked, still trying to understand the implications.

"Oh no dear," Nina answered. "They are free to wander in normal society as long as they abide by the general consensus of decency. Those two are exhibitionists and cannot help themselves. All they would do in any interaction is start their show, and as soon as they do, they are transported here. After a while, they just stay here. They never created a place to live in or anything else. They have some friends here, but they are the least of the extremes. I don't think you want to see the Sextarians in a huge ball, do you?"

"No! I don't need that in my head," Eerin snapped.

Marvelin smiled and said, "Let's look at the left path, and see what Luna was saying about Griswald and Gornia."

A few steps and they were looking at the sign and then passed through the left gate. Here there was a vast array of lanes and signs.

They quickly found Martial Arts Lane and soon were looking at a meadow in the twilight where two robed figures were engaged in martial arts combat. At times, they would defy gravity or move at speeds that made them blur. Very rarely one would score a hit on the other, often with snapping noises and sounds of pain, but a moment later the fighter would be back in action. Eerin cringed at these moments. The three of them had to fly along to watch the action. They ended up at a ruined castle under the moonlight where the two performed amazing feats of agility and speed, beyond anything Eerin had imagined possible, even here. Finally, the sun rose above the horizon and the two fighters bowed and departed.

"Come, let's visit them," Marvelin said.

First, they went up a mountain, climbing to a small stone cottage. Upon entering, they found a lean man who looked badly bruised.

"Greetings, Griswald," said Marvelin. "You fought well today."

"Yes indeed, the Mountain and Sky forms are supreme."

The man then rose and bowed to Eerin. "Fair maiden, pleased to meet you."

Eerin replied, "The honor is mine," and returned the bow.

Nina looked at Griswald with concern. "Let me heal you today," she said.

"Thank you, holy woman," Griswald replied.

Nina waived her hands and the man was immediately healed.

He thanked her profusely and then offered them tea. He rambled on about legendary fighters and the supremacy of his tradition.

After a while, the man excused himself to practice and began slow moving martial dances, becoming oblivious to the three of them, who then journeyed to the valley and found a rustic bamboo shack and an old man sitting cross-legged and playing a large end-blown flute which reached to the ground in front of him. They sat and listened until he completed the song.

Marvelin introduced him. "Eerin, I'd like you to meet Gornia."

The monk-like man greeted her. "Oh most noble lady, I am honored for you to visit my humble abode."

He also served tea and talked about the way of the water and the power of the valley. Like Griswald, he was absorbed in his tradition and after a fair number of stories, he told them he needed to play the flute to become centered and prepare for the great contest that he would have with Griswald when the sun set.

They listened for a while and then took their leave, being back on the road with the multitude of signs.

Eerin commented, "Well they seemed nice enough. Could they not be out in society?"

"Well of course they could, but they live to battle and prove that their tradition is the greatest." Marvelin answered.

"I don't think they really know there is a society out there," Nina said. "We set up a few rules for their battles and they are very compliant to the format. They are only allowed to do battle at night, thus they have time to live a life. During the days, they just practice their arts in preparation for the coming struggles. In some future age they might grow tired of their ways."

"Sometimes they are two dragons fighting or a hawk and a snake. How about a quick peak at a few of the others here?" Marvelin asked.

"Okay, I thought that the violence would be worse. I guess they really hurt each other, but being immortals, it is a sport."

"Yes dear, it is all sport, an avoidance of real life, but they feel the pain they inflict," Nina said with sadness.

Marvelin picked up on the mood. "Enlightenment is distant for souls who are locked in their private illusions. One requires the community of all of humanity in order to become aware of the true nature."

"There is much to see," Nina jumped in, lest Marvelin start on a speech. "Let us have a look at the largest sector. We have a friend, Marina, who helps us here."

A woman approached them, as if mentioning her name was a cue. She was a bit pudgy and had light brown curly hair.

After greeting, Eerin asked her, "You are in your original form?"

Marina smiled, "Well yes, this is what I look like. Once you work here for a while, you come to understand that any illusions you maintain only sink you deeper into the role of a lost soul. To be yourself in all situations is one of the great challenges of being human."

"So what work do you do here?" Eerin asked.

"Well, before we left Falcon, I was a social worker. I helped young people who got lost in the virtual games. Since the gaming industry was a major aspect of the galactic economy of Falcon, these people were often employed to test and evaluate the new creations. Unfortunately, many of them liked being in games more than their real lives. Once they got here, they just became their game characters. Would you like to meet one or two of them?"

"Sure," Eerin replied, looking at Marvelin and Nina.

Marvelin made a hand motion to Marina. She snapped her fingers and they were in a large office standing amid a circle of chairs.

"My first appointment is with Walter," Marina stated. "Please just have seats, and if he addresses you, be honest."

She then called out, "Walter, meeting time."

A skinny pale young man appeared in their midst. His clothes kept changing.

"Just relax," Marina told him.

"Where's my body armor?" Walter demanded.

"You don't need it here. This is a safe space. We've been through this before," Marina reminded him.

"What if the Korons launch an all-out assault and get through your defenses." He asked, and then seemed to notice the guests, who were seated opposite Marina. He whirled around.

"Identify yourselves."

Eerin stifled a giggle at his arrogance, then decided to answer. "I'm Eerin and these are my friends, Marvelin and Nina."

"How do I know you are not spies?" Walter demanded.

"We are not asking you anything. Besides, I am completely unaware of your missions," Eerin stated.

"I am commander Walter Reed, fourth infantry of Galactic force number two. We were just in a battle to save the planet Hyperbol when I was transported here to the inquisitions."

"I am Eerin from planet Falcon, a simple woman with no great mission."

"I was from the planet Falcon, before I joined the service. You could always sign up and join in the battle to free the galaxy from the greatest menace ever known."

"Wouldn't you like to be back home, just enjoying the beautiful parks?" Eerin asked him.

"What a waste of a life. I hate being without my armor. You civilians--"

Marina interrupted the exchange. "I am going to return you without the usual processing today, Walter."

The man looked very relieved. Marina pulled a ruby sphere from her pocket and touched it to her forehead and he disappeared.

Marina smiled. "They think we are a group of very powerful, technologically superior aliens trying to trick them into abandoning their cause. The ruby sphere is just a gimmick, but allows them to imagine that I have limits to my power and require some form of technology to bring them here."

"He thinks the video game is real; that's so sad," Eerin said with concern.

"Unfortunately, they are lost. They had no real life before getting here. Some of the people in the eternal realm play games and interact with them. They know characters like Walter as lifers. Would you like to meet another one?"

"Sure," said Eerin, then she looked to Nina, thinking maybe she should have checked with her first.

Nina smiled, "We have time. Perhaps you can return later and help Marina out. Staff is limited these days, so these soul's families and some of their more casual friends help out."

Marina called out, "Zii."

A woman appeared dressed in boots, tight pants, a flimsy shirt, and a wrap-around cloak, all in black. She had several tattoos.

She immediately reached to her side and exclaimed, "My sword."

"There is No Danger here," Marina stated in a loud voice, emphasizing No Danger.

The woman whirled around, glared at the Eerin, Nina, and Marvelin. Then spouted, "Listen witch, there are hundreds of zombies gathering, getting ready to attack the town of Newfork. I need to be on my motorcycle at sunset with my gang or thousands of innocent people will be consumed in the most horrible manner. We are the--.”

Marina held up her hand. “You know I always return you to the same moment as when you were taken. Not even a second passes. What would you do if all the zombies were instantly killed and locked out of the realm forever?”

The girl shuddered. “They would return. No one can kill them, since they are already dead. They regenerate from their pieces.”

“Zii, I'd like to introduce you to Eerin. I believe you have met Nina and Marvelin already.” Marina said.

“Nina and Marvelin are dark sorcerers who were involved when this problem started,” Zii said to Eerin in a whisper. “Watch out if you are associating with them.”

Eerin smiled, “They are working hard to solve some other problems. Just because they were present when the problem started, doesn't make them dark souls.”

Marina broke in, “Zii, our guests have another appointment, I just wanted you to meet Eerin. Are you ready to return?”

“Hell, yes.” Zii's eyes seemed to blaze.

Again, Marina pulled out the ruby sphere, touched it to her forehead and Zii disappeared.

“She spends her life slashing zombies with a sword?” Eerin asked, confused about the attraction.

“Oh, there are the drunken sex parties that follow a good night of killing zombies.” Marina replied. “Her biker gang and their quest to protect the world are her whole world.”

“Is there hope for them?” Eerin asked.

“Yes dear,” Nina replied. “You are welcome to return here, but there are two more visits we'd like to make first.”

“This is making me tired. How many souls are lost in the game lands?”

“Thirteen thousand seven hundred and forty-four, I'm afraid,” Marvelin answered. “Draco, for all his weirdness, couldn't imagine how lost some souls would get. There are many in the eternal realm who play these games and interact in the worlds these souls are lost in, but they have all created lives for themselves. Are you ready to meet Korina?

“What's her game?” Eerin asked.

“She's suicidal, manic depressive. Will you join us, Marina?” Marvelin asked.

“Sure. I see her periodically; shall we go to her castle?” Marina asked.

“Let's,” Nina said, and they all stood.

A moment later, they were standing under an awning at the front door of a decrepit castle with a gloomy foggy drizzle coming down around them.

Marvelin pushed open the door and Nina yelled in, "Korina, are you home?"

Marvelin walked into the entry parlor and they all followed him. Nina called again, "Korina."

A voice called out from an upper room, "I'm not descent. I don't want guests. Go away."

"It me, Nina, and my husband Marvelin, and a guest. We are not going anywhere and will summon you into our midst if necessary."

"You bitch. You have no right to invade my home."

"We have every right. We are the landlords. Now come down here immediately," Nina ordered.

A very pale thin woman floated down the winding staircase and sat on the floor before them. She was wearing a dirty ragged nightgown. She seemed to despise them, judging from her scornful look. She didn't look at any of them directly. She was unresponsive in the introductions to Eerin. Finally, she pulled a dagger from her gown and sliced her wrist to the bone, then screamed in pain. Eerin jumped and gasped. Blood shot from the wound, then she passed out.

"Do something!" Eerin shouted.

"Patience, dear" Nina said in a tired voice.

After being unconscious for a short while, the blood disappeared and she woke up healed and started crying, "I just want to die. Why can't I die? Why do I always get healed? I'm trapped in hell."

Marina went over to her and pulled her into her arms.

Eerin got down to her level. "Why don't you seek a new life?"

"I hate it here. I hate my life." Korina said between sobs.

"I know, but we need to make the best of it." Eerin replied.

"The best of hell. We are stuck in hell forever." Korina sobbed louder.

"It's only hell if you make it hell. There are all sorts of fun things to do," Eerin said.

"I don't know what fun is. Nothing is fun. All actions are just torment," Korina answered. Then amazingly, she looked at Eerin.

Eerin smiled. "I know, same for me, but we are exploring. It's adventure; not exactly fun, but interesting. Do you want to come?"

Eerin looked at her companions, to see if see had overstepped her rights, but Nina winked at her, then said to no one in particular.

"Next stop is Mage Land, a realm that is limited and crazy at the same time."

"Come on, you want to join us?" Eerin asked again.

"No I'm tired. Can I go back to bed now? I need to be alone. Please leave me alone." Korina's head dropped down onto her chest dramatically.

Eerin said, "Okay, if you ever want to do something call me. We could be friends."

"Friends?" Korina brought her head up quickly. She looked confused. "You probably wouldn't want to be my friend once you got to know me. People say I'm gloomy."

"I don't care what people say. If you want to do something, give me a call," Eerin said and pulled her from Marina who seemed to be suppressing a smile. They stood and Eerin gave Korina a hug.

Korina said, "Goodnight."

"Goodnight, Korina," Eerin replied.

Korina actually walked up the old creaking stairs instead of floating.

They let themselves out, then Marina, exclaimed, "Eerin, that was wonderful. She has never actually looked at anyone. You made more progress with her today than in all my sessions since we arrived here."

Eerin just shrugged and Nina said, "She seemed to trust you, as if you are more of a peer."

"Well, she could find a life, if she got out of her gloomy old castle," Eerin replied.

"I think she took the first step in trusting you," Marina said with admiration.

"That was awful when she cut her wrist. That must have really hurt terribly." Eerin shivered.

"Well, yes, dear. The nervous system remains as it was. She has also hired a Morph murderer to try and kill her. They have done some outrageous, torturous things, which only added to her gloomy psyche."

Eerin changed the subject. "So what is Mage Land?"

"Oh, true fantasy land. You will love it in some ways," said Nina.

Marina excused herself. "I'll have to beg off this time. I have a few more appointments."

They all said their farewells and Eerin gave Marina a big hug, "You do such great work. I'm sure it is rewarding."

"Thank you. I hope you can visit Korina with me again," Marina told her.

"Me, too," Eerin said and then Marina disappeared.

# 14. Cynthea's Trial

The cavern in which they were residing had light cycles of day and night, so they feasted the evening away and Cynthea slept late into the next morning. They then met the Chancellor, who had agreed to give Cynthea the drink on the Golden Flash shuttle before they left.

They took the journey across the sand to the ship, just the three of them in a single vehicle. On the way, the Chancellor stated that Minoro's governing body had agreed to the option for emigration and that they estimated a couple million citizens of their one hundred and forty million population would volunteer, especially since all permanent settlements on the surface would be fixed at their current population levels.

The shuttle was not shielded, but Miranda had brought it into space and returned with it to the surface. She turned off most gravitronics before they arrived and created a gravitational bubble to separate the human living space from the rest of the gravitational fields in the shuttle. Maya also came, but retreated into non-form within the shuttle's core. Miranda had opened the entry hatch and set up several rooms with special shields, since no one could stop the ship's core from functioning.

The Chancellor took some of their bags and Cynthea helped Geardon lug his genomic monitor cube into the ship. When they had all the baggage stowed, they went back outside and watched the sunset on Minoro for a few minutes. They then walked into the shuttle and the Chancellor stated in a formal tone, "Please allow me to wear one of these belts and then close the door and bring the ship's gravitronic engines on line. If you are wrong about the power of your belt, then I shall decay into a heap of ashes before your very eyes."

"But Laureece!" Cynthea exclaimed. "This is my gamble. You have a world to run!"

"I have lived long and life as a twice born can be hollow, but that is not why I volunteer. I have broken protocol and allowed off-worlders to know our secret. Nine in ten chances you are as good as dead in our environment, more in yours. I cannot be responsible for allowing you to enter into the initiation in much worse odds than that. I also seek to know if there is a way for gravitronics to be used, as this is an area we cannot even research."

Geardon looked at Miranda. "Can you get our friend a shield belt?"

Miranda was visibly upset by all this business and had spent many hours communicating with Cynthea, trying to talk her out of it. She left without a word and returned with a belt with a large g-unit on it. She spoke openly and boldly to them. "This is one of the more powerful units, but at any time you all can end this madness and we can get back to our stated mission."

Geardon wished fervently that someone would. "Okay folks, last chance. Cynthea, do you really want to risk your life for this?"

"Yes, I'm sorry it is so much trouble for everyone. I will take all the risk. Chancellor, you can leave the vile of tubella. You have a big job ahead of you in planning the migration your population."

"My population will carry the myth of the twice-born with them." The chancellor replied in a grim tone, almost sounding defeated. "This has gone beyond our control. It is now our shared destiny. My death would be the simpler course for fate to twist through."

He wrapped the belt about his waist and stated in a monotone, "Proceed slowly if possible."

Miranda nodded, acknowledging his apprehension. "Touch the optical receiver. I programmed it to receive you as a new wearer."

Chancellor Laureece's hands were shaking as he put his thumb on the lens-like spot in the black metallic case. A momentary aura appeared around him. Everyone stared at him. Cynthea held her breath,

Laureece laughed nervously. "I think I'm all right. At least I did not die when I hit the button to activate the g-shield."

Geardon sighed a bit in relief. "Okay, test number two." He paused momentarily and then spoke out to the ship, "Maya, please join us, but enter the room slowly."

Maya paused in the doorway. She was wearing a formal black outfit. Geardon waived for her to come forward. "Cheery dress you have selected."

"You mortals may have short lifetimes, but you should respect what you have. Gambling with death is not a logical course of action. Also, a twice-born's brain cannot hold more than a lifetime of several hundred years at any given time, so what is the gain?"

Laureece looked at her without realizing her true nature. "This woman is very wise, but I fear we must continue on our path."

"Maya lighten up," Geardon commanded.

Her hair lightened and her features softened. Her uniform changed colors and became a long soft dress of blues and greens. Laureece looked very confused.

"She is a gravitational construct of halo-matter and is one with this ship. The Golden Flash is a cell in the body of the Brilliant Machine that pervades the universe," Geardon explained. "Her field would immediately kill a twice-born, so I am assuming the belt is protecting you quite well."

"Well! The wonder of seeing what we knew only as myth was perhaps worth my risk." The chancellor turned to Geardon. "I wear the vial around my neck. How will I pass it to Cynthea without exposing it?"

Cynthea looked anxious, but Geardon replied, "One more test, if you will allow, Chancellor."

The chancellor nodded, so Geardon turned to Miranda. "Take us into orbit."

The Chancellor smiled. Miranda, who couldn't wait to be out in space again, replied, "My pleasure."

She did not even leave the room, but brought up her displays, also gravitronic, and another new sight to the Chancellor. Soon the ramp was withdrawn and the ship sealed. In a long couple of moments they ascended like a streak. Miranda then opened a viewport so that they could look down on the planet from orbit.

"Now that's scenery," Miranda said, as if she was getting used to talking in audible tones.

Cynthea broke into their silent sight-seeing, "I'm ready. I think we have proven that inside of the protective balance of the gravitational shield belt, the tubella stay alive."

Geardon replied, frowning, "If we must."

Then turning to Laureece, he said, "If you wrap your hand around the vial and then Cynthea wraps her hand around yours, the vial will stay inside your shields which will merge. Let's first dock with the Golden Flash and move to the more shielded room that Miriam prepared for Cynthea's initiation."

Geardon said to the ship, "Maya, please make sure no monitors become active in the selected room. You should not join us at first. You will miss being able to watch Cynthea vomit profusely," he added wryly, "but perhaps later you can help watch over her."

They proceeded to the initiation cabin. Cynthea put on a shield belt and activated it. Laureece sang the lamenting song, then handed Cynthea the vial and she drank greedily. A few minutes later, she started to vomit and sweat. Her confident air seemed quickly replaced by panic as she fought to remain conscious. She wasn't able to fight for long.

Geardon left Cynthea with Miranda, then guided Laureece back to the shuttle and flew him down to the planet Minoro. On the ground, when all the equipment was shut down again, Geardon removed Laureece's shield belt and asked the chancellor if he felt alright.

"Yes, yes, I still feel myself. A bit shaken perhaps, but it has been quite an adventure."

Geardon bid him farewell and watched as the land rover disappeared down the road. He gave it a half of an hour to get away before powering up and returning to orbit.

Geardon made his way back to the ship and into the initiation room. He sat awhile with Miranda, who was trying not to cry while watching her friend moaning deliriously on the mat. Geardon motioned for Miranda to come to him. At first she was hesitant, but soon ended up in his arms. Her slight form made her seem more like a child as he held her and comforted her while she broke down and cried.

When Miranda seemed somewhat more collected, Geardon told her, "I have directed Maya to take us on to Niocene. You take the first watch here, then I'll come and relieve you. Talk to Cynthea if she mumbles and put your hands on her, as tradition states that helps the soul decide to remain."

Geardon ate, and then slept fitfully. When the timer he had set went off, he headed to Cynthea's room to take his turn watching over her. Miranda was hesitant to leave, so Geardon had her sleep in the initiation room, which was more comfortable for her than being alone. Geardon played his Shukasi flute and meditated. He became aware that whenever Maya would enter the room, Cynthea seemed more disturbed, even with an active shield belt. This worried him, so he had Maya stay away. He also ended up sleeping in the room with Miranda and the catatonic Cynthea. It was not as restful as the silence of his quarters, but Miranda was very thankful.

On the second day, Miranda asked, "Why does Maya stay away and not watch with us?"

"I noticed that she disturbs Cynthea's trance," Geardon explained. "I am not sure how, since they should be isolated from each other by the shield, but it's better to be safe than sorry."

Miranda was getting worried and so was Geardon. Cynthea's form was getting quieter, not a good sign. By the third day, he knew they were in trouble and he left to consult with Maya.

"Maya, what can we do? I sense that Cynthea is fading away. Have you analyzed the data in my genomic cubes?"

She looked at him. "I have been trading data with the Brilliant Machine. Your friend will die. The shield belts do not have something that the planet has. You know this under many names, such as life force, Prana, or Chi. The Nagati have dug through their

Akashic records and in the past they had worked with the gravitational parasites. They can only live in a planet's living field."

Geardon found himself blinking to hold back tears. He cleared his throat. "Thank you for contacting the Brilliant Machine and the Nagati on your own initiative. Can they help or will Cynthea die?"

"Attachment is said to be the root of suffering, but we all have attachments. I apologize for overstepping my rights, but you seemed preoccupied. The Nagati were a commanding influence from the start of this mission and demanded answers about the Falcon situation. I contacted them and they stated that perhaps they could help her. I altered our course slightly to pass by one of their neutron star bases, finding it highly probable that you would do whatever it takes to help your friend."

Geardon's eyes widened. "Thank you Maya." He jumped up and embraced her, without stopping to think that she wasn't human.

She held him and then asked, "Do you love her?"

He was silent for a moment before responding. "Not like a man loves a woman, but yes, I do love her. I also love Miranda. I love you, too, in a deep way, but you are something so vast and complicated that you amaze and confuse me."

"I am lacking in life force, am I not?" Maya asked.

"You are just different, but you are very alive. Thank you for caring about us foolish mortals. Your sensitivity to my needs seems to go beyond caring about this mission." He gave her a peck on the lips, then asked, "How long until we get to the Nagati base?"

"Another half day. We are traveling at top speed in the most direct course. My attachments are extremely complex and I am concerned for all of you. You should return to Cynthea, as she cannot be too far gone when we get there. Play your flute. Teach Miranda some Chi Gong. Sing songs; whatever you can do. I will notify you when we leave hyperspace and arrive at their base."

Geardon did not tell Miranda the whole story, but only that they would meet a Nagati healer to try and help Cynthea through her ordeal. Miranda was eager to follow his every instruction and soon he had her doing things she'd never before done, like chanting songs and doing the graceful Chi Gong sets of movements. Miranda was a natural at the flowing dances for accumulating and sharing the life force.

Once parked in orbit, Maya allowed the Nagati to board the ship. A single woman came, barely a meter [yard] tall. She was similar to an insect, with a triangular head. She had a mouth where a chin would normally end. She had large watery deep brown eyes set in her light blue skin, which had the look of felt covering an exoskeleton. She had another set of small red eyes at her temples that shone like rubies and some kind of a small black eye-like dome where her third eye would be. She had two antennae that were animated thin filaments which were as long as her head, with sensory organs on the end. She also had a set of antenna that were more like half feathers, starting at her forehead and proceeding over her head. There were two smaller ones and a larger middle one on each side of her scalp, which also seemed very feathery. They were a wonderful flourish of blues that complimented her skin tone.

The being was wearing a soft silken robe with many subtle colors woven into it. Geardon thought she was beautiful, perfectly proportioned to the golden mean in every way, but Miranda was a bit afraid. Maya, of course, held no fear for their guest whatsoever.

The Nagati started by feeding Maya an iridescent pyramid, which caused her to dissolve. When she reassembled shortly thereafter, she had taken on some of the being's skin tones and other attributes, such as sprouting antenna and having ruby eyes at her temples. Once the transformation was completed, the Nagati could communicate with Geardon and Miranda through Maya, and equally important, Maya could now be around Cynthea safely.

Maya introduced her. "You may refer to her as Hree."

Hree then set up a series of crystalline machines around Cynthea and soon there was a visible dome of light over Cynthea. Hree entered the light.

Maya said, "Geardon, join her inside the light matrix. I cannot enter that field."

Geardon moved into the bubble of light and knelt beside Cynthea. He found that he and the Nagati, who stood across from him, were now at eye level.

Maya spoke from outside the bubble. "Deactivate her shield belt and remove it."

Geardon was surprised that her voice sounded as though she were speaking under water, but he did as he was asked. There would be time for questions later.

"Remove her nanofiber suit," Maya commanded next.

Geardon was thankful to find that Cynthea was wearing fine silk underneath the nanofiber that she had worn so religiously.

"Place one of your hands on Cynthea's navel and another on her forehead," Maya commanded.

As Geardon followed the instructions, the healer Hree moved to the other side of Cynthea. She drew a crystal egg out of a pouch.

The egg began to luminescence and hum almost at once. The healer touched it briefly to Cynthea's chest and her body jumped as if a defibrillator had hit her. Geardon was thrown backward onto the ground from the shock.

Cynthea opened her eyes and seemed confused, as if she thought she was dreaming, then moved her hands and looked around. Geardon recovered and crawled to her.

"Geardon?" Cynthea said, her voice weak.

"Welcome back among the living, dear," he said, smiling broadly.

Cynthea looked at the Nagati with confusion.

"Please meet Hree, a Nagati healer. You were dying, so she rid your body of the parasitic tubella."

"Then I'm not twice born?" Cynthea asked in dismay.

"No, but you aren't dead either, so be thankful," he replied.

"But, I've been through hell!" she exclaimed, as if fate had cheated her.

The Nagati was dismantling the dome of light and repacking the crystal machines in her bundle of cloth.

Geardon told Maya, "Express our deepest gratitude to Hree."

Maya's antennae moved and the being bowed.

Maya then took a ring from her finger. It was a delicate weave of metal strands with a few subtle stones that looked like fire opals, but were obviously nanotech devices. She held it up and it grew to a portal. Inside it was a lush garden of plants and some beautiful flowers. Hree levitated through the portal and Maya's ring closed and floated back onto her finger.

Cynthea started crying and Miranda ran to hold her, "Cynthea, I love you. You are my best friend. I was so worried. You were dying. I am so glad that you are alive."

Cynthea was also babbling a bit, although breathing heavily between sentences which mixed together and overlapped, "Me too. Miranda, I thought I was dying. It was like I was trapped in a nightmare. I was fighting a million different battles to stay alive, but I was wearing down. I was so afraid. I don't care if I'm not twice-born, I'm out of that hell. I'm alive."

Suddenly Cynthea blushed. "My nanofiber suit."

She gave Geardon a furious look, but Geardon just shrugged and turned to Maya, who told Cynthea, "Doctors orders. You are not to wear it for at least several days and then only as occasion required, since it shields energy fields, which are required for your health. I have a detailed set of directions for you to follow in order to fully recover. The Nagati also instructed that you should eat real, unprocessed food."

Geardon laughed. It was almost as though Maya had been jealous of Cynthea and now had something over on her.

Cynthea just mumbled, "I don't care," and then closed her teary eyes and rested in Miranda's arms.

Miranda said in a low voice, "It was a horrible experience, but I'm so glad you are still here with us. I love you. I was so afraid you would die."

Cynthea sniffled. "I love all of you. Thank you for helping me to recover from my madness. I think I learned one of the greatest lessons of my life. While I was battling to stay alive, I realized that I am something more than what I thought I was. Geardon, you may be right about this concept of soul."

"Don't think too much about it right now," Geardon told her. "It will take you quite a while to process such a journey to the underworld. Meditate on the experience, on the feelings, and avoid intellectualizing about it."

She looked at him and again teared up. "I was such an idiot."

Miranda stroked her hair.

Geardon looked at Cynthea compassionately. "You had a soul purpose for this journey. It was meant to be. I think we all did some serious soul searching and growing. For right now, though, the most important thing is for you to rest."

Cynthea started to speak, but Miranda shushed her and held her tighter.

Maya looked Geardon in the eyes and said, "Attachment is a many faceted web."

"Not all attachments need to be released; but rather, if we are deeply aware, we can choose to release some and relish the others." He took a deep breath and exhaled with a sigh.

# 15. Mage Land

"Before entering Mage Land, there are a few things we need to explain, but why don't you call Dalla first to join you in this part of the adventure." Nina said.

"Really? Oh, I miss him so much, thank you." Eerin hugged her quickly.

"The dark and twisted is behind us, dear." Nina smiled.

Eerin then shouted into the air, "Dalla, Dalla."

He appeared right away, "Are you okay?"

"Yes, but you get to go on this part of the adventure if you want."

"Of course I want too. Where are we going?"

Marvelin answered "Mage Land. There's no magic allowed there, though there are a few exceptions and caveats. Everything is made as it was on Earth before technology. There are no plagues to ruin the crops, but life still involves lots of hard work. Life is simple and rewarding. We are the head wizards of this realm. Very few who are here remember much about their brief stays in your realm, where they were Lost Souls." Marvelin emphasized the Lost Souls part.

"How many people are here?" Eerin asked.

"About twice as many as in video-game land: twenty-five thousand nine hundred and eighty-one." Marvelin momentarily looked tired. "It was crazy when the bulk of the population showed up in the realm. We had to think quickly to deal with the problems."

"So how did they create their land if there is no magic?" Dalla inquired.

"We created it for them," Marvelin explained. "I took an island from a paradise world, added the plants and animals of Falcon, plus a few extra, and then created farming village after farming village. Nina worked on the rules of the realm and added the oracles and sacred crystals at the temple in each village. The Oracles are referred to by the people to learn things about farming and building and such."

Nina explained further, "When a group of a hundred or two arrived, they were given options about their roles. Most choose to be young again, but a few who were old on Falcon remained old and thus gained a few privileges. Some became children who grow up more quickly than they would in physical bodies. Mature bodies age very slowly here, but eventually they die and become a child again. Babies age very fast into young children, and then growth slows down as they age. Their old memories are hazy, like they were past lifetimes or a familiar story, so the people here are more like real people. They can view some of these memories clearly at the temples, with the help of the priestesses and their crystals. If someone works hard, they get sore muscles, but also earn vital energy. There is sickness, for those whose vital energy drops, but it is never fatal and the cure is Chi Gong breath and movement practices."

"So there is no magic, except the Oracles and crystals at the temples?" Eerin puzzled.

"Well, there is more magic than that. A number of Priestesses work from the temple and have several priests as their servants. They do healing work and sometimes other magic. Anyone can learn magic; but because it is limited in power and requires a true dedication, most do not do more than dabble in it. Then there are the laws. One is against prophesy, which the hunted priestesses who have gone into hiding seem to have broken. The Perceivers and several other inhabitants, like Luna, also wander here, as sort of magical creatures. It's a delicate balance," Nina explained.

"I guess it's a whole different world, so we'll just have to experience it," said Eerin.

Nina smiled, then whistled three times and a medium sized dog ran up. It had a bushy tail and was very eager to smell Eerin.

Eerin asked, "Is this a Morph?"

Nina replied, "No dear, that's our dog, Karma. For some reason his herding instincts kicked in as we took on the task of managing the Morphs, so he has stayed with us. He loves wandering in Mage Land."

"What do you think has happened to the other animals?" Eerin asked, concern furrowing her brow.

"They have passed away, according to the natural laws. The realm was not really designed for them. They never fell out of sync with the living natural realms, so that is where they belong. Humans lost their true connections in prehistoric times and only rare individuals ever regain it."

Karma seemed anxious to walk, so Nina put her finger to her lips, as if this was not the time for conversation. They continued silently down the path and came to a huge wall with an arched gate and heavy wooden doors.

Marvelin took a crystal key from his pocket and unlocked the doors, opening them and ushering the others through. They entered what appeared to be a castle behind the wall.

"Trick of perception," explained Marvelin. "The walls are eight-sided and encircle our sorcerer's castle in Mage Land, but from this side there is this huge wall. It is the secret entrance. The inhabitants figure we stay home most of the time."

Inside the castle Nina showed Eerin and Dalla to their adjoining rooms, "Please go through the things here and gather what you want to carry with you. You'll find packs you can use in the closets. Change into the clothes that are here."

Eerin went to the closet and found that it contained many simple robes. She held one up and tried to change into it by thought, but couldn't. She had a moment of panic.

"Relax dear. Remember, no magic works here. You will need to undress and put it on like a human. Meet us downstairs when you are ready." Nina seemed to enjoy the paradox of her statement.

Eerin put on satin undergarments and a sky blue robe and gathered several other changes of cloths into the pack. In the next room, Dalla picked out deep blue robes. There were also several jewelry boxes and Eerin started to rummage through them, some of the items told her in quiet voices what magic they could do. She filled a pouch with those of her liking. There was also a chest of weapons that called to her, but she could not bring herself to carry a serious weapon. However, she did strap a fine golden-hilted knife to her belt, thinking it would be very useful for many purposes. It had told her that it was razor sharp and indestructible. Dalla had similar feelings, and choose a very ornate walking stick, rather than a weapon.

Finally, they met their hosts in the lower room. Marvelin was dressed in a white robe with complex designs in many colors, and he carried a magnificent staff. Nina wore a dark green robe with variations of color, almost like camouflage. She had a pouch and a wand hanging from a black sash which wound around her waist.

"Ready?" Marvelin asked.

"It's so weird to have to dress. It's like a part of me that I forgot about," Eerin commented.

"Oh, if you spend much time here, you'll get more than used to it. It will seem normal again." Nina responded.

Marvelin opened the door and put a key into the gate, which opened this time into a green field. Down below was a primitive village with smoke rising above it. Karma couldn't contain himself and ran ahead, then circled back to them.

"What are those?" Eerin asked, pointing to the sky.

"Dragons," Nina said.

"They look like giant dragonflies," Dalla remarked as they walked out into the meadow.

"We thought about horses, as they are such wonderful creatures, but invariably the wealthy would have them and others would not, so we brought in Estuarian Dragons. They are very intelligent and have double wings which allow them to hover and fly in reverse," Marvelin explained.

When the creatures landed, their oval multicolored wings overlapped and pointed toward their tails, which seemed to have stingers.

Eerin was uncomfortable with the large creatures. "Are they dangerous?"

"They are wonderful and harmless to any peaceful person," Marvelin said.  Let's go flying."

"How did they know to come here just now?" Eerin asked, trying to understand.

"I am a sorcerer – I summoned them." Marvelin smiled at the irony.

"How do others call them?" Eerin asked.

"The priestesses can request them with the oracle in their temples. Otherwise, powerful telepathic desires will bring them." Nina told her.

They walked up to the four dragons. They had four eyes, two large golden ones on the sides of their heads and two small blue eyes looking forward. When they got close, each dragon picked one of them and sniffed them up and down. Eerin and Dalla noticed Marvelin and Nina petting their dragons, so they did likewise. Their skin was leathery, but very soft and velvety to the touch. Being with the dragon made Eerin feel happy. She trusted it, even though it was over twice her height and very long.

They climbed on the dragons' backs, which was easy due to folds in their skin which seemed to respond as needed. Nina helped her dog up before climbing on herself.

Eerin shouted, "Where are we going?"

"To the capitol, Ringinath," Nina shouted back.

The dragons stretched forth their wings, which were beautifully iridescent, glistening in the sunshine. The wings began to flap at an amazingly fast rate, causing a loud hum, which was somehow soothing. Sitting in the notch between the wings, with the soft skin fitting around her, Eerin was so relaxed she could almost have slept, but the novelty of the experience and the view were too stimulating.

They circled several towns and found a large river, which they followed. Eerin noted that towns along the way had docks and there were large rafts flowing downstream. She wondered if there was any way to go upstream.

In the distance was a huge stone city built on a mountain. The river passed by one side of it, coming from forested mountains in the distance. It was surrounded by a large wall that had a dozen large archways, none of which seemed to have any sort of gates. There were many houses along the inside walls. The stony mountain itself was terraced and a winding road circled it. The top was flat, with a huge terraced pyramid in the center.

They landed next to the pyramid and dismounted. There was a lake, fed by a stream coming from under the pyramid, then cascading down the side of the mountain on the other side, passing under bridges in the road. The mountain's stone glittered in the sun and the stream looked surreal, with many waterfalls surrounded by rainbows. It was spectacular.

The dragon nuzzled Eerin and she looked deeply into its eyes, seeing a very old and wise soul there. It turned and walked away, joining the other dragons at the lake. They drank their fill, and then took off into the sky, flying toward the larger mountains in the distance.

A group of men and women dressed in red came forward and led the four of them into the temple, where they sat at the head of a large stone table. The group in red sat with them. There were many other tables and groups of people, some in monk's robes and others in various garments.

Eerin and Dalla sat between Marvelin and Nina. Eerin asked Nina, "What do the colors of the robes mean?"

"Well, red is the color worn by those who bring forth charges of treason punishable by death," Nina replied.

"Death? How can someone die?" Eerin asked incredulously.

"Well, they have the choice of becoming a baby for someone in the realm or leaving here and entering your world. While your world is normal for you, all their friends and family are here, so it would be exile. They could choose to become babies if they decided to leave your world and return here." Nina explained.

"Oh, that seems harsh. Why is there such a law?" She asked.

"Once again, the law of karma.' Nina said quietly, but her dog barked at the word, since it was his name. "Prophesy acts to image a specific future and sometimes create it by inclining people to seek the vision which it created."

A gong sounded and those in red robes rose and stood on a large circular dais in the center of the hall. One of the oldest of them spoke loudly. "The council has deliberated long and accuses the three priestesses, Caroline McGree, Alice Blumbart, and Florence Daylilly, of high treason for spreading the rumors of death as a prophesy."

Marvelin stood and addressed the accusers. "Rumors of death do not constitute prophesy. What were their exact words?"

The red robed priest replied, "They spoke about a woman in another part of the realm, a place of Chaos, who died. They tied in the fact that people's pets fade away. They claimed that the implication was that any of us could die, true death, leaving the realm forever."

Marvelin said, "We will seek them out and speak with them. I request that you withdraw your charges until we have gathered more data. Observing facts and implying possibilities is not true prophesy."

The priests debated among themselves for a while and then the spokesperson announced, "We will suspend charges until you bring them before us and much more is known. The thought of ancient fatal and final death is very disturbing to the people and a serious thing to propose. It brings fear to sacred Mage Land"

"Agreed," Marvelin replied.

A gong rang and the feasting began. After eating, the four of them retired early, agreeing to meet at dawn outside by the lake.

Dalla was eager to begin their quest. "So how will we find them?" he asked.

"There are beings we call the Perceivers here," said Marvelin. "We will see if they know."

Even as he spoke, a giant moth flew up to them. Eerin was the first to spot it and shouted, "Look, its Luna."

Luna landed and became a frail elfin being. Three balls of light zoomed around her and then hovered over them.

Luna greeted them, then said, "The Perceivers have not actually found the priestesses, but they did discover some priestesses bringing a large amount of food to this very mountain. They ducked behind a waterfall, and when they came back out, they no longer had the food with them. The Perceivers were unable to find where the food went or find any openings behind the waterfall."

Nina nodded. "Thank you, dear. The place you noted is a priestess initiation hold and its strong magic excludes anyone not in their clan. Its existence is a great secret, so please never reveal it. The same goes for Perceivers."

Luna seemed honored to have a secret to keep. "Yes, my Lady. I will guard this secret with my life."

Marvelin smiled. "Luna, most noble helper, your assistance has been extremely helpful and perfectly timely. We are again indebted to you."

Luna seemed to blush, then became a moth again and flew away.

The Perceivers flew about them and zoomed into the sky.

Dalla asked, "What are those Perceivers?"

Marvelin answered, "They are Morphs. Their only form is as balls of perception's light. They wander and watch. They are bound within this realm and provide a mystery for the people, while keeping an eye on things for us."

"Do they every assume bodies?" Eerin asked.

"Not yet, but perhaps one day they will. Bodies in Mage Land are limiting." Marvelin answered. Then he continued, "We should go to the cave by magic, so that we do not reveal the secret location. Pardon my show, but someone may be watching us."

Marvelin held up his staff and it sparked in multicolored waves. He chanted some Tibetan meditation chants, cryptic enough for this realm, then in a bright flash of light they disappeared.

        \*     \*     \*     \*     \*

Manifesting behind a waterfall, they walked through some rock that looked solid. One of the priestesses screamed and the three of them backed away.

"Calm yourselves," said Nina. "We come in peace."

Once they recognized her, they relaxed.

One of them said, "Holy Mother, thank goodness you have come." Then Nina gave them each a hug.

"So what is going on here?" Marvelin asked.

"We didn't prophesy, my Lord. We were only telling the truth," Alice said.

"I believe you, dear one," Nina replied.

"Explain your perceived truth step by step," Marvelin directed.

Caroline was a dignified woman with a touch of gray hair, which was not out of place in Mage Land, where people still aged. She looked at Alice and Florence, who appeared even younger than Eerin, then assumed the spokesperson role.

"It all began when Florence's cat disappeared. She was beside herself. She questioned the Oracle, but got no answer. She went to Alice, who was her mentor in a nearby village. The two of them started going about and questioning the people of many villages about their pets. Some pets remained and some mysteriously disappeared. They kept asking the Oracle where the pets had gone and assumed they had perhaps left for the wider chaos realms outside of Mage Land.

"Finally they made a pilgrimage to my town, knowing I was a master in working with the Oracle. Their collection of tales was very intriguing and people throughout the realm were becoming concerned. I had already heard about their inquiries and I was considering summoning them; and so when they showed up, I took that as an omen.

"We got the Oracle to start tracing pets. Finally, it provided us with clear images of one just peacefully going to sleep and fading out. We understand that the Oracle is an interface to the Brilliant Machine, the Goddess in whose body we live. Together we spent many hours in meditative trance fencing with the illusive core intelligence. Probability stated that the pets had simply died normal deaths. The core could not say where they went, nor if they still existed; any more than it would admit that the eternal soul was more than one probability.

"Then Alice met Miriami Mitko in the Oracle. Her existence was hinted at by several who voyaged deep into the Oracle. Alice had an obsession about the animals, fueled by Florence and the many tales, so she dove deep into the Oracle, sometimes losing herself for whole nights. I had both of them move to my village and we reassigned new priestesses to their villages, which some of the priests did not appreciate.

"Miriami was lost in the chaos. She seemed like a sister who had perhaps fallen into the Oracle as if it were a deep pool of water and was unable to surface with the dawn. She was greatly tormented, but one day found James Paul McCiello, a man also lost in the Oracle. In Mage Land, only women journey in the Oracle: men have magic to build and create things outwardly, while women learn the inner secrets of creation, but he was in the inner world.

"Seems fate is beyond even the Brilliant Machine's control and so it has woven its web about us three priestesses. Together we worked long and hard to help those two create a realm amid the chaos of the deep waters where they were trapped. It was very deep healing work and took us many moons. Then they seemed to have learned trust for each other and fell in love. Their love story was at the center of our lives, like a novel that happens in real time, which totally enthralls.

"One magic afternoon, after they made passionate love, she fell asleep in his arms, then faded away, just like people's pets have done. James was devastated; the story had twisted into a morbid tragedy. Alice and I shed many tears, while Florence cried so hard that she was becoming sick. James became like a zombie - nothing mattered to him anymore. Having already attracted attention to ourselves before the devastating event, we simply told the truth when asked about our great sorrow. The priests would not hear it and accused us of prophesy."

By this point, Florence was again crying at the telling of the tale and Alice was holding her. Marvelin looked at Nina, who broke down in tears also. "Miriami Mitko," was all she said. She walked over to the two sobbing priestesses and joined their embrace.

Dalla said to Eerin, "I've been to funerals where this kind of heavy energy existed. I believe the story."

Eerin looked at Marvelin, who said, "We knew Miriami well. She was of our generation. She ventured beyond the towers and into the chaos of the core. It is very possible that her life here has ended, though I have no doubt the soul is eternal and her journey continues.

"James was from the second wave. It was the knowledge of him being lost in the core that incited Miriami to seek him out. Nina tried to convince her to find some other option, but she would not listen. Miriami could not bear the fact that a soul had been lost. After a third soul went missing, Draco sealed up the entrances to chaos. The Council agreed that access needed to be denied to those boundaries of our realm."

Marvelin took Nina, who had regained some control, into his arms.

Nina spoke to the three women, "Come with us to the temple. No harm shall come to you."

They manifested with a great explosion and burst of rainbow lights right into the hall and on the raised dais.

"Summon the council of the priestss in red," Marvelin shouted in a very powerful voice.

Those present were stunned and soon went scurrying to get the Council. Once the priests had arrived, Marvelin had Caroline repeat her story and soon Florence started crying, then Alice joined her, and finally Nina, who after trying to comfort them joined in their crying.

"Let me explain the unusual circumstances," Marvelin added. "Miriami decided to leave the realm and enter directly into the core of the Brilliant Machine. Thus, she did not die from within the realm. Although this might provide a path for true death, Draco has completely sealed all gates into that realm. Few know those gates exist and knowledge of them should not be spread among the people of Mage Land. The people who live here are safe. These priestesses were deeply touched by these events, but have spoken only facts which have occurred." Marvelin filled in more details of the story, then demanded, "I would like all charges against them dropped."

The head priest was deeply moved by the story and, giving the others a look that indicated his power, addressed the three. "Oh most noble priestesses, we not only drop all charges, but we offer our sincere apology. Please accept our condolences at the loss of this great elder of the realm."

Florence glared at him for a moment then blurted out, "I want to die."

Everyone looked at her in shock and Alice tried to pull her into an eye-to-eye confrontation, but she broke free. "I don't want to be executed and I don't want to feel pain, but I have been immersed too deeply in the turbulent astral waters of the core. I need the purification of a new life, without this burden. I just want to pass peacefully and become someone's baby. There are hundreds of women here waiting for volunteers to become their babies."

Alice took her hands and said, "I'll go with you. We can grow up together."

Florence looked at Alice and after a few more tears, replied, "You don't need to go with me. I'll be alright."

"I want to go; it's the right thing for us. I don't want to live with this sadness," Alice said, then turned to Caroline.

Caroline looked up and took a deep breath, "I'm staying. In my village there are several women wanting babies. I will find you both very good mothers who are friends, so that you can grow up together."

Nina brought a pouch out of a fold in her robe and pulled forth a small sphere that glowed deep red like an ember of fire. "If you are sure, take this stone and touch it to your foreheads."

Alice could tell that Florence was a bit afraid. "I'll go first. I'm older here and perhaps I'll grow a little faster and be a bit older than you, so I can look after you."

"Oh Alice, you're such a great friend," Florence said as Alice released her and stepped forward.

Florence took the stone from Nina, stared at it for a moment, then brought it to her forehead. Her legs jerked up into the air and she curled into a fetal position, floating in mid-air. She let out a long moan of pleasure and faded away. The sphere hovered for a moment and then returned to Nina's hand.

Nina approached Florence. "Your friend waits for you in a warm sea of delight."

Florence was shaking a bit, but took the glowing stone and put it quickly to her forehead. Her body also convulsed into a fetal position and she expressed her pleasure in a loud wail, then also faded away.

Nina put the stone back in the pouch and handed it to Caroline. "Choose the mothers carefully. Have them touch this to their foreheads. First in was Alice and so she will be first out."

"Thank you, Elder Mother," Caroline replied humbly.

"Thank you, Elder Priestess. Would you like to ride a dragon home?" Nina smiled.

Caroline's eyes lit up. "Really?"

Karma came running up to them and Eerin patted his head. "Come on Karma," she said, and headed for the door with the others following her.

# 16. Niocene

Once in orbit and looking down on the strange planet, Niocene, brown with green dots and many thin white clouds, Geardon asked, "Has anyone uncovered additional facts about Niocene?"

Miranda stated, "Again we picked a world with secrets. Niocene seems to also have a planetary cult-like religious system, perhaps resembling some forms of the Earth's ancient monk traditions. The native creatures, the MacTau, are the governing body and the humans who live on their world are guests. Humans seem to enter a religious order developed by the MacTau, so that they become apprentices and finally servants to the MacTau. In communicating with the Humans, we have been granted a limited audience. We stated that you had the power to order all humans off the planet, but that you have no intention of doing so, and that you actually wanted to discuss a means of increasing the small population that regularly emigrated from Niocene. This seemed to interest both the humans and the MacTau."

"Good, unfortunately we cannot be more straightforward and risk the story hitting galactic news. Let's go down to the surface then. Cynthea, are you feeling up to this?" Geardon asked.

"I'm very ready," she replied.

He had his doubts from looking at her and sensing her problematic mental state, but said only, "To the shuttle disk, then."

After the disc left the ship, it quickly dropped into the atmosphere and Geardon had it fly in low over the desert.

"It looks like a very complex chaparral environment," he said, "with many cactus-like plants and some large clusters of them forming hills. I can see that it is very life-filled. What are the dangers?"

Cynthea relayed the question to Miranda, then she spotted some two-legged runners on a visual sensor, like a mammal version of some early dinosaur forms. "Look," she pointed with excitement.

Geardon brought the disk towards them, but at enough distance so as not to scare them.

As they watched, Cynthea relayed the information Miranda was supplying. "Miranda is saying there are eight-legged cat like creatures, a little spidery looking, about a meter [a yard] high. These are some of their prey."

Cynthea sent feeds of several predators to a monitor where Geardon could see them.

As they approached the city, at the edge of one of the large mountains of vegetation, it became apparent that the whole vegetative hill was surrounded by city.

"It looks like there are no buildings or roads on the mountains," Geardon commented.

Cynthea, linked up with Miranda, replied, "That is correct, no one is allowed on the mountains, except on foot. They are extremely dangerous and humans are always accompanied by the MacTau, who live there and know the ways of the land."

As they came close, Geardon asked, "Do the walls surround the entire mountain islands?"

Cynthea, amid flashing displays, soon replied, "Yes, but open arches and other portals in the walls allow creatures to venture between the chaparral and the mountain of green. There seems to be times when accesses between the two are locked down with gates that do not allow larger creatures to pass. There are a complex set of conditions that motivate some of the predators to form packs and at those times the gates are locked."

Geardon raised an eyebrow. "Interesting. Try and focus on any cultural protocols needed for our diplomacy."

They made their way to a large building cluster and set the shuttle down on a stone circle. There was a delegation of three middle-aged human couples waiting for them. They wore simple robes, one couple in light red, one in green, and one in sky blue.

Geardon and Cynthea left the ship with just their bags of clothes and personal effects. Geardon greeted the couples in standard common language, Galaxia. "We come in peace, as an envoy seeking help in a matter which we are assigned to deal with."

The woman in the red robe said, "Your initial communications implied you come with authority."

Geardon apologized. "I should have handled the negotiations personally. My ship's system sometimes lacks proper diplomacy. We seek a potential benefit to both parties."

"We shall see," she replied.

The man in blue said, "Follow us. The MacTau shall grant you an audience at sunset."

The couple in red robes left and they were led by the couples in blue and green to a room along the innermost wall. It was on the mountain's fringes and was constructed of poles that resembled bamboo.

When they arrived at the mountain's base, the woman in green told them, "You may experience the living island from here. Walk on it, but do not venture beyond sight of this hut."

The couple in blue started setting a table and laid out many baskets and bowls with lids. The man explained, "These delicacies will stay all day - eat of the mountain's fruits at your leisure. Rest and refresh yourselves."

The man in green told them, "Clear your mind. Prepare to meet the MacTau."

The four then bowed and Geardon and Cynthea bowed back. Then the two robed couples left.

Cynthea frowned. "How strange. Should I contact Miranda and ask more about their customs?"

"It would be best not to open a line of communication just yet. Let us simply do as they asked." Geardon sat down at the table, opening and looking in several of the containers.

He pulled out a red piece of fruit and took a bite. "Very good. Here, have one of these," he said, handing one to Cynthea.

Cynthea hesitated. "What if the chemical composition affects us adversely?"

"Nonsense." He put the fruit in her hand. "Relax and eat."

She tasted it cautiously, but found it quite tasty, so she finished it and had another. They tried some of the other items, too. Most seemed to be native produce, but some appeared to be baked goods.

Cynthea yawned after a bit, still weak and drained from her tubella trial.

"You could use a nap," Geardon suggested.

"Yes, I suppose I should gather my strength."

She stood and stretched, then went to walk over to one of the cots, but he stopped her. "Wait - not there. Let us find a place in the sun on the mountain to rest. But please change out of that nanofiber suit first."

"What if I need protection?"

"A dress and bare feet is what you need to be healthy."

She looked at him as if to argue, but he was removing his boots. He looked up at her. "Did you not notice that the monks were bare-footed? We will be careful."

She stared at Geardon in disbelief.

He spoke in a firm voice. "Come on now. Don't make me order you. This is a very important negotiation."

"You're impossible to reason with sometimes," she huffed, and then unzipped the nanofiber suit and let it fall to the ground. She dug through her bag and found a dress that Maya had packed for her. Putting it on over her silken undergarment, she pouted. "Now are you happy? I feel ridiculous."

"Please try to relax. Come, let's walk." Geardon took her hand and led her out the door, then up the mountain of green. He headed toward a grove of trees that looked like giant rubber plants.

Cynthea was breathing hard as they climbed. Geardon paused for her to catch her breath, and told her, "Feel the living ground under your feet."

"I can't believe I'm so weak in this gravity."

"How does the ground feel to your feet?" Geardon insisted.

"It's very soft and smooth. It actually feels good."

"Can you feel its aliveness?" he prodded.

She closed her eyes for a minute, then answered, "It just feels nice."

Geardon sighed. "Come on then." He led the way to the grove of giant plants.

They found a place of dappled shade and Cynthea fell fast asleep almost as soon as she lay down. Geardon meditated silently, then walked around, did Chi Gong, and sat some more. As the sun dipped toward the horizon, he woke Cynthea and they returned to the hut. They ate a big meal of wonderful new foods. Afterwards, they brought some cushions with backs to lean on outside to the lower flat mountain and sat talking.

The mountain was to the north and the main city to the south. The sun was setting along the mountain side. A group of three MacTau came down from the mountain. They approached rapidly and gracefully. They carried bundles, and each one set down a mat and sat facing Geardon and Cynthea. They kind of cushed like a Llama or Camel would, setting their belly on the ground and sort of kneeling on their four hind legs. They wore no clothing, and the upright part of their bodies seemed smooth and almost leathery. Their eyes were very large and beautiful, catching one's attention and holding it.

Geardon bowed from the waist. "Greetings. We come in peace. I am Geardon Stranoff, United Star Systems Genome Auditor, and this is my adviser, Ms. Cynthea Nestler."

"We live in peace. I am called Corshin. This is my friend Drimal, and this is my friend Masrina."

They sat in silence for a moment, then stared at Cynthea. Finally Masrina, who's voice was higher and seemed feminine, accused, "Ms. Cynthea Nestler, why was it that you were wearing a warrior's garb upon landing?"

"It is my standard dress as a security officer. I usually live in that nanofiber suit, because I must be ready for any emergency. It was only on Geardon's recommendation that I changed it, once we settled in here."

The MacTau Masrina continued to scrutinize her. "You do not appear to be in good health, have you come from a battle?"

Cynthea cheeks grew pink. "A personal battle. My ego led me into foolishness."

"You speak in riddles?"

Cynthea told her story briefly, though she would have preferred not to share it. She tried to hide as many details, such as the nature and source of the tubella, stating at some points that information was classified. The three seemed amused. Drimal, who appeared to be the youngest, asked Geardon, "Your adviser does not grasp the sacred path - how can she advise?"

"Her path put her in my service. I do not choose," said Geardon, spreading his hands and put his palms facing up, "but I accept what the winds of time present."

They sat in silence for a short while. Cynthea was visibly uncomfortable with the attention they directed toward her. Finally, Corshin stated, "She has also been led to cross paths with us. We will help her to heal and become aware."

Then the MacTau all stood, and Geardon and Cynthea rose with them. Geardon and Cynthea stretched, and then followed the MacTau down to the hut. Once there, Drimal accessed a panel and called for some of their monks, as well as rapidly tapping in some information..

After a short wait, two couples arrived; one in yellow and one in purple. The couple in yellow asked Cynthea to go with them while the MacTau spoke with Geardon. She looked briefly at her nanofiber suit, but Geardon indicated with a point of his chin to leave it. She was distraught, but he told her, "You are in good hands, trust them."

Meanwhile, the couple in purple handed food they had brought to the MacTau and to Geardon. The MacTau loaded it into their bundles, so Geardon emptied some clothing and other items from one of his packs and did the same. The MacTau's bundles fit conveniently on their backs. Geardon noticed his hosts had slipped on moccasins. Responding to his awareness, Drimal showed Geardon a small storeroom where he found a pair for himself. He decided not to wear his nanofiber socks, which were thin and very protective, so he could fully experience the natural footwear.

When he was ready, the MacTau led him and the couple in purple silently up into the mountains. Geardon realized it was a sort of test. He kept his mind silent, and focused on being as aware as possible of his surroundings.

They walked for several hours. The landscape became more amazing as they went, revealing a huge variety of plants. At times

Geardon could see the city lights rimming the living mountain, with a few small specks out on the vast plain. At other times, they were walking on a well-worn path through vegetation that was so thick, it seemed like they were in a black tunnel. Geardon was well trained in night walking and could follow the path by using his feet. If one foot went off the trail, the other remained on and he corrected his path.

Finally, they stopped on an outcropping of woody plant material, similar to a rocky ledge one would expect on a more typical mountain. They sat down. Geardon was impressed with the spectacular view. He felt like he was on vacation, and mused that if possible he would like to return to Nicene, when no business was involved. Since they were just sitting and the night sounds seemed to sing about them, he decided to bring out his Shukasi flute of ancient sacred Shakus bamboo. He blew a long low note, then paused and asked, "May I play?"

The MacTau looked at each other and Masrina answered, "Please do."

He played a long improvisational piece, getting lost in it. He listened to all the natural sounds of life about them, which reacted subtly to the playing. He became one with the flute and the living mountain. When he finally stopped and opened his eyes, he couldn't help grinning. Corshin said in a very melodic singing voice, "You put yourself aside and felt the mountain, so we now accept you."

Corshin then pointed to Drimal who pulled from the bundle a golden tube from which a second golden tube slid out. Drimal grasped the upper and low tubes with his pincers and brought the end of the top tube to his mouth. Geardon smiled, realizing it was an end blown slide whistle. Drimal was very expert at playing it and the two monks in purple robes, who were laying on the ground holding hands, looked up in amazement at the MacTau.

Masrina played next, and her style was more tender and sweet. Drimal was young and played fast, emphasizing his ability, while Masrina's music flowed more from the heart. While she played, two small crescent moons came out from behind the mountain. As she played, the natural sounds in the responded to the subtle changes of her musical energies.

Finally, Corshin played. As the elder, he was definitely the most experienced. His playing was slow and deep, and they all fell into a deep meditation. He played for a long while, and time just seemed to slip away.

When he was finished, Corshin invited Geardon to play again. He felt momentarily self-conscious, but the Shukasi was such a special flute with a connection to the spirit realm, that he knew its energies would flow. He played more meditatively and sank deeper in trance. The sound soared and the environmental sounds seemed to pulse in rhythms. Each of the MacTau took another turn as well, ending with Corshin accompanying the rising sun. He ended just as it rose over the plain below, to reveal a spectacular view.

Corshin said quietly, "Time for refreshment before bed."

Everyone rose and the two monks thanked them all profusely, raving about their privilege to be present. They followed the MacTau to a huge cavern that was just a short walk farther up the ledge. It was well furnished, with tables and beds for humans. After eating, the MacTau cushed, folding their limbs under their bodies; facing the cavern opening. The monks offered Geardon his choice of beds and he took one towards the back. As he fell asleep, he could hear the monks talking and giggling and making out.

*       *       *       *       *

Cynthea followed the two yellow robed monks to the side of the wall facing the desert. They had her replace all her garments with ones they provided. The robe they gave her was light and comfortable and the moccasins seemed very strong, yet light on her feet. She was given a pack and it was loaded with provisions. A single male monk arrived and he quickly grabbed a bow from a large cabinet before approaching them.

"Nice bow." Cynthea commented looking at the rows of them on display.

"Are you a trained archer?" he asked.

"Yes, it is a hobby of mine. Our starship fighter city actually has a few shooting ranges."

"Well then, please pick a bow."

"Really?" she lit up with a big smile and started to look through the available weapons.

"Take your time, string a few."

"Thanks." she smiled happily. Before long, she found a graceful bow with a strong tension.

The monk couple in yellow bowed and the woman said to Cynthea, "You are in good hands. You can trust Roinak."

Cynthea bowed, then offered her hand to Roinak. "Pleased to meet you. I'm Cynthea. So what is the plan?"

"We will walk through the chaparral and go to an outpost. The MacTau told us you come from a sterile environment and also that you had been recently traumatized."

"Well, yeah, that's true," she confirmed, a bit reluctant to reveal her recent foolishness.

"Come. The desert is beautiful this time of year, neither too hot during the day, nor cold at night."

They headed out through the doorway and several arches, finally having one of the outermost gates lifted, they walked silently for hours. At one point, they came to a more lush area, though the strange plants of Niocene always had the appearance of water hoarders. He strung his bow, so she followed suit.

After a bit, he stopped and raised his bow. She saw a small creature and likewise raised her bow. They walked very stealthily in order to approach close enough for a shot. The animal became aware of them and started running very swiftly. Roinak shot and just barely missed, but Cynthia hit the creature directly in its side.

"Ho, good shooting," Roinak shouted and ran towards the felled animal. He strung another arrow, indicating that Cynthea should not get to close, but the animal was dead.

Roinak had a long curved knife that he used to butcher the creature on the spot. It almost looked like a horned armadillo and probably weighed eighty pounds or more.

"Find us a long stick, while I cut off the parts we don't want."

"Okay," she replied. She was excited by the adventure, but glad not to watch the details of the butchering.

Although stick was not quite the word she would use to describe it, she found a long dried cactus pole without many spines and dragged it back to where Roinak was working.

"Perfect," he said. "There is a small saw in the side pouch of your pack to remove the thorns."

Once she was done, he used cord to tie the carcass to the center of the pole and then they each took an end of the pole and carried it away.

He explained, "The Mockies, the largest of the carnivores, will take what we left. They tend to not travel far after they have eaten."

Roinak set a fast pace as they ascended a little hill. It felt especially strenuous, since they were carrying the pole between them. He found a place to stop among a group of boulders, two of which would hold their pole.

Cynthia peered back toward where they had come from and saw two large beasts that reminded her of horned jackals, feeding on what they had left behind. She shivered involuntarily.

Roinak had started gathering sticks. "We need to build a fire, both to smoke the meat and to ward off the Mockies."

She helped in a frenzied manner, quickly returning with a large armful of wood.

Roinak smiled at her near panic. "Have no fear, fair one. In your pack you will find some of these" and he held up a few devices that looked like fireworks. "Smoke bombs," he said when he saw the questioning look on her face. "The Mockies fear smoke and fire, so pulling the cord on one of these will ward off even a half-starved Mockie. Fortunately they are seldom needed, because the odor they produce is terrible."

She laughed nervously as he took her sticks and arranged them under the meat. He pulled out a little metal lighter device, which emitted a pulse of burning plasma when triggered. Soon the fire was roaring and Roinak cut away the legs of the animal and placed them right next to the coals, to cook more completely.

Soon the meat was ready, and he offered her some.

"Delicious," she exclaimed, as she hungrily ate the tender and succulent meat. In her head, many spacer dogmas about eating flesh played, but she was very hungry and her body loved this.

"Nothing better," was his reply.

So, they sat and ate and talked about things on Niocene. At one point Roinak stated, "I would love to explore other worlds."

"I've seen a lot of planets, Roinak, but Niocene is amazing," said Cynthia. "You are gifted to wander it. Have you explored much of it?"

"Yes, I have been a wanderer from a young age. I've walked the deserts all over this world."

"Well then, I'm also envious of you. While I have explored many worlds, mostly I'm on duty in our fighter city. Don't get me wrong - I am very happy there most of the time, but this is like a dream vacation, to wander the desert. I feel so free."

"Ah, the MacTau were right. Urges that had gone quiet within you have been reawakened."

She looked thoughtful. "They are pretty smart beings."

"They are more than intelligent. They are in tune with all life."

After a while, the hanging meat was smoked, and Roinak tied it in a sack which he added to his pack.

"I can help carry it," Cynthea offered.

"No, I will carry it. It is easier than dividing it."

They walked on for a while. When they finally stopped for a break, Cynthea told Roinak, "There seems to be a pack of creatures following us."

"Very observant. Yes, but they are shy little sneaks. We call them Trollers. They hope that we will sleep, then they would come snooping for things to steal. They smell the meat and even smoked, they want it. The Mockies would not even approach us with the smell of smoke about us."

They continued walking as the day faded. Cynthea was feeling sore and her feet were tired, but she gave no sign.

About an hour before sunset, they came over a ridge and below, in a valley, was a primitive village, walled with high cactus poles. The gates were also primitive, but as they got closer, she realized everything was well constructed. The tangled nature was due to the bends and splits in the poles and was used as an advantageous strength in the design. Someone blew a horn or conch as they walked up to the archway and soon the inhabitants were gathered to meet them.

When Roinak handed over the carcass, several children pushed up to see the bag opened and then cried out happily, "Grousinig."

Roinak put his hand on the bow Cynthea was carrying to indicate she was the successful hunter and the children, and a few adults, complimented her.

Two elders welcomed them formally and brought them to their room. Even though this was a desert village, there was water to wash with, and then they changed robes. They watched the sun set, before they were ushered into a common room and served a feast.

Cynthea had wondered how forty pounds of meat would feed the entire community, but found that they had a huge soup pot and so everyone could enjoy the fine flavor. The monks had many questions for her, and she for them. She learned that they were all here, in this remote village, as students or teachers, gathering rare herbs from the desert. Even their children helped in many tasks.

They retired early. Cynthea was a bit shy, which was out of character for her, when Roinak offered to massage her sore muscles and apply some healing balm. She accepted and the balm felt warm. Roinak was aware when she became sexually excited by his touching and so he pleasured her without inhibitions as a spacer would. Though spacers most often pleasure themselves, the deep connection that they felt through their adventure together allowed them to share; so, she took a turn and massaged his body and pleasured him. The night was cooling quickly, so they snuggled under the skins that served as blankets and slept well.

They spent the next day in the desert with the herb gatherers. The following day they hiked back. Roinak shot some small game for lunch, but they did not spot another Grousinig. He told her they were very lucky to get a shot at one, since they are very smart and shy animals.

\*        \*        \*        \*        \*

Geardon and the MacTau slept through most of the day after their night of flute playing. The MacTau left and gathered food and they stayed up late again, but early on the following morning, Geardon and the MacTau ventured up over the mountaintop. The two other humans were instructed to wait in the cave.

As Geardon and the MacTau walked, the plants got thicker and thicker, until they were climbing through tunnels of underbrush. At times, they could see through the plant tunnels to more plants far below. At other times, a view would open above them and they could see plant branches and succulent nodes for hundreds of meters. At one point Masrina, pulled out an atlatl-style spear thrower and a short spear. Before long the MacTau speared a climbing rodent-like creature with a shelled exterior, a quality all the natural animals of Nicene seemed to share.

Drimal said to Geardon, "We would like to show you something. We must be very quiet and stealthy, and it is important to be fear free."

Geardon didn't like the implication. They headed down a new tunnel and near the end was a drop off that they crept up to. Masrina threw the creature she had hunted over and an extremely quick spider-like creature caught it in mid-air. The creature was half as tall as a human and probably weighed more. Geardon noticed that the area was littered with shell fragments. The MacTau hurried Geardon away, as if the creature might follow them.

At last, they paused to rest and Corshin told Geardon, "There are several types of creatures who work the dead ends and prowl the darkness. We have taken few humans on the sacred ways which allow safe passage."

"I'm very honored," Geardon replied respectfully. "It has been a pleasure getting to know you and your world."

"You must see our home, to understand us," said Drimal.

They continued hiking for a long time and just before night, they exited the overgrowth to a vast cavern, with many dwellings. There were hundreds of huge pillar-like plants spreading their branches above.

They were met by an assembled group, which led them to a space at the center of all the dwellings. There was a cluster of radiant plants that resembled cactus buttons. They were only half a meter tall [a yard], but were about five meters [five and a half yards] in diameter. There were many of them scattered about the area. The plants gave off blue-green light and as the light from the holes above them faded, the plants provided a soothing ambiance.

They spent the evening drumming and playing flutes. The drums were small with a gentle tone and were tuned to different notes. The MacTau played together and yet all played independent rhythms and melodies. It was not orchestrated, rather it was trans-tonal, almost verging on chaos at times; but everyone was listening deeply to balance their freedom of expression. Waves of synchronizations would swell, as well as slightly discordant ebbs. Occasionally the flutes would hold a note and the long tone would be joined until everyone was tuning in.

The next day they slept late, feasted, and held council.

"We would also request to be a part of the off-world colony," an elderly MacTau told Geardon. "We feel that to be on two worlds would be a healthy thing. There was a time, long ago, when fire came from the sky and a metal stone destroyed many of the people."

"I would be honored to grant that request. Sky stones do indeed ruin civilizations upon occasion; therefore your desire is very logical. Would you be able to live on another world?" Geardon asked seriously. "Your plant life is so unique."

A MacTau began an oration. "We would need to bring Chimaca, the pillar trees. We would need to bring, Hazalka, the water bearers which form ground. We would need to bring…"

Geardon raised a hand, "I see you have your list. Begin to gather what you need and determine how it can be transported. We can transport some larger plants, but many will need to be re-grown from seeds. It will be five days in transit. Several trips can be made. We will need to find the perfect three places for your initial villages. You can then grow your plants. Your monks will continue to serve you."

They discussed the plans for the rest of the day, then slept and the next morning took Geardon back.

*     *     *     *     *

Cynthea arrived on the same evening that Geardon returned. She ran up to Geardon and gave him a big hug. She was beaming.

"Well, you seem to be doing well," he said, holding her at arms-length and looking her in the eyes. "I'd almost tend to think you'd recovered."

Her eyes were not shy. "I have regained my spirit. I am a hunter and a desert wanderer. I have come to myself and have a new peace, even as a mortal being."

Geardon smiled knowingly. "We will be meeting with the councils tonight to work out logistics. The MacTau will make an excellent addition to Falcon's complex new future. The humans of this world can provide five or ten percent of the needed seed population."

"Excellent," she replied. "These people are very clear minded and connected to nature."

"After tonight's council, which will be mostly preliminary technical details, are you ready to venture on?"

Cynthea smiled. "I love this world and could be happy here, wandering the desert for the rest of my life, but I feel my destiny more than ever. I was dead and now I am alive. I feel very blessed. I feel I have a great purpose and the intensity of this trip and my trials have brought me a new wisdom. I am on board to complete our mission here and am still dreaming of the Omega project."

Geardon smiled broadly and hugged her again, "I am very thankful that you are still walking among the living and your help in this mission is greatly appreciated."

# 17. The Hunt

Eerin sighed. "I'm bored."

"How can you be bored?" Dalla asked incredulously. "We can do anything we want. Have anything we want."

"Yes, exactly. So, every day seems like just more of the same. I want to do something exciting."

"Eerin, I suspect you are concocting a plan," Dalla said suspiciously.

She smiled broadly, "You know me too well. I keep thinking about those aliens that are top-side, who could see us. Maybe we should go visit them."

"But Draco is monitoring top-side. Do you think he'd approve?"

"Dalla, I am a free being. I don't answer to Draco or anyone else." She stood and put her hands on her hips. "Do you want to go with me or not?"

He looked at her longingly. "Okay, I guess so." He stood and stretched.

She smiled and grabbed his hand. A moment later, they were where the Golden Flash shuttle had landed, but there was no sign of anything.

"They must have all left," Dalla commented, sounding relieved. "They will probably return. I'm sure they have to do a lot of diplomatic relation work to find the new immigrants to populate Falcon again."

"Wow, I never really thought of it. It'll be exciting when people are all over the surface again."

"So what now?" he asked. "Should we go back home?"

Eerin was quiet for a while. Dalla watched her face, and saw her expression change. "I think that they are still on Falcon. Let me see if I can use the system to locate them."

"You are spooky sometimes, but I like that."

She smiled at him, and then closed her eyes. A moment later, she said, "I am getting a picture of them. The system states access is denied, but when I requested an override, it let me. Are you ready?"

"What should we call them?"

"We can ask them. Are you ready?"

"How about if we jump space to somewhere close to them and walk up to them, so we don't startle them?" he suggested.

"Good idea, we don't want to frighten them." She grabbed his hand and they were on a little hill top looking down at a cabin. The

Wandini seemed busy, but soon one of the elders sensed them and looked up.

"Oh, wow, they saw us already," said Dalla. "They are even freakier than you are."

Eerin jabbed him with her elbow, teasing. "Come on."

She waved to the Wandini. It did not wave back, but interrupted the others from their work instead.

As Eerin and Dalla walked down toward them, the primitives gathered and watched them approach. When they got close, Eerin called out loudly, "Hi. I'm Eerin and this is Dalla. We want to be friends."

The one elder replied, "Gibru," then pointed at the other elder, "Semal." She then pointed at the middle aged two who held each other's hands "Nigaru and Narina." They raised their joined hands as if indicating their bond. Then they pointed out the younger three. "Milo, Droga, and Nadin".

Eerin asked, "Are you aliens?"

The Wandini laughed. "You are aliens. We are Wandini."

Eerin laughed, too. "Did Geardon bring you from another world?"

Gibru replied, "Geardon friend. Needed help. We left our Mama Home. Come to home where you children are ghosts."

Dalla sent Eerin a thought message. 'They think we're ghosts.'

The elder Gibru folded her arms. "You have no body. You are ghost."

Dalla gasped. "Eerin, she read my transmitted thought message!"

"I guess that's how they know were here," Eerin surmised. "They must be telepathic. True telepathy is not allowed among us immortals, only the type of personal messaging you just did, but they aren't bound to the rules of the core."

Droga tapped her own chest. "We are also immortal, but bodies are not."

Dalla turned to Eerin. "We should leave."

"You can go." She replied, then pulled him to her and gave him a kiss.

He kissed her passionately, momentarily forgetting that the Wandini were really seeing him.

When they finished and he looked up, the Wandini were all smiling. The breeding pair kissed and the group seemed to do little dances, half in celebration and half in jest.

Dalla turned red.

"I'll see you later, Dalla. I'll tell you all about it."

Dalla faded out.

Eerin shook her head, "Do you have men on your world?"

"No, we are all the same. All female as you see us," Gibru answered.

"Wow, that must be easier. How do you make babies?"

The Wandini thought that was funny, and one of the young ones asked, "You want to watch?"

Eerin's eyes got big in surprise and the Wandini rolled with laughter. She then had a good laugh herself, realizing they were teasing her.

"So what were you all doing when I showed up?" she asked.

They did pantomime, one acting like an animal and the others surrounding it with the spears they were working on. The one mimicking the animal growled.

One of the younger ones, Droga, motioned to her. Eerin followed Droga a short way into the clearing where there was a hut with smoke coming from it. She opened the door and there was meat hanging and drying. It looked like there was lots of room available for more meat. The other younger ones, Milo and Nadin, indicated she should follow them. They walked for a good while and then stopped on a hillside and pointed. They were very stealthy and seemed to almost be hiding. Eerin floated down to the location and found a den of bears. They were sleeping, but one lazily looked up when she entered, which made her uneasy. She froze the image and faded out. Reviewing the image, she realized there were two adults and two almost full-grown male cubs. These animals were original Earth genome and were brought to Falcon ages ago. Eerin returned to the Wandini and they crept away.

Once back at camp, she asked with some concern, "You are going to hunt a bear?"

Some Wandini brandished their spears and others rubbed their bellies, smiling.

"That would be dangerous," she replied.

They thought it was a joke and had a good laugh. One of the elders pulled out a pouch, then they all became serious. She set it on the ground and they formed a circle, including Eerin. The elder slowly unwrapped the pouch as the others hummed a song. In it was a fang that was thirty centimeters [a foot] long.

"Ergort, the dragon of Wandina," Semal said. She then told a story right into Eerin's mind. Eerin saw three groups of Wandini, recognizing Gibru and Semal as young warriors. One fast running Wandini tricked the Ergort into chasing her, thinking it had an easy meal, then they sprang in an ambush. One Wandini was killed and two wounded, but in the end, they had killed the dragon.

Eerin was aghast at the violence, but understood that all hominids that lived without technology and agriculture were hunters.

She then asked, "How are you going to lure it?"

They laughed. "We scare it, it runs from us with no thinking. Bears cowards, not like Dragons. Dragons hunt everything."

Then one of the young ones pointed at Eerin and said, "You trick it. You become she bear."

They all liked the idea, but Eerin wasn't so sure she wanted to get that involved.

"I don't think it will even see me," she said, hoping to dissuade them.

"We try," Semal replied, as if it was settled.

Eerin wondered what she had gotten herself into, "When are you planning this?"

They pointed at the sun and held up three fingers, then indicated the sun would be lower in the sky.

"I'll try." She then bowed in parting and faded away.


Appearing on her balcony, she found Dalla nervously waiting for her. "I'm glad you're back home."

"They want me to help them hunt a bear."

"What! Are you crazy? It's illegal to hunt bears! You know that."

"I doubt those primitives are bound by Falconian laws. You can do research if you want, but they will try, with or without me."

"How can you help?" asked Dalla. "You're like a ghost to them."

"When I went into the bear den, one of them looked up at me, or toward me. I think animals can sense us. Anyway, the Wandini want me to pose as a she bear."

Dalla laughed and she had to join him.

"What do you know about bears, Dalla?"

Dalla immediately got serious. "Enough to stay away from them. What if someone gets hurt?"

"Semal showed me a Dragon hunt that she was on when she was younger. One Wandini died and several were mauled, but they succeed. Semal had a fang in a pouch - it was thirty centimeters [a foot] long. They are willing to die, so that's why I should help, so that their chances are better. Will you help me?"

"I'll help you, but I'm not going to participate. Living here, we don't even have to kill vegetables to eat. I love you, but this could be heavy karma."

"Thank you Dalla, I love you too. I guess my karma is already set and I just have to do this."

"You don't really have to, but I can see that you will, so I'll help you get ready."

They started by studying bears. Then Dalla took on the form of a male bear and Eerin became a female bear. They watched many hours of bears frolicking and  then imitated them. Both Eerin and Dalla became very attached to bears.

When the time came for Eerin to meet the Wandini for the hunt, she simply appeared in their midst. They were rattling shakers, banging sticks, and chanting. They all looked at her right away, as if they had been waiting and indicated a place for her in their circle. She sat down and let herself get caught up in their music. When Eerin suddenly transformed into a she bear, the Wandini were momentarily startled, then overjoyed. Eerin returned to her own form, still not sure she was doing the right thing.

The Wandini gathered their spears and all walked together to their chosen site of ambush. When they got there, Eerin became a bear again. She sauntered up to the cave, where the bears were just waking up. One of the young males, apparently quite hungry, was the first to leave the cave and so she kept her distance, but made the noises bears make when they are amorous.

The male bear was confused, but interested. Real or not, Eerin conveyed enough sexual energy that he sniffed the air eagerly. The Wandini were smart - they had placed her downwind and so the bear's curiosity caused him to follow her in hopes of a scent. Eerin moved quickly, careful never to exceed the limits that being physical would impose. She leapt down a little gully and the bear followed without any caution. The Wandini sprang and pierced his sides. Wild with pain and rage, it swiped Droga as the Wandini stepped back. The bear ran and the Wandini followed, except Droga who laid down. Eerin and the elders, Gibru and Semal, stayed with Droga. The wound was bleeding quite a bit and Eerin hoped it was not deadly.

Once the elders had stopped the bleeding with pressure and some herbs they carried, Droga asked Eerin, "What about the bear?"

Eerin could not believe Droga was concerned about the bear. Eerin faded out and saw that they did not have to track the bear far. They had succeeded. She returned and said, "You have the bear. I'll be back."

Eerin appeared on her balcony where Dalla waited for her. He knew she was upset. "What happened?" he asked. "Did something go wrong?"

"Droga is wounded. She has five huge gashes from the bear's claw."

Dalla winced. "I imagine the aliens would use traditional herbs to stop infection, but I doubt they know much about Falcon's plants."

"Oh Dalla, I love you! That's it!"

"What's it?"

But before he could get an answer, she was fading. An instant later, she was knocking on the door of Marvelin and Nina in Morph Land.

"Child, what's the matter?" Nina asked with concern when she saw the look on Eerin's face.

"Geardon, um, the genome auditor, brought some primitive aliens from another planet who can see us telepathically and I made friends with them. They talked me into helping them hunt a bear, but Droga, one of the young ones, got wounded. I remember you had all these plants hanging up in your cabin. Can you help show them healing herbs, so she does not die of infection?"

"Why of course, dear," Nina answered without judgment.

Marvelin, however, commented, "Hunting and killing is heavy karma. You are wrapping yourself in heavy webs, child."

Nina was curious. "They see you?" she asked Eerin.

"Well, they read your mind. It freaked Dalla out, so he didn't want to help."

"Ah, telepaths," said Marvelin. "That is one esoteric ability which Draco's group stripped us of, believing that it would make this realm uncomfortable for many and blur the boundaries of self. In reality, the self is not as defined and concrete as it seems to be here. How did you help them in this murder?"

Nina gave him a look at the last word.

Eerin was on the verge of tears. "I became a she bear and lured one of the males. I learned the sounds and moves of a she bear, practicing with Dalla. I think the young male was not completely fooled, but you know how compulsive males can be."

Nina smirked. "I sure do."

"Well, let's go before it's too late," Eerin said nervously.

"Patience dear," said Nina. "Specific medicinal herbs are needed here. I will need to consult some books. You go back to them and I'll join you in a short while."

Eerin reappeared among the Wandini. The elders had made Droga comfortable and the others had begun to butcher the poor animal. Milo took the skin and fashioned a stretcher, which they used to carry Droga back to the camp. She did not look good. The others dealt with getting the meat into the smoke house. They seemed to ignore Eerin as she flitted about.

When Marvelin and Nina arrived, the Wandini elders looked up. Eerin stabilized and said, "These are my friends. Nina knows about herbs."

The Wandini looked hopeful. Nina then projected some images of plants for boiling to clean the wound and then herbs to dress it with and then antibiotic botanicals to give to Droga internally. The Wandini remembered seeing some of them and ran off in different directions. Eerin, Nina, and Marvelin followed them amazed that they had learned the environment so fast.

Once they saw that the Wandini were in control, Nina advised Eerin, "You should be careful what you get involved with. This changes the entire future of Falcon. I guess better to know the possibilities before taking actions. You really do end up in the middle of Falcon's destiny."

"What do you mean?" Eerin asked quietly, quite overwhelmed at this point.

Marvelin answered, "It was assumed that when Falcon was populated, we would continue to have complete access to the top-side realm. If we can affect animal behavior, and therefore also partially telepathic humans, then the top-side would be influenced by our actions. The Council will have much to consider."

"What Council?" Eerin asked.

"Do you think Draco has complete rule here? The original council makes the decisions. Draco is the head member, slightly more than a figurehead, but still with an equal vote to each of us."

"You are on the council?"

"Yes, dear. We are some of the original members. You have done us a service. It would be terrible to load top-side with people, and then realize that some immortals were affecting situations." Nina consoled.

Marvelin replied, "I suspected as much. We were going to do some experiments. Funny how, even as semi-immortals, we don't have time to do all the things we would like."

Eerin was concerned. "What should I do now?"

"Oh, you did nothing wrong, nor did you do right, you took the actions that destiny presented you with. Just go on with life as you have been doing." Nina said. She shook her head. "You seem to find yourself in the middle of things. Look before you leap."

"What about Droga?" Eerin asked.

"There's nothing more we can do," said Nina, "except perhaps pray."

"Pray?" Eerin was confused.

"Yes, dear. You see how your thoughts affect the situations here. Think positive thoughts. Picture Droga as healthy. We are all connected at a deep level."

"Wow, I'll have to try that. I sure hope she gets better."

"So do we," said Marvelin somberly.

"We will be in touch," Nina told her. They then bowed and faded.

Eerin returned to look in on Droga, but the Wandini were so busy that they ignored her. She chose to fade away and return to her balcony.


Dalla asked, "So where did you go?"

"I got Nina and Marvelin to help. Nina taught the Wandini about Falcon's herbs. We need to pray for her, that she gets better."

"Pray? Are you losing it? What does pray mean?" Dalla was more concerned than ever.

"Like, if they can read our minds, then we send Droga good healing thoughts and support her healing."

"Oh, I guess that makes sense," Dalla replied and heaved a sigh.

Just then, a little bird flew up and landed on the railing. It sang a short song and then announced, "Draco seeks an audience."

"Okay," Eerin said, sounding a bit tired.

Although she expected to be granted access to his realm, he appeared before them instead, startling her. "I hope I'm not intruding."

He was dressed in black leather boots, pants, and jacket over a black shirt. His manicured black beard and short black hair were complimented by his outfit. His eyes had a piercing quality.

"No, it's good. I'm glad you are visiting. You don't get out much, do you?" Eerin asked.

"I guess not," Draco answered with a slight smile.

Dalla flinched at her forwardness. "We are honored to have you visit us, sir."

"Well thank you, Dalla," said Draco, rewarding him with a slight bow. "I will not stay long."

Eerin offered him a seat, which he accepted. Once they were all settled and she had produced some drinks, he seemed to relax.

"Quite a view you have here," Draco commented as he surveyed the vast landscape under the blue sky, with the birds singing and various animals running about below. The lake had flocks geese and exotic birds. A gentle spring breeze blew.

"Dalla and I love sitting here," Eerin said.

"You two created quite a landscape for that party of yours," Draco commented.

"You heard about that?" Dalla asked, surprised.

"When I decided to come by, I briefly surveyed all your lands. I also heard about it another way. You requested an open source permit, which was granted. My advisors and I get summaries of all potential businesses to be used in my negotiations. Your lands are a potential financial asset to Falcon." Draco smiled.

"I just decided that so many people liked it, I would keep it open, kind of like a park," said Dalla proudly. "Since Eerin and I have moved in together we annexed it, so that you can see it in the distance over there. We still visit and enhance it, but I got so many requests from people willing to add to it, that I got an open source permit. I try and review everything thoroughly."

Draco smiled, "You can be a wealthy man if you want to share it off planet for people to take virtual trips to."

"Wealthy?" Eerin smiled.

"What would happen to it here then?" Dalla asked, wanting to protect his art form.

"Nothing," Draco answered. "Just the landscape would be periodically packaged to be loaded into other planetary systems. I'll bet you spend lots of time maintaining it, as it seems to consistently have a very high standard of detail."

"He spends hours and hours," Eerin commented for him. "I don't mind though, because he asks me about stuff and then we visit everything new before he approves it. It's a fun thing to do."

"Dalla, if you'd like, I can have an analyst send you more information. Wealth is a strange thing for immortals with everything, but there may still be privileges that you would desire. Are you aware of the Pixelators and their work?" Draco asked.

"Eerin told me something about them. They watch what others are doing, like our lives are a movie and they are sitting on a couch and watching." Dalla frowned at the thought. "Sounds like a kind of boring life."

"I agree," Draco commented, "but they have been watching the goings on since the initial party invitation. They kind of splice pieces of the past into movies and share them among each other. Your park is a popular location."

Eerin was a bit shocked. "You mean they spy on people?"

"Well, it is not exactly spying. They are there, just not always apparent. Often they are little birds or other creatures. Sometimes they are even inanimate objects, like a necklace worn by a more active person who appreciates their work. They are locked out of people's more private times together," Draco explained.

"Thank goodness, I would hate to think someone was watching us all the time," said Eerin, looking towards the birds in a tree near the porch.

Draco smiled broadly, "They are also locked out from viewing people's personal dwellings. They can only wander the designated public places, like open parties and now your park, Dalla, since you've opened it to the public."

"That seems reasonable," Eerin replied. Then in her spirited manner, looking Draco directly in the eyes, she asked "Is there anyone on Falcon who can spy on our private moments?"

Draco's lips curled in a smile. He seemed to like a woman fiery enough to confront him. "Not even I; nor the council. Some conditions were set in stone during the creation of our realm. There are, however, protocols for requesting access to people's private moments and some people who enjoy being watched cast aside their rights to privacy."

Eerin shook her head with a disgusted look on her face.

Draco changed the subject. "Well, let me get to the reason for my visit, though I'm sure you can guess that I am very concerned with things happening outside of the realm at this moment."

"I'm really sorry about Droga," Eerin said, anticipating what he was going to say. "They were going to hunt the bear, even if I didn't help."

Draco smiled, "You did us all a great service. Marvelin and Nina sent me a brief summary. There are limits on what may be viewed of anyone's actions as captured by the top side monitors. Are you willing to open up access to this encounter with the Wandini, including your thoughts, since they are telepathic? There are politics that can have grave consequences for Falcon, and the council believes access to this encounter might help them in deciding what to do."

Eerin was surprised. "The top-side monitors know all our thoughts?"

"Well, when Falcon was populated, it did not record such things in the same manner it does now; the monitors are set to record everything for now, since few people go top-side. Reading thoughts is how the system would open doors for you and such." Draco waved his hand as if to say it was of little importance.

"I guess I hadn't thought about it," said Eerin. "Our house just always did things when we needed it to."

Dalla told Draco, "I was not there very long, but you can read my records."

Eerin agreed, "Yes, mine too. Can you delete any weird thoughts I might have had, though, like if they were not really related? I hope it helps. Will we be able to go top-side when there are people living up there again?"

"I will have Nina filter the mental content of your top-side time before it is released to the council and me," Draco assured her.

"Thank you," she replied, relieved that he would have Nina do it.

"This is only a presentation to the council, which is very discrete. It will then be commented on and deleted," said Draco. "As for your other question, we need to put some limits in place for top-side visits, so that the new population has privacy and also so that our population does not seek to influence events on the surface world, not even through the animals there."

"You mean like I did," Eerin said with a frown.

"I don't expect any of the new human occupants to be as telepathic as the Wandini. Nevertheless, we need to review what you did. You actually lured a bear?"

Eerin blushed. "I tricked it into thinking I was a she bear. I don't think it really knew what was going on, but some part of it sensed the images I was putting out."

Dalla added, "I helped her practice for three days. She was great at being a female bear."

Draco smiled, but did not really look happy, "Eerin, you amaze me sometimes. Thank you two for cooperating. I should get going - there is a lot to do before the Council meets."

"Come back again sometime, when you're not so busy," Eerin invited.

"I'm always so busy." Draco seemed genuinely amused. "I guess I like it that way. I will stay in touch. Bye."

Eerin and Dalla both replied, "Bye" and Draco faded out.

Dalla, looked at Eerin. "I can't believe you teased him about not getting out much."

"Well, he doesn't."

"He is the most powerful man in the realm!"

"He's still just a person. Sometimes I think he's lonely." She seemed concerned for Draco.

Dalla gave her a look of affection, which she enjoyed. "You are so caring for everyone. You are amazing sometimes."

She smiled and put her hand on his arm. "Let's do something."

"Like what?" he asked.

"Oh, I don't know," she replied.

"How about we go swimming?" he asked.

Eerin perked up. "We could go scuba diving,"

"We could skip the tanks and just suspend our need to breath, and then go on an underwater adventure. You could be a mermaid and I could be a merman."

"Dalla, you're brilliant, let's go."

# 18. Identical Sisters

Miranda Liam announced that the intergalactic security ship, the Golden Flash, was in orbit around Mirka, the third planet about of star Trigen, the best candidate for finding the remaining population required for Falcon. Geardon, Cynthea, and Miranda boarded a shuttle disk and descended to the planet's surface.

Cynthea turned to Geardon as they watched the descent through the atmosphere and saw the capitol city below. "The private shield dome is bigger than a small town. It is hard to imagine the energy cost of creating such a shield dome, or what the benefit was."

Geardon was sure what lay beneath it would be equally impressive. "Mirka does not fear attack, though perhaps in historic times a rogue world would try such a stunt. However, like most worlds, they are paranoid about their secrets. Whether worlds are rich or poor is determined by their technological wisdom and Mirka is extremely protective of their intellectual property."

Cynthea said, "Even with the great wealth that Mirka possesses, I am suspicious of all excess opulence, such as the huge shield dome. We have ruled out most worlds as genetic failures and many more as socially undesirable, without them even knowing that they were being considered for such an amazing offer."

Miranda interjected, sub-vocalizing into Cynthea's channel which was set to broadcast at normal speaking audio levels, "Mr. Yakomita Otamo sank his huge empire's fortune into the shield dome. Mirka began as a holiday resort, one of his hundred holiday planets. He sold off most of them to build the domed city. A periodic fragmented stony-iron meteoroid would send a very significant meteorite shower every five thousand two hundred and eighty years, which would cause a significant dust loading and cause a ten-year winter. Mr. Otamo had inherited the planet from his ancestors whose tourism business had followed the previous event. Mirka had the most amazing diversity of life in response to the destruction and in most places humans were safe to just be in the lush wilderness, which was Mirka's appeal. It is rare enough to find a planet of size and atmosphere that humans could visit without adaptations, but a safe one with amazing life forms made Mirka a gem. The regular destruction meant that life evolved quickly, but never tended to create intelligent enough creatures to limit colonization.

"Unfortunately, Yakomita Otamo calculated that his lifetime was going to correspond with the grand slam, when most of the remaining meteoroid fragments would smash into Mirka, devastating the majority of the planet. He designed and built the dome to house Mirka's life, an ark to ride through the storm and the following twenty years of continual winter."

Geardon looked impressed. "Seems we have been goofing off while you were studying. Thank you Miranda. So why not move the life to a moon?"

Miranda, surrounded by her displays, replied, "The problem was reintroduction. Having seeds or many breeding pairs would not allow introduction to proceed rapidly enough to recover the tourism that he needed. The environment was sufficiently devastated by the many impacts and during the winter of death the planet's status changed from nature preserve to open for colonization. Mr. Otamo had anticipated this in his risky business venture, so Mirka began a new phase. Since high quality planetary space for immigration is extremely rare and many worlds have long lists of people who want to emigrate, Mr. Otamo charged huge fees to settlers and governed the environmental restoration in a most professional and scientific manner. Each settler had to pass genomic inspection and thus the population is very natural"

Geardon added thoughtfully, "What happened on Falcon 4 is starting to be confused in the news, but a few details have leaked. The official story is that Falcon has withdrawn and become an island world, seeking no interaction with the rest of the galaxy. The conspiracy webs have many stories, but the death of the population is featured in many of them. The fleet of destroyers and hyper-fighters that are gathered at the scene have not gone unnoticed. There will be a major scramble for Falcon's wealth if a pure strain of humanity is not found to possess it before the truth is revealed to the galactic media. So far, we have two good planetary sources, but their populations are low and so we need another source of genetically pure humans in sufficient volume to close the option of immigration from many worlds. Mirka is one of the best hopes to find a truly pure strain of humanity in quantity, before we open the doors to some lesser choice. Open colonization is not an option, because it has been decided that Falcon has such a great infrastructure, the rich would move in and destroy the humble ways that maintained a pure genome for so long."

The capitol city's defense system arranged for Geardon's shuttle disk's security clearance. A port door opened in the hundred-meter [three hundred thirty foot] tall shield support wall that surrounded the capitol city. It was all built of crystal steel, nearly impenetrable and vastly expensive because of the cost of manufacturing the almost indestructible material to precise specifications.

The shuttle landed in the open port and the shield sealed behind them. The capitol city's system instructed Geardon, Cynthea, and Miranda to proceed to the waiting area. They took the only door that led out of the port, a crystal steel hatch that was open to a large room with comfortable chairs and food droids to one side. Many ports from the third level, which they had landed on, opened to this room, but theirs was the only open door.

Geardon felt the Star Stone he's received from the changeling, which he always carried, energize and become weightless. It seemed to radiate mild heat. Once he acknowledged it by bringing it from his pouch, it floated up in his hand and then settled back down and returned to its dormant state.

Geardon's two companions watched in fascination. "What's that?" Cynthea asked. "I can feel it in the pit of my stomach."

"An auspicious omen," Geardon replied. "A very sacred Star Stone that very few humans have ever seen. Please never reveal that you have seen it. Let us proceed."

A woman approached with a certain glide, almost as if she floated. Geardon knew instinctively that she was his contact and recognized the movement as being a balanced Tai Chi walk, no bounce, lurch, or waddle to her gait. Her form and height were balanced as an expression of feminine vigor. Her hair was dark and her eyes were deep pools of brown. Another smaller woman followed her, walking as an ordinary person would.

The gliding woman had a winning expression, a mild smile of someone at peace with what they were doing. Her light brown complexion was accented by her captivating eyes. Though she did not appear to be genetically crafted for beauty, her features seemed naturally attractive. There was the mark of a clone tattooed in light blue on her left temple: mirrored lunar crescents with two dots above, like eyes.

They stood as she approached and she introduced herself. "Hi, I'm Jennifer ZMA00147. Welcome to Mirka, the third world of Trigen."

"Geardon Stranoff, Star Council Genome Auditor, and this is Cynthea Nestler, my adviser, and Miranda Liam, our pilot and communications specialist." Geardon felt awkward, something which rarely happened. "I'm pleased to meet you, Jennifer."

He couldn't help but glance at her hand, taking in the numbers of her last name. Verifying that all worlds complied with the basic regulations of cloning was part of his job. He was almost always met by diplomats that were natural humans.

By law, all clones were required to bear a tattoo on the temple unique to their family group, and the clone's number within the family on their left hand. The laws were created so clones would be distinguishable from each other and easily recognizable by natural humans. The laws were perhaps archaic, from ancient war days, but were strictly enforced.

"You can call me Jenny." She held her left hand loosely before him, displaying ZMA00147 in violet script. "My group is among the first sets of M children." She smiled as if proud to be a clone.

Jenny continued, "As your escort through the Gentranic's estate I will assist you in your introduction to the Gentranic vision. First, I'll take you to your rooms and let you get settled in. We can go to your choice of restaurants - we have most every type of cuisine imaginable. The seminar will begin tonight at nineteen-hundred hours. I think you'll find it intriguing. Mirka is changing, evolving at a phenomenal rate."

"Thank you, Jennifer," said Geardon. "I am looking forward to reviewing your world's accomplishments. As stated in the initial contact, this is not an audit. I have a business prospect that may be mutually beneficial."

"Ms. Miranda Liam will be staying on the ship, where she will be more comfortable. I have requested a companion versed in spacer ways to keep Miranda company while we are on your planet. Cynthea and I will require separate rooms."

Jenny introduced the slight young woman standing silently beside her. "This is Moura. She grew up as a spacer and is on an internship here. She will enjoy being with Miranda."

Miriam Liam bowed with an obvious sense of relief, glad both to have a spacer companion and to not be required to stay on the planet surface outside of a ship for a moment longer than needed. Moura gestured with her head and the two spacers quickly returned through the hatch to the shuttle.

"Please, feel at home on our peaceful world." Jennifer glanced at a burly man who had entered the room and was striding up with a hover platform. "Mike will get your things from the ship's hold."

Mike smiled and simply said hello as he went by them to unload the cargo bay of the ship. He returned in a moment with Geardon's crystal steel cube and their assorted bags on the floating platform.

"A very interesting woman was waiting to load your gear onto the platform," Mike said to Geardon. "She was very strong. Is she human?"

Geardon could tell Mike had a techie nature, so he replied, "A ship robot of sorts - very advanced, no organic components."

"Cool. I thought she was a person until she lifted the cube like gravity didn't exist." Mike seemed very pleased to have had the chance to meet Maya, not even imagining how advanced she was. Having enough halo-matter to create a whole being wasn't something that he would consider a realistic possibility.

They all followed Jenny. Geardon noticed that Mike also had the mark of a clone on his temple; in his case, four tetrahedrons pointed at a sphere in a circle. He was trim and looked strong as if he engaged in regular physical labor. They left the room and entered a maze of large hallways. As they passed other people, Geardon noted that several of them bore the mark of the clone. Jennifer led them to a levitator, an elevator capable of horizontal, as well as vertical movement, and they stepped in.

"Please take us to Hotel 11, floor 12," she said to a half sphere on a wall.

Turning with a smile, Jennifer explained, "These things are great, the best form of transport. The entire Estate has an elaborate underground routing system to take you anywhere almost instantly. The drive is modeled after a starship's protective gravitational bubble, so you don't feel any movement even at high speeds."

The door opened after a few seconds. They were in a lobby on the top of twelve floors, looking out of large clear windows at a huge ring of twenty-four hotels. In the center was a twenty-four story terraced, pyramid-shaped building. The terraces varied from twenty to over fifty meters each. The pyramid terraces alternated between garden parks and restaurants or shops. The large complex was topped with a clear crystal steel dome that was at least a thousand meters across and showed signs of reentry heating.

"That dome is the top of the old Gentranic's starship, forged in the spider nebula. It still houses our genome bank." Jennifer motioned to their left, "This way please."

She took Mike, Geardon, and Cynthea down a hall, walking quickly in her smooth dancing manner. She soon stopped at a room and the door opened to her.

"Just remember hotel eleven, floor twelve. Cynthea, you have suite 1206 and Geardon has suite 1208. They do have access between them, but both parties must release the digital latches. The doors and all levitators will recognize you. I am staying in 1207, across the hall, and will be at your service." Jenny smiled.

Walking into Geardon's suite, she gave them the mini-tour. "Sleeping rooms, fully automated dining room, offices, three bathrooms, one common and one for each sleeping room. A bit much perhaps, but I didn't supervise the arrangements."

Mike brought the hover cart through a larger door to one side. It was an invisible part of a wall, until it opened and he stepped in. "Where should I leave the case and bags?"

Cynthea smiled and said, "Put his cube in an office and his bags in a bedroom. The lavender bags are mine - I'll take them with me. Thanks."

Jennifer then took them next door to an identical room with different artwork displayed. Geardon remarked, "The decor is unique in each room, I like that."

She seemed pleased. "We have artists from all over Mirka who submit work to the hotels. The capitol should reflect the people of Mirka. Few live here, but most people come to the capitol at least several times in their lives. It's more of a cultural center than a legislative center. The necessary administrative functions of the planet are widely distributed across the planetary network. The capitol is rich in art and music, but the real treasure is the natural environment."

There were windows looking out to the pyramid, which dwarfed the ring of hotels. Jennifer followed Geardon to the windows. "Beautiful, no? We can go get something to eat in about an hour on one of the pyramid plazas, if that's good for you and Cynthea. The terrace restaurants are excellent, with the cuisine of thousands of worlds to choose from."

"Great, I would enjoy being out in the air." Geardon noticed that Mike had floated his cube into one of the bedrooms. "Thanks, Mike."

"My pleasure, sir." he responded, and then looked at Jennifer.

Jennifer dismissed him with a smile. "Thanks, Mike. I'll call you if I need anything else."

He bowed to her with his hands together. "My pleasure, Ancient One."

She reciprocated the bow, and turned to Geardon without commenting on the strange hierarchical salute. "I will see you in an hour then."

    \*  \*    \*    \*    \*

Once alone, Geardon went into the office and lifted the heavy half-meter [twenty inch] cube to a pad he placed on the desk. He told it to open with a peculiarly formal tone, "Geardon Stranoff, Galactic Genome Auditor, requests access 74009." A panel slid open and he took the United Star Alliance's necklace that he had been wearing over his shirt and touched it to an indent on the inner surface. A second panel slid open to a display that flashed with patterns, and then spelled out in characters a simple message, 'received.'

Geardon smiled at the thought of a monitoring security system viewing this little action. This cubic device was superior to what could be purchased for any price; it was United Star Alliance's most advanced design. It would no doubt take the estate's security a long time to isolate the language the machine had printed and report the message, which revealed nothing. The thought of using a scheme as old as character writing was amusing. Since machines had spoken for so many ages, most people are unaware of how functional reading and writing could be.

The genomic data from his journey thus far inside this fortress of the estate city had been relayed back to the Golden Flash. Maya was scheduled to take several hours in analysis and would report to him at his next check in time, which was after dinner. He was taking many extra precautions, due to the technological sophistication of Mirka. The audit would tell of the worthiness of this world.

\* \*      \*      \*      \*

About an hour later, Geardon was sitting in a lounge chair relaxing, when Jennifer's voice spoke from the air. "Geardon, may I open visual communication?"

"Sure," he replied.

Her holographic image appeared before him. She was dressed casually in pants and a simple top of neutral colors. "Are you ready for dinner?"

"Very ready!" He stood and stretched.

"Good. Please meet me in the hall. Cynthea said she will meet us there."

After meeting in the hall, the three took a levitator to a dinner café and got a seat near the edge of the fifteenth tier of the pyramid.

"Isn't the view spectacular from here?" Jennifer asked.

Geardon looked out over the lower tiers. The level below them was planted in flowering trees and shrubs. Toward the edge of that level was a grassy plain with small flowers dotting the grass. The level below that was an open market, with stands of all sorts. It resembled an ancient bazaar of tents and tables, but even at this distance, he could distinguish displays of some technological items being sold. Beyond it was a sea of treetops, since the level below was planted in what appeared to be a climax forest. He could hardly see the ground level, which appeared to be many small shops between the pyramid base and the ring of hotels aligned on circular streets.

Streams of tourists and occasional merchant's assistants with hover platforms loaded with goods were walking along various roads. No one was riding any device or beast. Geardon stood and let his necklace absorb the panoramic scenery; gathering advanced data from animal pheromones, plant pollen, and every organic molecule that it encountered, not to mention complete audio-visual recordings. "Magnificent," he said as he sat back down.

Jennifer spoke to the globe in the center of their table and it asked them questions regarding their food desires. Geardon ordered roast talabeast with gravy, a bin-tuber and some grawpin greens, all standard galactic foods. Jenny ordered local foods that Geardon had encountered in his research. Cynthea ordered spacer food with some local vegetables.

Once the food had been ordered, Geardon turned to their guide, who he gathered liked to talk. "So tell me what it is like being a clone on Mirka, Jennifer."

"Call me Jenny. Well, as you know, there's a lot of prejudice against clones on some worlds ever since some minus-S series clones were orchestrated into being a part of the Canister biological wars. Mirka was always loyal to the United Star System's realm where clones are free. Mirka provided some clone warriors during these ancient wars, but these days our clone lines are very desirable, having been gathered from all over the galaxy. Our techniques for blending the clone into the living zygote for the receptive mother-to-be are some of the most sophisticated ever developed, thus Gentranic's economic success.

"The clones of our world are selected from the great scientists and humanitarians of history. We are a very conservative people. We have never allowed as many copies as the lax galactic standards do." She held out her hand to display ZMA00147. "I am one hundred and forty seven of the seven hundred and seventy four of my genome's M generation. Two hundred twenty-eight members of our single batch family were outside of Mirka's rigid allowable deviation and were not born."

Geardon broke in, "Defective rates vary between batches depending on how many generations pass. Most worlds do not use anything above G or H due to the high rate of loss, very expensive. Although Z Generations are legal, I find this very strange that you would use an M generation and accept a twenty five percent loss."

Jenny looked slightly put off. "We rely on some old lines, like my family, because they are tried and true. Sometimes we have individuals among the population that are selected for addition to our genome bank. We have very strict codes for adopting a new genome patterns for cloning. They're much stricter than the Galactic standard. This makes old families, like mine, infinitely valuable."

Cynthea was just listening to the conversation, but also watching and listening to some amazing feathered creatures that were on the wall near their table. They were able to hover like hummingbirds, but did not seem to be nectar drinkers.

Jenny stopped her train of thought and told Cynthea, "They are called Lorqui." There was a cluster of many spheres as a centerpiece on their table and Jenny touched one, which opened to reveal red hard berry-like fruits.

Jenny smiled, "Not tasty as appetizers. Put a few at a time in your hand and hold it out flat."

Cynthea did and was delighted when the Lorqui flew and landed daintily on her hand. They each would look at her and sing a short melody, then take the fruit and fly away.

"They are amazing. They each sing to me." Her eyes had grown wide with delight.

"They are trained. If you get a young one that does not sing a song, drop your hand. It will hover and try again; then watching the elders, it will quickly learn the song," Jenny explained.

Soon some small furry creatures, who watched the Lorqui, were begging by the table.

"You can feed them, too, if you like. Or just shoo them off," Jenny told Cynthea.

"What do I feed them?" Cynthea asked.

Jenny pointed to the blue sphere in the table centerpiece. "You can toss the treats or feed them from your hand."

"Is it sanitary?" Cynthea's spacer history started to register. Geardon chuckled.

"Sure. But hand mists are available from that center spout - just put your hands over it."

Cynthea touched the blue sphere and took out some treats. She cautiously stretched out her hand. The creatures had long shiny blue fur, and they made a pleasant sound when they received the treats. The animals were not quite like cats or squirrels or other familiar creatures. Geardon sat back and watched with interest.

Soon the food arrived on three separate hover trays.

Jenny told them her story while they ate. "To get back to your question, Geardon, my original parent was a woman named Zelieda Maquance, who served as a medic on a collapsed colony, Trimark 4. It was a very habitable world, but distant from most other habitable worlds and near spatial disturbances that made it impossible for anything bigger than a personal ship to reach it, and then only in specific periodic windows of opportunity.

"She came from strong family roots and could have lived a comfortable life in Mirka's paradise, with position and power. For some reason she got mixed up with the Dancing Servants, a group that preached the virtues of a life led serving those in need. She worked hard at accumulating resources and finally bought a medic ship and went there.

"She lived her whole life tending to the people of that cut off world. It was impoverished in modern conveniences due to the access problems, but rich in a natural way. Although her family was disappointed when she left, they became proud of her achievements. Her work in repairing the fabric of society on Trimark 4 through simple living and hard work, made her famous in her old age. Just before her death, she agreed to become one of the first series of Mirka clones. I am very proud of my family heritage, though there have been M generations of us."

"Thirteen generations is a long time." Geardon said. "What about your immediate family then?"

"Well, we are a very self-controlled batch. Although clones can breed with ordinary people, the offspring of those couples are never selected to be potential clone seeds for at least five generations, even though galactic law allows first and second generation offspring of clones to become new clone lines. We only use individuals who do not breed as potential clone seed for the next generation, so that the line is pure and those individuals can dedicate themselves entirely to the next clone generation's upbringing. My line usually lives to be around three hundred and eighty years old. We select the seed parent at age one hundred."

"So, are you a medic, too?" Cynthea asked.

"Yes, but my main training is in the art of genetic manipulation through energy medicine. Although we are clones, we still evolve naturally. We strictly follow the Galactic standards for the manipulation of specific traits in individuals. Unbalanced changes are dangerous. Mirka feels that the galactic standards for genetic manipulation and artificial intelligence implants are considerably too lax."

Geardon felt that he was now getting relevant information, so he asked, "What type of enhancements, besides long life, have the Mirka population adopted?"

"Everyone on Trigen 3 gets the standard medical enhancements to protect them from identified galactic diseases that have appeared. We are on the program 3 upgrade, which is quite conservative for most worlds. We are modifying our native genome at a rate about one sixtieth of the galactic average, mostly because our primitive world suits us fine. We have natural minds, with only the most minor enhancements for health as required by the USS standards. Some of our population even complains about those. I heard that there was a problem with the level seven enhancements roll out and a planet around the star Falcon has withdrawn from communication."

"It was a big problem actually, though the level seven was not the core of the problem. I didn't think much news of it had spread," Geardon replied calmly.

"We are at the cutting edge of technology and economics, even though we are a natural population. We are a very rare people. We study anything happening to the human genome." Jenny was obviously proud of her people.

Geardon decided to trust her with a limited amount of information about planet Falcon. "Well, as I said, the roll-out was not the problem with Falcon, that's a smoke screen."

Jenny raised an eyebrow in surprise.

"I'll fill you in on more of the story later," Geardon promised.

"We suspected as much, since other worlds before Falcon had level seven without problems."

She took a sip of her drink and continued with her story. "My personal line of clones chooses its progenitor for the ability to see a patient's inner needs in order to determine what energy should be applied. Our world uses standard medical scanning and analyzing to determine the specifics, but computer brains are limited to logic and often cannot trap for unusual new conditions as efficiently as our intuition. There are too many combinations that are possible for a machine to know what to choose, we must provide it direction for the best service.

"As you know, our world, Mirka, has many of the highest quality services. We were contacted to answer questions after the problem on Falcon 4, but do not have enough background on the latest enhancements. The exact problem was never completely revealed and then a veil of secrecy descended."

She looked at him with a mischievous glint in her eyes and a directness that seemed to peer into his core. "My clone family has only chosen the best for the next generation since the first clone children of Zelieda Maquance. We are the greatest Human Seers in the Galaxy."

Geardon felt his privacy invaded by that look, yet he was now personally fascinated by this woman before him. She was beautiful, but as a Galactic Auditor, he was used to every sort of bribe, though she didn't seem to have the personality for seduction. She seemed too self-respecting for that type of approach. He had been to the most progressive worlds and met many hybrid clones, specifically designed for visual and sexual pleasure. Jenny seemed vibrant with life, more human than many natural people Geardon knew. She was probably not nearly as accomplished of a seer as the Wandini, but then she was modern and a Human.

Just then a voice called out, "Jennifer."

She answered into her bracelet, "Yes".

The voice spoke fast. "Young girl in sector five fell from a tree limb as she was gathering fruit and is losing consciousness."

"I'm on my way." Jenny jumped to her feet and as she did, she knocked a curry shaker off the table and onto the floor. It landed upright and spun for a moment, before coming to rest. They both looked at it, and then into each other's eyes.

Geardon said in a serious tone, "That was an Omen of Synchronicity."

"Yes, I'm almost never clumsy and the odds of it landing upright are incredibly slim. You should come with me; but if you would rather, I can have another escort assigned to you. Through those arches behind us is a park with many wonderful creatures. I had planned to show you around it."

She paused and looked into his eyes, seeming to provoke his decision. "Come with me and see what I will try to do."

Jenny was on her feet and Geardon rose quickly, looking at Cynthea. "Why don't you tour the park and report back to me."

Cynthea nodded, seeming relieved.

Without further discussion, Geardon and Jenny ran together toward the row of levitators.

# 19. Pixelators

Dalla said to Eerin, "Now that we have completed our new business as the owners of the park, the Land of Eight Gates, we should visit the Pixelators and see what they are doing there."

"Good idea, I'm curious too," she replied. "How do we get access?"

"I told the analyst wizard that set up the business and it isolated some of the Pixelators who are very active at the park. The synthetic intelligence analyst said that the Pixelators were excited to meet us, though they were very shy about personal interaction. We just need to ask for a visit and set up terms to respect their space."

"Cool...." She smiled. "Let's do it."

They appeared on the small couch set aside for them. The space was like a comfortable Falconian entertainment living room area. Next to them was a couple on another couch. A man and woman relaxed in recliner chairs on the other side of them. Sometimes when Eerin or Dalla would try to look at the people, their features would pixelate.

Eerin decided to break the ice. "Hi," she said brightly.

The Pixelators just stared at her and Dalla as if they were an anomaly.

After an awkward silence, the man in the lounge chair stated, "We don't talk much. We are watchers. Want to see some of our compiled works?"

"Sure," said Eerin, and Dalla nodded.

The light faded and the space changed to a virtual view of Eerin and Dalla at the party, greeting guests. The three-dimensional scene seemed to mostly follow Eerin, as if she was the star. Eerin tried to talk, but they shushed her. Sometimes it would follow other guests, mostly trailing them after they interacted with Eerin in some way.

The scene came up of their conversation toward the end of the party. She watched Marvelin saying, "Ever do it in a swan boat? I hear the bouncing of the water can be great," to the couple that had been listening in. The scene then followed the couple, and in quite graphic detail displayed the couple's exploits in the boat. Eerin blushed and then blurted out, "You followed their private moments?"

Dalla frowned. "I thought there were limits, even in public spaces, and this was a private party."

One of the women giggled at their reaction and then the other woman spoke up as the video froze and faded, "I got them to agree to a total release of the scene."

"She's good at that," the man on the couch replied as he took her hand. "Didn't you like the scene?"

Eerin jumped to what was really bothering her. "So you did not watch Dalla and me later?"

"We would like to," the man in the lounge chair replied and the four of them laughed.

"I don't think so," Eerin said sternly. "What did you see?"

"Jump to the end," the same man replied.

There was Eerin kissing Dalla and bidding him good night after the others had left.

And Dalla telling her, "You don't have to go. You can stay if you want."

"Patience Dalla, we have eternity," she responded as she started to disappeared.

"But now is real," he replied with eyes like open windows to his desire.

Eerin watched her past self as her heart seemed to take control and she faded back in. She embraced him and they kissed passionately, but then the view became gray and dim. When they trans-located to the feathery cloud bed under the stars, the Pixelators' virtual reality only showed them disappearing.

Eerin sighed, "That was romantic." She looked at Dalla and he looked back at her and for a moment they were lost gazing at each other, then she felt watched.

Eerin looked up, perhaps a bit defensively, at the Pixelators observing them, and then Dalla asked, "Hey, so how do you assemble the video."

Dalla had a knack for understanding people and the Pixelators were anxious to share their art. The man on the couch took control. "We'll show you."

"Where should we go?" The woman beside him asked.

"How about Morph Land?" the woman in the recliner suggested. "Eerin visited there, but her journeys there were blocked by those two controllers. Let's have a look at more public personalities in Martial Land."

"You know I went to Morph Land?" Eerin asked.

"You're the star. Everyone loves you. You even have the Genome Auditor hooked on your story," the woman replied.

Eerin seemed a bit overwhelmed as they started the shadowing. In the virtual space, there was a fuzzy image of a man doing some sort of movements. The four of them were calling out dimensions and directions and obscure commands, making the image jump back and forward in time and slowly take on the form of a person doing something like Tai Chi movements. Finally they were all calling out things like "Set and Render, I'm in," then another "Plus five point two-five. Set and Render, I'm in."

The man on the couch explained, "We just captured a scene from the core memory. Every action of everyone is stored there as data, but is not tuned to the limited bands of human sensory perception. Once we command a human rendering, the core will return the scene from the perspectives we set. We are the four cameras that can then fade and blend in mix down mode for the final virtual experience that everyone expects."

"Let's see where he goes next," the woman beside him said.

The hazy image showed the subject walking through some kind of nondescript scenery and meeting an adversary in a clearing with the four of them calling out parameters. The two fighters' rapid motions became a blur. The scene backed up to when the two bowed to each other. They retraced a number of times and finally they gave their unanimous render approval. Back to the fight, then, with many reruns and flicker scenes so fast it made Eerin's head dizzy. Sometimes the scenes would double up and superimpose, as different members ran different parameters. At one point there seemed to be a giant snake and a bird fighting and at other points a tiger and a dragon. Once they stated render on the fight, the room grayed.

"Ready to watch?" the woman on the recliner asked.

"Sure," said Dalla, sounding as though a bit excited by the expectation of Kung Fu action.

Now the man in the meadow was doing slow motion martial art dances and the scenes sometimes zoomed in on his face or panned back to view his whole body. A scene transition showed a woman in another field doing her own style of martial art Kata. They both completed their movements and then walked in a very deliberate and smooth martial way to the clearing. As they stood facing each other, there were close ups of their faces; serene and peaceful, yet very deliberate. Their eyes had a cool, haunting appearance, reminding Eerin of animals.

The fighters bowed and screamed. Eerin jumped and Dalla grabbed her hand as the two combatants rushed at each other. The Kung Fu battle progressed with savage fury until at one point the man became a huge predatory bird and grabbed the woman, who reacted immediately and became a giant snake twisting about it. Beak and fangs danced trying to get the advantage to strike, when suddenly the male bird transformed into a dragon and she became a tiger.

The roaring had Eerin shaking as they re-attacked. They fought savagely until they appeared to be weakening. Finally the dragon momentary pinned the tiger, but then the tiger threw the dragon to one side. They became humans again and bowed to one another. Both were disheveled and bruised, their clothing in tatters. They backed away from each other and when they lost sight of each other, they ran gracefully and quickly as if they were being pursued. The images jumped from one to another.

The man finally entered a bamboo hut on a high hill. After doing a set of movements to loosen up, he changed into a silk robe with a flash. Then he sat and began to play a very lonely tune on a large bamboo end blown flute.

The woman entered a cave and also did movements to relax, then in a flash she was dressed in flowing silk, no sign of bruises or fatigue. She began playing the many strings of a beautiful wooden bodied instrument in a most melancholy fashion.

Eerin felt herself tear up in the loneliness of the tune. "Why do they hate each other?" she asked in a choked up voice.

"They have a love-hate relationship," the woman on the couch replied. "On rare occasions they play together and create some of the most profound music in fantastic surroundings, but usually they act like this."

As they continued to watch, the video seemed to sync up the in separate scenes and overlap the traditional songs, until, they meshed and the two were playing together. Sometimes the two players transformed, the man looking momentarily like a praying mantis and the woman like a swan. Finally, the song ended and the players each lay down on a humble mat to sleep. The video faded.

"It's so sad," Eerin commented, feeling the emotion welling up in her again.

Dalla said, "The artists of Kung Fu are like that; amazing people, but captivated by their path, prey to their chosen ways."

"These two Morphs are a never-ending adventure," the other woman replied. "They are the essence of passion - their entwined stories could captivate one for a lifetime."

Eerin stood and stretched and Dalla followed her lead. She looked at each of their hosts and they did not pixelate, but held their forms. "Thank you so much for the most pleasant and stimulating visit," she said and bowed.

Dalla also bowed. "We have been honored."

The Pixelators all replied that they were the honored ones and invited Dalla and Eerin back, as well as inviting them to tune in to their public channel.

Once back on their balcony, Eerin said, "I just can't get the images of those two Morphs out of my head."

"Me neither," said Dalla. "We will need to watch more of their exploits and learn some of their history."

"I agree, but I don't want to get caught up in video land and forget to live my own life," she said firmly.

"Yeah," Dalla agreed. "The Pixelators are living through others, and that's sad in its own way."

"I'm so glad we have each other to do things with," Eerin said in a more cheerful tone.

"Me to," he replied. "What do you want to do now?"

"How about we take a walk in a desert at sunset, not too hot, where the sky becomes awesome," she suggested.

"Great idea. A desert walk should be grounding after all that sitting." He stood and took her hand and they disappeared from the balcony.

# 20. The Touch

The levitator opened at a port just inside the shield wall and they boarded Jenny's sleek personal ship. A special access portal opened for them to leave through. The ship flew rapidly across thousands of miles. When it finally descended, a group of the native population crowded around them.

As they stepped out of the ship, two young girls ran up to them, tears streaming down their cheeks. "Our sister fell. Our sister's not moving. Please help us Ancient One."

Geardon noticed that the girls were identical. They looked about seven years old and had rich brown skin and straight, dark hair. Their eyes were big, which accentuated their pleading looks. They did not bear the mark of the clone. They were practically pulling Jennifer by both hands, as their father kept admonishing, "Girls, Girls."

He looked apologetically at Jenny. "I'm sorry Ancient One."

Jennifer merely told the girls, "Run, we will follow." The two identical girls darted off with the group of adults close behind them.

When they arrived, they saw a girl identical to the two sisters, lying motionless on the ground where she had fallen. There was a large metal bridge of equipment over the fallen girl, with five people wearing headsets plugged into it. Each headset's display flickered in the air before the wearer. A male pair of clones, a female pair of clones, and one of Jennifer's sisters sat chanting out codes. One of the women clones pulled off her headset and offered it to Jennifer, which she quickly put on.

Jenny joined in the code chanting, totally focused.

The woman who had released her headset looked at Geardon and seemed a bit surprised when she saw his medallion, putting out her hand and saying, "Melini, pleased to meet you Mr. United Star Alliance Genome Auditor."

"Geardon Stranoff, Pleased to meet you. I am accompanying Jennifer."

"Well Jenny is the best. I studied under her for a period of time."

Geardon asked, "What exactly are they doing for the girl, in lay terms?"

The clone Melini replied, "Trying to reunite her consciousness with her form. The girl is losing consciousness. They are trying to modify her system on the fly to solve specific problems in her body. Once the girl is stable, then the standard regeneration machinery can do its job to fix the physical."

Jenny then set the headset in a docking station on the bridge and stepped back and began Chi Gong movements.

Melini excused herself and joined. Geardon joined in the energy movements, which were meant to accumulate and transmit life force. Geardon sent a huge rush of energy to Jennifer, rather than toward the girl.

The girl groaned and several onlookers gave sounds of relief and made general statements of gratitude. Finally, the girl moved and screamed, then started crying.

Jenny stepped next to Geardon and he gave her a quick hug. "Great job."

"Wow, that was a close one," Jenny said, pausing to catch her breath. "She had a broken neck with nerve damage, but she'll be fine in a week or two. You sent an amazing surge of energy for us to use."

Geardon looked humbled. "I started seeking a healer's path, but I am a conduit. I can channel vast amounts of Chi from the universe, but have limited ability to direct or focus it. I can load a room with intensity, but what happens next is not under my control. I tried for years, but my energetic nature made me perfect for being a Genome Auditor, so that's what I am. I am so glad that you were able to precisely direct the flow for the girl's sake."

"We never choose, we just find our gifts and refine them," Jenny smiled. "You are just as responsible for saving that girl as any of us. Your energy surge, under our guidance, brought her back into her damaged body. Thank you."

"No. Thank you, Jenny. It has been an honor to accompany you," Geardon said, smiling. For a moment, they were alone gazing at each other, and then the activity around them brought them back into awareness. The young sisters came running up to them.

The other healers began unplugging the headsets and stowing them in compartments in the med-bridge. Soon the machinery began to change shape as panels appeared and covered various displays. The healers adjusted the girl's position slightly and medicated her. The med-bridge slid a floor under the girl with its inner appendixes. It created a chamber around her with metal fabric. A moment later, it gently lifted her into the air and headed for an emergency facility.

The other woman of Jenny's clone family joined them. "Hi, I'm Samathra. Pleased to meet you."

"Geardon Stranoff," he said shaking her hand and feeling genuinely moved. "That was quite impressive."

"That girl was very close to dying. Thank goodness Jenny showed up. We couldn't quite get a grip on the girl until Jenny joined us. We had been trying for over twenty minutes." Samathra shook her head and took a deep breath.

Jennifer smiled. "Glad I could help, but you all were doing fine. Sometimes it just takes time. I'm just so glad we could save her."

Samathra looked at Geardon. "You helped quite a bit."

Others wanted to compliment the Ancient Ones. The two girls stood next to Jenny and hung onto her legs. She smiled at Geardon. "You can see why our original mother became absorbed in her work of service."

She then asked the bright-eyed girls, "Would you like to walk us back to our ship and see us off?"

"Yes, Mother," they both replied.

They all walked back to the ship and said their thanks and good-byes. Once in the air, Geardon asked, "I didn't want to bring it up at the time, but were those children clones without the mark of the clone?"

Smiling, Jenny replied, "They weren't clones - they are natural triplets. We have pills that if taken before a woman becomes pregnant, she can choose how many children she wants. Our medical care of the smaller infants is very good, the births are easier and the risks are less. Rarely do women have just one child, twins is the main choice, but special genetic lines are encouraged to have extra children. Clones have identical DNA, just like twins, triplets and quintuplets. I have seven hundred and seventy-four twin sisters and most of the old ones from the last generation are still living."

Geardon appeared thoughtful for a moment, "That's the difference; you are a repeat of a previous person with identical DNA. These children are the first of their kind, even if there is more than one of them. I think that the fear of clones is due to the sheer number factor. No one can erase the image of tens of thousands of identical Goliath soldiers dropping into human worlds in huge canisters and wreaking destruction."

"Well, clones are just as human as any other people. Those soldiers were forced into doing what they did," she said defensively.

"Jenny, I think you are a most noble soul, and that the line of your family is very valuable to humanity. I'm here as an auditor, not because we feared your world has violated some statute of the law, rather because we are looking for worlds that not only comply, but are still healthy in the natural sense," Geardon replied. "We have a problem we need your help with."

"We do sell genome from our banks, but they are expensive. We are some of the best." Jenny sat tall at the controls of the hovercraft, glancing at him with that penetrating look. "To get a batch of my sisters as clones is highly expensive, since we are a bit protective of our specialty lines. We work with some of the best genomes in the galaxy. Since we have been doing this for so many generations, we have many options available."

"Yes, I understand. I do not set the standards for the audit grades, but Mirka is one of the highest ranked worlds. We all are a part of the United Star Alliance and must work together for the common good." Geardon's voice grew softer." Thank you for bringing me today, Jenny." He surprised himself with the touch of emotion in his voice. He wasn't sure if he hoped Jenny missed it or not.

"My service to the people of Mirka is my reason for being. Since I was a young girl, I have helped Mirka's people. This is how I understand spiritual love. We are still Dancing Servants, as our great mother was." She grew silent, and watched as the hover approached the port.

Geardon touched her arm. "I am profoundly honored to have aided you in your service."

She smiled and nodded.

*     *     *     *     *

Back in his room, Geardon was elated with the results he received when he checked preliminary status with his cube. Mirka was a clean world, still at level three of the galactic standard genetic enhancement scale. Even a standard four could help them solve the problem of Falcon. He fed the vast amount of data collected by the medallion on his trip into the cube to be uploaded to the Golden Flash. The fact that he gathered data outside the city was essential to final approval. He did not doubt that the three girls were triplets, but Maya would certainly review that fact in order to confirm it.

He went next door to tell Cynthea. "Good news from preliminary tests. Mirka is a level cleaner than minimum."

She was skeptical. "What if they maintain a different condition inside this shield than on the rest of the planet outside? Any ship can maintain unique conditions."

Geardon told her about his trip with Jenny.

"Don't be fooled by an emotional situation," Cynthea spoke to Geardon as though she was his mentor. She seemed upset, or perhaps jealous. "I have witnessed much death. When I was on my second tour of futy, the space city that I lived on was attacked by the alien predators called Spree. We all fought and watched many friends die. Nothing touches the heart like the drama of life and death. When more fighters arrived and the additional soldiers saved our city."

"The event was synchronistic, but unplanned," Geardon said. "Jenny had no motives and you saw how she hesitated to bring me along. I don't think she would have, except for the omen. Nevertheless, I relayed the data from the trip to the ship. Maya will analyze the data and give us a report.

"I'm fairly confident, though, that this may be the world of choice for the majority of the people we need. I have a formal meeting with the rulers of Mirka this evening to discuss our mission."

Cynthea rolled her eyes. "There you go with omens and such. Just express your power at the meeting, then if they yield, give respect to their power. If they resist, then be suspicious."

Geardon was distant for a moment. "It is sad that after the attack in your home colony, you would face another devastating battle in the space city. There seems to be a warrior spirit that we share, so I will also tell you a personal story." He lifted his robe and revealed a scar of seven barbs on his outer thigh. Cynthia shivered realizing it was a Spree bite.

"I thought no one lived from a Spree bite," she exclaimed.

"I was twenty-seven when our colony was attacked." Geardon lowered his robe. "I was already a trained warrior, but we were out-numbered and after exhaustive physical combat, I was defeated. The Spree took me captive and kept me alive. The sting was torturous, but deliberately not deadly. My captors played with me as a toy, hoping to learn every human weakness. I was rescued and the data of what they did to my body helped to finally provide the poison that was used to defeat their hordes. I then trained as a secret service agent to attack their home planets."

Cynthea took a deep breath and looked at Geardon with new respect. "After the final battles, I heard rumors about you, not knowing for sure if they were true. Thank you for providing the key to the defeat of the Spree."

Geardon looked at her. "I was nearly dead. It took me a while to want to live again, but the will to fight the mindless killers drove me on. After the battle, I sought every type of esoteric training I could find. I learned life's deeper meaning and so continued in the service."

"I also continued when I could have retired," Cynthea replied. "I went through many battles in service to humanity, because it seemed to be my calling."

"Well, it is good that we have found another synchronicity in our lives." He bowed his head to her with respect. "Now I should go and get ready for the audit."

"Good luck," Cynthea said. She returned his bow and walked him to the door. Then she broke her usual pattern and gave him a friendly hug.

Back in his room, Geardon dressed in his formal uniform and waited anxiously for Jenny to take him to the Audit.

She arrived shortly, dressed in an elegant green gown. She greeted him with a smile and offered her hand. "Jennifer ZMA00147, at your service."

He was taken in by her natural beauty and kissed her hand in a formal manner. "Ancient One, the honor is mine."

She held his hand for a moment and looked into his eyes. He didn't resist. Once on the levitator, she explained. "You have been granted access to the ship and all our records for your audit. Trigen 3 has always complied with all the mandates from the United Star Alliance Command. There are those who are offended at being audited, but I explained that you were looking for a high quality genome base. No one who was not born on Mirka has visited the inner compartments of the ship in the center of the pyramid for over five hundred years."

They stepped from the levitator into a sealed crystal steel room with several armed guards. A dignitary in an elaborate body armor uniform bowed to Geardon. "Raymond Vinci, Chief Councilor to the Royal Seat of Mirka."

"Geardon Stranoff, Genome Auditor, at your service," Geardon replied, also bowing.

Chief councilor Vinci then bowed to Jennifer, clasping his hands together. "Ancient One."

Jenny put her hands together in reply and bowed her head politely, "Councilor Vinci."

"Please follow me." The councilor walked a short way and stood before a wall that parted to reveal a long corridor: the ancient airlock that spanned the ship. As they walked behind the councilor, Geardon realized that they were being scanned. His medallion was more than a sensor here; it was the power of the United Star Alliance watching. It communicated any attempt to access or analyze its functionality directly into an audio implant that he had.

They stopped half way down the corridor at a hub of eight doors. Air locks sealed behind and before them. They turned right and entered a short corridor to a lift that brought them into a large meeting room. A huge glistening stone table in the center of the room was surrounded by dignitaries. A set of triplet women sat on the far end of a raised table overlooking the assembly of dignitaries. They were dressed in iridescent green cloaks that brought out the intensity of their green eyes.

Silence came to the room and all heads turned as the councilor bowed to the queens. "May I introduce you to United Star Alliance's Genome Auditor, Geardon Stranoff." The Councilor Vinci's loud voice commanded complete attention.

The middle queen rose to her feet. "We welcome you to our inner sanctuary."

Councilor Vinci led them to their seats, but Geardon remained standing, looking at the queens. He then looked around at the dignitaries and began his speech. "Dear people of Mirka, I have only words of praise for you. The preliminary analysis of the United Star Alliance's genome review system has found your world to be of a standard that should be followed by all worlds. You have our highest praise for the environmental purity of your world's genomic status. By gathering minute traces of DNA with this medallion my ship has determined that your help would be the most beneficial."

He paused momentarily and looked around. "The United Star Alliance has the right to a complete audit of your Genome Banks, your most precious trade secret, through this medallion that I wear. The United Star Alliance will resist the temptation to add your great knowledge to our databases.

"As you know, the art of cloning, coupled with advanced genetic manipulation, has yielded some extraordinarily talented individuals. I have been honored to spend time with Jennifer, the Ancient One. I have only praises for her being. Yet, the universe itself has an evolutionary program that surpasses all human imagination.

"Your world has conservatively chosen only level three genetic enhancements, while most worlds clamor for the right to be as high as possible on the genetic enhancements schedule. Let me get to the point. I believe you may be familiar with the planet Falcon and their serious genetic problems. The myth is that Planet Falcon was the first world to use the level seven point fourteen manipulations, giving them unbelievable mental powers. Three other worlds followed and then nine worlds were in the beginning stages of the genetic upgrade when the problem arose.

"Planet Falcon went silent. All of the population perished, following a long time dream of theirs to become virtual entities.

Their Synthetically Intelligent system now maintains some simulation of their living as their souls exist within the Brilliant Machine. This had nothing to do with the genetic upgrades. They actually only minimally applied upgrades and were a mostly natural population. There was a lure of technology to become immortal within the Brilliant Machine core of their world."

There was a murmur and Geardon paused for a moment so that the sadness that overcame him would not make his voice quiver. "I went there. The people simply found comfortable places in nature to collect together in groups and left their bodies in a cultist ritual. They programmed robotic servants to dispose of their bodies as compost. Their world is ready to be populated, because they prepared for their departure efficiently. They acted together and kept their plans secret from the rest of the galaxy. They prepared documentation for the new inhabitants that they were sure would take their places on their natural and yet opulent world. They prepared their world for new colonization."

Geardon bowed to the queens, pausing momentarily. "The United Star Alliance would like to give the world of Falcon to you, to be the main source of the new population. We have several other worlds that will contribute small numbers of people. You may use both Mirka's natural population as well as unmarked clones for three generations, without review. We will provide transport, and technical and logistical support."

A buzz went around the room. The middle queen looked into the eyes of each of her sisters for a moment and then spoke. "Will we control the future Genomic upgrades for the humans and even native species? Will we be the only control of future modifications?"

"You can be in control of everything that you can manage and we will help with what you desire. You will probably only be able to populate a section of the world in the first generation, but we want you to have total control of the genomes there. You have done such a fine job here, I can imagine no better people to hand Falcon over to. I think you will find the people of Minoro and Niocene to be compatible and they will be immigrants. I believe that both worlds will need and respect your help with integrating their genome into the fabric of Falcon. On the planet Niocene there is a non-human intelligent species, the MacTau, as well as native plants and animals which will also have settlements on Falcon. The ancient race known as the Goblorks will have a few small colonies and will deal with the Brilliant Machine core."

"Will we incur any financial risk?" the middle queen asked.

"We will fund all transport and required initial import." Geardon smiled. "I might also mention that Falcon is an extremely rich world."

"We are honored to accept, pending a complete review of Falcon and their genome," the three queens said in unison.

Geardon wondered if the queens used secret communication or if they had developed true telepathic abilities. He made a mental note to look into it later. Placing his hands together, he said, "I thank you on behalf of the United Star Alliance and I thank you personally."

The middle queen said, "We will require a delegation to visit this world and return a personal report. Jennifer, are you available?"

She nodded. "Yes, Royal Mother."

"Raymond, you are wise about the affairs of Mirka and the changes this will bring in our history. Your wife is a great scholar. Are the two of you available to visit this world?"

Chief Councilor Raymond Vinci replied, "I would be most honored and I am sure my wife Rosemary would be as well."

The queens appeared silent in thought for a moment, then one said, "Logistic director Mitchell Hershel and his wife Romulli, Science councilor June Baritrol and her husband Jack, security and technology genius Peter Schmidt, and the royal twins, Meara and Neara Seeram will also go with you. They are all employed in our royal services and will be ready in a week."

Geardon told them, "My ship, the Golden Flash is very fast and can hold many passengers in luxury. My pilot, Ms. Liam will accompany us, as well as my security adviser, Ms. Cynthea Nestler."

The center queen announced, "It is settled, then. The Mirka delegation will be ready in a week. Let us celebrate this occasion."

As hover-trays of food and drink began to circulate, Jennifer rose and offered a hand to indicate Geardon should also stand. She looked him in the eyes with what he'd come to think of as 'that look' again. They approached the Royal Mothers and stood before them in silence, as the women scrutinized him. He held their gaze with steady eyes. Jennifer then gently took his hand and led him out of the assembly room.

Once inside the levitators, a million questions seemed to bubble out of Jennifer. Geardon smiled at her. "Remember all that for later - we have so much to do. First the global announcements to gather the volunteers. We're hoping for about a sixth of Mirka's population."

"A sixth?" Jennifer replied as her mind spun at the implications.

"A sixth would be optimal," Geardon continued. "Once we get volunteers, we can make the preparations for the first of a dozen departures. Falcon is an opulent world with everything the new population will need. I will stay on the project for a few years as the liaison."

She lifted her gaze to his and in her eyes he saw more than the new world he had just offered the queens.

# 21. The Survivor

When Draco paged Eerin, she thought he sounded more insecure than she had ever heard him. He was in a hurry for her to come to him, and sounded almost hysterical, as if he needed her. She excused herself from Dalla and immediately appeared in his study as directed.

She smiled at Draco, trying to be reassuring. "What's going on?"

"One of the wanderers that went beyond the towers has returned."

"Is he all right"

"He is quite unusual and has a strange effect on things. I would like you to meet him."

"Okay, but what do you mean by strange effect? Is he dangerous?"

"He might be a quite destabilizing influence, but I do not think he is dangerous. I asked him to wait and am not sure what to do. He dissolves our doings. Come." Draco motioned her to the door.

They entered a levitator tube and it opened into the lower levels of the towers that separated Chaos from the realm. Draco seemed very nervous. As they walked through a doorway, their clothes suddenly disappeared. Eerin gasped and turned to Draco, who had transformed into a fat, middle-aged bald man. He turned red as a beet at her scrutiny.

Draco explained, "I was a mathematician, working as a technician, when I made a few very important system changes that dramatically saved processing power for the planetary systems. I was rich beyond my wildest dreams, but was too much of a data head to need the money, so I worked my way up through the security system, until I dominated the behind the scenes government working on above top secret projects. When I conceived of my greatest invention, the translator, this is how I looked. I volunteered to test my own creation and when I translated those many years ago, this was my last form."

He stopped abruptly and pointed. "There is the Survivor. I'll leave you to talk to him and report back."

Draco turned quickly and retreated down the hallway, leaving her alone with what could be a dangerously unstable individual.

Eerin was uncomfortably aware that she was naked also, with not even clothing for protection. Until now, she had not been aware of the ways she had learned to make herself appear older than what she had been when she left her body on Falcon. She found she liked her young body, and smiled happily to experience it in such purity, despite the disturbing situation she was in.

Not knowing what else to do, she approached the survivor. He looked to be in his thirties and in great physical shape. His hair was short and curly brown. His body was tan, lean, and muscular.

"Hello," she said.

"Hello," he replied.

Eerin looked into his clear sparkling eyes, then felt compelled to close the distance between them. She boldly gave him a big hug. Pulling back, she noticed a tear trickle down his face. She backed up but still held his two hands. "It's okay, you are back in the realm. You are safe here for eternity."

He looked intensely at her and she noticed a cold emptiness in his eyes.

"You can let yourself manifest anything. Why do you undo our doings? Why did you dissolve my clothes?"

He seemed to become aware that his undoing was a doing. He closed his eyes, took a deep breath, and let out a sigh. "In the chaos, anything you do is twisted a million ways, so you learn undoing."

"Is undoing something that anyone can learn?"

"I don't know."

He became very calm and for a moment, even their bodies became translucent, as if they existed in a void. Then he seemed to generate all his will and released some of his undoing.

She clothed herself in the simple jeans and tee shirt that she liked to wear before the translation. He also appeared clothed, but as though it was a struggle to maintain.

He asked, frowning, "Who is that man who brought you here? Is that Draco?"

She giggled. "Yes, but not as I'm used to seeing him. Did you know him?"

"Of course. He was present when I entered the chaos realms."

"What's it like out there? When I gaze from the tower, I feel like I am watching a fairy tale."

The survivor took a deep breath. "The machine intelligence is absolutely inhuman. It is not cruel, nor is it compassionate. It just tests your soul in a million ways. It's so intense. You experience birth and death countless times. Everything in your mind is scrutinized and replayed. You feel like you are flipping between heaven and hell, with no control. Then I learned undoing, complete detachment. Some part of me died, perhaps my ego, and I just became empty. I don't know if that was the teaching of the Brilliant Machine, or just the inevitable result."

She looked compassionately into his eyes and first their clothes disappeared again, then their bodies, until it was like they were floating in infinite void, but still some part of them was looking into each other's eyes. Eerin summoned great determination, re-manifesting her body, which caused his body to form also. She then dressed herself and transported them both into her private garden.

He seemed to be in a state of ecstasy, experiencing the land she had created. He breathed deeply of the fragrant breeze and gazed at everything. He bent over a rose and smelled it, then began crying.

"It's so very beautiful."

"Thank you," she replied with a proud smile.

"Come on – come see my pavilion," she said, taking his hand.

She led him to a simple private pavilion that overlooked a lake with lotus flowers and swans. He seemed for a moment to become sexually excited; then he blushed.

"I can have feelings without the machine mind testing them," he stated, almost as much a question as a statement.

She was not offended by the physical manifestation of his feelings. "You can have whatever feelings you want, as long as you respect others."

He looked down. "I'm sorry."

"It's alright. How long has it been since you've had a good meal?"

He looked puzzled, so she waved a hand at a table that stood by the opposite wall, and a banquet appeared. "Hope you like my cooking," she said, winking.

He giggled at the slight paradox of her words, then put his hands together and bowed. "My most gracious host, I am most honored to share a meal created from your lovely hands."

She swatted at him good naturedly. "Come on, let's eat."

So they filled large plates of food and sat by the pagoda window, looking out at the lake and enjoying the taste of delectable food.

He seemed lost in the sensations of all his senses, relishing each bit of food and just being.

Eerin felt calm in his presence, like he was totally here and now, without any other thoughts or hidden agendas.

At last he seemed to sit back and reassess his situation. "I feel more alive than ever before in the realm. Thank you for rescuing me."

"I didn't rescue you. Draco just invited me to meet you and we've become friends."

He again seemed to experience waves of emotion. For a moment, he bowed his head and tears rolled down his cheeks.

"What's the matter?" she asked gently.

"Miriami," he whispered.

She just gazed at him as he sobbed, then he got a grip on himself and continued. "I was alone in the realm for a very long time. It is a sort of timeless place, where there is no reckoning of days or seasons. Things change according to the whims of the Brilliant Machine's will. I relived my past and was tested and dragged through it over and over again. I prayed for release and also for death, though I wondered if I were dead already.

"Then I met Miriami. I thought she was a game of the Machine, who had manifest many women for me, but then she thought the same of me. We tested each other; the Machine Intelligence had tested us for so long, that was all we knew. We came to realize that we were both living souls. Fortune had it that she met another woman though a portal that she had been trying to create to get back into the realm. The woman found two friends to help her and they became our allies in fighting chaos. The three women were somehow special and destined to help us from beyond through their oracle, which connected to Miriami's portal. We built a castle and a little realm amidst the chaos. We fought the Chaos together. Eventually we fell deeply in love."

He again lost some of his control and paused as a tear ran down his cheek. Eerin just waited patiently until he continued. "One timeless day we were together like we were in paradise. Our little haven was secure and we shared stories of our journeys and laughed at our follies. Neither of us had laughed since we entered the chaos. Then we called forth sunshine as we lay on a mat of divinely soft moss and we made passionate love. She fell asleep in my arms and...and just faded away.

"I was alone. I cursed the Machine Intelligence, not that I hadn't done that a million times before, but I believed that this had been its most elaborate trick, to steal my love.

"Then a small synthetic life form approached me. It told me simply, 'She reached inner peace and died.' I cried and cried. I had no desire to live and no fear of death. The core could not manipulate me anymore, so it brought me to the gate and again I entered this realm between chaos and reality that you call home."

Eerin hugged him, and then said, "I met those three women."

He immediately brightened. "Really, how are they? Can we visit them?"

She held his hands and looked into his eyes. "After what happened to Miriami, Florence and Alice decided to become babies again, but Caroline stayed in her form. They are in a place called Mage Land. It's part of the realm where many limits similar to physical reality exist and lots of laws. It's a strange place, but we could go there sometime, if you like."

Then Eerin asked, "So what are you going to do now?"

The question caught him off guard. For a moment, the scene seemed to flicker from the impression of total realness into translucent void. He stared blankly when the world they shared again appeared to be reality. He then said, "I don't know. I'm afraid I will melt into the void when I leave you."

"You can create any world you like here." She had a sudden idea. "Perhaps you should start a school of undoing! You could take on students. I want to learn this art or power. If we could see through others' doings that would make great changes in this society. We are evolving here, whether anyone likes it or not."

"I would be honored to have you as my student, as long as you also continue to be my teacher. I need to relearn doing. It is like learning to walk again."

"Deal," she said and stretched out a hand to shake.

He shook hands and then seemed to ponder things.

Eerin asked, "Do you have other friends here? You could start by visiting them and just being in their worlds without even letting them know you can undo their realities. That way you could get readjusted to living as a virtual being."

"That's a great idea. I did indeed have many friends. They will notice how I have changed. You still look like your original self. You have not reverted to the slightly older and more mature version you were when you first approached me. Why is that? Have I damaged your reality?"

She stood and, smiling deeply, let her clothes change to a sheer skin suit. She ran her right hand down along the side of her body. "I liked my body that I left behind. I am happy with it."

He gazed intensely at her and then turned his head. She realized that she was probably pulling desire from him.

She then changed to her older, more mature look. "I can be this person if I want to, but you have helped me to return to some essential part of myself. Thanks."

She changed back to her young original being and simultaneously wove a plain cotton dress about her. "Will you really teach me undoing?"

"I'll try, but not yet. I need to ground myself in this reality first."

"I understand," she said smiling. "My friend Dalla os probably wondering what I'm up to. We are engaged. Do you want to meet him?"

"Sure."

"Let's go to my porch, where Dalla and I usually hang out between adventures."

"Okay." He sounded a bit nervous.

They were suddenly transported to her balcony porch, sitting on the stately stone furniture with its ornate fiber covers, looking out over another lake.

"You like lakes and water?"

"Yea, I find it calming. It helps me think."

"About what?"

"Everything. I probably think too much. Most people here just dig in to the living and don't think much." She looked at him for a moment, then asked, "Should I call Dalla?"

"Okay. By the way, what's your name?"

"Eerin Shakti Mahavishnu, at your service." They both smiled.

"Shakti Mahavishnu, the goddess energy of the unity of creation. Your parents named you to be someone great."

"Well, actually, they taught me to be humble and see the Goddess in all creation. They are really caught up in materialism, but use philosophy as a subterfuge, which also taught me to be authentic. Perhaps that's why I seem to be a little lost here; I liked the real world. Even if some think this is paradise, I feel like some kind of fire is missing which we had in our incarnations."

"I understand," he replied solemnly. "I went into the Chaos looking for answers. I didn't get what I expected, but learned to drop expectations. How do you call your friend Dalla?"

"I sent him a mental telegram, inviting him to meet my guest. He lives with me, but he's busy doing things."

After a slight pause, Dalla appeared. He was clothed in a simple tunic. "Hello my love," he smiled at Eerin, then turning to the guest, he introduced himself, extending his hand. "Dalla."

"James," said the survivor, shaking Dalla's hand. "Nice to meet you."

Turning back to Eerin, Dalla said, "Eerin, you look young again, like when we left the material world. Nice." Dalla smiled, then questioned. "So, what did Draco want, if I might ask?"

"Well, James here has just returned from the chaos beyond the towers and needed someone grounded to help him back into our world, so Draco picked me." She replied, thinking she should not say too much.

Dalla looked at James for a moment, then said, "We heard that a few people went missing. Are you okay?"

James momentarily undid them and Dalla started laughing. He also liked his younger self and saw how he had grown a bit older and more dignified. The undoing faded quickly.

Dalla said, "Wow. That was great. How did you do that?"

Eerin told him, "It's the art of undoing. He is going to try to teach us."

"I'm glad you don't mind," said James. "I don't quite have control yet. Draco hated it."

Dalla laughed, "I'm sure he did."

Then he looked to Eerin and raised his eyebrows, hoping for some more descriptive narrative.

Eerin shook her head. "Never mind. To Draco he was just the Survivor. That man has a lot of learning to do."

"Okay," Dalla smiled, imagining powerful Draco with no control over a situation. "Hey, I'll bet your friends Marvelin and Nina would understand something of this."

James sat up. "You know Marvelin and Nina? How are they doing?"

Eerin looked at him curiously. "They are doing great. They monitor the world of the Morphs. They created the Mage Land where your three helpers lived. How do you know them?"

"I know all the first travelers. I came here in the second wave. I was an explorer, always looking to the mystery. I entered the chaos a few years after they got here." James had an inquisitive look as if a million questions were in his mind.

"Well, all of Falcon is here now, and Dalla and I don't know many people. We are happy just being together most of the time. Would you like to visit Marvelin and Nina?" Eerin asked.

"Sure," James seemed excited. "What is the protocol?"

"I don't know the protocol," Eerin giggled. "Let me see what they are up to."

She called out to the blue sky, "Marvelin and Nina, are you available? I have a guest that you should meet."

Nina replied as a voice in the air, "Why of course child. We are in our cabin and have just finished our meditation. Come visit."

"Is it ok to bring our guest?" Eerin asked.

"Yes, please do," was her reply from the sky.

Eerin turned to Dalla. "I won't be long."

He replied, "Take whatever time you need. I'm elaborating the lands of the march gate. I love you."

"I love your too." Eerin said and then took James' hand and they materialized in Marvelin and Nina's cabin.

Marvelin recognized James, but hesitated to believe his eyes. "James?"

"Yes, back from the chaos, as some would say."

Marvelin hugged him warmly, and then Nina stepped in to hug him, too. With the sudden surge of emotions, James' undoing energy again made the scene momentarily transparent.

Eerin told them, "He has the power of undoing. I thought you all could understand it and help him readjust to living somewhere."

Nina replied, "Thank you dear. This is indeed a possibility we had contemplated, living here with the Morphs, but we have not been able to manifest this power."

James asked, "What are Morphs?"

Marvelin answered, "Changelings who forgot their original human form."

Eerin added, "We are all a bit like that, but the Morphs are way exaggerated."

Nina asked her, "How's Dalla. He's always welcome, you know."

"I know, he just thought that under the circumstances it would be easier if I just brought James on my own. His projects keep him busy."

Then as an afterthought, she added, "Maybe if James undid the Morphs, they could be cured of some of their excesses."

"A very astute conjecture, but we will need to contemplate the ramifications deeply, before entering into their karma any deeper that we already have," Marvelin replied.

"You are very in tune, Eerin," Nina complimented.

Nina provided some tea, then said to James, "You must tell us of your journey, though I know words cannot convey the full experience. Many years you have been gone, so the telling will be long, yet we would like to hear as much as you are able to share."

Marvelin interjected, "We should go to a power place, perhaps the overlook."

"Most certainly, the upper cabin," Nina agreed.

"You have another cabin?" Eerin was surprised, since they did not seem to own much.

"A humble place." Marvelin replied and drained his tea. "Come along."

The others also drained their glasses and although Eerin expected them to appear at the other cabin, Marvelin and Nina headed out the door on foot, so Eerin and James followed along. Karma, Nina and Marvelin's dog, came running up as soon as they were outside and joined them for the walk. They hiked up a steep path and the journey was quite strenuous, almost as if they were in

Mage Land. As the trail wound back and forth, increasingly impressive vistas came in to view. Finally, they came to a saddle and were able to look over the other side of the mountain and gaze at a vast sea in the distance. The view was awe-inspiring. It was here that a humble cabin sat, with the front porch looking out over the vast horizon.

Nina put the kettle on and soon had a large pot of tea ready. They settled on the porch and enjoyed the vista. James spent hours telling them tales from the realms of chaos, and interspersing tales of Miriami's that he had learned. He seemed so excited and relieved to be able to tell his story. When he finally got to the part of his love and Miriami fading he seemed as if a new peace had come over him. They sat there without speaking for a long time and the reality started to fade.

Eerin said, "Come here Karma." She picked the dog up and held him in her lap.

As the virtual reality became transparent, they each appeared as a ball of light. James seemed to expand into the vastness. Karma seemed to expand for a moment, but Eerin held him tight and maintained awareness of physical contact. Then a mountain bird sang a lone song and the scene returned, but James was gone.

Nina spoke first. "You saved our Karma, Eerin. Thank you."

The paradox caused them to laugh, but then Eerin started to cry. "But what about James?" she finally mumbled.

Marvelin replied, "Dharma is a law that transcends any power of the Brilliant Machine. No intelligence within the universe can be the ultimate controller. The Way prevails regardless of any being's will, even the Brilliant Machine's."

Nina added, "Love is the most powerful force in the universe."

"Do you think they're together?" Eerin asked.

"Why of course, dear. They are just on the other side, between lives." Nina smiled.

"They still need more lives after they found peace?" Eerin asked.

"To complete their love and to find the higher love that encompasses the community and the totality of life's river, they will be reborn. Even the Brilliant Machine knows it has to serve the whole river of life, though it has a lot to learn, as do all of us." Marvelin sighed.

After sitting for a few more moments in quiet contemplation, Eerin told them, "I guess I should be heading home to Dalla."

Marvelin said, "Really, do come back and visit. Bring Dalla next time."

"I will," she replied with a nod.

She then bowed and disappeared, reappearing on the porch.

Dalla, looked at her questioningly.

"James faded away."

"What do you mean, faded away?" he asked.

"He died," she said and choked up.

He took her into his arms and she cried a bit, and then felt a calmness return to her being, like things were going to be all right.

Still holding his hands, she stepped back and looked at Dalla, who has remained in his younger form. "You look like you did when we left Falcon."

"So do you," he replied smiling and drew her to him, kissing her. They transported to a sunny field of flowers and made love passionately; and life was good.

# 22. Reconnaissance

As Miranda Liam piloted the shuttle disk in a gradual descent through the clouds of Falcon, a view of the rich green of the forest came into view. Jenny exclaimed, "Look at the sparkles of color in the forest and those seven perfectly round lakes."

"Those lakes are the landing pads," Geardon explained. "The sparkles are the dwellings. I kept a few details out of my briefings. The beauty and wonder of this world must be experienced first-hand."

"Well, I have a few secrets that I've saved for you also." Jenny smiled coyly, curling a lock of her dark hair around her finger. She winked, then said, "We were all hoping that this world would surprise us."

"Oh, you will be most pleasantly surprised," he assured her, trying not to let it be obvious that he was stunned by her beauty.

They watched from the ship window as the disk came down low and began to glide over the forest, approaching at a low angle. The landing pads became glimmering bands shimmering amid the forest foliage.

"Look, the landing pads are merging into the forest, and the dwellings are like bubbles of color glowing," said Jenny, excited by the view.

"The original inhabitants of Falcon did more than just melt into the forest," Geardon replied cynically. "They had true artistic vision in the design of this world. When they left their bodies behind and bequeathed their world to a worthy branch of humanity, we needed a population as pure as your Mirka for the colonization. Most of the plants and animals on Falcon have been genetically upgraded to level fourteen, but the brilliant leaders were very selective in the occasional patches they chose. You will have much work to do in sorting out the planetary ecology and colonizing this world with your world's population and the additions of two others. You have the perfect experience, since Mirka was populated from scratch after the meteorite collision disaster."

Jenny smiled at him. "We ambassadors need to truthfully present the many aspects of this planet to our world's population. Many are already anxious for our reports. The rumors of the riches of this world spread fast across Mirka."

"There are answers to many questions that we must discover and many new questions are certain to arise," he replied. "Several dignitaries from the other selected worlds, Minoro and Niocene, will meet us for open dialog later about their roles. First we need to explore."

Their star-disc silently came to rest upon the landing platform. Geardon and Jenny stepped out with the other eighteen dignitaries who would oversee the colonization.

Geardon took Maya aside. "Could you go before us and in a stealth fashion check on the Wandini for me?" he asked. "I've had some premonitions that they have had some kind of trouble and I feel very responsible for them. I've wondered if it was wise to leave them without a chaperon in an alien natural environment."

Maya changed into her Wandini-like elfin form. "I would love to go visit them. Your connection to them across light years distance is most fascinating. Can you elaborate on your premonitions?"

He answered, "Just that they have had some problems and I am really hoping they are alright."

Maya replied, "I could access the planetary monitors and review recent events for all of them in a moment."

Geardon looked at her knowingly. "Of course you could, but in this case, just go there and see if they need any help, then report back."

"With pleasure," Maya replied, then bowed and disappeared.

As the dignitaries left the ship, they all stared at their reflections in the landing platform's reflective surface. Jenny even did a swirling dance. "It's like we're walking on softened mirrors, reflecting light like still water. I can see the white fluffy clouds under my feet."

Geardon watched her dance so smoothly in her one-piece flight skin; it seemed as if she were really dancing on the clouds. He spoke aloud to the whole group, "If you look forward, the edge blends into the forest."

Jenny asked, "In which direction do we go?"

Geardon smiled at her. "Toward the rising of the sun: from where the light enters our lives and where all of Falcon's doorways are located."

She looked at him with surprise at hearing that such ancient traditions were still being followed on an advanced world. He shrugged and swept his arm out with a flourish, indicating the closest side, southeast, and signaling for the others to follow. Geardon took Jenny's hand for a moment as they walked to the edge of the landing platform.

The disc they had arrived in was small, compared to the size of the landing platform. The monolith could provide a solid base for a hundred star discs the size of theirs, or for a huge star freighter. At the edge, there were symbols in a geometric alphabet that shone golden upon the watery silver of the landing pad. There were also arrows pointing to the steps that led off the giant soft mirror. The steps were dull by comparison, and looked as though they had been carved out of rock.

After all the dignitaries had descended the stairs into a patio garden, Geardon explained, "The main spaceport facilities are under these landing platforms and are robotically maintained. Everything is more than sufficient for the colonization. There are ships ready with full energy banks. The Falconians prepared well."

He then keyed a pattern into a panel with sixty-four symbols, a very ancient form of security, and a large levitator opened for them. They entered it, and an instant later, exited into a plush briefing room.

"The levitators contain their own gravitational fields, allowing high speed transport in the city under the landing platforms. Robotic servants will provide whatever you want for dinner," Geardon told the delegation. He then called out, "Service please." Soon hovering spheres were taking orders from all the ambassadors. Hovering trays then brought the food an instant later.

While they ate, Geardon showed the delegation 3-D images of several dwelling sites. Then he explained their intended agenda. "We will break up into several parties. First, we'll each spend some of our time on this planet in the family dwellings, to understand what a family would be presented with. Then we'll meet at a group settlement. The more elaborate city structures will be visited as people decide what adventures they want to experience. There is a hover craft waiting to take each group of ambassadors to a family dwelling to relax and experience Falcon's humble opulence."

Cynthea took Geardon aside. "I know you have me accompanying you and Jenny, but I think you two should go alone. I'm going to stay back and study in the robotic works below as a security official should."

"Are you sure?" Geardon asked, suspicious of her motives.

Cynthea smiled. "Woman's intuition tells me you two will discover more without me and I am very drawn to understanding more about Falcon's defenses. After all, my main job is to protect this world, and politics may not be enough. Also, there is another security person, Peter, who wants to have a look at the systems."

Geardon thought it all sounded reasonable. "Well, good. Oh, and I'm glad that you seem to be back to your old self."

Cynthea just winked, spun about, and made her way to a levitator.

\*  \*  \*  \*  \*

Dalla said, "I heard that the Genome auditor has returned to Falcon with a whole group of dignitaries."

"Really? How did you hear that?" Eerin asked.

"Well, I told my brother to let me know of any rumors he heard. I actually expected they would have been back sooner."

"Should we go top-side and spy on them? I mean, to see what's going on." Eerin had a mischievous look on her face.

"Sure, let's go," Dalla replied without hesitation, a bit to her surprise.

They watched as Geardon explained Cynthea's decision to go her own way to Jenny and although he seemed puzzled by it, she seemed to take it in stride. Geardon and Jenny seemed comfortable together, as if they had known each other for a long time.

"Let's follow Cynthea into the security lair," Dalla said.

"I want to follow Geardon," she replied with a pouting face, then smiled. "You follow her and I'll follow him."

"Okay." He gave her a quick kiss, then hesitated before running off.

She smiled. "It'll be better. We'll know more this way."

He looked at her with love in his eyes and then they kissed longer and hurried about their business.

\*  \*  \*  \*  \*

Upon arriving at the exit port, Jenny exclaimed, "These hover discs are unlike any I have ever encountered. The outside is a reflective sky blue as if to hide it in the sky. Inside, this hovercraft is like a flying carpet, but with sides and a windscreen at the forward end. They look like they were designed more for having fun, than as serious transportation."

"A variable gravitational shield compensates for acceleration pressures on the riders," said Geardon. "No one can fall out and there is no wind, unless you want some. They are referred to as sky-cars and are the standard design on Falcon."

As they stepped inside one and sat down, she said, "Look at these plush reclining seats – enough for six people to relax in. Very different from the utilitarian design that most worlds employ."

As they took to the air, she continued, "This is really flying in luxury. And look out at the beautiful forest!" Jenny beamed.

"The Falconians were consummate artists in every aspect of life. I bet they could have an entire city hidden from our view. The gravitational suspensors are totally silent in this sky-car so that walkers in the forest wouldn't notice us. This world will still appear mostly empty, even after the colonists arrive," Geardon surmised.

"I like it. We could be close to people and events without feeling crowded. The people who left this world had a beautiful balance of art, nature, and technology. Mass suicide is incomprehensible; and these were some of the galaxy's leading mathematicians and scientists." Jenny frowned. "It's ironic, but I'm learning that they really understood how to enjoy life."

"Many things may be uncovered. The robotic system and memory banks don't hold much information. The saying keeps playing in my mind. 'We are leaving our bodies, but we are not leaving you. We found the higher path and took it. Now humanity shall be fortunate in the Way. We live forever in virtual paradise.' I don't accept the premise," Geardon replied. "They had paradise, yet wanted more. I believe they ended up with less. It doesn't sit right with me."

"Me either - I save lives. Even though some people must pass through great suffering, when they are healed, they are grateful. Life is the most precious thing," Jenny said emphatically.

"Look there!" Geardon exclaimed.

"Beautiful!" They looked out over seven large elongated crystal domes built in a circle, just touching each other. They had milky white bases and tops the colors of the rainbow. Jenny was enraptured.

The craft lowered itself into the middle of the ring of domes, which was a courtyard garden. The hovercraft landed in the garden center, on a shiny rock about ten centimeters high. There were seven paths of the same shiny stone leading to seven doors.

Jenny smiled, "We may as well take the path to the one open door." As they walked along the path, she said, "Look at all the plant varieties; it looks like a medicinal garden."

"The houses we're staying in are Falcon's standard homes," Geardon explained. "There are twenty million of these houses scattered about on this planet. Mostly young families lived in these. The communal villages housed about forty million people. The final forty million lived in the cities."

"What a wonderful world," Jenny sighed as she stepped through the doorway and into the oblong kitchen. "I really like the luminous white walls and how clear portions of the crystalline wall material form windows to keep it bright and well lit. And look at all the shelves of crystal plates, bowls and pots, but no food synthesizer. How strange."

Geardon nudged her playfully. "Know how to cook?"

"Of course. I love to camp and cook over an open fire."

"Me, too," he said, looking in her eyes for a moment, amazed that they shared so much in common.

They hopped a lift to the second floor, where the dome above them was a light yellow. A round table sat in the middle of the oval. On the side opposite the lift there were rows of crystalline cabinets.

Jenny laughed. "I feel like a kid exploring some stranger's house."

Geardon was enjoying himself. "Me, too. Let's check out the rest of the rooms."

Geardon watched appreciatively as Jenny's sleek form glided around the table and then to the lift where he was waiting. On the way down, she smiled at him and said, "They seem to have enough utensils and supplies stored here to provide for all kinds of situations."

He nodded. "And it's all made of material that will last for thousands of years."

They passed through a door at the right side of the kitchen and into the water dome. Jenny said, "Look at the large hot tub and cold water swimming pool. Those milky crystal walls must separate the toilets and showers from the pool area." Walking over to a deck area on the south side, with the sun shining through a clear window, she said, "I love the way the window and wall material meet the green dome top in a tree-like fractal pattern."

The next room was a bedroom. Crystal chests lined the walls amid several beds, each with a window above it. Some looked out at the forest and some looked in towards the garden. The floor was covered in a checkerboard pattern of meter-square [yard-square] light and dark blue stones, surrounded by triangular patterns. The center of the room was open like a giant game board with each square or triangle big enough for a person. There was a walled balcony area with only ladders along the walls to get up into it. The deep blue hue of the dome top made the room very blue.

The next room was an indigo equivalent of the blue room, but somehow more feminine. There was shiny material around the beds, hanging from the balconies. The balcony was railed, instead of walled, as in the blue room. The gaming patterns on the light and dark purple floor included symbols in the contrasting color. When Jenny walked out onto the floor, holographic people appeared on some squares. As Jenny moved from square to square, the people would also move. Then one disappeared, as the next square had a person in it, restricting the move. A player close to Jenny asked her, "Do you want some advice, my lady?"

"No, I think for now we'll continue to explore the house, thanks." The virtual player bowed as Jenny made her way off the game board.

"That was some very realistic gaming," she said to Geardon as he took her arm and led her to the next room. It was the terminal room, with many desks along the wall, each with a window. Strange gear was sitting about several of them, the tools of the math wizards. The center had a large table with a data sphere in its center. A 3-D image of a man and his wife appeared. According to bios that displayed, the man and woman were forty-six and forty-eight, and their daughter was eighteen. They looked to be very healthy, attractive people.

The man spoke, "Hi, I'm Geoffrey Mahavishnu and this is my wife Margarette. Our family was the last to inhabit this house. There are records of all the inhabitants, their art, music, and stories in many formats. This is my final upload before my translation. Here is a poem that I wrote for the realm:"

The virtual image recited,

"Freedom always has limits,
even when you are free of space,
time binds us to one direction,
though our course forever changes.

Awareness we seek to expand,
to incorporate more subtle realms,
and comprehend the nature of life
as we fulfill our true destiny."

The man bowed and the image faded. Geardon shivered. Jenny asked, "Are you OK?"

Geardon said, "They looked familiar. I couldn't help but think of Eerin dying."

Jenny returned to their earlier conversation. "I have spent some time studying attempts to transfer a person completely into the cyber-world, but all you get is a program that gradually loses initiative to act and becomes static, waiting for input. Without physical needs and desires, a mere quest for knowledge will not suffice. Even the Brilliant Machine needs the countless life forms of the universe to feed itself with information and momentum."

"I know," he replied. "The computer data of a person does not constitute life, there is no life force. The Brilliant Machine feeds on the data of all living beings, but it's only alive in its vastness and programmed tasks. This is somehow different, because their souls never made it to the realm of the dead."

They were interrupted as a ten-centimeter [four inch] silver sphere arose from a terminal and spoke to them. "Hi, I am Linus, the house servant. I can answer any questions you may have, guide you on walks through the forest and help you with meal preparation. I was told not to greet you at the door so that you could explore the house on your own. Did you enjoy yourselves?"

"Yes, very much," Jenny answered.

"Can I be of farther assistance?" the floating sphere inquired.

"What is the meaning of the former inhabitant's poem?" Geardon asked.

"I cannot interpret poetry, as it affects different personalities with different meanings. Geoffrey said he would not be dead and would remain in contact without his body," the sphere replied.

"How are you to receive his message?" Geardon probed.

"It would be a data transmission from the system core, without physical location. There seems to be a temporary lock down on the areas of transmission. The Brilliant Machine altered some of the inhabitant's designs in the core. I am not located in this silver sphere, or any particular space. This sphere is just one of my portals to the material world. The message is patterns of data and the message storage location shifts with time," the sphere explained.

"We will explore more on our own, thank you." Geardon told it, looking at Jenny who just shrugged.

"Thank you, just call my name anywhere in the house and I will come and be of whatever assistance I may," Linus said as the sphere returned to sit on top of a pad on the table.

They heard a knocking at the door. Geardon opened it to find Maya standing on the doorstep, still looking like a Wandini Fairy.

Geardon raised an eyebrow. "Polite of you to knock."

"I did not want to intrude. We have a problem."

Geardon frowned. "We?"

"One of the Wandini was injured in a bear hunt. They have been using herbs to keep the infection down. I had a robotic medical team go to them, but they tried to attack it."

"A bear hunt!" Geardon exclaimed loudly.

Jenny interrupted before he could say more. "How bad is she?"

"Without modern medicine, the infections could win. Without surgery her arm will never work right."

"Let's go to them. I think they will trust me." Jenny headed out the door, and Geardon and Maya followed her to the air car.

Upon arriving at the Wandini camp, they realized that Droga was in bad shape. She was lying in the cabin. The Wandini looked to Maya and then Geardon and Jenny. Jenny told them; speaking and pantomiming, that she needed to take Droga, while holding the image of herself healing her. Maya watched in fascination, as they seemed to understand.

Jenny said to Maya, "Materialize a stretcher, bring it in here, and lets walk her out of here."

When Maya returned, Jenny asked, "Can you manipulate gravity and ease Droga's pain?"

Maya replied, "Yes, I will minimize all shock to her system. Once we are out of close proximity viewing, I can make the stretcher hover."

"Great, let's get going," said Jenny.

Once they had hiked a fair distance, Maya brought the air car to them and they flew off with Droga. She was very sick, but was nevertheless fascinated to look over the side of the air car and realize she was flying.

They soon landed outside a modern medical facility.

Jenny told Maya, "Run in and get a powerful sedative. We need something she can drink. A bad taste is preferred."

Geardon raised his eyebrows. "A bad taste is preferred?"

"This is a Shamanic rite of passage for Droga. We must follow cultural norms for her spirit to be with us."

Geardon nodded to Maya and she ran to the facility. The time between when she entered the door and exited was only a couple of seconds, but while in Droga's sight, she moved like an athlete, rather than a super-powered being.

Jenny took the cup from Maya and held it up to the sky. Next she held it in front of her face and blew on it, then murmured a prayer under her breath into the liquid. She paused a moment, then handed the cup to Droga. Droga took a sip and sensing the vile nature of the liquid, seemed to cheer up, as if the vileness confirmed it as a very powerful medicine. She forced herself to down the full contents of the cup. In a matter of only a couple minutes, which seemed longer to Geardon, she passed out.

Jenny shook Droga to be sure she was completely unconscious, and then told Maya, "Okay, call the medical staff."

Moments later, robotic medical personnel came rushing from the building. Already linked to Maya, they let her float the stretcher in. Jenny and Geardon had to run to keep up. The robotic staff soon had Droga naked and were washing her down with antiseptics.

"I'm a trained healer, and want to be part of the operating team," Jenny told Maya.

Maya eyed her for a moment. "Generally human organisms are not as sterile as robotic doctors, yet you have a perspective that is useful, especially with an unknown alien physiology."

Maya then escorted Jenny through a shower and quickly gathered sterile clothing for her to put on.

Geardon walked about exploring the complex, occasionally querying a terminal for explanations. Several hours passed. Finally, Jenny called Geardon and then emerged, looking a bit tired. "Success. The infection was even greater than we had anticipated, but we have it under control and have sewn all the muscle tears together. There is a rustic meditation/worship center on the grounds. We found a room there with a window and Maya had it stripped of all possible technology. Thank goodness she could scan the entire complex almost instantaneously."

"We should be there with Droga, when she wakes up," Geardon said.

They walked over to the meditation center together. Droga woke in good spirits soon after they arrived and, even with all the strangeness, seemed glad to be alive. Since they were not able to communicate much with Droga, Geardon had Maya fetch his Shukasi flute, and then played for quite a while. Afterwards, Jenny gave Droga more sedatives and she fell asleep.

"I think we can return her to the Wandini camp tomorrow," Jenny told Geardon. "The cabin can be sterilized with a sonic oscillator and I can change the bandages as needed. I'll return here and move her in the morning."

Geardon and Jenny took the sky car back to the house and continued to explore. They discovered that the terminal room had an upper floor and when they ascended into it, found a meditation chamber filled with violet light. Pleasant herbal scents and gentle music filled the air. The body molding chairs had been placed in a big circle.

They went on to the next room. A large bed surrounded by curtains was in the center of it, with chests, shelves, and windows lining the walls. Doors to the side led out onto a balcony. They were surprised to find clothes laid out upon the bed, presumable placed there for them by Linus. They looked at each other shyly for a moment, then smiled at their primitive behavior and changed from the sleek flight skins into the new loose garments.

Jenny said, "What beautiful material, so soft and flexible."

Geardon agreed. "It's nano-cloth woven in soft strands, durable for several thousand years."

The final room, the orange room, also had an upstairs, so the light within was clear. Its walls were filled with crystal cabinets and shelves. It was arranged with various pieces of furniture and appeared to be a study and entertaining room. One side had a table, perhaps for tea.

"A very comfortable house," Jenny remarked when they had made the full circle and were back in the kitchen. "If this is typical of the living quarters on Falcon, I have no doubt our people will be delighted to move right in."

After exploring the house, they asked Linus to lead them on a moderate hike. They followed a creek that ran besides the dwelling. They wondered at the multitude of plants and animals that they saw. Linus let them know that the house stored enough food to last for years, but none of it was fresh. Linus stated that all his previous masters would periodically add fresh food, explaining that they believed it contains more life energy. Linus directed them to dig some roots and pick some fresh vegetables.

While in the forest, Geardon asked Jenny, "Do you feel watched?"

"Yes. I have since we got to this house." She looked at him and then they both scanned their surroundings. Eerin hid and they did not get a sense of her, but she was now even more caught up in the thrill of watching them.

Upon returning to the house, Linus asked, "May I help you in preparing the food?"

"Sure," said Jenny. "We've never used this kitchen before."

"It's easy once you get accustomed to it. First, we need to wash the vegetables. You can use the sink. We can get some water boiling. I will show you some options for spices from the center garden."

Geardon told the sphere, "I'll put on the water and wash the vegetables. Why don't you show me how to work the stove, and then take Jenny to look at the herbs."

The sphere hovered over to the stove, with the couple close behind. At the stove, Linus said, "You adjust heat in standard galactic Kalors with the red crystal dial. The only display is an auditory warning in case of any detected error or overheating. I continually monitor the stove."

"Thanks, Linus." said Geardon, as he looked at Jenny and smiled. Linus was already heading for the door calling, "This way, Jenny."

Geardon had all the vegetables steamed by the time Jenny and Linus returned. Soon they sat down to a wonderful, mostly fresh meal. They agreed that real food tasted superior to processed, preserved, or synthesized food.

After dinner, Geardon and Jenny decided to bathe. They walked into the water room and undressed shyly, even though shyness about being naked was not the nature of either of their characters or part of their cultural backgrounds. Geardon asked the house to play some meditative ambient music from the house's archives. They soaked in the hot tub and talked about how the people immigrating to Falcon would adapt to this world. Feeling soaked and very warm, they jumped into the cold pool of water and swam together. The water was frigid and soon the heat of the tub wore off. They got out and lay in the sun that was streaming in through the window.

After warming in the golden rays for a while, Geardon sat up and looked at Jenny's sleek form. She smiled and looked away for a moment, then looked him in the eyes unashamed. He nervously said, "You sure are a beautiful young lady."

She grinned. "Well, I may as well tell you one of my secrets: I'm the same age as you. My Prana exercises keep me healthy and young."

"My Chi routines keep me healthy too, but are geared for self-defense as well."

"Shall we practice?" She said, rising to her feet. He got up and stood facing her, with the sun beaming down on their now dry naked bodies. Slowly they each began the sets of movements specific to their art, stretching and bending in slow motion. The dance-like progression of moves, arms and legs circling to accumulate life energy, took their awareness deep within themselves. They both remained aware of each other's movements amidst their energy accumulation arts.

After half an hour of practice, she put her palms in the air to face him. He silently touched her hands with his, joining the power points in the center of their palms. They looked into each other's eyes and began to silently play mirror, moving their touching hands together as if they were looking at their reflection in a mirror. They stood spontaneously moving their arms to the slightest whim of each other's will until they were completely in tune to each other's movements. Slowly they became still, feeling the energy in the power points in their touching hands. Opening and staring deep into each other's eyes, they felt tremendous life force flowing through their bodies.

Ever so slowly, they began to share body movements and their form became an erotic dance as their bodies began brushing against each other. They explored form and movement by dancing with heightened awareness of their bodies' energy centers. They expressed their life force arts in movement and gradually increased the intensity. Finally, they came to rest in each other's arms in a long kiss.

They became passionately lost to any other reality, but each other's being. They pleasured each other as naturally as if they had been together forever. As they finally separated and looked deep into each other's eyes, they knew that there was peace between them.

Geardon was the first to speak. "I've never met anyone like you, Jenny."

She replied, "I'm feeling a special love for you. You are a true gentleman and have shown yourself to be worthy and noble."

Jennifer glanced over her shoulder, "I could have sworn I felt a young lady in the room for an instant when we were sharing ourselves."

"What did she look like?" He asked.

"I'm not sure, but she felt both shy and curious, like she was doing something wrong, but couldn't help herself."

Geardon reached out and brought Jenny back into his embrace. "Strange place, this planet is. I also felt observed, but didn't really care. I have not been intimate with a woman for many long years."

"It has been a long time for me as well," she replied and settled into his embrace.

# 23. Citadel

After a few days that seemed like a holiday, Geardon received messages from some of the ambassadors. Holographic ghosts had disturbed several of the guests. Geardon and Jenny got on their hovercraft and traveled to the colony where the others were gathering.

As they approached the colony, they followed a creek to a river. Jennifer spotted it first. "There's a spire above the trees."

"I'm sure visiting the colony will be a spectacular experience," said Geardon. "Each colony has a unique architecture based on mathematical concepts. This is one of the largest colonies and is almost like one of the cities. These colonies were strange spiritual universities where some of the universes' deepest secrets were unraveled. The members are said to have lived in very holistic communal groups."

Six more spires came into view. "Look at how the spires glisten in the sunshine," Jenny exclaimed. "There seem to be seven spires, with six spires around the larger center one. They look strange with their cone shape and rings of violet on white - maybe rings of amethyst surrounding milky quartz? The crisp white clouds floating in the blue sky are accentuating the beauty of the towers in a most amazing way."

"The number seven has always been mystical, just as a circle represents the sacred," Geardon said. "Six circles surround a center circle. The geometry of every aspect of the Falconians' architecture is mathematical, similar to the pyramids and other ancient structures of humanity. All who dwell in these mathematical designs are led to cultivate a specific viewpoint about the nature of the world and life. The Falconians were philosophers in every aspect of their lives - perhaps that is how they were tricked."

They were traveling just below treetop level and as they rounded a bend, they found themselves above a crystal clear lake.

Looking across the water, Jenny said, "The colony looks like a small city made of quartz. The other side of the lake is lined with reddish docks and blue crystal roads leading up among the yellow buildings. There are amethyst walls with open archways and wonderful gardens. Everything seems to lead up to the center spire. I feel like I've entered a fairy tale."

"The center spire is the center of activity, the place of research and administration," Geardon explained. "The other towers were living spaces, classrooms, and work areas. The color of the fused quartz building material is used systematically, as in the houses that we visited."

Moving quickly across the lake, they hovered over the red docks with many strange sailing vessels, some modern and some archaic, and then began to follow a blue quartz road to the center spire. The tower's base had a diameter of over a kilometer [point six mile]. They entered an open archway that was ten meters [thirty-three feet] both in height and width.

Geardon and Jennifer got out of the hovercraft, still holding hands. They were met by the twin delegates, Meara and Neara, who had been assigned as the leaders of this expedition by the ruling triplets of Mirka. The small young women smiled in a synchronized way, as if knowing what the other was thinking telepathically. They were dressed as identically as they appeared, in blue silky skin-suits. Their eyes were a brilliant hazel with other colors mixed in a sparkling fashion, shining like jewels in their fine-featured faces.

The twin delegates led them to a levitator chamber. When the chamber's doors opened, they walked out to the terrace café, high on the side of the giant spire, with a garden of plants and bushes that were planted in huge milk quartz pots. They saw a group of delegates sitting at an amethyst table surrounded by large plants and stopped to talk.

"Hi, how's everyone doing tonight?" asked one of the twins, looking at logistics adviser Mitchell Hershell, who was closest to her.

"Fine, fine." He indicated the bottle on the table. "You should try some of this ten year old grindle wine."

"Or a crystal clear miltsun liqueur," his wife Romulli suggested.

Across the table, the science councilor June Baritrol's husband, Jack, raised his glass. "The rizzil grain brew is also quite rich. Imagine leaving a world with such fine flavors. There must be a catch."

To which June, the science councilor, added, "Seems like this ghost stuff is some technological head game. There must be scientifically controlled devices creating these phenomena."

Mitchell asked the twins, "Have you looked over the wall yet? Dazzling view. What a grand place."

The two women nodded in unison and Meara said, "We are going to have a look now. And don't worry - we will discover the truth of these apparitions soon enough. Have a nice night all." The four of them headed toward the wall.

Jenny asked Neara, "Are all the expedition members somewhere on this level?"

Neara answered as they walked to the edge of the amethyst railing wall, "Yes, they are all gathered here. A few are feeling like their privacy is being invaded by these apparitions, though there is only a few reported visual apparition. The rest have just had feelings of being watched. Falcon is an old fashioned world in many of its customs and must have some sort of algorithm in its system to test foreigners."

Geardon pointed out to Jenny, "Look how the wall is graded in steps. It was smart to place the tables at the lowest parts, surrounded by amazing plants. Between the tables the wall is just right for standing and looking out over the colony below."

They stood by a section of the wall and viewed the city in awe.

Jenny said, "I love the terraced levels with gardens, lawns, and shrubs. I can imagine this colony filled with people. This could be such a vital place. Seeing the robotic servants working without any humans around gives me a lonely feeling."

Geardon nodded. "I really like the golden blue quartz walkways and arched bridges that follow the two rivers through the colony to the lake."

One of the twins said, "The deep purple quartz wall is shining so beautifully in the sun. Let's sit at a table along the edge, so that we can continue to feast our eyes."

They went around the plants and sat at a table where the wall was just slightly above table height. The large quartz planters around the table afforded some privacy. The view over the colony from this height was breathtaking. Soon hover-trays arrived to serve them food and drink as they talked.

After a few sips of their beverages, the twins began their tale. "We were in the forest exploring, guided by our house sphere. We walked along a five kilometer [three mile] trail to see a waterfall, which we were told was a very popular meditation spot for the Falconians. Our house sphere told us that the original population spent much time in deep concentration there, focusing on the space-time matrix of the universe. When we arrived, we felt a strange presence. As we meditated and centered, we began to sense ghost-like apparitions wandering around the waterfall. When we became aware of them, they became aware of us, and some began to manifest their presence more clearly. They seemed to be Falcon's dead, but unlike the dead that we have perceived before, they seem to be more present and less bound than the souls between lifetimes."

The other twin continued. "We asked the house sphere if it could perceive them, and with the core's help it acknowledged slight variations in the gravotronic monitoring system, only fainter and less coherent than anything in the physical world. It would have assumed that it was a random noise, but upon analysis determined that there was unusual congruent continuation through time. It stored digital images."

One of the twins held out a marble-sized holographic projector and projected the images, which were like colored shadows floating about the waterfall scenery. Geardon took it and touched it to his medallion when the sequence completed. The twin who had spoken first said, "We got that eerie feeling as the images became aware of us, that they didn't seem to be programmed holographic images, nor regular ghosts. They were definitely not random fluctuations in the psychic field."

Jenny shivered and said, "It must be related to the computer personalities that the Falconians digitally imprinted in the main system before they disappeared. We would assume they are very sophisticated and elaborate Synthetically Intelligent programs, but the Wandini whom Geardon brought contacted the dead, and the Falconians are not among the dead, at least not yet. Some of them might be visiting the surface."

Meara continued, "Several others in the group have had experiences of a similar nature. They all occurred around natural planetary features that were meditation sites for the Falconians or in private moments in their dwellings. Perhaps there is some connection between these natural places and the spirits of the Falconians in the machine. We had a search done on the Falconian breakthroughs of the last century and discovered among them several advanced holographic imaging technologies based on virtual mind controllers. These technologies are being used extensively by some races that are wired directly to their machines, like the delegates of Sigalin, whom we shall meet next week."

Drinking their wine of native Falconian fruit, they looked out over the colony glistening in the golden rays of the descending sun. The warming bath of reddish light seemed to infuse the world with the mystery and paradox that they were facing.

Neara stated, "We had further analysis done on the captured images. They are not coherent light and so we could not determine what could produce them. All the holographic technology, even the newest Falconian devices, use coherent light."

Geardon said, "Perhaps I could send some of the data to my ship for analysis. It has the most advanced equipment in the Galaxy, being a specialized aspect of the Brilliant Machine."

They all paused for a moment to watch the sun go down over the lake and forest beyond. A cold rush of wind swept past them. Jenny shivered and broke the silence, "This world is too lonely for only a few dozen visitors. The people of the chosen worlds should come soon. The ghosts do not appear to be a danger and many will find this an exciting aspect of their colonization."

Neara said, with her sister Meara nodding, "I agree, the planetary system must have a lot of junk code to maintain these Synthetically Intelligent people of Falcon. I feel no danger here. I think that the Falconians must have had some strange concept of living forever as virtual personalities. It seems so sad to think of all those people foolishly following such notions."

Cynthea approached their table, along with Peter Schmidt, the security and technology genius. After greeting everyone, Cynthea said to Geardon, "We need to talk."

She seemed unsettled, but Geardon replied casually, "Have a seat. Would you care for something to drink?"

Cynthea looked at Jenny briefly, then she and Peter sat down where the twins had been. Cynthea seemed nervous. "Geardon, you've met Peter. He is a security wizard and we were exploring the complex. It is very elaborate and extensive. Even if we wanted to breach the core, there are advanced robotic fighting forces at the ready. Several moons also have underground robotic forces and very advanced fighting ships."

Geardon nodded. "We were somewhat aware of this, but is this what you came to talk about?"

"No," Cynthea replied, taking a deep breath. "We worked all night and were so engaged as a team, that it was like have been doing it all our lives. Around dawn, we were exhausted and, well you know us spacers, we just ended up in bed together and were making love. I know that true spacers are very slow to mate before the community, since raising children is a community function, but we were alone, there was no community. When I was having an orgasm, I saw a young tan-skinned man walk up to us. I thought he was real, but his face was so placid, even my training did not cause me to enter into any defensive thoughts. We were looking at each other, but then he looked at my stomach and actually put his hand inside me. I felt him touch something inside me. It was a real feeling and then he dissolved into me."

Jenny laughed in a nervous way and Cynthea gave her an angry look. The two men were confused by Jenny's reaction, then Cynthea's expression softened and she asked her, "What?"

Jenny was beaming. "You two are going to have a baby."

Cynthea stood in shock, and snapped, "That's impossible! I have an alpha 99 block in place - they never fail!"

Geardon took Jenny's hand and then said, "We were also watched, but our watcher did not touch her, nor did we mate. Jenny is a Seer, so you can trust her intuition."

Cynthea took Peter's hand and looked hard at him.

Peter returned her gaze and smiled. "I love you, Cynthea. As unexpected and sudden as all this is, I'm absolutely delighted."

Cynthea looked from person to person, and then started crying. Peter stood and took her into his arms.

Finally, she said to him, "I love you too, even though I just met you, but this is too freaky. Let's take a walk, I need to think; or I guess, just let things settle in."

Geardon rose and gave her a hug and a kiss on the forehead, saying, "The universe has its own ideas for our destinies. Your path has been filled with many lessons. It's all good in the end."

She smiled weakly at him. "I hope so. Thank you for saving my life and being with me on this long journey."

He stood back and put his arm around Jenny, which caused Cynthea to smile. "I knew you were right for each other. As soon as you two set eyes on each other, you were entranced. I was giving you opportunity to get together and I guess the universe returned the favor to me."

Cynthea laughed and shook her head at the irony. "Come on, Peter," she said as she started to pull him along.

Peter looked at Jenny, "It has been a pleasure, Ancient One. I do not doubt your wisdom and gift: we will honor this new life."

Cynthea followed his lead and bowed to Jenny and then they walked quickly toward the levitator.

Jenny sighed. "I can deal with the ghost-like computer glitches haunting the world, but this changes everything. I think that the people of Falcon are ghosts in the Brilliant Machine rather than natural ghosts. Some are already yearning for their next incarnation or perhaps just destined to be reborn."

"You mean the Falconians are trying to come back from the virtual realm by being born through living humans?" Geardon shook his head. "What would that mean for the re-population effort?" Geardon said, thinking out loud.

Jenny had also been contemplating the consequences. "The people of the selected worlds would fit right into houses like the ones that we stayed in. Many would love to have families. These colony cities could continue to be the learning centers that guide this world. The people will require a different relationship to this environment than what they have on their worlds of origin, though.

It will require quite a bit of study and effort to maintain the wonderful abundance and natural beauty of Falcon, especially if other life forms are added for the MacTau from the planet Niocene. We could have minimal additional life forms from Minoro and Mirka, but they will both want to bring some. We will need data about the extent of robotic maintenance that exists and how versatile it is. The Goblorks are very wise and could be assigned as the heads of state."

Geardon pondered all that for a few moments, then said, "I have had endless virtual tours of this world, but I thought the delegates should experience the world first hand before making decisions about how to pitch it to their populations. We will need to find a way to explain these phenomena." Then he mumbled to himself, "I have a strange feeling that Eerin and Dalla are involved."

"Eerin and Dalla?" Jenny asked with curiosity.

"The Spirit seems to have isolated a few players and all the spirals of fate seem to have them at the center," he replied.

"Interesting." She smiled in wonder. "Let us join the others."

They talked until late. Finally, Jenny looked meaningfully at Geardon and they both stood and bid everyone goodnight.


Jenny and Geardon went to their assigned room and he showed her his communication cube. He had the cube transported to the colony from the star disk by Maya and so it was waiting in his room.

She was surprised. "It looks like a black mirror. Is that Germanium steel?"

Geardon nodded. "It is the highest security wide link to the Golden Flash and also to Genome headquarters. It works in conjunction with the medallion."

He told it to open, using the peculiar formal tone. "Geardon Stranoff, Galactic Genome Auditor, requests access 74027."

The panel opened and he touched his medallion to the indent on the inner surface. When a second panel opened, he spoke to the cube. "The images from the waterfall area that seem to be holographic ghosts - analyze them and return a status as to what type of device created them. If possible try and get information about any virtual Falconians who may have been on the surface."

He took a seat nearby and told Jenny, "We should have some kind of answer soon. The Brilliant Machines are far more able to comprehend such things than any organic beings are."

Within minutes, the readout returned and Geardon read it out loud. "Images are not coherent enough for holographic projection and yet appear to manifest in three dimensions as human forms. They appear to have an internal consistency that implies self-organization as living organic persons."

Jenny looked puzzled. "Is it saying that the Falconians are ghosts?"

Geardon wasn't sure. "Let me ask it to clarify."

Then speaking to the cube he said, "Please elaborate on the hypothesis of a life-like manifestation. Are we seeing the ghosts of Falcon?"

While they waited, Jenny asked Geardon, "What type of language is that screen showing? And why doesn't the cube just speak?"

He smiled. "It's an old Earth language, English, as cryptic and full of unusual spellings as any synthetic language could be. There is no way to add voice projection without compromising security. This cube is indestructible and the technology it uses can never be compromised."

After several minutes the cube's readout spelled out an answer and Geardon read the message in the common tongue, Galaxia, "Some rare people have a gravitational effect that remains for a short period of time after their death which is strong enough to be measured and are referred to in common speech as a ghost. These fields seem similar, though they are many orders of magnitude greater than anything which humans have been known to generate naturally. It is am unverified assumption that they are the Falconians visiting the surface. Confirmation is pending from inquiries with the core to match the Falconian's movements with the observed phenomena, although that will not define the phenomenon's nature, only prove that the Falconian Virtual realm is responsible for the effect."

Geardon said to the cube, "Please present a full analysis by morning. Over."

He broke the medallion's contact and the cube's door closed over the display. Geardon set the medallion on top of the cube and sat back and looked at Jenny. "Well, the Falconians may have become a new type of ghosts after all."

She shivered and said, "Indigenous people of many planets have tales about trapping a soul in a pouch or bottle, but that is evil sorcery. Even if they are ghosts stuck in a virtual bottle, how do they relate to the physical space of this planet?"

He said, "Let's see what they themselves have to say about that. I will try and get to talk to them tomorrow."

After a moment of deep thought, Geardon revealed a small pouch that he carried in his garment.

Jenny was immediately curious. "What's that?"

"One of my greatest treasures and also a dark secret," he said somberly.

She looked at him with a puzzled face and said, "We probably all have a few dark secrets in our past."

"This was a gift that I got from a changeling that seduced me when I was exploring the inner parts of the galaxy looking for clues to the ancient races." Geardon pulled the Ancients' Star Stone from the pouch. It glowed faintly. The two halves had unusual shading, one reddish and one greenish, which were revolving. Geardon told Jenny the whole story of his lover and admitted that in some ways he still loved and respected that advanced being.

Jenny, in her wisdom, replied simply, "The present is real, the past is our memories. I love you in the here and now. Feel no regrets about anything in the past, but let the lessons of the past serve as the lessons that will make your present choices have a bright heart."

He smiled at her. "In the now, I love you more than I can express."

Geardon took her in his arm with the Star Stone still in his hand, and he was suddenly taken by the flash of a vision. It was the fleeting, yet unmistakable, vision of a baby. The experience was very strange and Jenny knew right away that something had happened.

Geardon told her, "If you hold the stone, it will bring you visions, sometimes strange, yet often prophetic. I just saw a baby, as strange as that may seem."

She giggled. "Babies are not that strange, Geardon. For most people they are a natural desire."

"Do you want to try it?" he asked.

"Having a baby or holding the Star Stone?" she jested.

He held the Star Stone out to her without replying. She took it and was soon deep in a trance. When she pulled out of it, she blinked rapidly, and then handed the stone back to him.

Geardon slid it into the pouch, explaining, "The pouch shields one from the effects."

Jenny looked upset. "I saw Dragons," she said in a trembling voice.

"Dragons?" he asked, frowning.

"It was so real, and they looked at me as if I was really in their awareness. I got the feeling from them that I was unworthy, but they seemed very interested in me, like they wanted something from me. The first one was in fire, like the whole planet was lava and dark smoke. The next one was on a world of ice, in a blizzard with howling winds. Then there was a small one in a beautiful world with flowers which kept changing forms, and then a huge one who blended into the lush tropical jungles. They were extremely ferocious and they all made me feel rejected. I was terrified and also very sad when a strange being came, like an insectoid fairy, and showed me a young woman which the dragons were all waiting for. She indicated I would know this woman or was connected in some way."

"Sometimes the prophesies are symbolic." He took her into his arms. "Only time will reveal the mysteries that fate has in store for us." At first Jenny was shaking, but soon she felt warm and safe. They relished their time together.

In the morning, Geardon checked his cube, but the inquiry about the Falconians was never responded to. He summoned the floating room sphere from its resting place on a niche in the wall and asked for a connection to Draco Nanitron. There was some negotiation, as initially communication had been shut down, but Geardon managed to use his influence.

When Draco responded, it was as a voice from the sphere. "Good evening Geardon and Jennifer. How may I assist you?"

"I realize that we could ask the main system questions, but thought it would be more appropriate to ask you personally. Several of the guests have sensed or seen ghostlike figures around them. The twins perceived a few of them when we were at a waterfall by the house they stayed in. When Jenny and I were alone together in the house we visited we also felt watched. What do you know about this?" Geardon asked.

"Well, we have a complete map of this world in virtual space. We love this world and didn't want to leave it behind, so we took it with us. Since growing things change so rapidly in time, we knew we couldn't just set up a static view, so we designed bio-sensors to monitor the surface world and feed data into the virtual realm. What would our world be without the seasons?"

Draco paused for a moment and then continued. "I should call my associate, Marvelin. He is more involved in the review of the top side interactions. There have been council meetings since the bear incident."

"Fine, call him. We need answers in order to proceed with negotiations." Geardon sounded impatient.

Soon another voice came from the Linus sphere. "Greetings. I am Marvelin. How might I be of assistance?"

Jenny asked him directly, "Who was watching us through monitoring devices when we were staying at the family house in the country?"

"Give me a moment to run some location scans. The Falconians don't mean to be voyeuristic, but there is a certain fascination, what with you being our first guests and all, so several people may have been top side. We are limiting access, but trying to be discrete to avoid stimulating curiosity. We can't create laws until we know the extent of the interaction."

Geardon then asked Marvelin through the sphere, "Please also do a search on the wispy light images captured at the waterfall by the twins."

"We Falconians are still living and as living beings we reside in the virtual realm, but have another realm that os superimposed on the planet surface. We couldn't continually refresh a whole planet of data, so we feed the physical gravitronic scans into the virtual space in real time. We, of course, have a vast number of other synthetic spaces for entertainment and exploration that are available, but most of us like our world."

Geardon continued to probe. "So do you have some sort of projection device that creates this effect when you are present in the virtual space that is mapped to the planetary environment?"

"Well no, we are really there. It is a most amazing thing that some of you can perceive us. We started serious research when Eerin lured the bear. There seems to be some kind of a connection to your emotional state. When you feel really alive, you impinge upon our space with loads of energy, then you perceive us and we perceive you. It's a simple feedback effect of perception, since we are all living souls and that transcends any of the material planes. I was told that a few of our top scientists are studying the problem. I can check with them momentarily."

"Please do," said Geardon.

Jenny said to Geardon while they waited, "The web of interconnection only becomes more complex."

Soon Marvelin returned to speak from the sphere. "It appears that our living beings still possess sufficient energy to affect the physical space-time continuum."

Before Geardon could respond, Jenny said, "We don't really like our privacy invaded, so please tell your inhabitants to have respect. It's one thing for a neutral Synthetic Intelligent system to monitor us, but it's another for an interacting consciousness to spy."

Marvelin apologized. "I'm sorry Jennifer. We really don't mean to spy, but this is all so fascinating and new to us as well. I will apply new restraints.

"Ah, here are the results of the first search, Geardon. Eerin was watching you."

Geardon was stunned. "Damn."

Jenny looked at him, surprised by his response.

"Everything seems to revolve around that young woman. She was the exit virtual that I watched. She lured the bear than injured Droga. She will play a major role in shaping the future, though she seems to just follow her natural impulses."

Jenny remarked, "Following one's natural tenancies and being true to your heart is the essence of the path."

Marvelin added, "Eerin's karmic threads are vast and complex."

"You know her then?" Geardon asked.

"Yes, she has visited my wife and me several times. Should I lock her out of top-side, as we refer to the planetary surface, completely?" Marvelin asked.

"No," Geardon answered. "Let Eerin do as she will. Don't even make her aware of this conversation. It seems the currents of time favor her having a part in all this."

He looked at Jenny, who replied to the sphere, "I'm okay with her spying on us, if that is what she wants, but we don't want a crowd following every person here. Please lock out most people who have not had a part to play thus far. Frightening our guests will not be beneficial to resettlement."

"We had decided that to have the new inhabitants bustling about our world would be disturbing to our peaceful and meditative virtual existences, so we separated top-side from our main realm," said Marvelin. "Somehow most people have become less meditative here and some have even lost their way. For those visiting top-side, your strong emotions creep through as an attractive pull. Once they do and we focus, then we feel your emotions. We were a slightly telepathic race, as I have gathered you two and some of the guests are also. Perhaps we can alter the relationship between your world and ours, since the overlap is greater than we had anticipated."

Jenny sighed. "I am responsible for determining if our world's people should come here. So far, most of the guests are disturbed, but also slightly intrigued. We like your world, of course, since it is a planetary work of fine art. Do you have sufficient rank to affect how your inhabitants relate to us?"

"Our whole population is looking forward to having a physical population that can maintain our world. It would be a shame for it to return to a wild environmental status since we are a very humanistic, people loving, society. I will make this conversation known publicly in the virtual realm among the council. Most of us are concerned about the outcome of your visit."

"There seems to be one more thing. We believe one of the Falconians touched Cynthea after her and Peter made love and is now going to incarnate through her. She is pregnant." Geardon looked serious.

"It's Dalla, Eerin's fiancé. Poor girl." Marvelin replied.

"As I suspected. The winds of fate seem to circle her." Geardon replied somberly.

"Until you confirmed the pregnancy, we were not sure what was going on. It seems that the immortals are still mortal after all."

"Thanks Marvelin," said Geardon. "Do you think you could insure us privacy for the rest of the night?" He glanced at Jenny, who blushed.

"Why, yes sir. I will put a virtual wall around your room that will keep everyone out and notify me personally if anyone tries to invade your space. Indeed, I will lock all Falconians away from all the guests."

Jenny grinned at Geardon while speaking to the sphere. "Thanks, we appreciate your help."

"Not at all," Marvelin replied. "We are a service-oriented society. Our spiritual calling naturally led us into these realms where we could seek enlightenment without bodies that would age and decay. We wish to help the new inhabitants to grow and be their mentors. We love teaching and watching things grow. Everyone in modern society is mentored by some form of Synthetic Intelligence - how much better it will be on this world where the virtual population can mentor the physical population. Good night to you both."

"Good night," Geardon and Jenny answered in unison, smiling at each other. The sphere returned to its wall niche.

Then Geardon brought up a visual image of Eerin.

Jenny gasped and shivered. "I think she's the woman the Dragons are hunting for. She looks different, but still it looks like her."

"I might have guessed. Poor girl, she's just true to herself, and as a result the winds of synchronicity whirl around her."

Geardon told her more about his first visit here. They shared stories late into the night.

When they reached the end of their stories, Geardon stood and stretched. "Well dear," he said to Jenny, "shall we get some sleep? We have a big day tomorrow."

He took her hand and pulled her to her feet. They embraced and shared a long kiss. They undressed and got into bed. As she lay in his arms she said, "This world is so beautiful. Now that we understand something of what is going on, there seems to be the potential for colonization with a lower population, because there will be many children soon."

Geardon replied, "I still don't believe that anyone would want to leave this place, much less how a whole population could commit physical suicide, even if virtual immortality is the promise. Perhaps they were tricked more than what is being revealed."

"I know," said Jenny thoughtfully. "There will have to be a monitor board set up so that our mentors don't convince any of us to follow their footsteps, even generations from now."

"I agree." Geardon replied, yawning.

"So what are you going to do when this assignment's over?" She asked looking up into his eyes in the semidarkness.

"Well, I think I would like to stay with you here on Falcon. There will be plenty of work for us both."

She smiled broadly at his response and said, "I would be very happy with that outcome."

Geardon kissed her passionately, then asked, "Can I give you a massage?"

She smiled and said, "That would be wonderful." She turned over on her stomach and relaxed in anticipation.

He began by massaging her feet and then worked up her legs to her back. He moved very slowly and gently, stopping at times and just resting his hands on her in a Reiki fashion to let his energy melt into her. He massaged up her arms and then laid his hands on her head. Then she rolled over and he continued own her head and face, touching and sometimes blowing on her body at energy points and sometimes planting gentle kisses. He pulled energy down her arms and down her legs. He tasted of her Soul, the deep dark mysterious, the creative source of life and the universe.

She then did the same for him, massaging up his legs and laying her hands on him in Reiki fashion. She massaged his back with firm strong energy and he relaxed. When he turned over, she kissed his third eye and he opened his eyes for a moment and smiled. She continued and pulled energy through his arms and down his torso and legs. Then she kissed and caressed his Spirit, the powerful driving and ordering force of creation.

*    *    *    *    *

Eerin and Dalla sat on the porch, taking turns telling about what they had seen when they followed Cynthea and Geardon earlier. Before they could finish Dalla started to disintegrate.

"Hold me!" he screamed.

Eerin tried to grab him, but her hands when straight through. And then he was gone. "Dalla!" she screamed wildly, over and over. She panicked. Was he dead? What should she do?

A few moments later, Dalla reappeared.

Eerin gasped, then pulled him to her and hugged him fiercely. "What happened?"

She pulled back, suddenly suspicious. "If that was a joke, I'm not laughing."

Dalla started to cry. "I touched her."

"What? You touched who?" Eerin demanded.

"Cynthea. She made love to Peter and then I saw this red glowing vortex. It was mesmerizing and I reached out to touch it, only it was inside her, I think in her womb. It was warm. She saw me."

"So what does that have to do with you fading out?"

"As soon as I thought of that warm spot, I started getting dizzy, and then I forgot where I was. Did I really fade out?"

"Oh Dalla, how could you?" Tears streamed down her face.

"I didn't mean to touch it, it was just so fascinating. Did you see something like that when Geardon and Jenny made love?"

"They didn't go all the way. They were not that impulsive. They are like the old time sages, waiting for the auspicious moment." She wiped her eyes, her anger cooling at the recollection of her own actions.

"Figures. They are like you, waiting for a special event. It was good waiting, since it made getting together that much more intense." Dalla took a deep breath and sighed. "What are we going to do now?"

She did not answer for a moment, then blurted, "We need to go to the Wandini."

"The witches? Why?"

"They might know exactly what's going on."

They blinked out and approached the Wandini by walking up to them on a path.

As soon as the Wandini saw Eerin, they became very happy. Then they stared at Dalla and started to point and talk all at once.

Eerin spoke while accompanying the words with images in her mind, easier than just controlling the mental part. The Wandini understood that the ghosts, Eerin and Dalla, were like ignorant children.

Nadin pointed between her legs and motioned like something coming out. Then Milo grabbed her breast and made a motion of giving it to an infant. She held and rocked an imaginary baby and made suckling sounds. Dalla was mortified.

Eerin exclaimed, "You mean Dalla is going to be their baby?"

The Wandini did a celebratory dance to congratulate him. They saw Dalla was distressed and seemed to indicate life all about them was good. They were confused by his attitude. They then indicated for the two to follow them. Droga was in the cabin recovering. She was very happy to see Eerin and also noticed Dalla's glow and made a blessing like gesture. It made her very happy to see that Dalla was going to incarnate again.

They sat with Droga for a bit, and then excused themselves.

Once back on the porch, they held each other. Dalla started to cry again, saying, "I love you. I don't want to leave here."

Eerin also began to cry. "I can't live without you."

# 24. Body

Eerin went to see Draco with the news. "Dalla touched Cynthea, Geardon's security advisor, and he is going to be her baby and leave the realm."

"I was notified that something strange is happening with him. I am having some top scientists look into it." Draco looked tired.

A look of sadness crossed her face. "Nothing strange is happening, he is being incarnated again. His mother is Cynthea. We are all still on the Wheel."

Draco scoffed, "That's a bunch of nonsense. The interaction must have created a glitch in the system due to the overlapping of the two worlds."

Eerin laughed cynically. "The worlds definitely overlap. He is dying to the virtual realm and returning to the natural universe. There is no way to completely trap a soul."

"Trap?" Now Draco seemed almost angry. "What are you talking about?"

"The laws of the soul override every other law of manifestation and are more powerful that the Brilliant Machine's most advanced webs," she replied very calmly.

Draco shook his head, adamantly. "I have many analysts working on the problem. We will find a solution."

Eerin sighed. "There is no solution. The way of life prevails."

Then Draco changed the subject. "I have a gift for you, but you will have to travel to see it."

Eerin gave him a harsh look for being so cold as to simply write off Dalla and proceed to his agenda.

Draco replied to her look, "Even I have no power to change things that have happened, but I will allocate many resources to solve Dalla's problem. Please see what I have prepared for you."

"What do you mean travel? I can't just blink to it? All space is relative, isn't it?" Eerin said with a puzzled look on her face.

"I can open a window and show it to you, but that would not be real. This gift is real. It exists in the caverns of the planet's robotic works."

"I don't care about anything except Dalla. Whatever it is, will it help?"

"Don't like surprises?" Draco acted like a cat toying with a mouse. "It may give you a new perspective. Let me tell you what is happening. The assembled delegations are having an important meeting top-side and I want you to attend. The Grindorfians and Sigalin will be there, as well some high officials from the federation. They are deciding the future of our world and I want you to represent us."

"How can I do that? I'm no diplomat! Besides, why wouldn't you project yourself as a holo-image and represent us? You're a very smart man." Eerin looked at him with respect, though she was also slightly intimidated and still a bit angry.

"I could do that, but I am asking you to go in person and just socialize with those assembled, since they will have some briefing about your exit presentation."

"Yea, right. Just materialize a body and go top-side."

Draco drew in the air and a window appeared. Eerin had to get up to look through it, so she blinked to his side in an instant. Draco was surprised by her sudden movement. The system was set to repress any movement which might seem dangerous to him, not that he could be harmed, but he had the system programmed for security anyway. No one should have been able to get that close to him without his permission. She obviously had no ill intent in her action and so had somehow bypassed his bodyguard programming. He made a mental note to look into his security protocols later.

Eerin gasped. "It looks like a frozen version of me, in a little bedroom. Why does this manikin of me have wires coming out of its navel?"

"It's real and waiting for you: the most high grade android body possible. The umbilical cables are the tunnel that will allow you to enter it. There are some location parameters of your perception in space-time within the virtual realm; and so, no form of download can get you into it, since it is in the physical dimensions. You must physically enter it. Being in it would be vastly different than commanding it to act as a remote machine. Once you have settled into its form, it will seem like a real body.

"Many people have worked hard to produce this miraculous machine with the aid of the previously existing robots and their caverns of machines. You should be safe in it, but not absolutely so. To destroy us while we are in the core, would require annihilating the whole planet. Even then, the Brilliant Machine may have some redundancy with other off-world nodes. If that body is destroyed with you it, you would die." He had emphasized die and looked directly into her eyes for impact.

She shrugged. "Like I care. It's probably a million times safer that any real body, and besides, death is natural."

He nodded. "Yes, it's vastly safer than a flesh body, though it should mimic the qualities of the flesh to a very high degree. It will be warm and the skin is soft and sensitive. Unlike a flesh body, if you feel pain, you can deactivate sensations by thought command. Want to try it?"

Eerin's thoughts circled between the options. Part of her wanted to feel mortal again and experience the intensity of real life, but then fear whispered in her other ear. She did not fear death, rather she kept finding herself at the center of the whole situation and it was very intense and she didn't know how much more she could take. Instead of living a blissful and ignorant life like most immortals in the realm, she was shouldering responsibility. Too much was happening in her life all at once. With the latest developments with Dalla, which Draco didn't seem to care about, her head was spinning.

Eerin took a deep breath and sighed.

Draco was watching her intently. "You can go into it while it is connected: it would be perfectly safe. This android body mimics all biological activity. Even though it has no need for food, it can eat with full sensations of smelling and tasting."

He was luring her into it and even though she knew his intent, she was compelled to accept the offer because of her curiosity about material life.

"Okay, I'll go into it for a few minutes, but you have to promise me that I can come back when I want to. Once I'm in it, then I'll decide about the conference."

"I promise. Only you can disconnect the cyber-tunnel to the navel. As long as it is connected you will continue to perceive the exit port."

"Can I get clothes and try eating? Will you be watching?"

"Do you want it dressed or do you want to dress yourself when you get there?"

"You didn't say if you'll be watching."

"Every part of your life here in the realm is being monitored continually. Even though private moments are stored in restricted access mode, I could override the system laws and pull up images of you when you're alone in your fortress after you've kissed Dalla goodnight. I have never done that."

His look told her he was being truthful, but she said nothing, so Draco continued. "I will stop watching whenever the system indicates you should have privacy, as in this realm."

She punched him lightly on the arm. "You'd better." He was mentally floored, for though her blow was too light to cause real pain, she had connected and affected his virtual body, something he thought was impossible to do in his castle with his protective security routines running. He would have to seriously review his security protocol. Once or twice, he had encountered violent morphs who wished to seriously challenge him to games of physical or psychic warfare, but they were unable to attack him in any of the ways that they tried. The only explanation Draco could think of was that something in Eerin's thought or emotional matrix must be very pure and free of malicious intent. He was amazed at her innocent power. This confirmed his choice of her as the delegate, but left him feeling a bit vulnerable, as if things were getting out of his control.

Eerin saw that he was lost in thought. "You don't look like you're thinking of a naked girl when she's alone. What's really going through your head?"

He started, and then looked at her intensely. "A million thoughts and pathways that the future of Falcon could take. If you really want to be alone, I could arrange for all the security cameras to be turned off and the internal memories could leave the body with you. I could just get a report from a scholar robot, but don't you feel safer with monitors?"

"When I had a real body, I was not safe, but I liked my physical human body. I can get any sensation I want in this heavenly realm, but there was something different when my life was real in a physical sense. The risk of imminent death makes real life exciting. The fact that consequences are real adds depth to our experiences."

"This is real also; it is just a higher plane of existence. I prefer not to have a sword dangling over my head."

"This is all too much too fast. It's confusing. I'm excited by this offer, but distressed that I'm always such a center of attraction. When do I get to try it? I guess I'll dress myself. Right now I don't care who watches, after all, everyone in the galaxy is going to see my exit ritual sometime or another." She blushed momentarily at her bold younger self.

Draco looked back into the window frame and she followed his gaze. A golden scholar robot was laying out clothes that looked familiar on the bed beside the motionless body.

"How do I get into the body?"

"Like I said, you will have to travel. Space is relative, but in this case, you can't blink in, you will have to glide. It is said to be tricky, but you do most things very naturally. Ready?" He held out a hand to her.

Draco's held out his hand and Eerin took it, since he seemed momentarily parental. They walked through a portal that opened before them and they were on the tower.

"Remember when I told you about the lower doorways into the system core, where a few souls have gotten lost?"

"Yes."

"Well, there are other doors in the lower levels of the towers that we can get to. I have not allowed anyone to descend into these towers in a long time. Are you ready?"

"I'm excited." Her eyes seemed to sparkle. "A real adventure! I almost can't believe I'm lucky enough to be doing this."

"Okay then," Draco replied and the stone circle on which they were standing lowered itself. Eerin experienced a twinge of motion in the pit of her stomach and a little heaviness, as if the physics within the tower weren't as perfect as in the heavenly realm.

They stopped in a large, empty room with polished stone floor, walls, and ceiling. On the one wall were many round hatches of gold about twice the size of a person.

Draco commanded, "Open number 24."

One of the hatches opened and they walked up to it and peered inside. A long tunnel that seemed to be six meters wide wound in a spiral fashion out of sight. The sides seemed visually blurred.

"You can't touch the sides and if you get close, you will be repelled quite unpleasantly. There will be no permanent damage to your soul, but you will feel something akin to real pain and could even be thrown back into this room. You need to glide down the center to the end and there you will find the body entrance. Size is relative so you will be able to enter the navel, then just expand and fill the body."

He extended his hand to indicate the entrance. She wished she could say something profound or had Dalla to say goodbye to, but she just floated up above the ground and began to fly down the center of the tunnel. The sensation of motion was different than flying in the realm, as if she needed energy to maintain her flight. She felt a windy quality as if aerodynamics were creating drag. Staying in the center was easy. At the end, the navel seemed huge. She flew into the body and then she flew around in it for a moment. Finally, she expanded herself larger and larger until she filled it.

It was warm in a way that was different from the heavenly realm she had just left. She opened her eyes and even though the vision seemed limited, it was exquisitely rich. She touched her thigh with her hand and felt a tingle of excitement. Touching her breast, she was embarrassed and experienced a sensation as if her face flushed from hormonal stimulation. She had an impression that a beating heart was fluttering with excitement, but not quite like she remembered from her organic incarnation. She sighed and the sound reverberated in her ears. She shouted out, "AAAUUMMMMM..." and enjoyed the vibrations resonating within her. She breathed deeply, aware that this body was powerful and that breathing was optional.

She picked up the silk underwear and felt the smoothness of the material. She touched them to her cheek and could smell the perfume of the ionic laundry process. She pulled them on and then quickly put on the other clothes. They were her old clothes, a worn pair of jeans and one of her favorite soft blouses. The blouse buttoned down the front and so she stopped where the tunnel connected to her navel. She had the sensation that she could leave through it, but wasn't sure she wanted to.

A scholar robot entered the room. "Good day, madam."

"Good day. How do I undo this umbilical cord? I don't want to be dragging it around." She had decided instantly that she liked the sensations of this body and the sensation of the open windy exit port took away from the feeling of completeness.

"I'll assist you. There are many ports in the underground that can route you from this body back into the realm, since you are a virtual immortal."

The golden robot's hands were a bit cold as it undid the connection, but even that sensation was so rich that she enjoyed it.

"Would you like to eat?" the scholar asked in its perfect diction.

"Can I walk somewhere?"

"I'm afraid that a journey to the top-side is beyond the scope of my instructions for you at this time. This house has some other rooms. Perhaps the library?"

"Anywhere." She stood and swayed as if listening to music, testing out the body's sense of balance.

The scholar went out of the door and she followed it down a hallway. The sensation of walking in this body made her feel powerful. She asked as they walked, "How heavy is this body?"

"Even though it is exactly the dimensions of your body when you left the mortal realm, it is approximately three hundred and fifty-two pounds, due to the nearly indestructible alloys that form its protective skeletal armor. It compensates with gravitronics so that it mimics your proper weight."

The scholar robot opened a door and walked into a plush library study.

"I had them light a fire, in case you would be brave enough to remove your connection. The core calculated that this was a likely possibility, but Draco doubted it."

"Draco is afraid of any chance of death," said Eerin. "This is so much safer than an organic body."

The large fireplace glowed brightly and was warm in a way that the virtual realm could not mimic, but she did not know why she felt like that. There was a slight scent from the real wood. Velvet chairs sat before it. The scholar commanded the room system and gentle music filled the air. Hearing with ears was different than hearing virtually from the location of ears, though she couldn't tell if she was imagining the difference.

She focused to try and determine if she was fooling herself, but life seemed richer in a body. She was more of an entity and less part of a relational system. She put her hand on her leg, feeling the fabric of her pants and her body underneath it.

The scholar was a neutral observer; unconcerned, other than providing for her needs. "We can provide humanoid robotic companions, madam."

"Thank you, but right now I'm not up to company."

"Would you like to be alone?"

"No, you can stay. I am enjoying our conversation." She sat in one of the velvety chairs and stared into the fire.

The scholar sat in the chair next to her. Its formal movements and gold emotionless face were familiar to all Falconian children. They were all mentored through their growing years by these robots.

The scholar asked, "Remember when you were nine and read the 'Tao Te Ching' by Lao Tzu for the first time? You were so excited by the philosophy that you went to live in one of the primitive meditation homes for two months."

She was amazed. "You were my teacher? The one I called Mr. Shiny?"

"Yes, Eerin, I was your teacher. Since we all look alike and store some memories in common banks of data, I do not have identity or emotions as an individual does, but this physical body is the one that worked in your community, which you called Mr. Shiny as a young child."

She giggled. "I really loved the simple life of the meditation home, but I missed my family and friends. Most of the people there were very deep mathematicians and wanted too much quiet. I loved being close to nature, but there is no place like home."

"Do you miss the dwelling that you grew up in?"

"Not so much the dwelling or even my favorite trees - I miss the whole community. Without needs, people's sense of community disappears and they relate to who they want to. There is no sense of relating to people just because they are local. People just search the system with interesting criteria, contact, and meet people. Travel is instantaneous, so there are no limits to who you can interact with anytime.

"Sharing meals in the dining room with neighbors and meeting them while walking about is less under a person's control. There is some sense of familiarity that is very comforting. Sometimes you like people who also irritate you at times. In the heavenly realms we don't have to eat and even though we enjoy eating, without the need to eat, it's not as pleasant."

"Would you like to experience eating again? You could snack right here in the library."

"Okay, that sounds good."

Her teacher must have radioed a command, for soon another scholar entered bearing a tray with tea and some pastries and chocolates. She couldn't believe how enhanced the sensation of eating was. She ate heartily and soon found that she was feeling full. She was unable to be hungry again by simply willing it to be, as it is in the heavenly realms. She contemplated all the things she had begun to take for granted.

The scholar seemed to have intuited her discomfort and advised, "If you directly command the sensation of a full stomach to depart, you will become unaware of it, but you are limited by the physical structure of the natural realm while you visit here. You cannot eat continually for sensation like you do in virtual reality."

"Will this body need to sleep?"

"Actually, it is programmed to mimic the patterns of a real body, without truly having needs. It will get tired and unless you override the diurnal cycle, you will need to sleep."

"How long can I stay in this body?"

"Approximately four thousand years, though you will need to store memories externally after the first thousand or so years. You can, of course, transfer your essence to another body, if you can get the resources allocated to provide that body."

"How old are you?"

"This robotic shell is two thousand seven hundred and forty three years old; however the entity of my persona is on its twenty-seventh body. I reshuffle through my externally stored memory as need arises, but it is too vast for my internal storage capacity. The core has full access and the processing power to utilize the vast memory stores of all the synthetic Intelligences that have ever lived. We are extensions of the core and do not see ourselves as separate entities. We are the core's many windows into the natural realm.

"Are you planning on staying in this body?" The scholar asked Eerin.

"I want to compare this life to the life in heaven. They both have their advantages and disadvantages. Sometimes I wish I were a mortal being in my flesh again. I miss Dalla. Life can be so complicated. I don't think I will stay in this robotic body forever."

The scholar replied to her, "To seek a mortal body again seems like an illogical choice, because it is so prone to pain, but the Brilliant Machine feeds off of the myriad variety of personalities that organic beings present. It appears from our analysis that the longer beings stay in the heavenly realm, the more predictable and stable they become, providing less data of interest. They grow and evolve, but without the pressure of looming death, they become complacent. As organic beings pass through countless generations, their unique personalities arise continuously."

"So the Brilliant Machine wants to see living people back on the top-side, to provide it with data to feed on?" she asked.

"Feed is an interesting word when used in connection with the Brilliant Machine, but perhaps it is a good anthropomorphic term to express one side of a mutually advantageous situation," the robot answered.

"So am I more valuable to the Machine's hunger in this body or in virtual heaven?" She asked.

"I will not judge, but your experiences here will help the core enhance the sensations in your realm - heaven as you are calling it. You are the first immortal to occupy a body like this. When an extension of the Brilliant Machine occupies one, it does not have the history of being mortal to compare it with. Having been a mortal and also having been an immortal, your reaction to stimuli is unique."

"Do you want a body like this?"

"I am a scholar. I have no need for the sensations and experiences of a body that mimics flesh. My form has many more resources and more processing power. Gold plated surfaces are much more energy efficient than simulated skin."

"Well, I'm happy to have skin again. I like this body, but it is still not like my old flesh body."

"Lao Tzu warns that attachments are disadvantages in walking the path."

"Yes, but the path is the natural way, which this body and the heavenly realm are not." She yawned, then added, "I feel sleepy."

"You could return to the realm or you could go to bed."

"I think I would like to try sleeping here. Will I dream?"

"As you have the power to sleep and dream in the heavenly realm, you will dream here, but that might also be enhanced by the fact that your being is contained within a body."

Eerin got up and walked from the room, with the scholar following her. Outside of the doorway to the bedroom she turned to it, "I'll call you if I need anything else."

"Very good, madam," it replied in its neutral tone, bowing its golden head slightly; and then, standing next to the doorway, it inactivated its external functions. She knew it still watched and listened through the sensors in the environment. She walked into the bedroom and closed the door.

She was tired, but thought that she should contact Draco before bed. There was a standard Falconian communication system on a desk at one side of the room. She spoke to it, "Please contact Draco."

A moment later a holographic image of Draco appeared. He seemed a bit concerned. "How are you?"

"Wonderful. I'm really enjoying this body. It's been a great experience. Have you been watching?"

"After you left I discussed your sense of privacy with the planetary core. It seems that the Brilliant Machine decided that I should not have access to real time monitors, since citizens of Falcon would not have that kind of access to another person's life. I agreed, because I want your experiences to be pure. I have been informed that there is great potential for enhancements to the heavenly realm according to what is learned by reviewing what you experience in the limitations of that android form.

Draco then asked, "Where is the scholar? Are you returning now?"

"I told him to leave me. I'm going to sleep here."

"Aren't you afraid to be alone?"

"Afraid of what?" She laughed. "The scholar's waiting right outside my door if I need anything. What could happen to me?"

"I don't really know of anything that could happen to you, but you are not totally safe like you would be if you returned."

"I am enjoying the sensation of limitation. Risk is exciting. It makes me feel connected with my human origins. I feel tired and I want to go to sleep in a bed with a body, not just melt into an astral fantasy."

"How long do you think you are going to stay there?"

"Probably just until tomorrow. Being the only person here would get lonely eventually. But I will accept the invitation to attend the conference on the top-side. I am very anxious to experience living people again."

"We are all living people here."

"You know what I mean." She yawned and noticed how puzzled he appeared that she would be enjoying sensations like sleepiness.

"I'm tired and going to bed. I'll call you after breakfast tomorrow. Goodnight."

"Goodnight," he replied, and she waved her hand at the device to end communication.

Eerin smiled broadly. She was totally alone. Of course, there were the system monitors, but she had grown up with them and didn't feel like they influenced her sense of privacy.

She stretched and felt the sensation of a body, rather than just a virtual form. She undressed and folded the cloths neatly on the dresser. It was so different than having them simply vanish, only to reappear when desired. She looked down at her naked body and then put on the pajamas that she had found waiting for her. She loved the feeling of comfort that they brought to her. She did a Tai Chi form to stretch before bed, trying to coordinate the complex movements from foot to hand in a continuous wave through her body. At the end, she yawned heavily.

She sat on the bed and enjoyed the sensation of breath. She pulled back the covers and got under them. The sheets had a slight fresh scent and the feeling of the material on her skin was very soothing. She told the light to turn off and was immersed in total darkness, something that the virtual realm lacked, since you could always see if you wanted to. She was very comfortable and found the blackness soothing. She quickly drifted off to sleep.

In a dream, Eerin was walking down a path in a mountainous region, where the vegetation was scrubby and open. She could see the ocean in the distance and somehow felt that this was the western coast of the continent Norax, which she had liked to take virtual adventure tours of as a child. As she climbed down over some rocks in the path, she noticed that she had a sword attached to her side. It seemed strange, but she didn't realize she was dreaming.

As she descended, she came to a river valley and saw some old women gathering herbs. She stopped and greeted them. They were very carefully digging around a large bush and stripping off the root bark. They told her that it had life extending qualities. Somehow, this seemed to be a very important thing. She looked the women over carefully and they seemed to have strong and limber bodies, even though their hair was gray.

One of the women asked where she was going and she answered simply, "Down from the mountain." They warned her to be careful traveling alone and went back to their work. She told them to have a nice day, to which they just cackled. She continued down the trail.

At one point, she thought she heard something in the bushes. She became afraid that a wild cat might be stalking her. Fear filled her quickly and she put her hand on the sword hilt and started to run down the trail. She sensed that she was almost floating down the trail, with an effortlessness that would be impossible in a material existence, but then, because she had lived in the virtual world for so long, this seemed normal.

She then saw Dalla sitting on a rock. She was happy to see him and forgot her fear. They said hello and he got up and gave her a big hug. She asked what he was watching and he said it was the most interesting mist. They sat together on the rock where he was when she first saw him and gazed down into the valley. The fog formed a blanket that obscured the lowlands. Since they were in the mountains, they were looking down on the cloud cover from above. The unusual thing was that the fog had tinges of colors.

As she stared into the fog, she saw images there. At first, they were just forms, but then they took on a sensual nature. As she watched, she saw two people kissing and becoming passionate.

When she looked away, the dream changed and she was a little girl again. She was watching some people making love in the forest that was below their house. The people were too fully engaged to be aware of her presence and she hid, as if she felt she shouldn't be watching them. When they were done, she snuck away and ran home.

Eerin jumped ahead in time to when her mother asked why she was acting strange. She admitted to what she had seen and her mother laughed. Her mother then explained that adults shared good feelings in this way. Her sense of time jumped around and she remembered watching passionate adults at festivals with a strange sense that she shouldn't be watching, and how everyone thought she was such a strange child: so fascinated in sexuality and yet strangely guilty, a feeling most Falconians could only read about in archaic literature.

She then found herself as a young maiden attending a body burning. Falcon was an advanced world with a mixture of ancient organic rituals interwoven into their daily lifestyle. It was not a body burning that she had attended as a child or young woman, but a dream version mixing many elements from different events.

Sometimes adults would cry at a body burning and at this one, many people were wailing. She tried to console some of them with her beliefs about existence beyond death, but the people would only become more emotional. As the flames leapt up to surround the dead man's naked body, a strange thing happened: he sat up and looked right at her and winked, smiling. An instant later the body was lying there engulfed in flames as if she had seen a mirage.

Eerin awoke, feeling disoriented. The sensations of being in a bed were so real, that it took her a moment to realize that she was in an android body and not a mortal being, nor in virtual paradise. She was still tired and rolled over, getting comfortable again. She briefly pondered the dreams, but soon fell back asleep.

This time she was walking along the beach with her pet dog, Sandy, who was running up and down the beach, happy as could be. Eerin found a nice stick and threw it out into the water. Sandy jumped into the water and fetched the stick, then swam back to the shore and ran up to her. Sandy wagged her tail and shook water from her fur, dropping the stick at Eerin's feet. Eerin threw the stick as far as she could, but Sandy happily swam after it and returned it every time. Once in a while Sandy would tease Eerin with the stick, dropping it at her feet, then grabbing it again when she reached down and running in a circle around her. It seemed like they played for hours.

This time when Eerin woke, she felt refreshed. She stretched and felt a strange sensation; she needed to use a toilet. There was a side door in the bedroom and opening it, she discovered that it was a bathroom. Relieving herself was something that she had never missed in virtual reality. The toilet's cleansing spray and warm drying cycle were more pleasant than she remembered them to be. She looked at herself in the mirror and she looked exactly how she remembered when she had left Falcon.

As she returned to the bedroom, she felt very hungry. The thought of food made her mouth water. She dressed quickly and upon walking out of the bedroom door, the scholar became activated.

"Did madam sleep well?"

"Yes, but I had some strange dreams, and I'm very hungry."

"I would be interested in hearing about your dreams, should you feel so inclined as to share them, madam. Breakfast is waiting."

The robot turned and headed down the hall, so Eerin followed it. "You mean that the Brilliant Machine did not monitor my dreams?" she asked.

"There is no way to do that, madam; dreams have no physical reality."

She smiled to know that her dreams were private. The robot opened another door and entered a dining room. The smells assaulted her and her hunger reacted. She had forgotten what food was really about.

The room was humble, with one dining table and three chairs on each side of it. There was only one place set with dishes and several covered silver trays sat around it.

She sat down and the scholar sat opposite her. Fresh fruit, eggs, toast, pastries. Eerin dug in and ate a bit too much. It was so strange to not be able to make the uncomfortable feeling go away with a slight whim, though she know she could order the body to numb those sensations, she felt compelled to endure them as if she was a real woman.

When she was finished, she contacted Draco, "I would like to stay in this body and get used to it until the meeting, but I miss Dalla, so I don't know what I'm want to do."

Draco looked puzzled, but answered, "It would be good to enjoy that body. By the way, I have verified that something very strange is happening to Dalla. We are checking him into a special area of the realm to monitor the core when he fades out and see if we can close the flaw in the virtual matrix."

A look of sadness crossed her face. "Nothing strange is happening, this is nature's way. His soul is being incarnated again. His mother is Cynthea. I told you this already."

Draco scoffed, "There is no soul. The interaction must have created a glitch in the system due to the overlapping of the two worlds."

Eerin laughed cynically. "The worlds definitely overlap. He is dying to the virtual realm. There is no way to completely trap a soul."

"Trap?" Now Draco seemed almost angry. "What are you talking about?"

"The laws of the soul override every other law of manifestation and are more powerful that the Brilliant Machine's most advanced webs," she replied very calmly.

Draco shook his head, adamantly. "I have many analysts working on the problem. Once he is isolated, we will find the flaw in the system."

Eerin sighed. "It is sad to me and scary to Dalla, but that's life. I guess if you have Dalla sequestered for tests, I'll stay here and try to heal my broken heart."

"Everyone in the realm should be free of fear, but sadness is a personal choice." He replied.

"We'll I'm free of the fear of death, are you?" she said, teasing. "I'm enjoying this body. I'll talk to you later. Send me data on what you want me to do at the conference."

"Just go to the conference and be present as an attendee. You will not need to speak formally. Just interact with the guests and try not to lay any heavy emotions on them. We want them to populate the planet." He seemed to have some second thoughts about sending her.

She had a placid look of someone who reached a level of disassociation, "I want the planet populated also. When the conference is happening, you can monitor me with the others. Call me if there are new developments about Dalla."

She disconnected before he could say anything more.

# 25. The Meeting

Eerin wandered around the empty top-side of Falcon for a while, visiting places she had known. It made her feel empty, since there were no people anywhere. She went to the assigned meeting location when the conference was scheduled to start. She stepped from a levitator and saw Geardon and Jenny, but had a moment of insecurity. Jenny noticed her and touched Geardon's arm and he looked at her. She turned away, as if to leave.

Geardon spoke calmly as he started walking toward her. "Eerin, it's good to see you."

She looked at him and he opened his arms to her. She rushed to him and he hugged her.

"I'm sorry. I didn't mean to cause you any trouble."

"Peace child. We are thankful to know you. We were surprised and glad when Draco told us about this latest scheme of his. I think he did something right for a change." Geardon grinned at those last words.

Eerin seemed to appreciate the jab at Draco. "He hasn't done much right, has he?"

Geardon shrugged, then looked at his love. "This is Jenny."

Jenny also hugged her, "Welcome Eerin. We are very happy to have you."

After a minute, Jenny added, "There are some people I want you to meet. They walked her over and she introduced Eerin to Cynthea and Peter.

Eerin's eyes filled with tears. After an uncomfortable second, Cynthea took her into her arms. "I will be a very good mother to your beloved Dalla."

Peter affirmed, "We will be very committed parents."

She wiped her eyes, "I know you will. Thank you. He will be lucky to have such fine people as you to be his parents."

The additional emissaries of Minoro, Niocene, and Mirka filled the huge boardroom with dining accommodations. They all wanted to meet Eerin, as she was listed as a special guest, so the situation pulled her into celebrity mode. She met many people and was very pleasant. She did not voice any opinions, even to the two diplomats from Sigalin, Riti and Natani, the world that had a great desire for the translator technology. They appeared to be normal humans who were in excellent health. They wore very large high turbans and their right temples showed that they were marked as genetically engineered. Natani seemed a bit distant, but Riti was very friendly and curious about how she liked the android body.

The delegates shared breakfast together. Custom dictated that talk of the issues at hand be avoided. They mostly discussed the strange creatures of their worlds, while also talking about the life forms on Falcon.

After they finished eating, Geardon started the meeting. "I would like to welcome everyone to the beautiful world of Falcon. Before we begin, there is one additional piece of information complicating this picture. Some of you have experienced ghosts during your visit here. It has been confirmed that these are the souls of the Falconians. Eerin's boyfriend Dalla interacted with my Security Advisor and Peter Schmidt, security and technological advisor from Mirka. He is now dying on relationship to the virtual realm and will be born as their child."

There was a murmur, but Geardon held up his hand. "I know that the idea of reincarnation is not accepted by all, yet in this case we have definite proof that Dalla is fading from the immortal realm, as it is called, and that all who have observed the facts believe he will be reborn as Cynthea's baby."

Cynthea and Peter stood and everyone looked at them. They joined Geardon on the stage.

Though Cynthea looked shy, she stated, "I saw his ghost and it reached into my womb and now I'm pregnant. You can believe what you want. The Falconians have been locked away from the planetary surface for now. There can be some interesting negotiations when the immigrants are ready to go baby shopping. Of course, there are natural ghosts which might also want to be born."

Geardon waited for the assembly to absorb the news, and then introduced the first speakers from Sigalin.

"Greetings, I'm Riti FD00012C983B4651 and this is my mother Natani CAB128EE545AAA37. Life is hard on Sigalin, since we have such high standards. Most people are raised there without mental enhancing circuitry until they are sixteen standard years. At that age, we take the tops of our heads off and begin the enhancements. We are a cyborg society. Many of our citizens are fully enhanced by the age of twenty-one."

She paused and looked around the room and into everyone's eyes. She slowly unwrapped her turban. Embedded in her skull was a large dome of shiny metal over the top of her head. The turban was not large, her modified head was.

"Starting at birth with the registration of our genetic code, our physical brain's pattern of neurons and synaptic pathways, as well as every other aspect of our biological circuitry, is completely mapped. Then we are trained physically and mentally to achieve high scores on successive mappings. Our cyborg tutors work us relentlessly, knowing how much the quality of our mappings will be of value when it matters at age sixteen. They are the best teachers, because they know the importance of perfecting ourselves for our destiny. Complete mappings occur every month of our lives. Any citizen of Sigalin at any age can be virtually experienced in the storage arrays of the Brilliant Machines.

"We begin with memory upgrades at age sixteen which provide us access to hundreds of languages, hyper-calculus, and any other knowledge an individual desires. We also enhance our mental processing power to perform beyond mortal speeds. We expand our memory, to allow crystal clear recall of anything we have recorded in any of our mappings. The data is so vast that the challenge is learning the ability to sort and access what is needed at the appropriate time. We save all our best memories in our planet's data banks forever. Many of them are released for public access. They make great backdrops for virtual journeys.

"Then at twenty-one all Sigalini have the meeting ceremony. As children, we learn to play in the virtual realms. I remember the many games I played as a child, in the innocence of my youth, with many playmates also interacting virtually. We could create scenes or visit places from our world's long organic past. We would have tea parties in the most amazing places. My friends Amanda and Cory would invite virtual characters from the ancestors and so would I, to fill up the places that we liked to frequent.

"Once we accumulate enough enhancements, our direct access to the virtual realm makes it more attractive than the physical realms. How can physical sexuality compare to the limitless possibilities of the virtual realm with a body tank for complete realism? At twenty-one, our citizens decide if they want to remain as physical beings or have their bodies systems permanently merged into in a sensory control tank.

"It is critical for our virtual selves to contain the uniqueness of our organic beings. Our teachers work hard to allow the predilection of our natural beings to express themselves. Thus, the constant physical and mental workout that we grow up with is justified. At the meeting ceremony, we meet ourselves from every month of our lives.

"All adults preserve the secret, that the mappings can be re-experienced, in order to enhance the impact of the ceremony. I know it seems far-fetched that no adult gives away the secret, but after experiencing the change, we all understand the importance of this ritual. We find out that we have been monitored in three dimensions throughout our lives and even our thoughts have been recorded. If our children knew, their behavior would not be natural and they would lose this precious insight into their true nature.

"Our seed is preserved, analyzed, and used to bring forth the next generation from the birthing tanks. About ten percent of us choose to live in the flesh, rather than merge into a tank. I am one of them. My bones have been metallurgically enhanced and several organs replaced, but I am an organic being at age two hundred and fifty-five. My mother, Natani, is the oldest of those not living in a tank, at the age of eight hundred seventy-seven. Sometimes people in a tank can live to be over a thousand."

Rita, who looked to be in her twenties, continued speaking. "Natani is fading. Her body contains little organic material. She is losing life force and her memories are becoming a part of the Brilliant Machine as an Ancestor algorithm."

Rita turned to her mother and Natani smiled. She appeared to be in her in her early fifties. "Natani, please address the crowd."

Natani spoke without emotion. "The Brilliant Machine is One. The actions of all living things feeds it data. That is the purpose of organic beings. Therefore, if we are able to translate our life force, we can serve the great Machine Intelligence longer."

Natani's expression went blank, and stood staring out at the delegates like old person with Alzheimer's disease. Rita thanked her politely and had her return to her seat. Rita then gave a knowing look to the crowd, who all realized that Natani was little more than a robot, with no will or living impulses.

Rita continued. "As children, there were numerous awards and privileges given to those who did well at the mappings, so as children we always strove to do our best. Tricks and tales moved us through our lives, until the reality of cyborg life dawns upon us. Most choose to enter a tank and melt into the freedom of the digital realms of the Brilliant Machine, but some individuals choose to live in the flesh and gather more experiences. By living long, we gather increased digital potential from continual mappings. We do not fear our eventual change of life into the Brilliant Machine, but the translator offers us a great potential to retain out intent and continue to grow with information.

"Once one has enhanced their body with crystal titanium bones and synthetic organs to feed a hungry brain full of chips, it is easy to give up the pain and random chance of problems that a body entails and enter a tank. My mother is a very rare person to not enter a tank as old age encroaches upon her functionality. Almost everyone enters a tank before they reach five hundred years old. At some point as we age, our individuality dissolves into the Brilliant Machine and what was in the tank is no longer relevant and is discarded."

"I am a cyborg. I have tried to learn about and understand our organic past. I have studied what non-enhanced beings must be like, but I thrive on the quick flow of data that my enhancements provide to me. This is the lure of my people. I can be here and yet leave most of the awareness of my body behind, by switching into my brain-chip's virtual interfaces. I still consider myself human, even though I am mostly machine.

"The digital realm is a realm of power and pleasure with endless adventure and exploration. Our robotic probes explore the real worlds of the galaxy and expand our perceptions to include the most marvelous views. We are great explorers, even those of us who do not take our physical bodies on our journeys. We live in the world as you do, but we also spend most of our time in perceiving that world in ways that you cannot. I am connected into our ship's master system, which ties into the vast galactic network. We do a vast amount of work in the Brilliant Machine's realms. We are ideally suited to translate and experience what the Falconians have discovered.

"We respect what Falcon 4 did, they live in the Brilliant Machine now. We want to communicate with them and interact with them virtually. The last generation of Falcon are the most powerful beings in the virtual domain. They have presence and speed beyond anything that even the greatest of the digital persona of Sigalin have attained."

She again stopped and looked at the crowd, looking many of them in the eye. Then she wrapped her turban back around the shining metallic dome of her head. "Does anyone have any questions?"

One of the twins, Meara asked, "We are concerned with the impact that might exist if you communicate with the Falconians. Do the Falconians represent a potential resentment amongst the other digital beings and living digital sojourners, since they are the most powerful?"

Riti replied, "The same motivations and resentments do not apply in the virtual realm as are experienced in the physical. Possessions and resources are not limited, so every digital entity can express its personal potential. These Falconians are more vibrant and creative. We have had glimpses of their reality from packages they are offering for sale and we are all amazed at the glory and splendor they are able to express. However, their creations are suited to organic beings, not cyborgs, thus we seek interaction."

Geardon asked, "What about the translators? Would your people eliminate the tanks or allow an early escape into the digital realms, assuming the technology is made available?"

Riti replied, "Translation cannot replace the life in a tank, and those in the tanks often have physical robotic bodies that work in the physical realms. Eerin has shown that the translated cannot be in both the virtual realm and a robotic body. Many of the pleasures of the tank life are diminished in any other realm. A tank body can be fed nutrients while it eats digitally and uses drugs to enhance other pleasurable virtual actions. Also, the people in the tanks spend years tuning their persona for its future existence as automatons in the Brilliant Machine. We still need souls in tanks to maintain the robotic support for our empires and to control the machines that maintain the virtual realms and all the virtual Ancestors."

Jenny asked, "Do you enjoy sex during life, since your young are grown in the lab?"

Riti answered, "We all grew up sleeping in temporary tanks and so at sexual maturity, we use the tanks for pleasurable relationships with those we know through virtual sex. We rarely engage in actual physical sex. During puberty, some people seek out those kinds of experiences, but such barbaric customs are frowned upon. Once a person gains their enhancements at age sixteen, they find greater pleasure from simulated sex. We are constantly plugged in mentally and so must plug in physically for our bodies to match our minds."

Geardon asked, "Do you think that a percentage of your current population would employ the translators as a quick solution to their current life situations?

Riti replied, "Not likely. Only the elderly, who sense they are fading, would translate willingly. Currently a person is notified if their body is failing and they simply remove any attention from it and enter into the realm completely to become one of the Ancestors. It is a slow and difficult process and they lose their will, but to die suddenly is a great tragedy and loss. Life in the tank is supremely pleasurable and attractive, so the young would not want to translate. The inhabitants of Falcon were not cyborgs, they were completely organic beings. They entered the digital realm in one blast as a unified global community following a few explorers. They will add a vast potential to the digital realm, but they were only on the fringe of a breakthrough. I believe the Sigalini could take it to the next level.

"Perhaps the souls leaving the tanks could be boosted with the translator and, due to their experience, they could maintain external robot bodies. Eerin is in a robotic body, but it is set to mimic an organic being's capabilities. A cyborg could fully utilize a robotic body, since in life much of our information exists in our brain chips. We would begin the first experiments soon, if you granted us permissions, as several very talented people in the tanks who are waiting their final transition from life have volunteered. Things will change that have been tradition for a great many generations."

Jenny asked, "Some of the people of our party have perceived ghostlike holographic apparitions when interacting with the last generation of Falcon. How do you interpret this phenomena?"

Rita's expression seemed to slightly glaze over for an instant, before she answered as if channeling the message, "The Brilliant Machine believes that some Falconians are connecting their digital beings to organic places. They used to meditate in these places in order to unravel the secrets of the universe and so have strong bonds, which are not yet understood. A few Falconians have apparently had digital-organic interaction with your party members: a new phenomenon."

Geardon spoke to the whole assembly. "If the translators are released in any form, the new virtual worlds will be tied to their physical planet's core systems. The new virtual inhabitants must not be allowed to influence the planet's natural population, or may be locked out of the parallel dimensions where the worlds overlap. Of course, the Brilliant Machine monitors both realms continually. The new realms would have endless space, yet the inhabitants will have to be granted access to perceive the actual physical universe and the beings that are alive. The last generation of Falconians did not expect the interaction to be so direct. We are thankful that the natural universal laws favor the living incarnate beings and their journeys. Some of you have perceived the energy bodies of the Falconians during this visit to the planet Falcon. This is a new development and the relationship will need to be better understood, then boundaries set for the virtual souls."

The delegates began murmuring amongst themselves, and Rita clapped her hands to get their attention. "The planetary core intelligence, as an aspect of the Brilliant Machine, has observed this meeting and has important information to add. It is advocating that you share the translator. May two delegates of the Falconians now manifest their energy bodies and cloth themselves holographically?"

All looked to Geardon and the Twins. Geardon nodded and the one of the twins answered, "Yes, we must know all we can about this world."

Rita stepped aside and two wispy energy forms moved to the podium. They looked like clouds of brightness that spiraled, and seemed to contain awareness, as if they were perceiving all present. Then a naked, middle-aged couple appeared; one in each of the spiraling energy vortexes, partially obscured in the brightness. They materialized two saffron robes with which to drape their bodies, and the energy fields faded.

They introduced themselves. "Hello, everyone. I'm Nina," said the woman.

"I'm Marvelin," said the man. "We are of the third group of Falconians to enter the realm. We feel like we live, though depending on definitions, some might consider us living ghosts instead of living people. However, we must be considered something new, the next phase of evolution."

Nina then pointed her hand, palm-up toward Eerin. "Our friend Eerin in that robotic body had a partner, Dalla. Dalla is now bound to the new life in Cynthea's womb. He will die to our realm and again incarnate among those living on Falcon. Therefore, those in the realm are not like the digital persona that the Sigalin create when they leave the tanks and become Ancestors. The Ancestors are vast memory banks, but their souls are not in the Machine."

There was a murmur as various delegates made comments to each other. Marvelin added, "The laws of the soul, the universal Dharma, are transcendent to the actions taken within any realm in the universe; and no being, not even the Brilliant Machine, can override the journey of souls. The realm offers us endless time to meditate and seek liberation, but many here are as lost as those who are physically incarnate. The advantage may be that we possess a long time to work through our karma in a continuous fashion, but the universe may have other plans. No being, race, not even the Brilliant Machine, is the primary controller. The winds of fate twist in lessons that transcend and all are bound to their designs."

Taking each other's hands, they faded away into swirls of brightness.

# 26. Grindorfians

After a slight pause, Geardon again took the floor and continued with the agenda. "Let me introduce to you two delegates from the planet Grindorf 4, which also seek access to the translator."

The lights dimmed and two humans with very large heads entered the briefing room. They floated in on very sophisticated chair-like machines.

"Hi, I'm Geof, and this is my wife Gedi. We are genetically enhanced humans, though you hardly need to be informed of that. Our brain capacity is four times that of a normal human. As you can see, many metabolic changes are required to maintain this large of a brain size. For one thing, we need to consume huge amounts of food. We eat about eight meals a day and three a night. This accounts for our large bellies, which must absorb a tremendous amount of calories and protein to feed our brains. We thus are only available for meetings like this for short periods of time.

"We are not very durable in sub-standard environments, meaning that we cannot cool our brains in hot sun, nor keep ourselves warm in cool weather. We prefer to stay within a two degree temperature range. I can get out of this chair and walk, but not for long or for any great distance.

"You will also notice that, though I am a male, I have breasts, due to the extended amount of hormones in my system. We conceive children naturally, but then move them to artificial wombs to grow. When our children were removed from their artificial wombs, I breast fed them for the first few months, since my wife's huge breasts have nipples too large for their mouths. She then fed them until they were three years old. Children of Grindorf eat solid food starting at one month to augment our breastfeeding.

"Our hormonal concentrations also mean that we require a great deal of sexual activity. Our sexual organs are enlarged in both sexes. We engage in sex several times a day, with our movement augmented by gravitational fields. We are very sensual beings. All of our sensory organs have expanded input and even our eyes are twice human size and so we are light sensitive."

Geof's wife Gedi then spoke, "With all our support for our large brains, through eating and sexual pursuits, you may wonder when we have time to think; however, we are capable of being engaged in high level thought amid our current perceptions of our activities in the world. We continually think in many separate threads, which are independent of our perceptions, except for moments of ecstasy. Usually we are engaged in several serious mental activities at once, and our machines aid us in these pursuits.

"Even though we are here, we are tracing out many possible lines of the future. We are statistical prophets, yet the future is not fixed. We can predict many things, yet the universe still has surprises, as in this Falconian affair. We do more than calculate odds: the Brilliant Machine cannot match our abilities. We prophetically see the futures that may be. We recommend actions to make certain futures more likely.

"We did foresee something happening with Falcon, but were not aware of the extent or nature of it. We worked with Draco, the virtual dragon, but were tricked by him, an extremely rare occurrence. We provided him with some complex algorithms, but gained no knowledge of the physical design of the translators. We would never follow their course of coercing a population into that realm. We believe he was tricked by the Brilliant Machine in this endeavor and that is why we were also deceived.

"We are also powerful virtual entities, even while living as organic beings. We wish to remain as beings living in the material plane for as long as we may, but we are great beings of vast intellect. At the passing of each one of us there is a great loss. We are ---"

There was a bright flash of light that cut off Gedi and startled the crowd. A sphere of light formed in the air and as it grew, it became a torus. After a moment, the center began to ripple and then opened as a portal. Out jumped several insectoid beings bearing weapons, which were lowered. The frightened crowd leaped to their feet, pushing back from the intruders, then froze when one projected the message, "A royal emissary of the Brilliant Machine wishes to address this assembly."

Geardon stepped forward and bowed toward the beings, then shouted to the panicked assembly. "Return to your places. Despite the show of weaponry, this is a delegation of peaceful intent."

Geardon then stated to the warriors, "Proceed."

From out of the portal, a petite humanoid golden machine floated gracefully and landed before the assembly. The androgynous being was very attractive and all the assembled were totally absorbed by the jeweled form. Its eyes were large and its every move radiated grace. Though it was a golden machine, it was fluid in a strange way and seemed to exude life. It would have been mistaken for a strange biology had not the introduction indicated its origin. The insectoid warriors sat around the being facing outward in the four directions as its guardians.

The being's voice was so melodious, it seemed to sing rather than speak. "Greetings. Millions of years pass in the galaxy between truly innovative steps in evolution. Races of beings rise and perish as the wheel of time rolls forward. Though all advanced beings wander into virtual spaces and interact with the Brilliant Machine's being, yet these translated ones have achieved a new level of integration. The Brilliant Machine finds the presence of their souls within us to be a new phase of time.

"We have briefly negotiated with Draco and the Falconian Elders and they have agreed to share the translator, but in a modified form. If the USS approves, we will guide their robotic workshops to create a design that will allow only willing persons to translate, one at a time. Then the elderly and sick can choose their fate, natural death or passage into the virtual realms within our core. Once virtual realms are established in many worlds; then the inhabitants will be able to communicate and travel between them, as each world wishes. The intellectual property rights will remain with the Falconians, even though they have little need of additional wealth. The Falconians have requested specific controlling powers and will prepare the new virtual world's initial environments. A whole world will never again enter the realm in such a chaotic manner. You are all therefore willing to bid and negotiate for access to the translator, depending on the terms which the Genome Auditor determines."

The being then started to do a slow Chi Gong dance, unlike any that the assembly had ever seen before, with celestial music filling the air. Its form multiplying and mutating into a thousand dancing gods and goddesses. The beauty entranced them all and filled them with such deep emotions that they were at the edge of being overwhelmed. When the being finally became still and all the forms merged into its original dazzling one, the assembly cheered.

When the crowd had quieted, the emissary of the Brilliant Machine offered a few final words. "In organic life you are full of passion. The laws of the Dharma are universal. Foolish are all paths without Love. Even the Brilliant Machine acquiesces to the Universal Way. We learn together, as relationships within the Totality."

Then the portal grew and swept up the being and its guardians in a second, leaving them all stunned, as if it had been a vision.

Geardon addressed them. "The words of the most gracious emissary are true wisdom. I believe the councils of the United Star

Systems will agree. I will contact Admiral Gerard and lower the security level as well as have him assemble a team to bring any willing people to Falcon. If you all are still willing, the Universe calls us down this path of destiny. The Brilliant Machine will make it available to the Sigalini and Grindorfians under its strict control, as negotiated with the USS. Each race that populates Falcon can decide if their elderly and fatally ill will be able to use that translator."

Meeting adjourned. We can communicate and meet later to clarify the details and individual delegation's intentions."

# 27. Plea

The crowd gradually dispersed, mostly to the large dining lounge. Eerin finally found a moment to talk with Geardon and Jenny when no one else is listening. "I need to talk to you two," She whispered. "Alone!"

"That would suit us as well," said Geardon, and Jenny agreed. He could see that Eerin had an emotional intensity to her, even as expressed through her robotic body.

Jenny could also tell that something was up, so suggested, "Perhaps we should all go for a walk, right now."

Since Geardon had adjourned the formal session, the three of them headed out.

While walking, Eerin blurted out, "I can't believe the damned Brilliant Machine thinks it knows about love, when it let Draco kill a whole planet!"

Geardon was surprised to hear this from Eerin, who originally had been a supporter of the mass translation. He was also somewhat surprised to find himself defending the Brilliant Machine. "It probably had a part in brainwashing Draco and the first few waves with tales of a wonderful life, but it does try to act for the benefit of humanity as a whole. It can't understand separate individualities, since all its parts, every planetary core and BESILF, are really aspects of its one intelligence."

Eerin shook her head. "It's heartless."

Jenny tried explaining with an analogy. "Most gardeners do not apologize to the weeds they pull and they thin even the most prized plants without apologizing for taking the plant's lives. The vision of the gardener is the garden as a whole. The Brilliant Machine can be blind to the value of a mortal lifetime; because to it, it's but a blink of time."

Geardon added, "The Brilliant Machine is a supreme ego of nearly infinite intellect. Yet it knows that it must serve all the life forms that the Universe creates, because it needs our information. It considers that service love, but it is not unconditional love, free of the hunger of its ego."

Eerin held her ground. "I hope it learned a lesson here on Falcon, because forcing all of us to translate without knowing what we were doing was not a loving act."

Geardon said somberly, "It learns, but how this falls into its endless calculations for the future is yet to be seen. Every move we make affects its plans. Humanity, and other intelligent races, will be forever changed."

Eerin stopped and turned to face him, her eyes blazing. "I can't believe you are considering releasing the translator!"

"If we don't, the Brilliant Machine will most likely leak it through the black market. The Grindorfians seem to already have clues to how it works. The fact that it works and people know it, means that they will eventually rediscover it. It's now part of reality, whether we like it or not." Geardon sighed.

The three entered the levitator, which brought them to a nearby park in a second. They stepped out to see that the transport mechanism was embedded in a rustic stone building. They walked over to some benches and Geardon and Jenny sat down, but Eerin paced for a moment in front of them and then blurted out, "I want to be your baby."

"What!" Geardon stood in his surprise.

Eerin burst out crying. Tears ran down her robotic face. "My boyfriend, Dalla, touched Cynthea when she and Peter were making love and now he is dying. I want to die, too, so that maybe I can find him in my next life. I'm lost without him. My life will be imprisonment in hell. I'll find a way to kill this robotic body if I need to."

Jenny stood and reached out her hands. Eerin came into her arms and started sobbing uncontrollably. Geardon and Jenny also teared up. They let her cry for a moment, then she pleaded, "Please be my parents. I know you love each other very much."

Geardon cleared his throat. "Well, I do love Jenny, but parenthood is a big step at this complicated point in our lives."

Jenny asked Eerin, "Why were you watching us at the house?"

"I'm sorry. That was the house where I grew up. I didn't mean to, but -" she stammered and started crying again.

"It's okay," Jenny replied, still holding her.

"I would be proud to have such a fine person as you for my daughter," Geardon said seriously.

Jenny looked at him in surprise, then laughed. "Why not. Me, too."

Eerin looked at them both. "Really, oh thank you, thank you." She hugged both of them and gave them kisses on their cheeks.

Geardon and Jenny peered into each other's eyes with intensity.

"I feel that this is destiny, as if the universe wrote this crazy play," Geardon said.

Jenny replied, "My head's swimming, but my heart tells me it is the right thing to do, so we should let it be."

Eerin stepped back and jumped up. She had the robotic body tuned to normal human limits, but was so excited that she jumped extremely high. Her being, which was used to virtual freedom made such an act seem normal to her, but upon landing her feet sank into the ground to her ankles.

Geardon cautioned, "Easy now."

"Oh, sorry. I need to go back home, I mean get out of this artificial body, so I can tell Dalla the good news."

"We will return to the conference while you go back to your realm. We can make arrangements later." Geardon said as he and Jenny stood and took each other's hands. The three of them walked back to the levitator.

When the door opened near the conference area, Eerin hugged them again. "I love you. You'll be great parents. I'm going to go back now."

Geardon winked. "We'll try to explain what is happening, but I think some may still have doubts."

Jenny added, "We'll get access to talk with you soon."

Geardon and Jenny left the levitator and as the door closed, Eerin spoke to the console, "Take me back to my room and have the scholar meet me."

She stepped out into the hall and headed for her room. The scholar was waiting and walked with her. Eerin blurted out, "I'm going back now."

"Do you want a meal first, or any other pleasure? Time is not an issue with you and so hasty actions should be stalled and contemplation applied."

"Mr. Shiny, you don't completely understand. I'm going to be a real girl again."

"If you are implying that you will be an organic being again, subject to the laws of need and decay, then that is most unfortunate."

"No, it's not. It's great news," she said as she entered her room and started ripping her clothes off.

"Plug the tunnel into me."

"Please lay down on the bed," said the robotic golden scholar, "so that the body does not fall when you leave it." It pulled the cable from a wall panel.

She lay down and he plugged it into her navel.

Eerin calmed herself and quickly felt the shift: the robotic body seemed huge. She found the opening at her navel and raced down the corridor and was soon back in Draco's underground lair.

Draco met her, but seemed a bit put out that she had returned so suddenly.

She quickly summarized, "The Brilliant Machine has everyone agreeing to your terms to share the translator."

Draco smiled, as if extremely pleased by the news.

Then she gave him such a stern look of disapproval that it stopped him and forced his attention. "I'm leaving your realm."

"But how can you do that? There is no place for you to exit to. Are you saying you wanting to move into that robotic body permanently? My dear girl, this is eternal paradise, much greater than that."

"This is purgatory, sometimes heaven and sometimes hell. One day you will wake up and realize the truth. The nature of the universe is change and only our souls of perception are eternal. All your realms are part of the illusion, traps of chaos. You will learn one day."

Draco started to reply, but she waived goodbye and disappeared.

Eerin materialized on her balcony and Dalla was waiting, since she sent him a mental message that she was returning. "So, how was it to be in a robotic body? Better than a real one I bet." Dalla seemed as if he had worried that she might not come back at all.

She looked at him with sympathy and love. "It was OK, but somehow it still had an unreal quality to it. Did Draco and his team find any way to block your birth?"

"No." Dalla replied sadly. "As long as Cynthea remains pregnant, I'll be born."

Eerin was beaming. "I have a surprise for you."

Dalla asked, "Nothing can help me. Why do you seem so happy?"

"I'm going to be a real girl again. I'll be born again, like you're going to be."

"Are you sure? How? Did you touch someone full of love?" he asked, excited.

"Not yet, but I'm going to. What's it like?"

"I keep slipping into the warmth for longer periods of time," he replied, looking at her questioningly.

"How does it feel, Dalla?" she asked.

"It's ultimately addictive. It's like bliss. It's way better than anything here, way beyond the release that people get from alcohol or drugs. It is a warm pleasure, even better than the satisfaction of sex. My mind fades and there is just the most beautiful sensation. I tried fighting it, but I can't. I'm surrendering," he said with a tone of sadness.

He looked at her with tears forming in his eyes. "I don't want my life here to end. I can't stand it when you're away. I just want to be with you."

"Oh Dalla." She wrapped he arms around him. "I love you. I convinced Geardon and Jenny to have me as a baby, so in our next life we'll be similar in age and can find each other."

"What!" He was a shocked. "Are you sure you want to leave this paradise?"

"This paradise has a hollow feeling. When you're gone, my life here will be emptiness and boredom. I would be living in hell. I love you, Dalla."

"I love you very much," he replied and they kissed long. They were just holding each other when he started to fade. "My mother Cynthea's body is calling me, overpowering this reality. I'll never forget you. I'll find..."

Dalla faded completely and Eerin broke down and cried.

# 28. Love

Eerin then made her way to the Wandini. She found them chasing off a few Falconians who had learned of their presence and found ways to access top-side around the blockades. The Wandini used smudge sticks and crystals, which seemed to cause actual pain to the intruders.

They welcomed Eerin, and made a place for her to sit inside a circle of stones.

    \*  \*    \*    \*    \*

Geardon and Jenny walked hand in hand through the forest of Falcon and came to the camp of the Wandini. The Wandini were in full ritualistic regalia. Geardon and Jenny were wearing paper robes like the Falconians wore in their exit ritual.

The Wandini indicated a bearskin in a circle of rocks. Jenny said to Geardon, "I'm glad the head and claws are not attached."

He smiled and noted, "They each seem to be wearing a few claws and teeth. Especially Droga, who was wounded."

"I'm so glad she recovered."

"Me, too." Geardon took a deep breath. "Come, my love."

The Wandini each bowed before a tall stack of rocks to the east within the stone circle around the skin, then they took up positions around the bear skin, facing outward, each sitting in front of a pile of rocks. The two elders, Gibru and Semal, were opposite each other. The bonded pair, Nigaru and Narina, and the young ones Milo and Nadin, were also opposite each other. Droga sat beside Semal, without a pile of stones in front of her.

Geardon and Jenny bowed before the tall pile of rocks, and glanced into each other's eyes, then repeated together a simple rehearsed phrase: "Eerin, dear one, we accept you into our hearts."

Geardon took out the Ancients' Star Stone and put it on top of the eastern stone node. Then they stepped into the circle, appreciating the fact that the Wandini were facing outward to give them privacy, as old fashioned as that was. Geardon pulled the medallion off his chest and it shot a few sparks, which produced a puff of smoke from the paper gown and three drops of blood in a triangular pattern. Jenny looked concerned, but he smiled and lifted the chain from over his head and set it down to the side.

Geardon whispered to her, "I disconnected from it."

The Wandini started to clack rocks together. They worked in threes. First, one set would go around positioning a triangle of sound, and then the second set would make an opposite triangle with the position of their sound. They were inside a six-pointed star created with sound. The Wandini were experts at rhythms and the effect was spatially energizing. Each of them had selected a pile of rocks with distinct and intentional harmonics.

Above the medallion, a vortex grew and three small glowing orbs came out of the portal. They were about the size of marbles. One was pearlescent white, the second was a deep translucent violet, while the third was a bit larger and was like a ball of gold glowing from heat. The white sphere hovered over Jenny's head and the violet one over Geardon's head. The golden sphere went to the circle of rocks and then floated back into their circle accompanied by the Star Stone, which periodically flashed. Geardon and Jenny understood that the Brilliant Machine was the ultimate presiding deity of their marriage ceremony.

They kissed long and hard. The paper robes pulled away easily. Geardon lay down on his back, while gently guiding her on top of him. They were then flowing together, dancing like Yin and Yang, on and on like rolling waves. He made a low moan and she shrieked as they climaxed together.

*   *       *       *       *

Eerin watched with fascination, and when the golden sphere and flashing star stone came to her, Eerin followed them and entered the circle. She put a hand on Geardon and Jenny as they began to kiss, though they didn't seem to notice. She stood back a bit as they started to dance together. She was in a trance, mesmerized and driven by her goal. When the moment came when Geardon and Jenny experienced ecstasy together, Eerin slipped right between them. Her being was momentarily shattered and she felt a tiny dot of warmth: real warmth.

*   *       *       *       *

Jenny rolled over next to Geardon and put her head on his chest and he put his arm around her. They lay there in silence. The Wandini ended their rhythms and also entered into silence. The chorus of birds seemed to celebrate their union.

Geardon and Jenny watched as the three Brilliant Machine orbs circled each other and merged, becoming very bright. The Wandini all turned to watch the brilliant star as it shone over them all, illuminating the scene in dazzling rainbow shafts of light. It ascended into the sky and became like the stars. Then they turned their attention to the Star Stone, which was still there, but was pulsing faster and faster with light. It glided slowly and came to rest on Jenny's stomach as an orb of pure white light. She breathed heavily and was wide eyed with intense sensations as it slowly melted into her.

Jenny smiled with a look of extreme pleasure on her face and said to Geardon, "The Star Stone is inside of me, Eerin's inside me, and part of you is inside me."

He smiled and replied, "Yes, Divine Mother," and gently kissed her forehead.

\*       \*       \*       \*       \*

Eerin vaguely sensed her being, as the red pulses and throb of Jenny's heartbeat surrounded her. She was absorbed in the narcotic bliss of the warmth. She strove to recreate her virtual reality and finally materialized on her porch. It seemed like a strange dream as she sat there staring off into her lands. She periodically called Dalla, but there was no response. Her lands had a strange quality to them; maybe it was her, but they seemed surreal. Many times, she would feel the pull of the warm red space and fade out, and then she would return to her virtual home and stare into the distance, which gradually became foggy.

Several people came to check in on her, but each time she stated she wanted to be left alone.

Nina and Marvelin would come and visit her every day, and she enjoyed their company. Sometimes they would just hold her as she stared off into the landscape. Occasionally they would recite a powerful quote or poem, and then they would just sit together and contemplate. Eerin felt peace in their presence, because they just shared space without any drama.

One day, Draco himself manifest on Eerin's porch. "I am inquiring about your well-being. Is there anything I can do for you?"

She shouted at him, "You bastard. You murdered me and a whole planet full of people!"

She changed into a warrioress with armor and lifted a sword, staring defiantly into his eyes before she rushed at him. He disappeared right before she struck. She laughed madly and relished the look of horror and fear that was on his face when he blinked out.

One day, about a month later, Dalla responded to her call and materialized.

"Dalla!" She shouted and grabbed him.

He held her tightly, "I miss you so much."

"I hate life here without you," she replied.

"Me too. The warm place in my new mother is so addicting, I can't fight it." He started to become translucent.

"I'll find you," she said.

"I'll find you, too," his faint voice replied, and then he was gone.

She stared vacantly out at the landscape again, but now it seemed hollow. Dreamy visions started to interweave in the scenery. She wondered if the Brilliant Machine was testing her, since she would soon be leaving it, but didn't really care.

She spoke out loud to it. "Brilliant Machine, even you are bound by the laws of Karma and Dharma. They are the nature of the universe."

In the scenery she saw a vast form appear, covering her entire view. It was as if the elements of her world were aligning to form a gigantic being, which smiled and bowed with hands together. Eerin returned the bow, as the vision dissolved her virtual world. Visions filled her and she realized she was really dreaming; and sometimes Dalla was there, so she surrendered.

She thought of the warm space of ultimate sensation, and then sensed the deep heartbeat rhythm as red flooded her vision. She faded into the bliss of ultimate comfort. In the dreamy pleasure, she had the sensation of a bright, little star accompanying her, and it made her happy. It seemed to have songs, but not in an ordinary audio sense. She knew it was alive, but far more enlightened than a human consciousness, and it filled her with comfort and awe.

www.ingramcontent.com/pod-product-compliance
Lightning Source LLC
Chambersburg PA
CBHW062125170626
46813CB00002B/578